PRAISE FO

"Danger, desire, an
the razor's edge of

"[A] must-buy series for paranormal romance lovers."
—n Vixen

"Stellar world build
Weekly

"Ashley's Shiftertow
bet in
paranormal romance
stars)

"With her usual gift for imaginative plots fueled by scorch-
ingly sensual chemistry, RITA Award–winning Ashley begins a new
sexy paranormal series that neatly combines high-adrenaline suspense with humor." —*Booklist*

"Engaging paranormal romance." —Smexy Books

"One of my top paranormal romance series, with its complex po-
litical and social issues and some intense, hot romances."
—All Things Urban Fantasy

"[A] first-rate hero, exceptional storytelling, and a seductive and
sweet romance to satisfy any fan." —Fresh Fiction

"This novel [seemed] as though it was superglued to my hands,
because I couldn't pry it from my fingers." —Rabid Reads

"Wickedly sexy. . . . Are you new to the Shifters Unbound series?
Already a fan? Either way, I think you'll enjoy your time with
these rambunctious, charismatic, loyal Shifters."
—Harlequin Junkie

RED WOLF

JENNIFER ASHLEY

BERKLEY SENSATION
New York

BERKLEY SENSATION
Published by Berkley
An imprint of Penguin Random House LLC
375 Hudson Street, New York, New York 10014

ISBN: 9780425281376

First Edition: May 2017

Printed in the United States of America
1 3 5 7 9 10 8 6 4 2

Cover art by Tony Mauro

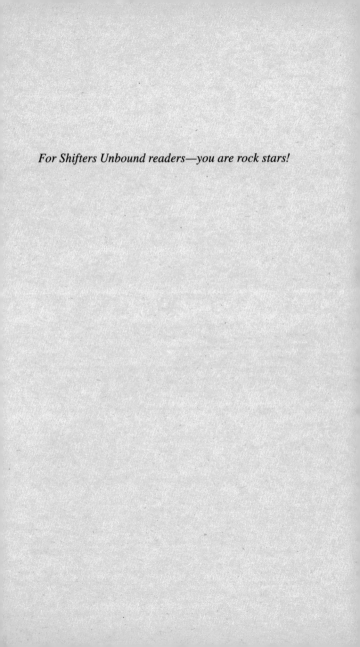

For Shifters Unbound readers—you are rock stars!

CHAPTER ONE

"Come on," the Lupine Shifter drawled. "Show us what you can do, c-c-c-coyote." He exaggerated the stammer, his eyes full of meanness.

Not coyote, asshole. Red wolf.

Dimitri knew he'd never say that without mangling it, so he gave the Lupine the universal sign with his third finger.

The crowd around them roared with laughter. The Lupine was naked, and so was Dimitri, as they both stood in the cement block–lined ring in the open-walled barn that was the fight club. Dimitri had never seen the Lupine before, but that wasn't surprising. Shifters came from all over South Texas and beyond to try their luck in the ring.

The refs for this fight—a jaguar called Spike, a huge bear named Ronan, and a wolf called Corey—backed away, clearing the space around them. "Fight!" Ronan said in his giant Kodiak voice.

The Lupine struck immediately. His Collar, the chain that in theory kept Shifters subdued, sparked like blue fire. The Collar that lay around Dimitri's neck was fake and did nothing.

Dimitri opened his arms and caught the Lupine in mid-spring. The Lupine shifted on the way, and Dimitri went down under a writhing, snarling, biting gray wolf.

Dimitri rolled with the impact, digging his fingers into the Lupine's fur. He avoided the claws, teeth, and sparks from the wolf's Collar as he kicked and shoved the Lupine off him.

Dimitri didn't like to shift too early in the fight. When he did that, his wild tendencies took over—he had no Collar to suppress him and fighting frenzy came easily. He wanted like anything to best this asshole, but if Dimitri let the frenzy come, he might kill the Lupine before anyone could stop him.

Dimitri rolled to his feet. The wolf rushed him, but too recklessly. Dimitri had time to sidestep, grab the Lupine, and use the wolf's momentum to send him flying to the other side of the ring.

The Lupine skittered, facedown, into the low cement wall. The crowd who'd bet on Dimitri laughed and cheered, loving it.

The Lupine's friends booed. "Man up, fucking coyote!" someone yelled. "Fucking coy—*oof*!" His grunt of pain was lost in the noise, but Dimitri saw a Feline quietly fold in half.

He grinned. Jaycee was here.

She appeared just outside the wall in sweatpants and a tank top that hugged her curves. "Kick his *ass*, Dimitri!" she yelled. "Or I'll come in there and do it myself."

The crowd's boos turned to her. "Keep your woman under control, coyote," someone shouted.

Dimitri didn't respond, waiting until the refs made sure the wolf was still in good shape to fight. If the jeering Shifters wanted to take on Jaycee, good luck to them. Their funeral.

Dimitri waited in the middle of the ring, lacing his fingers and stretching them, his bare feet brushing dirt aside. The wolf's claws had raked Dimitri's side, but not deeply, the cuts barely stinging.

Ronan said something to the wolf, then nodded and backed off. "Fight!" Ronan called.

The wolf sprang instantly. Dimitri knew he wouldn't fall for the sidestepping trick again, so he reached out, grabbed the wolf around the neck as he leapt, and started squeezing.

Claws scrabbled on Dimitri's bare flesh. Dimitri felt his shift come, his beast instinctively protecting itself. The wolf's claws met fur, though Dimitri's hands remained human as he became his between-beast.

The two went down in a tangle of dust, claws, and teeth. The Lupine's Collar sparked hard, the electric arcs singeing Dimitri's furred flesh.

The Lupine's gaze went to Dimitri's Collar, which lay dormant. Dimitri slammed the wolf to the ground with his between-beast strength, then became fully wolf.

Let the jackass call him coyote *now*. Dimitri savagely bit and clawed, and the wolf bit and clawed in return. They tumbled in a ball of fur and teeth, hitting the wall and then rolling away from it. Dimly Dimitri heard the crowd roaring, and his mate's shout.

"Dimitri, *get him!*"

Dimitri rolled the wolf over, pinning him with his large red wolf paws. His wild state was taking over—it told him to kill the threat and walk away. Only a lifetime of discipline allowed Dimitri to tamp down his instincts and remember this was a fight for enjoyment. Not real.

The Lupine snarled his rage. He knew he was losing, knew he'd underestimated the odd-looking red-furred wolf with the stammer.

Dimitri opened his jaw to go for the Lupine's throat. He was aware of the refs' feet—two pairs of motorcycle boots and one pair of running shoes—surrounding them. The refs would call the fight and pull Dimitri off before he could kill the Lupine. Maybe.

Dimitri struck. At the same time, he felt a prick in his belly, like a claw had scratched him, and then a strange lassitude filled his brain.

It wasn't quite like a tranq, which could knock out a

Shifter in a few seconds. A calm peacefulness stole over Dimitri, one that made him want to back off the wolf, let him go, maybe embrace him when they regained their feet.

He looked down at the Lupine, who had half shifted back to human. The man-beast wore a self-satisfied look.

Drugging an opponent was against the rules. Hell, it wasn't even done when fighting in the wild.

"You t-t-total b-b-b-b . . ." Dimitri couldn't get the word out.

The refs hadn't yet caught on that there was something wrong. Only a second had gone by, though it was stretching for Dimitri. The refs were giving Dimitri a chance to finish the fight, or for the Lupine to throw off Dimitri and continue.

Dimitri heard an uproar at the side of the ring, but he couldn't make out what anyone was shouting. Words slurred into one another, and Dimitri's grasp of English deserted him. Russian started going as well. Pretty soon, he'd be able only to growl in wolf.

A streak of fur zoomed into the ring. The refs reached for the leopard who'd sprung in, but she writhed and twisted away from their clutching hands.

She pushed between Dimitri and the Lupine and slammed her strong paw to the Lupine's half-beast face. The Lupine must have had only one dose of the drug, because instead of trying to tranq the leopard, he shifted back to full wolf and lunged for the leopard's throat.

The leopard sprang straight into the air as only cats can, and the wolf's teeth snapped on nothing. The leopard landed behind the wolf, grabbed him by the scruff, and shook him. She growled as the sparks from his Collar went into her mouth, but she didn't let go.

The ref Spike, with jaguar speed, went for her. Before he reached her, the leopard shook the wolf one more time, dropped him to the ground, and smacked him with her paw. The wolf went limp.

Spike as jaguar planted himself in front of the leopard, his ears flat, his fangs bared in a snarl. The leopard regarded him with disdain, sat down on her haunches, and delicately licked one paw.

Dimitri rolled over onto his back, wanting to laugh his ass off. The laughter came out as a wavering wolf howl.

Some in the crowd cheered, enjoying the show. The rest of them were roaring in fury. Even the humans who'd come out to watch Shifters fighting each other were shouting with rage.

"The match is a draw," Ronan said in his big voice. He sounded regretful.

"Stupid bitch ruined the fight!" a Shifter called out.

"'S why women aren't allowed in the ring," another chimed in. He was bolstered by many voices yelling agreement.

"Get her out of there!" another shouted.

The crowd surged forward. Two Lupines hauled themselves over the cement blocks and went for the leopard. Spike was right there, intercepting one, but the second made it through, the other refs too far away to stop him.

Whatever drug had laid Dimitri out faded and died as he saw the threat to his mate. He surged up, heat burning away the last of the sedative, and he rushed in a low wolf run to the Lupine heading for the leopard.

Jaycee had turned around, facing the Lupine with a leopard snarl. Dimitri bowled her over, sending her, surprised, to the dust, and then launched himself at the Lupine.

The Lupine, still in human form, went down. Those in the crowd cheered or booed, and then they streamed forward to join in the fight.

Dimitri's instincts changed from protective rage to alarm. The Shifters were blowing off the rules and storming the ring, becoming a mob. Humans gleefully joined in.

When Shifters didn't stop themselves, they became destructive killing machines, uncaring as to who they took down. This was what they'd been bred for centuries ago, why the Fae had won so many battles with Shifters at the forefront.

Dimitri whirled for Jaycee, driving her back from the crowd, herding her with snarls and snaps of teeth out of the ring on the other side.

Jaycee had a hot temper and could be reckless, but she was no fool. She bounded out ahead of Dimitri, then shifted back to human form, rising into a beautiful naked woman.

Dimitri tamped down on his need to admire her full breasts and the curve of her hips, her wheat-colored hair that was always messy, and her tawny leopard eyes. She rubbed Dimitri's fur in a quick stroke, then moved off to make sure the more vulnerable humans and young Shifters got out of the way of the now-crazed crowd.

The Shifters didn't care that their original target had just walked away from them. They started fighting the refs, Dimitri, one another.

Ronan had gone Kodiak bear, the huge creature bellowing as he shoved wolves and wildcats out of his way. Spike was fighting with the honed swiftness of a Feline, taking down Shifters with one strike each. Spike was the undefeated fighter of this fight club for good reason.

The third ref, a wolf called Corey McNaughton, was younger than the others, less experienced. Dimitri put himself with Corey, snarling and fighting, protecting as he battled.

The place became chaos. Dimitri fought in silence, anger making him fierce. If the police got wind of the free-for-all and showed up, they'd be screwed—tranqued, rounded up, possibly killed. Dimitri's Collar was fake, as was Jaycee's. Other Shifters from Dimitri's enclave also had false Collars, which they put on when they had to interact with humans. If the humans in authority found out about the fakes, they'd all be up shit creek. This riot had to cease.

Shifters in fighting frenzy, though, were all but impossible to stop. This was what the humans feared—Shifters out of control, going on killing rampages, slaughtering humans and taking over. Stupid, because there were far more humans in the world than Shifters, and Shifters rarely worked themselves up into this kind of collective frenzy. But right now Dimitri could understand their worry.

Dimitri tripped over the Lupine who'd been his original opponent, the one Jaycee had knocked out. The Lupine was coming around, human now. Dimitri shifted back to human, hauled the man to his feet, and shoved him toward a relatively calm part of the ring.

"Get out of here," Dimitri snarled, speaking with the

clarity he achieved when his emotions were at their most intense. "Asshole."

The Lupine gave him a look of sly amusement. What the hell was so funny, Dimitri didn't know. He pushed the man to the side of the ring and over the blocks.

The Lupine turned to study Dimitri from the other side of the wall. "Yeah," he said, nodding. "You'll be perfect."

"For what?" Dimitri yelled, not sure he'd heard him over the crowd.

The Lupine smirked and walked away, his shoulders back in arrogance; then he disappeared into the darkness beyond the arena's flaring light.

Another Shifter smacked into Dimitri, carrying him sideways. Dimitri gave up on the Lupine and rolled back into the fight.

Jaycee was yelling at a couple of Shifters who were barely past their Transitions—their fighting blood would be at its hottest. Dimitri waded over to help her.

Behind him, a truck was pulling up, a big thing, unmarked, with a water hose coiled behind it. *Shit, where had a Shifter found . . . ?*

He stopped worrying about it. Dylan, the most powerful Shifter in South Texas—or his son Sean, a Guardian; or Kendrick, Dimitri's leader—would have the resources to come up with a water truck on the spur of the moment.

Dimitri reached Jaycee and the overgrown cubs. They were Collared, from the Austin Shiftertown, and eager to fight.

"Time to go," Dimitri said. He swept open his arms, carrying Jaycee and the two younger Shifters out from under the old barn that was their arena and into the night.

Behind him, squeals and howls rose as a hundred Shifters suddenly got very, very wet.

"Jaycee," Dimitri said.

She turned from shoving the younger Shifters into the trees at the edge of the clearing, inquiry on her face.

Dimitri wanted to yell at her. He wanted to demand to know what the hell she was thinking rushing into the ring like that, breaking every rule of the fight club. She'd put herself in danger not only from the crazy Lupine fighting Dimitri but from every Shifter in the place.

He thought about how she'd fought the wolf, almost casually avoiding his attack and then smacking him down into unconsciousness.

"What?" Jaycee asked when he didn't speak. "You mean, why am I such an idiot?" Sometimes she'd talk for him, so he wouldn't have to struggle with what he wanted to say.

Dimitri shook his head. He reached for Jaycee and dragged her to him, her fine flesh bare against his. He tucked his hand under her soft hair and turned her startled face up to him, his mouth coming down on hers in a long, hard kiss.

Around them, pandemonium reigned, Shifters shouting and furious as the water truck cooled down the hot mob. None of that reached Dimitri, in a bubble of calm with Jaycee.

Her mouth was hot, her body the same, her kiss holding her fire. She wrapped her arms around him and stepped closer, letting him know she could give into mating frenzy if he did. Her breasts were firm against his chest, her nipples tight, her skin smooth as he slid his hand down to the round softness of her buttocks.

The chill in the air to either side of them kicked Dimitri out of the warm place into which he'd been sinking.

He lifted his head to find Kendrick, his leader, a white tiger Shifter, on his left, the hilt of the Sword of the Guardian rising above his shoulder. On Dimitri's other side was Dylan Morrissey, a Feline every Shifter around answered to.

Jaycee looked up, color flooding her face. She kept close to Dimitri, hiding her body, her sudden shyness making Dimitri's protectiveness surge.

"Dimitri," Kendrick said in his growling voice, which was deceptively soft. "Jaycee. We need to talk."

CHAPTER TWO

Jaycee had never been comfortable around Dylan. Jaycee was Kendrick's Shifter, which meant she obeyed no orders unless they came from him. She was fourth in the hierarchy of Kendrick's Shifters, after Dimitri, who was third, and Seamus, who was Kendrick's second, and she was happy with that order. She'd lived with this state of things since she'd passed her Transition.

Dylan, on the other hand, expected *everyone* to obey him, no matter what. He didn't bluster and snarl; he simply stared at you with those hard blue eyes and *willed* you to do what he said. Dylan technically didn't have authority—he'd once been the leader of the Austin Shiftertown, but he'd stepped aside to let his son take his place. He was supposedly retired, happy staying at home with his mate, his second son and *his* mate, and his grandson, but common knowledge said the retirement part wasn't strictly true.

Dylan wore a Collar, a real one. Jaycee had seen it spark on him, even though he controlled it well. Jaycee didn't wear a Collar at all, and neither did Dimitri nor Kendrick—unless they put on fakes to mingle with other Shifters and humans.

So why did everyone worry about what Dylan would do if they disobeyed him?

Jaycee didn't know. All she understood was that he was one frigging scary Feline, and she avoided meeting him without Dimitri or Kendrick nearby.

Now both Kendrick and Dimitri flanked her, Kendrick quietly strong as he moved to sit on the bench in the back of the van Dylan led them to.

Dimitri lounged next to Jaycee on her seat opposite Kendrick, Dimitri's arm stretched across the back behind her shoulders. He'd been allowed to stop and put on clothes—a loose pair of sweatpants and a T-shirt that clung to his torso. Dimitri looked comfortable, unworried, while Jaycee was nervous and perspiring.

Damn him for never letting anything bother him.

Dimitri's red hair was still tangled from the fight, though he'd brushed it back from his forehead with a strong hand in an attempt to flatten it. Jaycee resisted the urge to reach up and smooth his hair for him—he'd only growl at her.

Dylan entered the van, settling himself on a jump seat that folded from behind the closed door. This let him sit alone, apart from them. A jump seat was the extra chair, for that last person who didn't quite fit, a place for the vulnerable. Dylan used it to make himself different from them, reminding them of his power.

"Jaycee Bordeaux," Dylan said, the lilt of Ireland in his voice marked. "Tonight you broke almost every rule of the fight club. Rules put in place to keep Shifters safe. Might have broken them all if Sean hadn't showed up with the water truck."

Dimitri chuckled, a warm sound. "You sh-should have s-seen them, all w-w-w- . . . and . . ." He trailed off, his tongue failing him, but he kept laughing.

"Wet and pissed off," Jaycee finished. "Yeah, that was funny." Very wet cats and wolves had shaken themselves, fury in their eyes, Shifters in human forms cursing. Only the bears had basked in it, acting like idiots as they'd enjoyed the cooling shower.

Dylan didn't smile, though Kendrick's lips twitched. "They were pissed off for more than being wet," Dylan said.

"Oh, come on." Jaycee sat forward in her seat, her heart beating faster. "I went into the ring because that asshole drugged Dimitri. *He* didn't follow the rules. He had a tranq— I saw the syringe. He was going to tear Dimitri apart, and the refs were doing nothing. Besides, females not being allowed to fight is just stupid. We wouldn't do it if we were pregnant or had tiny cubs—we're not complete fools—but we can best any opponent you can throw at us. I think I proved that."

Dylan's gaze remained steady. "Females fighting in an arena full of drunk males could trigger the mating frenzy. The females would have to run for their lives."

Jaycee made a derisive noise. "Only because male Shifters are perverts." She folded her arms and thumped back in her seat.

Dimitri leaned to whisper into her ear. "Peace, Jase."

Jaycee didn't like that she shivered when his warm breath touched her, that his deep voice tickled down inside her. She hadn't been the same since Dimitri had yelled that he mate-claimed her in the middle of an argument in front of half a dozen Shifters. Jaycee hadn't given him a straight answer about that yet—hadn't accepted but hadn't turned him down.

Dimitri hadn't bugged her about it. He hadn't even touched her since that night. Therefore, their fate was undecided. No sun and moon ceremonies scheduled—who knew if they'd ever be?

Even so, Jaycee couldn't help liking Dimitri next to her, couldn't help warming at his touch. His stammer vanished when he whispered to her, not that the stammer ever bothered her at all. It was just the way Dimitri talked.

Kendrick broke in, jerking Jaycee from the cocoon of Dimitri's nearness. "The Shifters weren't as angry about a woman fighting as they were about your entering the ring during the bout," he pointed out. "Any outside interference cancels the match."

"And they l-l-lose b-bets," Dimitri finished. "Shifters *hate* that."

"Exactly," Dylan said. "So here I am, expected to discipline you."

"That Lupine was blatantly cheating," Jaycee said hotly. "Why aren't you disciplining *him*?"

Kendrick's green eyes glinted. "Oh, we have something in mind for him, don't worry."

"H-he said s-something weird to me," Dimitri added. "B-before he left. He s-said, *You'll be perfect.*"

Dimitri took on the growl and tone of the Lupine he'd fought, repeating his words without hesitation.

"And he's right," Kendrick said. "You *will* be perfect. You and Jaycee."

Jaycee's eyes narrowed. "Perfect for what?"

"To stop something before it becomes impossible to contain," Dylan said. "Though it might already be too late."

Dimitri came alert. He didn't move, but Jaycee felt his muscles tense, his breathing quiet. "That's reassuring."

Dylan's gaze took in all three of them. "This June, I led some of the Austin trackers up to Washington state," he said. "The Olympic Peninsula. There was a fight."

Dimitri gave him a nod. "Heard ab-bout it."

"Rogue Shifters, most feral, had set up an encampment there, with help from human survivalists," Dylan went on. "We attacked them and thought we had them cornered and beaten. These same ferals had been terrorizing humans in the remote mountains for a while."

Dimitri nodded in acknowledgment, though this was the first Jaycee was learning about it, to her irritation.

"What we didn't know was that these ferals had set up camp on a ley line," Dylan said. "On a gateway to Faerie. They were hiding reserves of Shifters just on the other side of that gate. When we thought we had them conquered, suddenly out popped a huge number of Shifters and human fighters from the gateway. We barely escaped. Thanks to the healer, Zander, the ferals were driven back, and we got away. Tiger and I went back up there a few weeks ago to scout around, but the ferals were gone. Wherever their gateway was, we couldn't find it. But gates to Faerie are magical and we don't much understand them. We have someone working on that."

Jaycee listened, her mouth hanging open. "Shifters were hiding inside *Faerie*? What the hell? Shifters don't work with the Fae."

Kendrick nodded, his tiger voice a growl. "Exactly what we said. But these Shifters appeared to be coming and going through the gate at will. I doubt they did it without Fae help."

"Don't you need a device of some kind to cross?" Jaycee asked. "Not that I know a lot about it, but I thought you had to have Fae silver, or a Guardian's sword, or something like that."

"You do," Dylan answered. "We don't know what they had, or what sort of deal they made. We don't know if this was a one-off or if more Shifters are doing deals like this . . ."

"And you want us to f-find out," Dimitri concluded for him.

"We want you to find out whatever you can," Dylan corrected him sternly. "There may be nothing to learn, which is what I hope. I need more eyes and ears—and noses—among Shifters who have become disgruntled with how we live, those who might think working with the Fae is the lesser evil."

"We need to know whether these Shifters are just griping or if it's a true threat," Kendrick put in. "Dylan has already had to deal with one Shifter rebellion instigated by the Fae. We want to make sure another doesn't start. There's more going on here than Shifters who want to overturn the hierarchy." He paused, looking troubled. "We *think*. We need to know."

Jaycee nodded. "I get that. But what makes you think Dimitri and I can find out anything? Everyone knows we're Kendrick's loyal trackers. Who would believe we'd turn against him?"

Dylan gave her a small smile. "You might not turn against your own leader, but you, lass, have no problem breaking the rules. You demonstrated that well tonight. You're both relatively new to the Shifters in this region, so you are an unknown factor. You don't wear true Collars. You don't like Shiftertowns and Shifter laws. Tonight you proved you weren't above blatantly breaking established rules. You are exactly the sort of Shifters a splinter group would want. So find one. Join them. And tell me what they're up to."

"Oh, is that all?" Jaycee said, her eyes widening. "Doesn't sound dangerous or anything. And what if we can't find a splinter group? Or we do and they won't tell us a damned thing?"

Dylan shrugged. "Then they don't. But we need to try, before shite rains down on us that we can't stop. I don't know what's going on. That bothers me."

A blatant understatement. The look deep in Dylan's eyes was one of intense rage. Dylan liked to have his paw on the pulse of every plot that went on in South Texas—his *paw*, not his finger, so that he could rip out throats when he needed to.

Dimitri glanced at Jaycee but spoke to Kendrick. "Too d-d-dangerous." He closed his eyes to get out the last word.

"I know," Kendrick said. "I can't force you to do this, Dimitri. You don't answer to Dylan. It has to be your choice."

Dylan didn't look pleased with this, but he said nothing. He couldn't tell Kendrick's trackers what to do without challenging Kendrick's leadership, and Dylan wasn't fool enough to do that. Kendrick was a powerful white tiger, un-Collared, and a Guardian. The very large broadsword at Kendrick's feet was a silent reminder that part of his job was to send dead or dying Shifters to the afterlife, the Summerland. Plunging the sword through the Shifter's heart rendered the bodies dust and set the soul free.

"Dimitri means dangerous for *me*," Jaycee broke in. "Dimitri is happy to jump down rogue Shifters' throats and charge in front of Fae swords all day. *I'm* supposed to stay home and knit or something. He's become annoyingly protective."

Did Dimitri look angry or even embarrassed by this? No, his handsome face and gray eyes settled into lines of amusement. He'd claimed Jaycee as mate. Now he got to be an asshole about it.

"That is true," Kendrick said to Dylan. "I can't compel

Dimitri to put Jaycee in danger. I can ask *him* to go, but not Jaycee."

Dylan lifted his fingers, which rested on his knee, the slightest bit. "Then we will wait for Dimitri's decision."

Jaycee rolled her eyes. "For the Goddess' sake. I haven't accepted the mate-claim yet. I've been a tracker for twenty years. I've fought plenty of Shifters. I can handle myself."

"You can," Dimitri acknowledged with a nod, his eyes holding both respect and heat.

Jaycee warmed, suddenly disarmed. "Thank you."

"To a p-point," Dimitri said. He gave Jaycee the ghost of a grin, knowing exactly how to make her mad. He turned to Dylan. "Jase is a rule b-breaker. True. What about m-me? W-why will they b-believe that I w-w-w- . . ." He closed his eyes again, halting. He did that when his mouth wouldn't let him speak, waiting until everything worked again.

"He means why will these rogue Shifters believe *Dimitri* wants to join them?" Jaycee asked. "Dimitri follows all the rules. Drives me bat-crap crazy."

Dylan and Kendrick exchanged a glance. "Because other Shifters ridicule you," Kendrick said, his deep voice gentle. "They mock the way you speak."

Dimitri opened his eyes, looking amazed. "So? I don't give a r-rat's ass."

Kendrick fixed him with a stare. "They ridicule you, *and it upsets you very much*."

Dimitri blinked, and then a grin broke over his face. "Oh, right. Yeah, I c-cry all night."

"And they claim you're a coyote," Jaycee said.

Dimitri's eyes flashed fury. "Now *that* pisses me off." No stumbling over those words.

"There you go." Jaycee waved a hand at him. "Much more believable."

Dimitri curled his lip in a very soft snarl.

Kendrick continued to watch Dimitri. "Will you do it? And allow Jaycee to help you?"

"*Allow* . . ." Jaycee moved in her seat, but Dimitri put a quelling hand on her arm.

"We b-both go."

"Gee, thank you." Jaycee sent him a scowl, pretending not to like the heat and pressure of his hand holding her wrist.

"She'll n-never let me hear the end of it if we d-don't," Dimitri continued.

"Shithead," Jaycee growled. Dimitri only kept on grinning.

"Another thing," Dylan said to Jaycee.

His gaze was hard to take. Jaycee wanted to look away, and because she did, she made herself meet his eyes. Not to challenge. Just to let him know she wasn't easily cowed.

"You'll have to be punished for tonight's transgression," Dylan said. "You broke the rules. That has to be answered."

Dimitri's amusement evaporated in an instant. His soft snarl grew louder.

"Dylan won't touch you," Kendrick said quickly to Jaycee, his glance taking in Dimitri as well. "I'm your leader, responsible for you."

Dylan didn't look as though he agreed completely, but he said nothing.

Kendrick did have the right to punish his Shifters for disobedience, which he'd done with Jaycee in the past. She'd always been one to push her boundaries, especially when she'd been in her Transition.

Kendrick's punishments had been mild, but what had hurt Jaycee most was that he'd been disappointed in her. She'd come away from the discipline vowing to do better. Kendrick had always kept the punishment private as well, not inflicting the public humiliations she knew other leaders sometimes employed on their Shifters.

Dimitri's growls escalated. He sat forward, his drowsing Lupine act over.

Kendrick switched his gaze to him. "The mate, of course, has the first right to punish."

Dimitri's growls cut off. He looked at Jaycee with sudden interest.

Now Jaycee's snarls came. "No way in hell!"

"It's his right," Kendrick said quietly. "He's made the mate-claim. And it's going to have to look good, you two. One more convincing part for your cover."

"Then you should do it, Kendrick," Jaycee said rapidly. "*You* punish me, and Dimitri can be angry at you because *he* should have done it."

"A good idea," Kendrick said, "except . . ."

"Except I won't let him," Dimitri broke in. "If he touches you, Jase, I won't hold back."

Kendrick made a *see?* motion at Jaycee.

"Then forget it." Jaycee slammed her arms over her chest. "Dimitri will get all possessive and mess it up."

"No, I won't." Dimitri's voice was hard, as were his eyes.

"You can refuse his mate-claim," Kendrick said in a kind voice. "Right now, if you want. That is *your* right."

All three males fixed their eyes on her. Dark blue and bright green of Dylan and Kendrick, dark gray and bloody stubborn of Dimitri.

Jaycee could do it. Refuse the claim, be finished with Dimitri. Walk away, back to freedom.

But if she did that, she knew it would be the end of their easy friendship. Dimitri would never again give her that flash of warm smile, the thumbs-up when he was pleased with her. They'd never go back to teasing each other, insulting each other, arguing and battling it out, then making up. Their comradeship would be at an end. They could try, but there would always be the barrier of the rejected mate-claim between them.

Dimitri would then find some other female who didn't mind finishing his sentences for him, who warmed when he gave her that hot look from his gray eyes. Jaycee's hands curled to fists. She already wanted to rip out that female's throat.

She met Dimitri's gaze as he waited, tense, for her to kick him in the face in front of the two most alpha Shifters they knew. Dimitri pretended to be unworried, but she saw in his eyes that he braced for her refusal. He expected it.

That realization hit her hard. Dimitri expected Jaycee to hurt him. Her heart began to burn.

"All right." Jaycee lifted her hands, putting as much resignation into the words as she could. "I'll stick with the claim for now. Dimitri can punish me." Goddess help me. "What do you want me to do?"

CHAPTER THREE

Jaycee's "punishment" was acted out in the Austin Shiftertown in the common area that opened out behind the house of the leader, Liam Morrissey.

Dimitri waited for Jaycee under the live oaks, hiding his unease by folding his arms and assuming a relaxed stance. He wasn't uneasy for himself—he was unhappy for Jaycee. This would be hard on her. But she was doing it, bravely, because it was her job. Jaycee had a lot of loyalty in her and a high sense of duty, no matter how much she might bitch about this later.

Liam stood on the back porch of his house, his brother, this Shiftertown's Guardian, next to him. They would be witnesses, as would the Shifters who were drifting in from all over. Shifters never stayed home and minded their own business if something interesting was going on.

Kendrick had decided the discipline should take place here, where it would be very public—much more so than if they'd done it at the ranch where Kendrick's Shifters lived. Word would spread—quickly if Dimitri knew Shifters—

that Jaycee had been singled out, making Jaycee's decision to seek rebel groups more plausible.

Kendrick joined Liam and Sean on the porch, his presence a comfort. At least Dylan hadn't elected to attend. He knew he was intimidating, plus he'd told Kendrick he didn't want it known that the punishment had been his idea. Shifters should talk about the errant Jaycee and how disobedient she was, not how Dylan had staged the discipline.

At the precise moment the sun cleared the trees and shone straight down into the clearing, Jaycee walked along the strip of land behind the houses to meet Dimitri. The Shifters of this town watched, some displeased, some curious, some believing Jaycee was getting her due for her antics at the fight club.

Jaycee walked slowly toward the clearing and Dimitri. There was a storm in her tawny eyes, rage that she had to endure this humiliation, but also a determination to play her part.

Make it look good, Kendrick had told Dimitri on the drive in.

She's going to kill me, Dimitri had answered.

Kendrick, the dickhead, had grinned. *Probably,* he'd said.

Jaycee stopped in front of Dimitri, her head high. She'd arrived separately, driven here by Kendrick's mate, Addie. Addie had vehemently opposed the idea of the punishment ritual, but she'd at last conceded, understanding the why of it, if not approving. However, she'd decided Jaycee should not come alone.

The conversation in Addie's car must have been rich. Dimitri had sworn he felt his wolf's red furry ears burning.

Jaycee had pulled her thick and sleek brown gold hair into a ponytail, which emphasized the smooth sweetness of her face. She had leopard's eyes, which were golden but with a shot of darkness. Dimitri studied the lips that could be gentle and loving on his, and the body that knocked him off his feet, sometimes literally.

She is so fucking beautiful . . .

The ritual began as soon as Jaycee stepped into the pool

of sunshine between the trees. Dimitri went forward to meet her, placed his hands on her shoulders, and started to push her to her knees.

Jaycee resisted. Dimitri glared at her, and Jaycee glared right back.

"Go down," Dimitri said in a fierce whisper. They'd rehearsed this—she was to kneel, to show the Shifters Dimitri had mastery over his mate.

But practicing the ritual in the dining room, laughing with Kendrick's cubs, was completely different from standing in front of dozens of gleeful Shifters waiting for the take-no-shit Jaycee to get her comeuppance.

Jaycee, with a scowl, finally allowed herself to fall to her knees. She refused to bow her head, though.

Kendrick came off the porch. He halted a respectful distance from Dimitri and Jaycee, making sure he didn't interfere with Dimitri's position of dominance, and spoke.

"Jaycee Bordeaux," Kendrick rumbled. "Do you acknowledge that you broke the rules of the Shifter fight club, designed to protect the safety of all Shifters?"

They'd agreed that Kendrick would do the talking—Dimitri knew he'd never get through a long speech in front of other Shifters.

Jaycee answered Dimitri, not Kendrick. "Yes," she said, voice hard.

Kendrick went on. "Do you acknowledge that you endangered all Shifters your disobedience might touch, and do you accept the punishment for your actions?"

Jaycee took longer to answer this time. Her eyes sparked dangerously as she looked up at Dimitri. "Yes."

Kendrick fell back, finished. It was up to Dimitri now.

Dimitri lifted his hand. He let his fingers become wolf claws, gleaming in the morning sunlight. Jaycee continued to glare at him, knowing what was coming.

"You're supposed to be s-submissive," Dimitri whispered to her.

Jaycee's eyes narrowed; then, at last, she stiffly bowed her head, looking about as submissive as an enraged rhino.

But then, Jaycee wasn't a Lupine. Lupines knew how to look submissive even as they were plotting their enemy's drawn-out demise. Felines just said *fuck you*.

Dimitri lowered his wolf hand to Jaycee's back, moving all the way down to her hips. Abruptly he dragged his claws up her spine, just enough to lay open her shirt and expose her flesh.

In the bad old days in the wild, a Shifter male disciplining his mate would have sunk his claws into her skin itself. Even these days more brutal Shifters would do it. Dimitri would never hurt Jaycee though. Not his girl.

In the wild, Dimitri could have done anything he wanted, if Jaycee had warranted a punishment in his opinion, and been considered justified by the rest of the Shifter community. He could even push her facedown and screw her in front of everybody, even kill her if she didn't submit.

But those were the faraway times when Shifters had been slaves of the Fae, bred for savagery. Nowadays, most Shifters wouldn't dream of cruelty to the females. There were too few females, for one thing; they were too dear. For the other, the females could turn around and slice the males open. Not that this hadn't happened in the bad old days as well. Females might have been regarded as below males in the hierarchy, but they'd never been considered *weak*.

"Jaycee," Dimitri said, making his voice so quiet only Jaycee would hear. "You're a bad k-kitty."

Jaycee flashed a look up at him, slightly less enraged, her slow smile hot. She bowed her head again and bent to press her face to the ground.

Dimitri moved forward, placing his feet on either side of her and resting one hand on her bared back. This could be sexy if a bunch of Shifters weren't watching, eager to see what Dimitri would do. Maybe Jaycee was right, and Shifters were pervs.

Dimitri leaned down and pressed his mouth to the back of Jaycee's neck. If they'd taken their animal forms, he'd have turned her over and closed his jaws around her throat, not pressing, but showing her he could kill her if he wanted to. Dimitri and Jaycee had chosen to remain in human form for the ritual, because Jaycee hadn't been sure she could make her leopard roll over and accept the dominant bite of a wolf.

Dimitri lifted his head and fixed his stare on the watchers. He shifted into his half-wolf form, feeling his T-shirt rip on his back, and gave them a snarl.

In his between-beast form, Dimitri didn't stammer. He wasn't sure why, but figured the wolf in him started to take over all parts of his brain, including his speech. "Jaycee has acknowledged her wrong," he told the waiting Shifters, "and has submitted to me. It is done."

As the Shifters' murmurs came to him like waves of wind, Dimitri leaned down and pulled Jaycee to her feet. He shifted back to his human form to draw her into his arms and hold her close, his hands on her warm back.

Jaycee finally relaxed and leaned into him, and Dimitri rested his cheek on her sun-drenched and fragrant hair.

The Shifters applauded. Some cheered. The punishment ritual meant the disobedient one had been exposed to the group's scrutiny and then accepted back into the pack.

The Shifters drifted away and then did what Shifters had done for centuries once a ritual was finished. They got out the beer and started to party.

Jaycee wrapped her arms around Dimitri, her body warm and supple. She rose on tiptoe to nip his earlobe and said quietly, "If you enjoyed that, I'm going to kill you."

"Yeah, I figured." Dimitri held her close, running his hands up and down her back to comfort her, and pressed a kiss to her hair. "I didn't enjoy it, Jase. It was for show." He laughed softly. "Okay, maybe just a l-little."

Jaycee drew back to look at him, but she kept her arms around him. "You won't know when, Dimitri, but my revenge will be coming. I'm a tracker, not stupid enough to screw up an op, but when it's over . . ."

She let it hang. Dimitri grinned, his blood heating in anticipation. He kissed her on the mouth and let her go. "Looking forward to it, sweetheart."

* * *

Jaycee didn't know how they were supposed to find the Lupine who'd tried to tranq Dimitri in the ring. At a roadhouse? A mall? An Austin coffeehouse? Hang around on street corners until he stumbled upon them? How did Shifters plotting to work with the Fae meet up?

Dimitri, damn him, didn't look worried about it. Back home at the ranch that night, he shrugged and said they would carry on as usual—the guy would likely find them.

Jaycee didn't know how he could be so patient. She wanted to find the dickbrain who'd stuck a needle into her mate and seriously kick his ass.

No—find said dickbrain and figure out what he knew. That was her job. Jaycee had been a tracker long enough to know she had to put aside her personal feelings to hunt and scout, kick ass later. She'd made a pledge to serve and protect her leader and all the Shifters that leader was responsible for. Even if waiting made her crazy.

The ranch house Kendrick had taken over for his group of un-Collared Shifters was run by a human called Charlie. Charlie was the original owner of the house, which had once been a bed-and-breakfast. He technically still owned it, but he ran it for Kendrick, keeping the Shifters stocked in food, beer, and other necessities of life.

Charlie was in his sixties, a Vietnam vet, and had once lived in a commune. He liked to joke that all this had been good practice for looking after a bunch of unruly Shifters.

Jaycee had taken to helping Charlie close down the house at night, check the grounds to make sure all was well. The one horse in the barn still wasn't certain of Jaycee—it knew she was a leopard at heart—but it had calmed enough to let her feed it and secure it for the night.

"Waiting drives me insane," Jaycee said impatiently to Charlie after they finished the chores. They walked together through the barn, which was basically a long breezeway with open doors on either end. "Dimitri acts like we have all the time in the world."

"Well, you do, really." Charlie led Jaycee out, and they climbed to the top of the rise behind the barn. From there they could gaze down at the ranch house and the smaller houses that had recently sprung up for Shifters and their families. There was plenty of space between the houses, but Charlie's ranch had the room. "From what Kendrick says, sounds like this rogue Shifter thing has been going on a while."

"Yes, but I didn't know about it then," Jaycee returned. "Now that I know, I want to *do* something."

Charlie chuckled, late-afternoon sunshine glinting on his graying hair, short locks of which moved in the wind. "That's because you're a cat. You get your focus on a thing, and you want to pounce. Your Dimitri is a wolf. Wolves can lie in wait for a long time. I've seen that on documentaries."

"Cats are superior stalkers," Jaycee said with certainty.

"Only until they run out of patience." Charlie winked at her. "Which you do very fast, my dear."

Jaycee sighed. "I know." She found it easy to talk to Charlie, which had surprised her at first. She'd never had much interaction with humans. Charlie was unbelievably understanding, though he wasn't a pushover. He'd agreed to let Kendrick and his Shifters live here for a substantial amount of money, but he didn't put up with any shit from them.

"I'm not going to give you the BS that you should listen to your man 'cause he knows best," Charlie said. "Lord knows, my Edna never listened to me. Good thing too, or we'd probably have been broke with nothing to eat. But don't dismiss Dimitri. He's a good guy."

"I can't dismiss Dimitri," Jaycee said glumly. "He won't let me."

Charlie grinned. "No, he's pretty gone on you. But he's trying not to push you."

Jaycee stared at him. "Are you kidding me? Dimitri is seriously pushy. Sticks by me wherever I go, reminds me day and night he's mate-claimed me, snarls at any male who even comes near me."

Charlie shook his head. "He knows it riles you up, honey.

He likes to see how far he can go before you explode. And he does it because he's afraid that you might give him the heave-ho. He's reassuring himself."

"Huh." Jaycee folded her arms over her chest. "Dimitri's not afraid of anything. If I turn down the mate-claim, he'll just find another female to run after him. He won't be single long. I see them eyeing him already, hoping I'll get out of the way."

She finished bitterly. The females under Kendrick's rule, even those she'd thought were her friends, were hot to land Dimitri. He was high in the hierarchy, Kendrick's third in command. While males outnumbered females, a strong Shifter like Dimitri drew a lot of attention.

Jaycee had noticed lately how the Shifter ladies watched Dimitri whenever he appeared, managed to wear little clothing around him, and swayed their hips when they walked past him. Dimitri, always friendly, didn't admonish them. He didn't respond, either, but in Jaycee's angry state, this fact didn't comfort her.

The mate-claim meant Jaycee was off-limits to other males, but it didn't necessarily mean Dimitri was off-limits to females. In the mating dance, females had a lot of power, even if they couldn't instigate the mate-claim. Before the Shifter-Fae war that had freed the Shifters centuries ago, males had often mate-claimed several females at once, which had been necessary in order for Shifters to produce as many offspring as they could.

Therefore, female instinct didn't worry about whether a male was already in a relationship—they chased his ass until the male went through the mating ceremonies with his chosen one. The mate-claimed female could be vicious, however, fighting off the other females with savagery. Blood had been drawn over male mates before this.

"I wouldn't worry," Charlie said. "I only ever see Dimitri looking at *you*." He spoke cheerfully, confident that everything would work out. "There he is now." He waved at Dimitri, who'd come out onto the back porch. Dimitri looked up the hill, shading his eyes against the setting sun.

Jaycee's heart squeezed into a tight ball. Dimitri stood

straight and tall, his hard body outlined by jeans and a T-shirt, his red hair burnished by the sun. He hadn't shaved in a day or two, and the shadow of whiskers outlined his jaw. Dimitri didn't wave back, only stood watching, but he didn't have to do much of anything to arrest Jaycee's attention.

She'd spent a while in her younger days being infatuated with Kendrick, but Jaycee knew now this was because Kendrick was a natural leader and had made her feel safe. He'd taken her in when she'd been a scared but unruly cub, nurturing her until her terrors had gone away. She'd hero-worshiped Kendrick, and this idolization had lasted past her Transition into adulthood.

Even so, she'd always turned her head to look when Dimitri walked by. She'd resisted her attraction to him for a long time, telling herself she betrayed Kendrick with her thoughts, but she'd enjoyed watching Dimitri—and fantasizing. Then she'd tease the hell out of Dimitri to make herself feel less ashamed of the fantasies, which were usually about Dimitri naked, often wet and glistening in the sunlight. In these waking dreams, Dimitri would lay Jaycee down wherever they happened to be—beside a bathtub, on a riverbank, on a beach—and make hot love to her. The fiercer the fantasy, the harder Jaycee gave him hell to compensate.

Dimitri gave her hell right back, never letting her get away with anything.

Jaycee kept her hands balled into fists as she and Charlie walked steadily down the hill toward the house. Dimitri waited for them, resting his hands on the porch railing, his body taut, yet he had a lightness in his stance that came from the wild animal inside him.

Jaycee hadn't spoken to him since the punishment ritual. Now, as she approached the porch, her mouth went dry and her palms began to perspire. She probably looked less than attractive, with her jeans and shirt covered with dust, bits of hay, and, she was willing to bet, a little horse poop.

Dimitri gave her a once-over with his gray eyes as she mounted the porch steps, Charlie hanging back to let her go first, as humans did.

"Hey, s-sweetie." Dimitri's voice was a rumbling growl. "Kendrick's sending us to the roadhouse to see if we can snare some Sh-Shifters. Go make yourself sexy—*er.*"

Jaycee did her best not to flush as she reached the porch. She had to slide around Dimitri's body to get to the door, and Dimitri wasn't about to move. He looked down at her, fire in his eyes, as Jaycee turned sideways to go past and tried not to look up at him.

She was fully aware of every inch of him, though, and the heat of his body through his thin T-shirt, the sensation like a caress. Dimitri didn't touch her and said nothing, only stood like a rock while she, the stream, tried to flow around him.

She finally made it to the door and inside, feeling Dimitri's gaze on her all the way. His laughter at something Charlie said warmed her as she hurried down the hall to her bedroom and shut him out.

Jaycee leaned against the door, out of breath, her skin on fire. "Damn you," she whispered.

The vivid sensation flooded her of Dimitri standing over her in the grass in Shiftertown, his legs around her, his hand and mouth on the back of her neck. Jaycee had wanted to combust. Dimitri had been in total command, but Jaycee had known in her heart he'd never hurt her. He'd made her feel protected but wanted, sensual and alive.

He'd held her close when he'd raised her to her feet, his gray eyes dark with emotion. Jaycee had clung to him, feeling his heartbeat against her chest, enclosing herself in his heat.

"*Damn* it." Jaycee was going to burn up and die, and Dimitri would only laugh.

His mate was the sexiest thing in this bar, which both pleased and alarmed Dimitri. A mate-claim was hell.

The Shifters in the roadhouse knew she was mate-claimed—they'd have scented Dimitri on her and understood what it meant. And still they ogled her.

Dimitri couldn't blame them. Female Shifters were few

and far between, and Jaycee was worth a second look—a third and fourth one too.

She was also driving them wild. Jaycee danced by herself in the middle of the floor, and the Shifter males gathered around her. She'd chosen a brief skirt that showed off her legs and a body-hugging tank top with skinny straps that allowed the thicker straps of her lacy bra to show. The tank's white fabric let everyone know the bra beneath it was dark blue. More enticing, in Dimitri's opinion, than if she'd left the bra off altogether. It made the Shifters around her wonder what it would be like to unwrap the package.

She'd been wearing shoes when she'd climbed into the truck Dimitri had acquired a few months ago, but Jaycee was now barefoot, the shoes tucked somewhere under the bar's counter.

Dimitri, at the bar, had his hands around a mug of beer as his heart burned, reflecting absently that roadhouse draft tasted like watery piss. But it was no good asking for a craft beer in a place like this.

He turned to watch Jaycee as she swayed to the music. She was a great dancer, as lithe and graceful as her leopard. A Collar winked around her neck—fake, but it only enhanced the curve of her throat. Men, both human and Shifter, moved closer to her, and Dimitri growled, his rage building.

"Man, I feel for you." A Lupine Shifter, one Dimitri had never seen before, slid onto the barstool next to his. The Lupine's dark hair was scruffy but not dirty, and his light gray eyes held sympathy. "She's a beauty," he said. "You want to tame her but not break her, am I right?"

Dimitri knew he didn't have a snowball's chance of taming Jaycee, but he nodded. "She's a w-w-wild one."

"Makes life exciting." The Lupine nodded at the bartender, a human, who set a beer in front of him. "You're Dimitri, right?"

Dimitri hid his start of unease. This was not the Shifter he'd fought in the ring, the one who'd stuck him with a tranq, but that didn't mean the Lupine wasn't dangerous.

The Lupine grinned, the wolf showing in his eyes. "Don't

worry, you've never met me. But I saw you fight the other night. You're good."

"Then you saw me get m-my ass kicked." Dimitri forced himself to calmly take a sip of beer and not to make a face at the taste.

"Yeah, but you held out. You'd have won if your lady hadn't barged in. Man, I laughed my butt off."

"Like I said, she's a w-wild one." Dimitri shook his head, but his heartbeat quickened. Was this Lupine simply making conversation or did he have something to do with the Lupine from the ring? He might be in the same pack or clan, or a friend . . . or he might have nothing to do with him at all.

"She's a good fighter," the Shifter said, watching Jaycee again. "I heard your leader made you humiliate her in front of the entire Austin Shiftertown. Too bad. She didn't deserve that."

"No, sh-she didn't." Dimitri stuck to the literal truth—Shifters could scent lies.

He felt no surprise that this Lupine knew exactly what had happened with Jaycee this morning. Gossip flew through Shiftertowns and out their other side with the thoroughness of a tornado, which was the reason Dylan had decreed they'd do the discipline ritual in public. It would spread the idea that Jaycee constantly needed to be reined in, which was not far from the truth. Dylan and Kendrick had probably spent the rest of the day spreading stories about the punishment as well.

The Lupine watched Jaycee in appreciation. Jaycee turned toward them, her arms aloft while she gyrated slowly, her body pressing against the tank top, her hips moving. Fire seared Dimitri's blood.

The Lupine laughed. "Down, son. Before every Shifter in the bar is fighting you for her." He gave Dimitri a reassuring look. "Oh, you don't have to worry about me. I'm mated. I'm Casey, by the way."

He didn't offer a hand for a shake like a human might. He simply held Dimitri's gaze, assessing him, trying to decide where Dimitri fit in the relative hierarchy of all Shifters.

This Lupine might have nothing to do with rogues or the

shit who'd tranquilized Dimitri. He might just be a fight fan. Or he might be the leader of whoever was organizing Shifters to work with the Fae. Who the hell knew?

Only one way to find out. Dimitri instinctively sensed that he outranked Casey, but he dropped his gaze after a few seconds. He needed to show he was strong but not too strong, compliant but not too compliant. A fine line to walk.

"N-nice to meet you," Dimitri said.

"Want to go a round with me?" Casey asked. "Just you—can you keep your mate from interfering?" His eyes sparkled with good humor.

Dimitri slowed his quickening heartbeat—a Shifter would sense that too. "Sure," he said.

"Great." Casey took a few large gulps of his beer and slammed the glass down on the bar. "Let's go."

CHAPTER FOUR

Jaycee almost missed Dimitri slipping out with the Lupine. She turned in the dancing—she loved to dance—to see him giving her a long look before he followed the other Shifter across the bar to the front door.

Jaycee growled in her throat, sent a wide smile to her dozen dance partners, and turned sideways to slide through them, intent on grabbing her shoes and following Dimitri.

One Shifter, a Feline, put a hand out and grabbed her arm. "Forget him, angel," the Feline, a leopard, said, pinning her with hazel eyes. "I'll Challenge him if you want me to. Or we'll just stay here while he runs off with his new boyfriend."

Jaycee's growl was drowned out by the music, but the Feline must have seen her eyes change.

"What, now you're going to fight me, bitch?" he demanded. "Fine by me. We'll spar, then I'll take you when we go down."

Oh, for the Goddess' sake. Jaycee could easily slam the guy to the floor, but his eleven friends might object. Jaycee could hold her own, but not against a dozen—she wasn't that optimistic.

Dimitri was waiting at the door, a scowl on his face. Any

second now, he'd come storming over here, and then this stupid Feline would Challenge Dimitri's mate-claim, and the floor would get very bloody very quickly.

Jaycee softened her glare into a smile. "Sure thing, honeybunch. What's your clan? I'm not sure what mine is—I'm an orphan. Who knows? We might be long lost cousins."

The Feline blinked and backed a step. It was taboo for Shifters of the same clan to mate—the instinct to keep the gene pool strong was bred deep inside every Shifter.

Jaycee took advantage of his hesitation to shake him off. She sent him a wink, as though she understood his worry, hurried to the bar to grab the shoes she'd shoved underneath, and turned to follow Dimitri, hopping to slide the heels onto her feet.

Another Shifter stepped in front of her. "*I'm* not in your clan," he said with the rough growl of a grizzly bear.

Terrific. Jaycee didn't like fighting bears—she was faster than they were, but they were *big*. One swat of a paw and she could go soaring across the room. Then Dimitri would storm over, and the bloodbath would ensue.

Dimitri, however, only made a faint gesture with his fingers. Instantly, ten other Shifters rose from chairs and stools and surrounded the bear.

"She's from *our* clan," said a tall Lupine who lived at Kendrick's ranch.

Friends were good things to have. Jaycee flashed her fellow Shifters a grin, left the bear spluttering, and joined Dimitri.

"How were our guys in place to help me out?" she asked as she joined Dimitri at the door. The Shifter Dimitri had taken up with was already outside, waiting for them in the middle of the lot. "Just happened to be here, were they?"

"It pays to have b-backup," Dimitri said without inflection. He didn't change expression, but Jaycee could see he was pleased with himself.

"Yeah, you're brilliant. Who is this guy?" Jaycee let her voice drop to nothing as they stepped out into the hot parking lot. The temperature that afternoon had been in the hundreds, and now heat wafted back from the asphalt.

"He wants to fight me," Dimitri said. "Spar, I mean. Name's C-C-C—" He broke off, face twisting in frustration. *"Shit."*

Dimitri always had trouble when pronouncing unfamiliar words. It was as though he had to learn painstakingly what others picked up easily. Jaycee wasn't sure whether this was because he hadn't spoken English until the age of ten or if some trauma had cut into his speech. She'd heard that bad situations in childhood could lead to stammering and speech impairment, but she had no idea if that had been the case with Dimitri. He never spoke much about his life before he'd come to live with Kendrick.

Jaycee squeezed Dimitri's hand and moved past him. "I'm Jaycee," she said as she approached the unfamiliar Shifter.

"Casey," he said.

He was Lupine. Gray or black wolf, Jaycee couldn't tell, though gray was most common. Lupines had been created to be the best of all species of wolves, but they tended toward one type or the other, as did Felines.

Dimitri was the oddity. Not many red wolves around. It made him lonely, Jaycee knew, but it also made him unique— only one of him. She liked that.

Dimitri motioned to his pickup, and Casey gave him a nod, agreeing to go with them instead of insisting he drive. Casey would know they didn't trust him, but that was fine. Shifters trusting each other too quickly would be suspicious.

Dimitri opened the passenger door of his truck, checked that all was well inside, and helped Jaycee in. His grip on her arm was firmer than necessary, and his grim face told her the Shifters surrounding Jaycee in the bar had angered him more than he'd let on. His touch was possessive, his eyes betraying his rage. Jaycee touched his hand as she climbed inside, caressing it to soothe him.

Dimitri's gaze flicked to hers, his usual good-natured warmth gone. He was a Shifter who needed his mate, ready to ruthlessly battle those who stood in his way.

Jaycee gave his hand another caress, feeling the energy

and wrath inside him. One day it would all come spilling out, bad luck to anyone who got in his way.

Dimitri sucked in a breath, gave her a hot stare, then withdrew, leaving Jaycee breathless.

She had the presence of mind to slide over and give Casey room before he climbed inside behind her. Dimitri, with his customary swiftness, had already made it to the driver's side and was in as Casey closed the passenger door.

"Where to?" Dimitri asked as he turned over the motor.

Casey shrugged, leaning back to look at him around Jaycee. "Fight club arena?"

"Too public." Dimitri drove slowly out of the lot. There were no scheduled fights tonight, but Shifters often went to the arena to spar between bouts.

"Where, then?" Casey asked.

Dimitri thought silently for a moment, then said, "Lake T-Travis. I know some s-spots."

"Shifters aren't allowed," Casey answered automatically.

Jaycee laughed. "Shifters aren't allowed to do a lot of crap. That shouldn't stop us."

Casey flashed her an approving look. "Hey, I like the way you think."

Dimitri drove west out of Austin on the 2222 until it could go no farther, then turned onto a narrow road and headed out into darkness.

Much development had encroached on the lake even in the few years Jaycee and Dimitri had lived in and around Hill Country. Still, there were remote spots along the Colorado where Shifters could run, and Dimitri knew how to find them. Jaycee came out here with him often, the two of them scouting or simply enjoying the solitude. They'd leave their fake Collars off and pretend to be ordinary joggers or boaters while human, then shift and run through the wilderness, reveling in the freedom of it.

Dimitri pulled onto another narrow road, where the darkness was complete. His headlights cut through brush, startling rabbits and flashing in the yellow eyes of coyotes. After a time, Dimitri pulled off the road, stopped the truck, and shut off the engine.

A half-moon hung in the southeast, and the light of stars bathed the ground in faint white light. A glow to the east showed Austin and its surrounding towns, another to the south indicating San Antonio.

"Light pollution," Casey grunted. "When I was a cub, you could see all the stars no matter where you stood. Now we have to search for darkness."

"Yep," Dimitri agreed. He slid out of the truck. "Sucks."

Jaycee scrambled out the driver's side after him. She knew exactly where they were, her Shifter vision showing her the outline of a familiar bluff overlooking a wide bend of river. She and Dimitri had come out here to run many times.

Casey climbed out and joined them, looking wary. They'd brought him far from the city, a long way from his pack, his friends, his Shiftertown. "What is this place?" he asked.

Dimitri studied the skies, his body in silhouette, then he walked to a fairly flat place on the ground and started pulling off his boots. He was finished with words, Jaycee knew.

"We come here a lot," she answered for Dimitri. "It's far enough from human communities for privacy, especially at night. If you're worried, we can take you back to the road-house."

She gave Casey a look that said she only wanted to be friendly and helpful. Addie, Kendrick's mate, had taught her the benefit of the cheerful, sympathetic tone of voice.

"No, it's fine," Casey said.

He toed off his running shoes and began to strip. Jaycee found a boulder to rest on, drawing her feet up. She'd be ref, was the unspoken agreement.

At the moment, she was busy watching Dimitri undress. He'd dragged his T-shirt from his broad shoulders and back, which were scarred from his bouts in the fight-club ring. Now he unself-consciously unbuttoned and unzipped his jeans, dropping them down his legs and kicking them away. Dimitri was a fine sight standing up in nothing but his tight boxer briefs, made even finer when he pulled those off as well.

He walked to a rock-free spot on the open ground. Moonlight glistened on his fake Collar and his strong body, his red hair dark under the white light. He waited, hands on hips, unaware he looked like a god. Or at least what Jaycee thought a god should look like—strong, agile, balancing on bare feet on the dirt, his hands loose while he sized up Casey, who'd finished removing his clothes.

"To first blood?" Casey asked.

"M-might be a f-fast fight. For me." Dimitri tapped his Collar. "Only fair to t-tell you. Doesn't work."

"I noticed that." Casey studied first Dimitri's Collar, then Jaycee's. "Doesn't matter. I've trained myself to not worry about my Collar much. To first blood. Your lady stops us if we get frenzied."

Dimitri nodded once, as though that sounded reasonable.

Jaycee rose from her place to move to the fighting area, but she clenched her hands, nervous. Casey could be up to any number of things—or he could simply be a Shifter who wanted to see what he could do against a good fighter.

Regardless, Jaycee knew she wouldn't be able to break up two males in the throes of fighting frenzy. Shifters could become what humans called *berserk*—a reference to Norsemen who fought with mindless ferocity. When Shifters got too far into fighting, nothing could stop them short of a heavy dose of tranquilizer. Jaycee had a small syringe in her pocket tonight, tucked there in case they found Shifters who objected to being spied upon, but getting close enough to use it would be the problem.

She cleared her throat, willing to go along with the charade for now. "Ready?" she asked. When Dimitri and then Casey nodded, Jaycee lifted her hand and brought it down. *"Fight."*

Dimitri went instantly into a half crouch. He began moving in a slow circle, fists quiet, scrutinizing his target. Casey did the same, analyzing Dimitri's fighting stance, looking for weaknesses.

Dimitri, as usual, waited for his opponent to make the first move. Frustrated Jaycee when he did, but Dimitri said

fighters often gave themselves away in the first few seconds
of the bout. After that, it was just cleanup.

Casey lunged, shifting to his half beast to strike.

Dimitri spun out of his way, shifting fully as he went.
He came down as a thick-furred red wolf and met Casey's
attack.

The contrast between the two wolves was marked. Casey
was a gray, the muzzle of his half beast showing white mot-
tling in gray fur. Dimitri's fur was red fading to tawny at
his chest, his tail tipped with black.

The difference between them didn't stop at fur color.
Dimitri's ears were more rounded, his muzzle sharper than
that of a gray or black wolf. His physique was why other
Lupines mockingly called him *coyote*, but red wolves weren't
coyotes at all. Jaycee had looked that up a long time ago. They
were rare, however, especially among Shifters.

Casey closed on Dimitri, claws lashing. His Collar
sparked, but he'd spoken the truth when he'd said he could
ignore it. Electricity bit into Casey's neck but he never flinched
as he dug huge paws into Dimitri and tried to yank him off
his feet.

Shifters were extremely strong in their half-man, half-
beast forms, usually stronger than their full animals. Why
Dimitri was remaining in his wolf form while Casey fought
as half beast, Jaycee didn't understand.

Wait, yes, she did. Dimitri had reasoned that being Collar-
free gave him an edge, and he was trying to compensate to
keep the fight even. He was playing fair. Dimitri did things
like that, which made Jaycee want to yell at him. He could
get himself killed playing fair.

Dimitri leapt at Casey, didn't matter that Casey was busy
trying to pound him into the dirt. Dimitri dodged under the
half beast's longer reach, slammed his body into Casey's
chest, and then pushed off him, raking all four claws into
Casey's torso as he went. Gray fur flew, but no blood appeared.

Casey's Collar sparked still more as he leapt in retalia-
tion at Dimitri. Dimitri spun in a fury of dust and red fur,

aimed beneath Casey's reach again, and launched himself into the other man's body. This time Dimitri closed his teeth around the loose wolf skin between Casey's chest and throat.

Casey howled and shook himself. Dimitri's body flopped as Casey's strength flung him around until Dimitri, pried loose, tumbled away. Dimitri came up with a mouthful of wolf hair, his muzzle stained with Casey's blood.

Blood flowed from the wound Dimitri had left, but Casey didn't halt. He roared in rage and lunged for Dimitri.

Jaycee slammed herself in front of Casey. He was a nightmare beast, half shifted, his eyes red with rage, but Jaycee stood her ground.

"First blood," she shouted up at him. "Fight's over."

Casey started for her, ready to battle Jaycee if she didn't get out of his way. Jaycee didn't move. She'd stared down plenty of out-of-control pissed-off Shifters in her time—stared them down and won. She'd perfected the *don't-mess-with-me-you-shithead* glare, and she used it now.

Casey was fairly dominant, she could see, but not as dominant as Jaycee. He snarled at her but halted his attack. After a moment under her steady gaze the crazed fury left his eyes, and then he shifted to human and took a long breath.

Dimitri hadn't moved from where he'd taken up his stance as the victor of the fight. He hadn't come forward to defend Jaycee but he'd watched every movement Casey made, every twitch of his muscle.

Jaycee knew Dimitri would have been on Casey in an instant if he'd attacked her. Dimitri let Jaycee hold her own, but he was always there to back her up the moment she needed it. The feeling of being guarded warmed her.

Dimitri, still in wolf form, walked to Jaycee's side and sat down, his fur warm against her legs.

"Good fight," Casey said, breathing hard.

Dimitri gave him a conceding growl; then he let his tongue loll out as he began to pant.

"Dimitri agrees," Jaycee said. She wasn't quite sure how

to continue the conversation by herself, but Dimitri apparently was going to stay wolf a while.

But, oh well, they weren't out here to be social. If Casey was a villain, he'd reveal himself sooner or later. If not, then they'd go back to the bar, have more beer, and the two guys would relive every move of the fight, ad nauseam, as males were wont to do. Jaycee would listen until she rolled her eyes and then went back out to dance.

Casey glanced at the moon, which had risen higher as they'd sparred. "We should give thanks to the Goddess," he said. "Well fought, no injuries."

Dimitri didn't move, didn't blink. Casey switched his gaze to Jaycee, waiting for her to answer.

Jaycee wondered if this was a test of some kind—if the way she responded would decide whether Casey would open up with all kinds of information about Shifters who worked with the Fae. Or, again, he might simply be a normal Shifter, one who liked to show respect for the Goddess.

"Sure," Jaycee said uncertainly. All Shifters performed rituals to the Goddess, from private meditation and prayer to big public ceremonies such as matings or send-offs for the dead. Some Shifters were more devout than others, but all shared faith. "Nothing wrong with honoring the Goddess."

Casey relaxed, and Jaycee congratulated herself on saying the right thing. Casey reached for her and took her hand, not in an intrusive or suggestive way, but as though they were friends, Shifters together under the sky. Didn't matter that he was stark naked and Jaycee fully clothed—their natural forms were nothing to be ashamed of. For Shifters, being nude didn't automatically equate to a need for sex.

Casey apparently had nothing sexual in mind as he led Jaycee to the top of the bluff overlooking the river. The Colorado narrowed here, glittering under the moonlight in its long journey from West Texas to the Gulf.

Dimitri walked close to Jaycee's other side, his wolf body in contact with hers, his strength easing her worries.

Formal prayers to the Goddess usually involved fire— Shifters connected with the Goddess through her gift of warmth and light in the night. As far as Jaycee knew, Dimitri hadn't packed a brazier in his new truck. Starting a fire on the ground would attract attention, and could easily become an uncontrollable wildfire through the dry Texas lands. Even a lighter or a candle would show in the clear air for miles, so they'd be doing this prayer in the dark.

The lack of fire didn't seem to bother Casey. He simply looked out over the river, his hand in Jaycee's, while Jaycee rested her palm on Dimitri's furry head.

Casey abruptly raised his and Jaycee's joined hands high. "Goddess, we thank thee for the beauty of the earth and your light to guide us in the darkness," he proclaimed to the sky. "And for the strength of the Shifters, so that we may survive to enjoy your world."

Dimitri moved against Jaycee's side and shot her a glance. Casey's wasn't a highly unusual prayer, though most Shifters kept prayers focused on friends and family.

Casey lowered their hands. The three stood in silence, watching the night. Stars glittered, and the moon bathed them in cool light.

A meteor streaked across the sky, a brief shaft of light that quickly died. Another followed, and one more. Then darkness descended again.

Casey let out a breath. "Did you see that? The Goddess blesses us."

Dimitri sat down on his haunches, his huff faint, but Jaycee heard it. It was a snort of derision, Dimitri's opinion on Shifters who believed the Goddess controlled every tiny detail of the entire universe. Casey didn't seem to notice, his face turned up to the stars.

After a time, Casey released Jaycee's hand and faced Dimitri, relaxed and calm. "Good fight," he said again. His chest bore faint red gouges from Dimitri's teeth, but the wound was fading and closing. Dimitri hadn't bitten him very deeply, and Shifters healed quickly. Casey gave him a rueful look. "Guess I got too cocky."

Under Jaycee's hand the red wolf began to move and change, big ears receding, muzzle shortening, tail disappearing. Cartilage cracked, and after a few moments, Dimitri the man stood at Jaycee's side in a body that made her mouth dry.

Dimitri smoothed his short red hair with one hand and gave Casey a grin. "We all d-do."

Casey frowned at him. "It's unusual to find a Shifter with any imperfection. No offense," he added quickly.

"You mean my st-stammer?" Dimitri shrugged. "Only in English, and only when I'm h-human. I d-don't think of it as an . . . im-imp—" He shook his head, unable to spit out the word.

"I know someone who might be able to help you," Casey said. "Well, I don't *know* if he can. If the Goddess has decided you should stutter, maybe there's a reason for it. But if it's only a problem with English or a confidence thing, I think this guy can help."

"What guy?" Jaycee asked sharply. She didn't like other people talking about Dimitri and his stammer, especially when they looked at him as though he were a lab experiment. "A Shifter?"

"Yes, a Shifter." Casey gave her a reassuring nod. "You won't know him. He's not from around here."

Hmm. *You are exactly the sort of Shifters a splinter group would want,* Dylan had instructed Jaycee and Dimitri. *So find one. Join them. And tell me what they're up to.*

Following up on Casey and his friend not from around here was exactly the task she and Dimitri had been charged to do. If they had to pretend Dimitri was worried about his stutter, then they did, as much as Jaycee disliked others discussing it. There was nothing *wrong* with Dimitri—he was fine the way he was.

"What Sh-Shiftertown are you f-from?" Dimitri asked Casey.

"New Orleans." Casey saw how closely they were watching him and gave a short laugh. "You don't trust me, and I don't blame you. We're Shifters. We don't trust easily. But the human woman called Bree Fayette—she came to Austin and mated with one of your friends. Seamus, right? She knows me from New Orleans. Ask her about me."

Seamus, who was one higher in the hierarchy than Dimitri, had recently mated with a human woman who'd once been a Shifter groupie. Bree, when she'd lived in New Orleans, had put on makeup and fake cat's ears and gone to Shifter bars to be around Shifters. She'd given all that up to settle down with Seamus, but Bree retained a vast store of knowledge about Shifters, more than some Shifters knew themselves.

Jaycee liked Bree, who was fun and funny, who'd been through a lot but had compassion by the ton. She made a great mate for Seamus, who'd always been a bit of a loner.

Jaycee had never had much use for human women before, but in the past six months, she'd become good friends with two of them—Bree and Addison. Funny how life could change so swiftly.

She gave Casey a nod. "All right, I'll talk to her. What about this other Shifter you mentioned? Is he from New Orleans too?"

Casey hesitated, looking uncomfortable. "I won't say right now. He's a good person, but . . ." He fell silent, obviously choosing his words. "I can't ask you to trust me yet. You ask Bree about me, then if you want to talk to me again, you call me. I'm heading back to New Orleans tonight. Call me there, and we'll get together again."

Dimitri gave him a clear-eyed look, as though he didn't have a suspicious thought in his head. "S-sounds good to m-me."

"I swear he can fix that." Casey waved in the general direction of Dimitri's mouth. "If you want him to."

Dimitri's smile flared. "S-so I can say sweet n-nothings to my girl?"

"Thanks a lot," Jaycee said to Casey in a dry voice. "He talks too much as it is."

Casey's worried look evaporated. "You know, I like you two. I hope we can meet again." He stepped to Dimitri and spread his arms. Dimitri went to him, and the two closed into a hug.

It wasn't bad watching two very hot, well-muscled, bare male Shifters pull each other close. Casey wasn't feigning—he held Dimitri tightly, soaking in Dimitri's strength, one Shifter drawing comfort from another. Dimitri hugged him as firmly, rubbing Casey's back with his fist.

When they broke the embrace, Casey took a step back and squeezed Dimitri's shoulders. He looked more at ease now, Dimitri's dominance helping to calm him.

He turned to Jaycee. "Mind?" he asked Dimitri.

"Up t-to her." Dimitri shrugged. "I better warn you, she might k-kill you."

"Shut up," Jaycee said. She didn't really want to hug Casey, but she went to him without hesitation and stepped into his embrace.

Casey was a good hugger—Jaycee had to give him that. His body was hot against the cooling night, his hold strong but not sexual. Jaycee found herself unwinding, the thought forming that maybe they really had made a friend. Shifters didn't trust easily, as Casey had indicated, but Casey had a quality that said he only wanted to make everything better for the world.

Jaycee didn't pull away until Casey released her. Dimitri was watching closely, his eyes narrowed, but he said nothing. If jealousy stirred inside him, he hid it well.

They walked together back to the site of the fight, where the two males dressed. It was a shame to cover such male goodness, Jaycee thought, watching Dimitri settle his jeans over his fine backside, but they didn't have much choice.

When they reached the truck, Casey pulled out a scrap of paper and wrote his phone number on it. "Drop me anywhere," he said as he handed the number to Jaycee. "No need to go out of your way. I can walk back to the road-house."

"Nah," Dimitri said. "I g-gotcha."

The three didn't speak much as they drove the winding roads back through the outlying towns, Jaycee sitting against

Dimitri again, Casey on her other side. The traffic, even in Austin, had thinned this late, and it didn't take Dimitri long to make it through the city and down the Bastrop highway to the roadhouse. Casey pointed out a black Harley with polished chrome in the roadhouse parking lot, and Dimitri pulled to a halt beside it.

Casey said good night, squeezing both Jaycee's and Dimitri's hands before he climbed out of the truck and mounted the bike. Jaycee watched as Casey started up and rolled out, lifting his hand to them in a parting wave.

She let out her breath. "Damn it, I can't tell if he's an evil mastermind or just a nice guy."

"Or a serial k-killer," Dimitri said. "I hear they're n-nice."

Jaycee gave him a look of exasperation. "What do we tell Kendrick? That we got to know a Shifter who likes to fight and then pray to the Goddess? Who might know a Shifter who's good at speech therapy? I think we wasted the evening."

"N-night's not over yet." Dimitri slanted Jaycee a glance that made her shiver. "Come in and dance with me."

CHAPTER FIVE

Music crashed into Dimitri's senses, too loud to make much sense of the melody or lyrics. Didn't matter. The beat beneath it, thumping through the club, was what the dancers came for.

Like primal beasts, he thought as he seized Jaycee's hand and pulled her against him. Pounding drums in the night caught the need to pulse with the rhythm. Both humans and Shifters responded to it.

Makes us think of another rhythm, Dimitri's thoughts went on as Jaycee began to move against him. *It's why males and females go into bars separately and leave together.*

Fighting Casey had fired Dimitri's blood. They'd broken off long before a fight would end at the fight club, and his body hadn't had time to cool. Having Jaycee squashed next to him in the truck driving back hadn't helped.

Dimitri tugged her close as she tried to whirl away. Jaycee glanced up at him, startled, then smiled and laced her arms around his neck.

Growls welled in Dimitri's throat. The truncated fight

and Jaycee near was enough to trigger the frenzy that told him to take her somewhere private and not come out for days. Shifter instinct. A bitch to fight.

So why did they bother holding back? Cubs who came to mate-claimed mates, even before they were officially joined in the sun and moon ceremonies, were accepted. None of the human born-out-of-wedlock constraint. All cubs were welcome anytime—no shame was attached. Why were cubs to blame if their parents were impatient?

Jaycee didn't look particularly interested in doing anything but dancing. She swayed against Dimitri, her breasts cushioned on his chest. Did she do it to drive him crazy? Or was she simply enjoying the music?

A Shifter groupie—a male—spun slowly up to them. He was dressed as a wolf enthusiast, with a headband with fake wolf's ears, yellow contacts in his eyes, and his face painted with gray and white markings and whiskers. Jaycee turned, releasing Dimitri, and undulated her hips toward him. The man moved his leather-clad body in near-perfect imitation.

A few seconds later, the groupie was right against Jaycee, dancing body to body with her. Dimitri lunged at the man, letting out a fierce wolf snarl. *Back off.*

Instead of looking scared or angry, the groupie grinned with delight—happy a Shifter had acted like a Shifter. He beamed at Dimitri, gave him a thumbs-up, and danced away.

Jaycee turned to Dimitri, shaking with laughter. "Silly red wolf. He wasn't interested in *me*."

Dimitri felt a moment's surprise that all beings with testosterone wouldn't crave Jaycee, and then he shrugged. He pulled Jaycee against him again, his momentary rage having done nothing to sate his hunger.

Jaycee was still laughing, smiling with her wide mouth, her eyes sparkling under the dim lights. Dimitri leaned down and kissed her.

Jaycee started; then she wrapped her arms around him and kissed him back, as only Jaycee could kiss.

The music spun around them, the late-night dancers

melding into the darkness. Dimitri sensed their needs, Shifters never shy about them, but they faded to nothing against the fires of Dimitri's own desires.

He licked through Jaycee's mouth, tasting her spice. She crushed against him, a warm armful, her breasts soft against him. She pulled back the slightest bit, smiled up at him, and then brushed her tongue across his mouth.

Dimitri growled. He dragged her closer, the music surging through him, his heart speeding with it. He saw an answering spark in Jaycee's eyes as her body ceased swaying, the two of them going still in the middle of the gyrating couples.

Jaycee touched his face. Flickering lights played in her eyes, hiding what she thought. Dimitri leaned to her once more, his next kiss deeper, opening her mouth to his.

The music abruptly died and the lights snapped on. Dimitri blinked and jerked his head up, looking for danger, but it was only the club owner trying to close up.

Jaycee laughed at him. She'd been doing that since they were cubs.

Dimitri took her by the hand and led her out, speeding his steps as he got closer and closer to the door. He and Jaycee ran out together into the night, which was finally cool after a day of heat. The parking lot was mostly deserted, the space where Dimitri had left his truck, dark.

He halted with Jaycee on the passenger side of the pickup, pressed her back against the door, and leaned into her to kiss the side of her neck.

"You take my breath away," he whispered.

He expected Jaycee to make some quip, a joke at his expense, but when Dimitri raised his head, her eyes were gentle.

"I wish . . ." Her words died along with her smile, and she closed her mouth.

At any other time, Dimitri might have prodded her to finish the sentence. Tonight, he didn't have the patience.

He lifted her hands over her head, pinning her against the truck while he resumed kissing her. Jaycee's mouth moved with his, as did her body. She was pliant against him but strong, vibrant.

He hadn't made love to her since the night a couple of months ago when Kendrick had first mated with Addie. Kendrick's mating frenzy down the hall had touched Dimitri and Jaycee, and they'd had a fine time in Jaycee's room. Jaycee had been a little panicked about it in the morning, but she hadn't kicked him out.

Dimitri had then mate-claimed Jaycee when she'd been ready to race into grave danger to save Kendrick's life—the mate-claim meant Dimitri could refuse to let her put herself in peril. Not that she'd listened to him. Jaycee hadn't yet accepted the claim, but she hadn't rejected it either.

Of course, Jaycee would never be an obedient, docile, submissive female, mate-claim or not. She didn't obey without question and had no trouble telling alpha male Shifters, Dimitri included, what she thought of them.

Dimitri hadn't pressed her into making a final choice with the mate-claim or to come to his bed. He wasn't an asshole who was going to lock her up until she gave in to his will and became his sweet little submissive mate.

Although that might be fun. The thought made him want to smile, and to kiss her harder.

Jaycee made a faint noise in her throat as she struggled against his hold on her wrists. Then noise turned to a hum as she relaxed against him.

Dimitri eased back from the kiss, but he didn't let her go. He moved his kisses to her throat, inhaling her warmth. He licked the hollow of her collarbone, just below her fake Collar. The silver links were warm, and he bit them.

Jaycee's pulse beat hard beneath his mouth. Dimitri released her hands, but only so he could skim his under her tank top, finding the heat of her skin, the lace of the dark blue bra she wore. Her eyes half closed as he found and unhooked the fastening, then slid his hands around to cup the weight of her breasts.

Her skin was soft, the heat of her intoxicating. Jaycee wrapped her arms around him as she had inside, rocking a little as though they still danced. Dimitri kissed her as he swept his thumbs across her breasts, her nipples tightening under his touch.

Dimitri jumped when he felt her fingers sliding beneath his waistband, then the heat of them on his backside. He stepped more firmly against her, sacrificing one hand's hold of her beautiful breast to scoop her closer.

Jaycee's kiss turned fierce, her longing palpable.

Mate-claimed. Mine. Dimitri growled in his throat. The wolf in him needed her, wanted for them to curl up together and shut out the world.

You and me, his thoughts rolled. *It's always been you and me.* Dimitri wished he could say that to her without his tongue getting tangled.

Jaycee didn't seem to mind his tongue right now. She was sucking on it.

Dimitri held her against the cool side of the truck. A warm breeze blew around them, stirring Jaycee's hair.

Jaycee broke the kiss, regarding him with languid eyes. "You kiss nice, wolf."

Dimitri couldn't answer—his mouth wouldn't cooperate. If he could ramble on poetically or at least toss off the sexy lines of the heroes in the books she liked to read, he was sure he'd have been taking her on the truck's front seat by now.

"Jase," was all he could manage.

She pressed a finger to his lips. "*Shh.* Talking causes all kinds of trouble."

It did—she was right. Jaycee moved again, dancing against him though there was no music. Just starlight and a Texas breeze, and a beautiful woman with her hand down the back of his pants.

Dimitri braced himself with his fist on the side of the truck and curved over her. She smiled up at him, eyes sparkling, as she moved her hand from his backside and around his waist to close it on his cock.

"Oh, fucking hell," Dimitri said. No problem with those words.

Jaycee squeezed him, no room to stroke, but it didn't

matter. Her fingers were firm points of heat, sending fires up his spine to explode into his brain.

"I'm a cat," Jaycee said softly, leaning into him. "I like to play."

Her legs, bare most of the way under her short skirt, were hot against his. Dimitri couldn't move, and he didn't want to. "I'm wolf. We're m-more d-d-dir . . . *shit*."

"Direct," Jaycee said. "I know."

He loved that she always knew exactly what he was trying to say. No one else did. Dimitri usually wanted to swipe his paw at others who grew impatient and tried to finish his sentences, because they invariably got them wrong. Jaycee never did.

Be with me for always. Not just playing. Not just scratching an itch.

Dimitri gave up on words and kissed her again. Better things to do with his mouth than talking.

Jaycee's fingers stoked the madness in him. She met his kisses with strength, the two of them locked together in the night.

"Hey," a voice behind them said. Jaycee stilled, but neither of them broke the kiss, neither of them turned. It was the club's manager, the human who ran the place. "Cops will be coming," he said apologetically. "They always do, to make sure Shifters aren't here after curfew."

Shifters should have gone to their Shiftertowns hours ago. Being found outside would lead to arrest and who knew what else. If the cops and Shifter Bureau discovered Jaycee's and Dimitri's Collars were fake, that could lead to complete disaster.

Jaycee slid her hand from Dimitri's jeans, turned her head to break the kiss, and let out a sigh. "Gotcha. Thanks."

Dimitri stepped back from Jaycee as the man moved on. Words bubbled up in his mouth but were unable to come out.

If he and Jaycee didn't have to wear Collars, they could stay out all night, do whatever they pleased, like the rest of the humans around here. But Kendrick had decided his group would pretend to be Collared Shifters so they could interact with the Shifters in captivity—and Kendrick's word was law in their little band.

While Dimitri struggled with speech and his anger, Jaycee dipped her hands into his front pocket and came up with keys jingling from her fingers. "I'll drive," she said.

She was around the truck and inside before Dimitri could grab her. The truck roared to life and began to roll forward. Dimitri snarled, grabbed at the passenger door, and got himself inside the instant before Jaycee put her foot down on the gas and squealed out of the parking lot.

"Son of a bitch, Jase, you drive like a *mamuna*."
Jaycee turned her head to look at Dimitri next to her. He was hanging on to the seat, sinews standing out on his arms. "A what?"

"A she-demon. Would you watch the road?"

Jaycee turned back in time to avoid hitting a car that had slowed for a turn. She'd seen it, but she liked to mess with Dimitri, who believed her the world's worst driver.

"Is that Russian?" she asked.

"S-Slavic. *Jase.*"

Jaycee moved around more cars and kept roaring down Ben White toward the west side of Austin and out into the countryside beyond, heading for Kendrick's ranch. The city had built up a lot even in the short time she and Dimitri had lived in South Texas, and development seemed to follow them as she drove through the night. She turned south after a time, heading into ranch country west of San Antonio.

She could still feel the imprint of Dimitri's hands on her breasts, his mouth on hers. She hadn't been able to stop herself from touching him, had needed to pull him into her right then and there.

Jaycee was going to lose herself in Dimitri if she wasn't careful. Lose herself and never come back.

She made herself feel better by driving like a maniac. Jaycee was actually a very good driver, extremely careful while seeming not to be. It made Dimitri crazy—so much fun.

"Stupid curfews," Jaycee growled. "I wanted to dance all night." *With you.*

"It doesn't hurt us to be c-careful around humans," Dimitri said. He slapped his hands on the dashboard as Jaycee slammed on the brakes to make a turn. He growled. "Yeah, I hate it too."

"Kendrick gives in to Dylan too much," Jaycee said, though Dimitri already knew her opinion. "Dylan's covert ops could get us all killed."

"Kendrick and Dylan are f-friends now," Dimitri reminded her.

"And we're just the lowly trackers." Jaycee decelerated to keep her eye on the very straight road. Animals could rush across without warning, and she had no wish to hit an innocent. "We have to do what we're told."

She felt Dimitri's glance of surprise. "You love being a t-tracker. P-proud. You're one of the only females allowed to b-be one."

"I know." Jaycee let out a sigh. "But it isn't enough anymore." She shook herself. "Don't listen to me. It's not like I want to quit, or think what we do isn't important." She simply wanted . . . *something.*

It called to her. What? Freedom? Dimitri? The mating instinct? She had no idea.

"That's okay," Dimitri said. "I d-don't listen to you anyway."

"Shithead."

Dimitri only laughed and fell silent.

They were in darkness now, making Jaycee feel better. She never liked being cooped up in a town. Even better when they pulled up to the ranch.

The ranch house was big and sprawling, built to accommodate large numbers of people. Kendrick and a few of his top trackers lived in the house; most of the other Shifters lived in the small cottages beyond it. At the moment, nocturnal Shifters were roaming the grounds, wolves and wildcats enjoying the night or, in a few cases, each other.

Jaycee lived in the house, where she could better keep an eye on Addie and the cubs, while Dimitri had elected to build his own place. It helped his sanity, he said, to have a retreat from the chaos of the larger house.

Jaycee liked the chaos. She'd been orphaned as a cub, and though taken in by a Feline family, she'd spent too much time alone and feeling alienated. Then, just before her Transition, her foster pride had been captured and Collared, caught in the massive roundup of Shifters twenty or so years ago.

The morning before Shifter Bureau came to take them, Jaycee had gotten into a fight with the alpha male of the pride, which she often did, and had run off alone to cool down. When she'd finally come home, the entire family was gone. The next-door neighbors, human, had told Jaycee what had happened. They'd offered to hide her, but Jaycee, terrified, had run away.

Kendrick had found her after she'd been hiding out for weeks, stealing food to survive. He'd taken her to his compound, where he'd already stashed dozens of Shifters who were escaping the roundup. Jaycee, beginning her Transition from cubhood to adulthood, had been volatile and confused, afraid and withdrawn.

She'd fallen quickly in love with Kendrick, the first male ever to be kind to her. Her foster father had always made sure Jaycee knew she wasn't one of the family, at the bottom of their group. Kendrick, by contrast, was an alpha who treated everyone fairly and recognized that Jaycee was quite dominant. He'd also recognized her fighting ability and trained her to be a tracker.

Dimitri, about her same age, had befriended her from the start. They'd suffered through the high emotions of their Transitions together and had shared their first sexual encounter when both of them came out of the Transition to rampaging mating need. They'd decided, after the clumsiness of that, to never speak of it and be friends only.

Dimitri had been an exceedingly good friend. He'd had Jaycee's back whenever and wherever she needed it, and she'd returned the favor. When Dimitri had too much trouble speaking, Jaycee didn't mind sitting in silence with him.

They'd been through twenty years of protecting Kendrick and his Shifters, living through every danger, every emergency, every hasty relocation, every hardship. When their first leader had gone insane—Kendrick had been the leader's second as well as the Guardian—and Kendrick had taken over, Dimitri and Jaycee had been side by side behind him.

The *we're just friends* thing between Jaycee and Dimitri had changed over time, the two of them becoming closer and closer. Once Jaycee got it through her thick head that her feelings for Kendrick had been only a girlhood crush, she'd looked at Dimitri differently, realizing what a special part of her life he was.

Now their relationship was at a crossroads. Jaycee knew if she did reject Dimitri's mate-claim, she would have no second chance with him. She and Dimitri could no longer have the closeness they'd shared, the friendship that had been quiet in its strength.

But if Jaycee accepted, then she'd be his forever. Bound. The mate always came first, so Jaycee would have to do what was best for Dimitri over all else.

Of course, Dimitri would then be obligated to do what was best for *Jaycee*. The responsibility went both ways.

As they reached the bottom step of the front porch, Dimitri, instead of mounting the stairs, pulled Jaycee back into the shadows. His arms went around her, and his mouth came down on hers in a hard kiss.

The kiss was hot and possessive, filled with the raw longing they'd shared at the roadhouse. Jaycee had loved holding him in her hand, feeling how ready he was for her. She deepened the kiss, opening for him, trying to show she wouldn't mind if they skipped the house and went together back to his cottage.

His hard cock pressed her through his jeans, Dimitri still wanting her. Jaycee pulled him closer.

Dimitri broke off with a suddenness that made Jaycee gasp, shot her a grin, and went on up the steps. His jeans were tight over his ass, his back straight with Lupine grace. *Shithead.*

Jaycee's heart pounded, but not in anger. Longing filled every part of her, turning her blood molten.

Damn it, why couldn't he be hideous-looking and a total jerk? It would be easy for Jaycee to tell Dimitri to get lost if he were sniveling and mean with a perpetually runny nose.

"Uncle Dimitri! Aunt Jaycee!" The cry came from inside the house, and then two cubs tumbled out the front door, barely missing Dimitri. They were followed more slowly by an older boy who tried to look admonishing at the younger two.

Jaycee spread her arms. "Hey, sweet things!"

The two youngest, little boys with mottled black and white hair and very green eyes, hurtled themselves at Jaycee and climbed into her arms. The older boy, a Lupine called Robbie, hung back until Dimitri held out both fists. Robbie grinned in sudden pleasure and thumped his fists to Dimitri's.

"What are you three doing up?" Jaycee demanded, trying to look stern. Difficult when all three were so adorably cute.

"Waiting with me," a deeper voice behind them said.

CHAPTER SIX

Kendrick came out behind the cubs onto the porch. The two younger ones, Brett and Zane, clung happily to Jaycee, but Robbie, older than they were and trying to be cool, folded his arms and remained next to Dimitri.

"Put the cubs to bed, Jaycee," Kendrick rumbled. He gave Jaycee a long look as though he knew both her exhaustion and restlessness. "Dimitri can give me your report."

"Only if he tells it right," Jaycee said. She stuck her tongue out at Dimitri, who only gave her a knowing look in return. Jaycee thought about how eagerly she'd stuck said tongue into his mouth, flushed, and sucked it back in.

The younger boys, who were both white tiger Shifters like their father, wriggled in Jaycee's arms but didn't try to get down. "We'll go to bed if *you* say, Jaycee. Right, Robbie?"

Robbie, an orphaned Lupine Kendrick had taken in, looked reluctant. He wanted to stay up and discuss tracker business with the grown-ups.

"Come help me, Robbie," Jaycee said, setting the cubs on their feet. "Your brothers are getting to be a handful."

Robbie didn't want to, she knew, but he straightened his

shoulders, liking that Jaycee put him in the same class as herself—those who looked after Kendrick and his family. Being a tracker involved more than scouting and intrigue. They were the leader's right-hand men . . . and women.

Dimitri stepped in front of Jaycee before she could lead the cubs inside. He put one hand on her shoulder, his strength unnerving, and gave her a swift kiss on the mouth. She couldn't help kissing him back. And then he was gone—just like that—starting to tell Kendrick what they'd found out. Kendrick gave Jaycee a long look but said nothing.

Still shaking from the kiss, Jaycee hustled the three boys into the house.

The door opposite the cubs' room opened and Kendrick's mate emerged. She wore a sleep shirt, and her thick dark hair was tousled, but she was wide awake, her blue eyes alert.

"If you can get them to go to sleep, I'll kiss you," Addison said to Jaycee.

"No, you need to kiss *us*!" Zane bellowed. "We'll be good, Addie."

"Speak for yourself," Brett answered.

"Come on." Jaycee pulled Brett and Zane into the bedroom, where they scampered away from her to their bunk beds.

Robbie followed at a more dignified pace to his single bed across the room but looked as anxious as his little brothers to be kissed good night and told a story.

Between Addie and Jaycee, they had the cubs tucked in, a story told, the lights finally turned off. Addie held on to the doorknob as she closed the door and slanted Jaycee a look. "Wine?"

Jaycee let out a breath. "Would be nice."

Addie led Jaycee to the kitchen, now deserted, found the stash of wine she kept for herself and Kendrick, and took out a bottle and two glasses.

There was no sign of Dimitri and Kendrick, and Jaycee couldn't hear them either. They'd probably gone for a walk, or to Dimitri's small house to speak in private.

Addie poured Jaycee a large measure of red wine, but she filled her own glass with bottled water. Addie was pregnant.

The blatant evidence that Addie was Kendrick's mate once would have made Jaycee miserable. But she'd come to realize that Addison and Kendrick were not only deeply in love, they were meant for each other—Kendrick was happier than she'd seen him in years. Addie was good for Kendrick and for their Shifters in general. She was also a fun person with extraordinary kindness, and Jaycee now counted Addie as one of her closest friends.

"Rough night?" Addie asked as Jaycee took a gulp of wine and closed her eyes to savor the rich taste. Charlie knew how to choose a good bottle.

"Confusing night." Jaycee told Addison about their encounter with Casey, keeping her voice low so any Shifter passing outside wouldn't hear. Kendrick shared everything with Addie and had instructed his trackers to as well, but Jaycee couldn't be certain which Shifters he wanted let in on this knowledge.

"I can see you don't know what to make of this Casey," Addie said when Jaycee finished. "Friend or foe? Scouting for converts or innocent bystander?"

"If Dylan hadn't put the suspicion into our heads, we might consider him a new friend." Jaycee sighed and sipped wine. "Sometimes it sucks being a tracker."

"I bet most bodyguards feel the same way," Addison said. "Can't let yourself trust anyone, because they might be bamboozling you to get close to the person you're protecting."

"Something like that." Jaycee rested her arms on the table, toying with the stem of her wineglass.

"There's more going on with you, though, isn't there?" Addie asked. "More on your mind than this assignment."

Addie knew, with Shifter-like perception, when things weren't well in Jaycee's world.

"You know Dimitri drives me crazy," Jaycee said with a little growl. "He keeps pushing me to accept the mate-claim, but what then? I don't know if I'm cut out to be an alpha's submissive little mate. But if I refuse Dimitri—I'll lose him.

Plus I'd have to see him every day, work with him." She balled her fists on the table. "Why'd he have to make the claim? Things were so much easier before."

Addie gave her a wise look. "No, they weren't. He still drove you crazy. You weren't sure how he felt about you. Or how *you* felt."

"Don't rub it in." Jaycee deflated. "You're saying I've always been confused about Dimitri. Well, you're right. Anyway, he made the claim because he wanted to tell me what to do. Remember? He didn't want me endangering myself protecting you and made the claim so he could forbid me to do things. See how well that worked? But he won't take it back."

Addie listened without expression, but Jaycee spied a twinkle deep in her eyes. "I was uncertain when I met Kendrick," Addie said. "You know that. Once I realized it was meant to be—everything was fine."

"Oh, right." Jaycee narrowed her eyes. "I was there, Addie. It wasn't fine at all. Getting you two together was a lot of work."

Addison flushed. "I know. But in my heart, all was good. If you look at your heart, you'll know."

Jaycee groaned and rested her head on the table. "I was just thinking it would be easier on me if he wasn't so *hot*."

"No, it wouldn't," Addie said briskly. "You like *him*, the man behind the hotness." She traced a design on her water glass as Jaycee lifted her head. "But, you know, having the guy you're lusting after be sexy really doesn't hurt." She flushed, dropping her gaze to her fingers on the glass.

Jaycee burst out laughing. Kendrick and Addie went at it with great enthusiasm and sometimes wall-shaking noise.

"Look at you blushing," Jaycee said. "Now I know why everyone was awake when we got home. You weren't waiting up in worry, were you? You and Kendrick were locked in a love crush, and the cubs were running around with no one to stop them."

Addie had not yet grown used to the blatant way Shifters

teased each other about sex. She turned redder, which made Jaycee laugh even more.

"It's all right, honey," Jaycee said. "You're madly in love. So is Kendrick. I'm really glad. I know I used to hope I'd be the one to make him this happy, but I knew I never could. I'm too much of a bitch. *You* are a sweetie."

Maybe it was the wine, on top of dancing with Dimitri after her heart-pounding worry watching him fight an unknown Shifter, that made Jaycee sappy. She slid from her chair, caught up Addie, and dragged her into a hard hug. Addie had Kendrick's scent on her and his warmth—no doubt at *all* what they'd been doing.

"You're the best, Addie." Jaycee laid her head on the taller woman's shoulder. "I'm so glad Kendrick found you."

Addison wrapped her arms around Jaycee in return. "And I'm glad I found *you*," she said. "I need a friend."

Jaycee released her and wiped her eyes, which were wet for some reason. "Yeah, me too." She took Addie's hand in hers. "We chicks need to stand together against all these *Shifters*."

Kendrick and Dimitri chose that moment to rattle into the house, still talking. They stopped just inside the door to the kitchen when they saw Jaycee and Addie.

Jaycee and Addie looked back at them and collapsed into laughter. Kendrick frowned, perplexed, and Dimitri's eyes narrowed as Addie and Jaycee hung on to each other.

Still laughing, Addie broke away and went to Kendrick, but Jaycee walked hurriedly down the hall to her room, not sure she could face saying good night to Dimitri again. Her heart beat swiftly as she closed the door and leaned back against it.

"Nope," she whispered to herself. "Not at all a hardship that he's *hot*."

Dimitri strode in through the house and knocked on Jaycee's door early the next morning. At her muffled "Come in," he entered without hesitation.

She was sitting up in bed, in the act of dragging her thick hair back from her face with one hand, a tight tank top covering her essentials.

Was she trying to kill him? She looked beautiful all sleepy and tousled. He so needed to wake up next to that.

Jaycee glared at him, but she had to have known it was Dimitri at the door. He'd knocked their special knock and her sense of scent and hearing was very good.

"Morning, gorgeous." Dimitri let his smile stretch as her glare turned to a scowl. "We're off to N-new Orleans."

Jaycee's sudden perplexity erased all other expressions. "Kendrick's sending us? Already?"

"He's intrigued. And worried. It's either that or w-wait around the f-fight club for someone else to tranq me."

"Did Kendrick talk to Bree?" Jaycee reached for pants but didn't throw off the covers.

"Seamus did." Dimitri spoke quickly so he'd stumble over fewer words. "She doesn't know m-much. She saw C-Casey around at the New Orleans clubs, but he didn't seem to be any better or worse than any other Shifter. Never hit on her, she says—apparently wasn't interested in h-humans."

"What about the other guy, the one Casey implied could help your stutter?"

Dimitri shrugged. "Bree didn't know who he was t-talking about."

Jaycee gave him an incredulous look. "So we go to New Orleans, hang around *their* fight club, and see if someone tries to tranq us?"

"More or l-less. Wait for C-Casey anyway." Dimitri leaned on the doorframe, pretending to be relaxed. "We have a house to stay in outside of t-town. P-perfect for s-s-surv-v . . ." He closed his eyes and let the word go.

"Surveillance—yeah, I get that. I guess all that's left is for us to go."

"P-pack light," Dimitri said. "Going on my b-bike."

"Seriously?" Jaycee pushed her hair from her face again. "Hours and hours hanging on your back?"

"Yep." Dimitri flashed her a gleeful look. "Get your lazy butt out of bed. We gotta g-go."

Jaycee didn't take long to pack. Dimitri leaned on his motorcycle's seat and watched her exit the house, a backpack slung over her shoulder. She'd put a light jacket over her tank top to break the wind and leather pants to protect her legs, low boots over those. With her hair pulled back and her sunglasses on against the glare of the morning sun, she was the sexiest thing he'd ever seen.

Kendrick came to see them off. It was early, not long after sunup—the nocturnal Shifters had finally fallen groggily into bed and those who loved the day were just opening their eyes.

Kendrick looked fresh for having been awake most of the night. Dimitri felt like shit, but he'd not been able to sleep much. Jaycee's laughing with Addie in the kitchen last night, Jaycee's eyes lit with mirth, had made him itch too much to go tamely to bed. He'd shifted and gone out for a run instead, grabbing shut-eye under the open sky.

Jaycee too looked great for someone who hadn't had much sleep. But then, she always looked good.

"No unnecessary risks," Kendrick was saying in his deep rumble. "Find out what this Casey is up to, if anything, and report. If he's not part of any shit going on, then come home. Understand?"

Jaycee slid off her sunglasses and tilted her head to study Kendrick. "He means don't go into New Orleans and party until we can't walk. Kendrick is all business, all the time."

Kendrick gave her a deprecating look. "You can party when we're sure we're safe."

"Which will be never," Jaycee said. She shoved the glasses back on. "Thanks, Kendrick. I'll remember this on your next birthday."

Dimitri swung onto the bike and lifted his helmet. "I'll keep her in l-line."

"I was thinking Jaycee would keep *you* in line," Kendrick remonstrated. He softened his tone. "Go easy, my friends."

He went to Jaycee and hugged her. Dimitri watched Jaycee hug him back, Kendrick giving her comfort. It was different now, the way they hugged. Before, Jaycee might have tried to make it seductive, with Kendrick breaking the contact before she could go too far. These days, the embrace was of a Feline leader reassuring a pride member, and that pride member responding with gratitude.

Kendrick came to Dimitri and clasped his wrist, Shifter fashion, Dimitri taking Kendrick's in return. "Goddess go with you."

"With you t-too," Dimitri answered. Behind the formal words, he felt the mystical bond between himself and Kendrick, who was both leader and Guardian. Kendrick had left the Guardian's sword in the house, under the protection of his mate, for this brief good-bye, but he radiated the Guardian magic that would be there for them, right until the end.

Kendrick released Dimitri, helped Jaycee climb onto the bike, and stepped away. Dimitri started up. Jaycee slid a helmet onto her head, clasped Dimitri's hips, and lifted her feet as Dimitri glided the bike down the drive.

He glanced back to see Kendrick standing like a sentinel in front of the house. Behind him, on the porch, was Addison, his mate, never far away. Addie lifted her hand in a wave. Dimitri waved back, and then they were on the road.

The eight hours from Kendrick's ranch to New Orleans was hot, heavy with traffic in places, and distracting for Dimitri. Jaycee's soft body behind him constantly took his mind off the road—he kept having to snap his focus back to riding.

They stopped in Houston to eat, blending in with other bikers in a café near the freeway. Dimitri and Jaycee had taken off and stashed their fake Collars before leaving Kendrick's so they could go where humans did. Anyone who knew anything about Shifters would recognize them as such, but if they kept themselves under control and didn't look anyone in the eye, they could pass for human well enough.

The local bikers eyed them curiously, but Dimitri used his friendliest grin and indicated that he and his lady were only passing through. The men eyed Dimitri's fighter's body and left him alone. The women eyed Dimitri as well, but then saw Jaycee's careful look and decided to leave him alone too.

Jaycee insisted on driving a stretch. Dimitri let her with trepidation, leaping on behind her before she could do something smart-ass like drive away without him. Jaycee laughed at him, knowing his thoughts, then let the motorcycle leap forward, nearly dislodging him.

Jaycee took the insane speed she liked, weaving in and out of traffic with heart-stopping ruthlessness. Dimitri kept an eye out for cops, and he knew Jaycee did too. She liked to enjoy herself, but Dimitri had to admit she was cautious while pretending not to be.

The sun was at its hottest in the July sky when they turned south at Baton Rouge and followed the wide river. Just shy of New Orleans, Dimitri, having wrested control of the bike back from Jaycee some miles ago, took them down a smaller road along the river toward the house that would be their secret headquarters.

Earlier this year, a Lupine called Mason, youngest of the wild McNaughton brothers, had taken a mate. That mate was a human woman, Jasmine, who owned this house, an ancient mansion from the bygone plantation days. Jazz was currently living in the Austin Shiftertown with Mason, and she'd graciously offered the house to Shifters who needed a place to stay when they ventured to New Orleans.

"Well, this is nice." Off the bike, Jaycee tucked her helmet under her arm and slung her backpack over her shoulder to admire the house.

A wide front porch ran the length of the brick and stucco structure, the porch decorated with white wrought-iron railings between brick posts, the roof hung with brackets, spindles, and other curlicued items. Rose vines and ivy entwined everything, a riot of red and yellow blossoms among the green.

The air hung heavy with moisture, the river not far away. However, the smell of river water, plus the encroaching industry, seemed to vanish in this place, the scent of roses taking over.

Jaycee walked up the stone steps of the porch, the ring of keys Jasmine had sent to Kendrick jingling in her hands. Dimitri followed close behind, both protectively and so he could admire her backside.

A soon as Dimitri set foot on the porch, the entire floor trembled. He drew back with a snarl, ready to grab Jaycee and drag her away from the house if the earthquake continued.

But nothing else was rocking. The heavy lantern that hung from the porch ceiling was utterly still. Dimitri moved forward on wary feet, but the movement had ceased.

Jaycee was fumbling with the lock. "I think Jazz gave us the wrong keys. None of them fit." She touched the key she held to the lock, but it was obviously too wide for the hole.

As soon as the key made contact with the big iron lock, the porch floor trembled again. The door clicked and then began to open slowly, with a faint but ominous creak.

Jaycee, key still frozen between her fingers, glanced inside with Dimitri at the wide, shadowed hall that ran the length of the very large house.

"So," Jaycee said, her voice subdued. "This is creepy."

CHAPTER SEVEN

J aycee entered the house, ignoring Dimitri, who tried to get in front of her like the alpha male he was. She brushed by him, his body heat warming her in the sudden chill, but her hackles rose as she moved down the quiet hall. Her leopard wanted to come out so she could sniff, sniff, sniff, and figure out what was up with this place.

Doors lined the hall, all closed, the house overlaid with the stuffy odor of an abode not used in months. Halfway along, the hall widened to the right, where a large staircase rose from the ground floor up three flights to the top of the house.

A ponderous iron chandelier hung from the ceiling high above, the bulk of it hovering between the second and third floors. Jaycee spied switches on the wall and flicked them on.

The chandelier came to light, burnishing the mahogany of the staircase and its railings. Oil paintings depicting the house, the countryside as it must have looked centuries ago, and people in their best clothing hung at intervals along the pale white moiré-patterned wallpaper.

"Pretty," Jaycee said, craning her head to look up the stairs.

"What happened to c-creepy?" Dimitri asked from directly behind her. "Which it is."

"It's just an old house," Jaycee said, trying to make herself believe that. "I know Shifters older than it is."

All was quiet. No one else was here—Jaycee would have scented another living being and so would Dimitri.

Leaving the light on, she continued down the hall to the back door. This bolt and chain easily came undone, and Jaycee stepped out onto the rear porch.

She breathed a sigh of relief, the tranquility of the setting beginning to overwhelm her uneasiness. "Even nicer," she said. "I could get used to this."

The veranda ran the length of the house, the green shutters on the windows contrasting nicely with the white paint on the house's trim. A gazebo jutted from the porch, forming an outdoor room complete with benches and a bookcase. The benches and bookcase were empty, Jasmine having taken her things, but she'd told Jaycee where the cushions for the seats were kept.

A light wind blew down the veranda, rustling the leaves, yellow roses, and wind chimes. Peaceful. Jaycee hadn't liked how the front door had opened as though *it* had decided to, but standing here in the cool breeze soothed the ruffled fur of her leopard and calmed her.

Jaycee set down her pack and helmet and rested her hands on the railing, looking out to the setting sun and the rest of the property. A few outbuildings were scattered in the back, screened by trees, but a glimmer of water caught her attention.

Her hot body urged her to see what it was. A fountain that would cool the air? A little babbling stream?

A stream would attract snakes, Jaycee told herself as she walked down the stairs toward the gleam, Dimitri coming close behind her. But oh well. She'd put up with snakes to dip her feet in cool water.

She moved around the thin stand of trees and then halted, smiling in delight. "A swimming pool. Hot damn."

Jasmine had said nothing about a pool, but it must belong

to the house. The next house was too far away for the pool to be meant for it, and the other properties around Jasmine's held warehouses for cargo from the river.

The pool sparkled in the evening light, the water clean and inviting. Jaycee lost no time in stripping down, tossing her sweaty, dusty clothes to the ground. She hadn't brought a bathing suit, but Shifters didn't need bathing suits.

She dove in, the water embracing her like cool silk. A perfect ending to a hot journey.

"I thought cats hated w-water." Dimitri stood at the edge of the pool, having rid himself of his backpack, helmet, and sunglasses. He put his hands on his hips and watched her, his gaze taking in her bareness.

"*Cats* hate it." Jaycee treaded water, keeping her head above the surface. "I don't."

Dimitri didn't answer. He watched her, the setting sun glinting on his eyes, which were lightening to the white-gray of his wolf. Jaycee continued to tread water, not wanting to swim away and have Dimitri make snide remarks about her backside bobbing on the surface.

Dimitri didn't say a word. He silently peeled off his shirt, then his jeans and boots, his underwear and socks. This pool was isolated, hidden from the outside world, allowing them to be completely alone.

The thought made Jaycee's heart pound. So did the sight of Dimitri's intoxicating body coming into view, tall and strong.

He didn't dive in as Jaycee had done; he waded in using the wide steps at the shallow end, walking down, down into the pool. The water lapped his calves, then his thighs, his belly, his chest, as he came on toward her.

He wasn't going to stop. No breaking into a swim to stroke to the other side or splashing around to annoy her. Dimitri simply walked to Jaycee, his gaze on her as though daring her to flee.

Jaycee stood her ground—or at least floated in place. Dimitri was tall enough to stand with his feet flat on the bottom, water up to his neck, while Jaycee had to paddle.

Her arms were getting tired but she didn't want to move to shallower water.

Dimitri just looked at her. He didn't reach for her, only watched, his gaze intent on her.

"What?" Jaycee asked irritably when he didn't move. Why didn't he grab her, try to kiss her as he had at the club last night—anything?

"I was thinking how beautiful you look in the sunshine," Dimitri said.

No stammering, no pause while he struggled over a word.

"Don't," Jaycee said quickly.

Dimitri frowned. "Don't w-what?"

"Melt my heart."

Slowly Dimitri reached out and placed his hand between her breasts. "So you do have a h-heart in there?"

It sped under his touch. "You know damn well I do."

Dimitri moved his hand up her chest to her collarbone, then back down again. "I feel it beating."

His gaze sharpened, eyes fixed on hers. Dimitri wasn't like other male Shifters who blatantly ogled Jaycee's body— Dimitri looked her in the eye. Meant he was more dominant than the others but also that he cared about Jaycee's reaction to him.

Jaycee had seen Dimitri's body plenty over the years— she should be used to it by now. Shifters took off clothes before shifting and didn't hide themselves. Naked was their natural state.

Jaycee had known Dimitri's bare body when he'd been a lanky youth, then noticed when his limbs started becoming muscular and honed. He'd grown bulkier and harder after his Transition, and now he was a beautiful specimen of a man.

She couldn't help but put her hands on his shoulders as he stood before her now, feeling the heat of him, the minute movement when he shifted his feet on the pool's bottom. His skin was sleek with water, water darkening the red hair that brushed his chest.

"Dimitri, if we start . . ." she began softly.

His eyes darkened. "If we start what?"

"We'll never get out of here and find Casey."

Dimitri rubbed between her breasts again. The heat of his hand built the fires in Jaycee's heart.

"The mission always c-comes first," he said in a low voice.

"It's our job," Jaycee said. "What we signed up for."

"I know. It w-wasn't a question."

"The mission will always come first," Jaycee echoed, hearing the regret in her voice.

"I just s-said that."

"I was wondering when *we* would come first." Jaycee caressed Dimitri's shoulders, loving the slick, smooth skin over tight muscle. "You and me."

Dimitri shrugged, an enticing ripple under her fingers. "When all Shifters are free of their Collars and living in peace in the human world. When the Fae gates are sealed so the bastards don't keep popping out and giving us hell."

Jaycee sighed. "Not anytime soon, then."

"We don't know that." Dimitri stroked the side of her breast with his thumb. "This C-Casey might be k-key to defeating the Fae and freeing all Sh-Sh-Sh . . ." He swallowed the word, closing his mouth.

"Right." Jaycee slid her hands down his chest, then let her fingers fall away. "Or Casey might take us square dancing." She let out another unhappy breath. "If we have to go meet him, why do you keep touching me?"

A fierce light entered Dimitri's gray eyes. "I don't care if the world goes to hell," he said, his voice savage. "I don't care if Shifters go with it. I won't stop touching you, Jase. You're my girl. Always have been."

Dimitri had come closer somehow, his hips now against hers. In the water they seemed to be nearly the same height, Dimitri having to bend only a little as he lifted his hand from her chest and closed both arms around her, pulling her closer still.

He studied Jaycee as they hung face-to-face in the water, then he lifted her up to him and kissed her.

Heat flowed down into Jaycee, cutting the coolness of the

pool's water. This kiss held the ferocity she remembered from the night at the fight club, when she'd leapt into the ring to his rescue. While everyone else had yelled at Jaycee for ruining the match, Dimitri had helped her get the younger Shifters to safety, and then he'd kissed her. And such a kiss.

They'd been body to body then as now, his mouth commanding, not punishing. Dimitri kissed Jaycee to enjoy her, not to subdue her.

He held her chin between thumb and finger, pulling away to look down at her. The strength in his grip, gentling, told her he could take what he wanted whenever he wanted, and Jaycee couldn't stop him. She could fight like hell, and be good at it, but Dimitri would win. He was stronger, a merciless fighter, skilled and able. He'd best her without trying very hard—Jaycee knew that in her heart.

Dimitri's eyes softened. He released her chin and moved his hand to her back, pulling her against him. The tenderness in the touch showed Jaycee his other side—he might be able to take her anytime he wished, but he wouldn't be cruel, wouldn't hurt her.

Dimitri lifted her in his embrace, moving his mouth to her shoulder, lips on her skin. He inhaled her scent and licked the curve of her neck.

Jaycee tilted her head, wanting his burning touch, his kiss. His body pressed the length of hers, the hard ridge of his cock firm against her abdomen.

It would be so easy to float upward, to wrap her legs around his waist and let herself take him deep inside. Make love to him here in the shadowy dusk, then lead him to the house, to a bedroom upstairs and have him love her again.

Who cared about Casey and his mysterious friend? Who cared that he might be the link to the troublemaking Shifters Dylan wanted to spy on? Why couldn't the world leave her and Dimitri alone?

Do it.

The suggestion seemed to come from outside herself, and Jaycee jerked her head up. Dimitri raised his head at the same time, confusion in his eyes.

"Did you say s-something?" he asked her.

"No." Jaycee unwound her arms but rested her hands on his shoulders, unable to make herself push away. "Know anyone with telepathy?"

"T-telepathy's not real." Dimitri scanned the area around the pool, alert. The light was fading now, the sun having slipped over the horizon while they kissed. "Maybe C-Casey . . ." He trailed off, uneasy.

"Casey doesn't know we're here," Jaycee said. "Unless he put a GPS tracker on us or something." Probably he hadn't—they would have scented a device. "Besides, why would Casey want us to have sex all night?"

Dimitri rumbled in his throat. "I don't know."

Jaycee rubbed his shoulders. "Well, the sooner we find this guy and drag him to Dylan or decide he's harmless, the sooner we can kick back, hang out in the pool, drink some beers, relieve the tension . . ."

She expected Dimitri to relax, smile, tell her that was a great idea. Instead, his eyes narrowed.

"It's not *relieving tension*." His voice was strong and clear. "Never that with you. When you're with me, Jase, it will always be far more than relieving tension." He hauled her up into his arms, bringing his mouth down on hers in a powerful kiss.

Jaycee could tell he meant to give her a single bruising kiss to show her how much her declaration had pissed him off, but the kiss lengthened, Dimitri enfolding her in his unbreakable grip. Jaycee's mouth opened readily for his, her entire being wanting to hold him, kiss him—screw the mission.

Dimitri broke the kiss, his eyes Shifter gray, the wolf in him growling. He released her abruptly and leapt backward into the water with a crashing splash. "Let's go find this son of a bitch so I can come back here with you and show you *exactly* how it's going to be."

He backstroked to the edge of the pool, then turned around and heaved himself straight out, not bothering with the steps. His body rose, water streaming from it, back straight, legs firm, buttocks tight. Dimitri landed lightly on his feet and bent to retrieve his clothes without looking at Jaycee. Not bothering to dress, he balled up his clothes in one hand and strode up the walk toward the house.

Jaycee watched him go, her heart beating so fast it rocked her, her mouth raw from his kiss. The evening light touched Dimitri's backside as he went, flaring every desire Jaycee had for him to unbearable incandescence.

When they tried to leave the house, the front door wouldn't open. Dimitri, whose body was already shaking with annoyance that he hadn't grabbed Jaycee in the pool and made hard love to her, pounded his fist on the wooden panels.

"What the hell is wrong with this thing?"

"Did you unlock it?" Jaycee asked demurely behind him.

Dimitri swung around. "Hell yes, I unlocked it, smart-ass."

Jaycee slid around him, jiggled the bolt, and turned the handle. The lock and the latch slid smoothly back, but the door itself refused to budge.

"Must be stuck," Jaycee said, her reasonable tone irritating him. "We'll go out the back."

Dimitri snarled and didn't answer. He tramped after Jaycee's enticing body down the long hall and to the door that led to the veranda. Jaycee undid the dead bolts she'd latched when she'd returned from swimming and turned the handle.

The door didn't move. Dimitri's heart beat rapidly. He didn't like being trapped. Not for any reason.

"What the hell?" he said in a near shout.

Jaycee thoughtfully studied the walls, then moved down the hall to the front door again. Dimitri didn't know why she was so calm.

Trapped, lost, can't get out . . .

The memory came at him from nowhere, tapping at his subconscious.

Windows. This house had a ton of them. Dimitri shoved his way into a room, which turned out to be a dining room, the table and chairs draped with dust covers. Dimitri shoved back the heavy curtains, unlocked the window, and strained to shove the heavy sash upward.

Nothing. Even his Shifter strength couldn't move it.

He turned around, lifted a chair, and prepared to break his way out. The fire was coming. Burning all around him. *No! Don't leave me here! Let me out!*

It was a cub's voice, Dimitri's. Walls in his mind hastily descended, blocking the glare of the flames. The panic didn't recede. He had to get out of here before it was too late . . .

"Dimitri!" Jaycee's voice broke through like light warming a cold room.

Dimitri closed his eyes and dragged in a breath. There was no fire, no evil people locking him in. Just Jaycee, her golden eyes wide, the silence of the empty house, and Dimitri holding a chair.

"If you break the windows, Jazz will kill us," Jaycee said, unruffled. "Let me try something."

Sucking in a deep breath, Dimitri made himself lower the chair to the floor. His hands were trembling.

Jaycee walked back to the hall, Dimitri right behind her. She chose a space between the interior doors and put her hand on the wall.

"We'll be back," she said, looking up at the ceiling. "There's something we need to take care of, but we're coming right back. I know it's lonely here without Jasmine."

Dimitri opened his mouth to ask Jaycee who the hell she was talking to, when a breath of air streamed down the hall. With a sound like a sigh, the front door silently swung open.

CHAPTER EIGHT

Dimitri grabbed Jaycee's hand and shot toward the open door, dragging her outside. The door closed slowly behind them, the lock clicking audibly into place.

Dimitri pulled Jaycee all the way down the porch stairs, where he halted breathlessly. "What. The. Fuck?"

Jaycee calmly detached herself from Dimitri, but there was a bright look in her eyes. "Jazz told me the house was haunted. But also that if it likes us, it will treat us well."

"Jazz is a crazy woman who thinks she's ps-psychic," Dimitri said. He'd met Jazz only once, at her mating ceremony to Mason. Zander, the insane polar bear, spoke highly of her.

"Jazz *is* a psychic," Jaycee returned. "I didn't believe it either, but the house is doing exactly what she said it would. Well, she didn't know *exactly*, but she told me staying here would be weird."

"She's got that right." Dimitri gave the house a wary eye.

Jaycee caressed the newel post at the bottom of the steps. "I'm thinking that if you want a place to stay tonight, you'd better be nice to it."

Dimitri stepped back until he could see the entire house. It looked innocent enough, an old plantation home restored and ready for Old South tours. As he peered at it closely, he saw that the middle of the porch roof sagged a little, something he hadn't noticed before, making the house look like it was smiling.

Dimitri gave the place a scowl and moved quickly to his motorcycle. "Come on. Shifters will be coming out to play now that the sun's down."

Jaycee stroked the porch post again, then finally turned away to join Dimitri. She gave him an odd look as she climbed on behind him, but Dimitri started the motorcycle before she could ask questions. The roar of the motor precluded any talking.

Haunted, right. Shifters didn't believe in ghosts. There was life, and there was the Summerland for your soul when you were done living. That was it. The soul could be stolen and enslaved, true, but you weren't exactly a ghost when that happened—more in limbo between one state and the next, hoping like hell a Guardian would stab his sword through your body and release you.

But Shifters didn't hang around and haunt houses. Humans didn't either, in spite of all their stories. Humans might be feeling the residue of violence or great sorrow in certain places, but Dimitri was certain no actual spirits of the deceased were there.

Even so, *something* had been going on in Jazz's house. He'd go through it when they returned and look for webcams or monitors—humans had all kinds of crazy gadgets that let them remotely manipulate things in their houses. Jazz or Mason might have set up something as a joke. Or Zander— he had a bizarre sense of humor.

Dimitri drove out to the highway that followed the river into the city. The road grew busy quickly, people flowing from the outer areas to the city in the encroaching darkness, light blooming in the distance. Jaycee easily balanced behind Dimitri as they rode, her arms lightly around his waist.

The Shiftertown in southern Louisiana lay south and west of New Orleans near Thibodaux. Bree had told them, however, that the bars popular with Shifters were inside the city. New Orleans, she said, was a little more tolerant of

Shifters, looking upon them as an exotic species to attract tourists and their money. There were even "vampire" bars here, Dimitri had heard, for those who wanted to believe bloodsuckers were crawling all over southern Louisiana.

Shifter bars were different from the vampire variety. For one thing, Shifters were real. Second, there was no theme in a Shifter bar—no weird drinks that looked like blood, no black walls, no videos of wolves and wildcats caught in the act of shifting. Dimitri had seen all these things at a so-called Shifter bar up north where no Shifters actually went. Groupies had loved it, though. Dimitri had looked in out of curiosity when he'd lived nearby, then left it before anyone realized he was a real Shifter.

The Shifter bar where Casey said he would meet them when Dimitri had called him was in a wilder part of New Orleans, well off the tourist paths. Plenty of people apparently came here—they were spilling out the front door into the street around it. A sign in front, painted in bright letters, stated: "Shifters Welcome."

Dimitri left his bike in an area where he'd be reasonably certain it would still be there when they came out, steadied Jaycee as she dismounted, and walked a little ahead of her to the bar. They wore their fake Collars in order to blend in.

Shifters weren't supposed to leave their home states without permission, but as Dimitri scanned the crowd bulging from the multistory bar in the crammed street, he decided that plenty of Shifters from outside Louisiana must be here. Louisiana had only two small Shiftertowns, and not all their residents would make the drive every night to hang out in this bar. Some Shifters had lives.

As Dimitri entered, Jaycee followed a few steps behind him, letting him lead without arguing, for once. The Shifters inside looked them over, instantly alert that new and unfamiliar Shifters had arrived. Dimitri knew without turning his head which of the Shifters were local; those Shifters considered this their territory and dominated without trying. Those from out of town, in order to keep the peace, remained neutral, not challenging the locals.

The bar was several stories high, each floor comprising a

large balcony encircling an open stairwell. Shifters filled every level, the ones above drinking and talking, the ones on the ground level dancing with one another or with human groupies.

The male Shifters instantly homed in on Jaycee, though they'd know, just as the Shifters in the roadhouse outside Austin had, that she was mate-claimed. Not only by scent, but there was an indefinable *something* about mate-claimed Shifters that made other Shifters instinctively know a female and male belonged together. In the old days, a mate-claim had been enough, with no extra ceremonies or official matings by the clan leader. The happy mating ceremonies under sun and moon in front of the community had been imposed in later years, when Shifters had started trying to be civilized.

Jaycee eyed males and females, Shifters and humans alike without worry. No male would mess with her with Dimitri there—no male would mess with Jaycee anyway, not the sensible ones at least. She could be friendly and open, but Goddess help the Shifter who tried to corner her for a quick grope.

Dimitri moved to the bar's counter and signaled for the bartender's attention. He was human, as was the case in all Shifter bars, because Shifters weren't allowed to serve drinks. The bartender jerked his chin when Dimitri ordered and turned away to fetch bottles of cold beer.

"New in town?" a half-drunk Feline Shifter next to Dimitri slurred.

Dimitri wanted to answer with something like, *What gave it away?* But he didn't trust himself to speak. He'd found that when strangers first heard him talk, they took his speech impediment for weakness. Dimitri merely gave the Feline a nod, pinning him with a gaze that showed where he was in his hierarchy.

The Feline understood and flicked his gaze downward, conceding Dimitri's dominance, but that didn't stop him from sniffing in Dimitri's direction.

"What are you?" he asked, wrinkling his nose.

For answer, Dimitri gave him a very Lupine growl.

"I know that," the Feline snapped. "But you don't look like no Lupine I've ever seen."

There was a flash and breath of wind, and Jaycee was around Dimitri and in front of the Feline. "He's a red wolf, cat breath," she said clearly. "And can eat you for breakfast."

Dimitri smothered a laugh. The Feline hunched a little lower into himself, snarling under his breath.

"Dimitri!"

The name sailed across the room over the thumping music. Casey walked through the crowd, his arms open, a welcoming look on his face.

The Feline ducked aside before Casey reached them and beat a hasty retreat. Casey came on as though he'd never noticed the Feline there and pulled Dimitri into a rough hug, demonstrating to the entire club that Dimitri was a friend, trusted.

The watching Shifters didn't relax, however, until Dimitri returned the embrace. Casey tightened the hug, then let him go, turning to Jaycee in delight.

"Jaycee. So glad you came." Casey wrapped his arms around Jaycee and tugged her close. Dimitri hovered near, but as he'd done in Austin, Casey didn't give her anything more than a Shifter hug of greeting.

Jaycee returned the embrace with enthusiasm, pretending not to be wary. The other Shifters, seeing the two accepted by Casey, went back to drinking, talking, dancing.

"Come and meet my mate," Casey said.

Casey had mentioned he was mated when Dimitri had met him at the roadhouse, but hadn't said anything more about his partner. Unusual, as male Shifters liked to boast about their mates—how beautiful they were, how smart, how sexy, how many cubs they had given the males. Shifters enjoyed rubbing their success in other Shifters' faces. Casey, on the other hand, hadn't mentioned his mate again until now.

Dimitri didn't glance at Jaycee for confirmation, but he saw her twitch a finger, which meant, *Sure, let's see who this woman is.*

Dimitri gave Casey a nod. Casey, looking pleased, gestured for them to follow him through the bar to a door in the back wall.

Dimitri walked directly behind Casey, Jaycee following

them. Dimitri and Jaycee weren't simply using Shifter protocol of the male going first, protecting the female—Jaycee was a hell of a good rearguard. No one would sneak up on Dimitri with Jaycee behind him.

Casey opened a door marked "Private" without knocking. As they walked inside the dingy office beyond, a woman rose from a sagging sofa to face them.

She was Shifter, older than Jaycee and Dimitri, probably in her hundreds. She was older than Casey as well, though not by much. A Feline of some kind, she was tall, with ropy muscles and thick blond hair that glistened under the room's one fluorescent light.

Most Shifters greeted those they didn't know with wariness, but not this woman. She bathed Dimitri and Jaycee in a wide smile and started for them as Casey shut the door.

"Casey told me about you," she said. "Welcome. I'm Maeve."

Maeve's eyes were green, framed by light-colored lashes. She went to Dimitri and embraced him.

Casey looked on fondly as Maeve hugged Dimitri, her arms strong and wiry. The hug wasn't demanding—it was maternal—and she didn't expect him to return it.

Dimitri, with a glance at Jaycee, embraced her politely. Jaycee watched, not angry, not jealous, but vigilant, in case the woman produced a knife and tried to plunge it into Dimitri's back. Then Jaycee could step in to stop her . . . or not. Dimitri imagined Jaycee studying her fingernails and considering whether to save Dimitri from the fatal stab wound.

Maeve released Dimitri and turned the same motherliness to Jaycee. "So happy to meet you." She drew Jaycee into her arms, sounding genuinely pleased.

Jaycee shot a bewildered look at Dimitri as Maeve hugged Jaycee and released her, keeping hold of Jaycee's hand. "Don't worry," Maeve said. "We're not as crazy as you think we are."

"Do we think you're crazy?" Jaycee asked, sounding uncertain.

Maeve gave her a wise look. "I know what you're thinking. Are they rogue Shifters? Defying Shiftertown leaders? Trying to break the system? What are they up to?"

Dimitri shrugged. "You h-hear things."

Maeve laughed. She released Jaycee's hand and drifted back to Casey. "It's not what you think. Casey, you should have explained things better."

Dimitri's heart beat faster. Had they found the villains Dylan was looking for already? Maeve seemed to know Dimitri and Jaycee were searching for rogues. Were *they* rogues? Or, like Jaycee and Dimitri, trying to find and stop them?

Dimitri longed for the good old days when all he had to do was keep Kendrick's Shifters safe. No deciding which "side" Shifters were on. They should all be on the same side—the Shifter side.

"It's complicated," Casey said. "I wasn't kidding when I said I wanted to introduce you to someone you should meet. I didn't mean Maeve." He put his arm around his mate and she sank against him, the two comfortable with each other. Intimate.

"Wh-who, then?" Dimitri asked. "You c-can't blame us for being s-s-s—" He coughed.

"Suspicious," Jaycee said. "All this covertness is making me itch."

"I completely understand," Casey said. "I'll take you to him. But . . ." His amusement died, his expression turning serious. "He won't meet just anyone. You'll have to do something for him in order to prove you can be trusted."

Dimitri's skin prickled. Jaycee edged closer to him, her warmth overlapping his, faint growls in her throat.

"W-what?" Dimitri asked.

Casey drew a breath, pressing his hands together. Maeve looked worried. "Your leader," Casey said. "Kendrick."

Dimitri desperately tamped down his instinctive reaction to defend, and sensed Jaycee doing the same. Some undercover operatives *they* made. They could barely hold themselves calm at the barest hint of threat in Casey's voice.

"He has cubs," Casey said, his voice going hard. "My leader wants you to bring him one of them. And to kill it."

CHAPTER NINE

Jaycee's ferocious snarls filled the room, the rage that tore through her hotter than she'd ever experienced. She would to rip out Casey's and Maeve's throats right now and drag their bodies to Kendrick and Dylan. Problem solved. No Shifter who wasn't insane would ask them to kill a cub.

Dimitri didn't hesitate. He went for Casey.

Maeve rushed in front of Dimitri to guard Casey, her face changing to a wildcat's that was more mixed than most Felines.

Dimitri didn't slow simply because a female had intercepted him. His hands changed to clawed paws, and he said viciously, "I'll kill you before I let you hurt a cub."

Casey yanked Maeve out of the way, then dropped to his knees in front of Dimitri, his head bending in submission. Dimitri wouldn't stop even for that, Jaycee saw. His wolf claws swept down, on their way to Casey's exposed neck.

Jaycee had enough presence of mind to grab Dimitri by the arms and jerk him backward. Dimitri struggled, furious, but Jaycee held him hard. If they killed Casey and Maeve in this club owned by humans, they'd bring danger to every

Shifter in this part of the country. They needed to first drag Maeve and Casey off somewhere the bodies wouldn't be found.

Maeve, interestingly, had backed away, no longer trying to defend Casey. She only watched as though curious to see what Jaycee and Dimitri would do.

"Peace," Casey panted. "That was your test. You passed. If you'd said you'd agree to do harm to a cub, I would have had to kill you."

Jaycee blinked. "What?" She clamped down on Dimitri, who was about to go berserk.

"We were supposed to tell you to go after one of your leader's cubs to see how you'd react," Casey said in a rush. "We don't want you to—believe me! You're *supposed* to be upset with us. It's a good thing. Like I said, you passed the test."

Dimitri's snarls continued unabated. "Who the fuck would even think of something like that?"

"He would."

Casey pointed to the door, which had opened soundlessly. Jaycee jerked her attention to it, unnerved she hadn't smelled or heard anyone coming. She released Dimitri, wanting him unencumbered if they needed to fight.

A Shifter stood in the doorway, quietly watching. He was tall and bulking—a bear, Jaycee realized. He entered the room and closed the door, the overhead light shining on his deep brown hair, trimmed beard, and glittering dark eyes. The light also glistened on the tranq rifle he held at his side.

"Forgive me," the newcomer said in the deep voice achieved only by bear Shifters. His timbre was rich and thick, his tone regretful. "I had to know whether you were true Shifters or monsters. You'd be amazed at what some Shifters are willing to do."

"Who the hell are you?" Dimitri demanded.

"Name's Brice." The man halted, not offering greeting hugs or even for them to come close to him. "Dimitri Kashnikov and Jaycee Bordeaux."

It wasn't a question. He knew exactly who they were. Jaycee definitely didn't like that.

Dimitri, on the other hand, was staring at him almost in recognition, as though things were clicking together in his brain.

Brice gave Jaycee a nod as he felt her scrutiny. "You can run back to Kendrick and ask him all about me if you want. He won't know. Neither will Dylan. That's fine. Dylan's a good man, in his way. He takes care of his people. But he doesn't really understand what we're trying to do. He will. In time."

"Why the hell did you ask us to go after his *cubs*?" Jaycee could barely get the words out. She thought about Zane, Brett, and Robbie, and felt sick. She sent a hasty prayer to the Goddess to keep them safe.

"Experience," Brice said. "I'm so sorry, Jaycee. I didn't mean to upset you. I assure you, I'd never have let you carry out such a thing. I'd have stopped you." He lifted the tranq gun. "I'd have made sure Kendrick dealt with you for even considering it."

Jaycee took deep, gulping breaths. "Well, I'm going to be unhappy for a while. That was a horrible thing to do."

Brice gave her a tight smile. He walked to the middle of the room and deliberately laid the tranq gun on a table. The rifle was now within reach of Dimitri and also Jaycee if she lunged quickly enough.

"My apologies," Brice said. "But I had to know what kind of Shifters I was dealing with. What I really want is to talk to you, get to know you. Have you get to know me."

Dimitri was rigid. Jaycee knew they needed to focus on the mission, to smoke out this guy and his followers. It was tough though. Dimitri looked like he wanted to snatch up the tranq rifle and bash Brice over the head with it.

But Dimitri relaxed suddenly, his infectious grin blossoming, though Jaycee sensed his tension, knew he was faking it. "S-sure. As long as we can s-sling back some b-brews while we do. C-Casey, I think you can g-get up now."

Casey looked to Brice for confirmation. He didn't raise his gaze to Brice but eyeballed him somewhere in the gut.

Brice walked to Casey, stopping a foot from Dimitri, raised Casey to his feet, and enfolded the smaller man in a hug. Brice was big—bears were. Casey was lost in the man's embrace, but his body sagged in relief.

When Brice let him go, Casey straightened up, standing stronger. Brice gave him a nod.

"You did good, Casey." Brice pivoted to face Dimitri, moving into Dimitri's personal space. "Brews? Sure. But not here. Are you willing to follow us out?" Brice looked Dimitri in the eye, then pinned Jaycee with an equally intense gaze. "We'll go someplace we can let our hair down, so to speak."

Jaycee folded her arms. "You're trusting us a lot."

"Not really." Brice's voice was deep and filled the room. "I don't yet *know* whether I can trust you. But I want to find out." He rested a hand on Dimitri's shoulder and then Jaycee's. "I learned long ago, my friends, that if you live in fear, they've already won."

Jaycee wasn't sure who *they* were, but Brice was turning away, finished with the conversation. He picked up the tranq gun and tossed it to Maeve. "Lock that up for me, love. Shall we go?"

Dimitri's uneasiness grew as he rode his motorcycle through the streets of New Orleans, following Brice, along with Casey and Maeve. Jaycee leaned into Dimitri's back, her arms around him, comfort in the darkness, though he felt her uneasiness as well.

Brice was trusting that Dimitri would follow them and not disappear into the night, bringing Dylan and crew back with him. But Brice hadn't actually done anything terrible yet. Just because his presence stirred something troubling in Dimitri's brain didn't mean the man was the embodiment of evil. Brice had come up with the scheme of asking Dimitri and Jaycee to kill cubs in order to discover whether *they* were the embodiments of evil.

Dimitri didn't like people who played games. He'd almost killed Casey, which had seemed to please Brice and even Casey's mate. Something was going on here, and it made Dimitri's fur itch.

Dimitri didn't know this city well enough to figure out where they were going. Brice, on a gleaming black Harley, led them south and west into streets of large old houses, well preserved on quiet streets. This area was too genteel for Shifters, Dimitri knew, but Brice slowed in front of a tall mansion and rode up the driveway and around the back. He'd already dismounted his bike, as had Casey and Maeve, by the time Dimitri and Jaycee reached him.

There were no lights in the front of the house, but the back windows, covered with pale, opaque shades, glowed. Brice unlocked a door with stained glass in its top half and opened it.

"Come on in," he said. "I have plenty."

Plenty of what? Dimitri and Jaycee left their helmets on Dimitri's motorcycle and walked behind Brice into the house. Dimitri led, and again, Jaycee let him.

Casey and Maeve hung back, as though uncertain, oddly. They were not very dominant, Dimitri had learned tonight. They'd quickly turned to Brice for reassurance and not tried to engage Dimitri when he'd gone into fighting frenzy. Only Jaycee had been strong enough to hold Dimitri back. If she hadn't, Casey would be in the hospital by now.

There seemed to be a party going on. The narrow back hall Brice led them along opened out into a larger hall that bisected the house, giving onto living and dining spaces. Shifters lounged in the living room and prowled from dining room to the kitchen behind it, eating, drinking, talking. The reason the front of the house was dark, Dimitri saw, was because the windows overlooking the street were covered with blackout curtains.

Music thumped over the conversations. The music con-

tinued even as the talking dimmed, Shifters aware that
newcomers had arrived.

Dimitri didn't know any of them. Shifters turned to him,
males and females, Lupines, Felines, and bears watching,
testing scent, listening. All were full adults—no cubs or
young Shifters before or even just after their Transition were
present.

What were they doing here? Besides what Shifters nor-
mally did—drink beer, laugh and talk, find someone to be
horizontal with if both felt the need.

Except there wasn't much laughter. Nor were any Shifters pairing off, no mates together, no males and females
eyeing each other and making discreet signals. For a Shifter
party, this one was amazingly staid.

"Stick with me," Brice said. "You'll be all right."

Jaycee slanted Dimitri a glance, raising her brows. Dimitri said nothing, every nerve in him alert.

The Shifters noted his alertness. They were rising, tensing, ready to throw out the newcomers if necessary. Shifters
weren't big on accepting strangers out of the blue. You had
to earn acceptance. Jaycee and Dimitri, living in isolation
for twenty years with very few new Shifters joining them,
had never had an easy time with acceptance either.

"This is Dimitri," Brice said in a loud voice. "And Jaycee.
Casey found them. I have cleared them."

The Shifters relaxed, but not by much. It would be a while
before they were beer-drinking buddies, Dimitri could see.

"It is almost time, my friends."

Someone killed the music, and silence descended under
the spell of Brice's deep voice. Brice didn't elaborate, but
Shifters came downstairs and out of back rooms, filling the
spaces.

Two Shifters carried a brazier out from the kitchen.
Dimitri hoped they weren't crazy enough to light a brazier
indoors—the smoke would choke them.

The two Shifters set the brazier in the living room
fireplace—at least they had that much sense. The way they
eased it in, carefully placing it on the grate and packing wood

chips around it so it wouldn't move, told Dimitri they'd done this before.

They lit the brazier, feeding it until a flame burned high. Once the fire was going, all eyes turned to Brice. The Shifters were packed into the living room now, standing in silence.

Brice raised his hands. "We give thanks to the Goddess," he said in a sonorous voice. "May all her blessings be upon you. I welcome her children, Dimitri and Jaycee, into this meeting, and hope one day to welcome them into our clan."

No word from the Shifters, but Dimitri sensed them relax further, trusting Brice.

Brice gave a nod to someone across the room, and the lights went out. The brazier gave the only illumination, the fire flickering across faces, the scent of burning wood drifting over the crowd. The scent nearly but didn't quite cover the smell of forty Shifters crammed into one small space.

They gave Brice enough room to stand in front of the brazier with a yard or so of empty air around him. He put his hands toward the flames—closer, closer—then he closed his eyes and extended his fingers closer still.

Dimitri's skin crawled. He shouldn't care whether this weird bear stuck his hand into the fire to be burned—idiot—but for some reason, it brought growls to clog his throat. He was never good with fire anyway, always stood in the back when it was brazier-lighting time at Kendrick's place, but watching Brice deliberately invite third-degree burns was driving him crazy. He growled and twitched, flashes of darkness darting across his vision.

Jaycee's cool touch sliced through his tension. Dimitri glanced down at her to find her gazing up at him in concern. He shook his head ever so slightly, but Jaycee's frown didn't vanish.

Dimitri flinched as a flame licked around Brice's hand, and the bear sucked in a breath of pain. The big man closed his eyes, sweat on his face, his mouth tight. He swayed a little, his hand shaking but still in the fire.

No one around him leapt to help him, to drag him from

danger. They watched, eyes fixed on their leader, as he let his hand be surrounded by flame.

Dimitri couldn't take it anymore. He shoved his way through the surrounding Shifters, grabbed Brice, and hauled him from the brazier.

Dimitri swung him around, seizing Brice's wrist and raising his hand. "What are you—stupid?"

Brice opened his eyes, which were streaming with water. His face was red from the fire's heat, perspiration coating his face, but he looked unworried.

The hand Dimitri held up was unmarred, he saw in amazement. It should have been shriveled and burned, or at least red and blistered. However, it looked perfectly healthy, the flesh intact.

The Shifters around Dimitri growled and moved restlessly. Brice lifted his free hand in a gesture that told them to stay put.

"It's all right. He doesn't know." He turned a kind look on Dimitri. "The Goddess protects her own, my friend. I don't recommend anyone try this at home"—Brice gave the room a faint smile—"but she won't hurt me. One day, perhaps, she won't hurt you either."

Dimitri stared into Brice's eyes, looking for lies, but the man's gaze, scent, and body language indicated he was telling the truth. Or at least that he believed sticking his hand straight into fire wouldn't burn him.

The flames were too close for Dimitri's taste. If Brice believed Dimitri would ever plunge his hand into a lit brazier, he was insane.

Dimitri gave one last growl, released Brice's wrist, and stepped back, though he kept looking into Brice's eyes. He wasn't going to drop his gaze and cower, as Casey had done.

Dimitri found Jaycee right behind him. She'd crossed the room with him, ready to back him up, no matter what crazy thing he was about to do. His heart warmed even as his skin prickled under the stares of Brice's Shifters.

Brice gave Dimitri a faint smile, turned back to the brazier, closed his eyes again, and stuck his hand into the flame once more.

Dimitri quivered, his fists balling. Jaycee's touch helped a little, but he found he had to keep his gaze averted from the fire leaping around Brice's hand.

Brice closed his eyes and began to chant, a low, throaty sound that rumbled over the room. The language he spoke was musical and full of complex syllables, beautiful and rippling.

A prayer to the Goddess, Dimitri recognized. He didn't understand the words of the traditional chants, which were in a Celtic language, something he'd never gotten around to studying. Learning Celtic was somewhere down on his bucket list, right after culturing yogurt.

The Shifters who were better linguists swayed in time to the chant, or perhaps they were simply mesmerized by Brice's voice. Jaycee's fingers bit down on Dimitri's wrist, she as unnerved as he was.

Smoke began to trickle into the room, not from the brazier. Someone had lit an incense stick. More than one—the thick scent of sandalwood and sage began to move through the air. To cover the odor of nervous Shifters? Or as part of the show?

The scent began to relax Dimitri in spite of himself. It was easier to let his mind drift on the smoke instead of fighting it, and to be lulled by the sound of Brice's voice. Dimitri felt a calm steal over him, but he didn't scent anything narcotic in the smoke. It was sage and other herbs, nothing more.

Brice's prayer continued, a few of the Shifters whispering along. Prayers to the Goddess were beautiful, conveying the admiration of Shifters for the benevolent mother-goddess who watched over them and welcomed them into the Summerland.

Dimitri found his body swaying, his eyes closing as he became caught up in the trance of the moment.

A bite on his flesh made his eyes pop open. Jaycee was

glaring up at him, her fingers twined with his, her nails pressing his skin. Dimitri jolted, realizing he'd been floating away on Brice's words and the scented smoke. He gave Jaycee a nod to let her know he was all right, but she didn't look away.

Brice at last removed his hand from the brazier, his words dropping away to silence. Again, his flesh looked perfectly fine, not burned and blackened.

Brice displayed his unharmed hand to the Shifters. They didn't cheer, only watched reverently. "And now for the sacrifice," Brice continued.

Dimitri didn't like the sound of *that*. His hackles rose, and Jaycee stiffened beside him.

"Who gives his blood tonight?" Brice asked. "I am willing, but I will step aside for another if you so desire."

To Dimitri's consternation, many pleas sounded, from males and females alike. Brice looked his followers over, then turned to Dimitri and Jaycee. "Why not one of our new friends?"

Some of the Shifters liked this idea; others didn't, but no one offered an argument.

"Jaycee?" Brice asked, reaching toward her with the hand that hadn't been in the fire. "Will you give of yourself?" He withdrew a knife, flames glittering on its long, thick blade.

Dimitri shook off the last of his stupor. "No way in hell," he snarled, putting himself between Brice and Jaycee. "If you're going to c-cut anyone with that thing, it's going to be m-me."

CHAPTER TEN

J aycee tried to move around Dimitri, but the stubborn wolf
wouldn't budge. He stood his ground like a brick wall,
folding his arms and becoming immovable.

Brice only regarded Dimitri thoughtfully. "Of course.
Dimitri. Come."

"He asked *me* first." Jaycee tried to slid around him again,
hampered by other Shifters and Dimitri's strength.

He snarled at her. "Stay back."

The command was that of a protective mate and a tracker,
one above her in the hierarchy. Every cell in Jaycee's body
was programmed to obey, and she fought it hard. Dimitri
didn't wait for her to debate—he simply pushed his way to
Brice.

Jaycee heaved an exasperated sigh and went after him.
They were supposed to be undercover, discovering what
Brice was up to, but no way in hell did she want to let Brice
touch him.

Dimitri halted before he reached Brice and the brazier,
his back quivering—he didn't like being near an open flame,

Jaycee knew. Dimitri had always been squirrelly around fire.

"Our little group is bonded only by trust," Brice said to him. "Any one of us may leave and not return, though we hope you will keep details about our gatherings to yourselves. The human police can be so obdurate." He smiled with patience for the poor, deluded police. "The blood sacrifice is a showing of trust. Will you trust us, Dimitri?"

Jaycee watched Dimitri stiffen, but his tone remained casual. "D-depends on what you p-plan to do with that knife."

Brice gave him a kind look. "I won't hurt you, I promise. If you don't believe me or don't trust us, you may walk out the door, unimpeded." He pointed the knife's tip at the exit. "Jaycee can choose whether to stay or go, regardless of what you decide. She is a free woman."

Jaycee hid a start of surprise, not so much at Brice's words, but at the Shifters' reaction to the statement—they didn't so much as blink. While male Shifters acknowledged that females pretty much did what they wanted to anyway, obedience to the mate and the clan leader was deeply ingrained in all Shifters. It was a rare Shifter male who didn't argue when it was suggested a female could ignore her mate's command or break unspoken rules of female behavior when she felt like it. The rage of the Shifters at the fight club when Jaycee had jumped into the ring was testimony to that.

These Shifters regarded Jaycee as though Brice's words were perfectly reasonable. As though her position with them was not dependent on her place in the Shifter hierarchy or whether she was mated and to whom. As though Jaycee was a person in her own right.

Jaycee had always believed this inside herself and acted accordingly, but it was a weird feeling to be accepted by these unknown Shifters for herself, not as a female defined by Dimitri or Kendrick.

Brice was waiting for her decision. "I'll stay," Jaycee said quickly. Not because of obligation, but because it was her choice. She wasn't about to leave Dimitri alone here.

Dimitri growled at her. He wanted her well out of danger, but too bad. Jaycee scowled at him and stayed put.

"Dimitri." Brice's voice held a touch of impatience. The other Shifters were waiting expectantly.

Dimitri squared his shoulders and walked forward. He stopped two paces from the fire, his hands curling to tight fists. Brice's expression said that he understood Dimitri's trepidation.

"In time, you will fear nothing," Brice said to him. "The Goddess will never hurt her children. Hold out your hand."

Dimitri obviously didn't want to, but he resolutely uncurled his fingers and lifted his hand, palm upward, toward Brice, his arm rock steady. Maeve came forward with a brass bowl that gleamed in the flames' light.

Brice laid the knife's edge on Dimitri's palm but didn't cut it. "Mother Goddess, hear our prayer."

He began to chant in Celtic once more, put a steadying hand on Dimitri's arm, and quickly sliced the knife across Dimitri's palm.

Jaycee leapt forward with a snarl. Two Shifter males stopped her by stepping in front of her and facing her, unmoving. Jaycee glared at them, but they remained a fixed barrier.

Brice flipped Dimitri's hand over and let the blood from the cut trickle into the bowl Maeve held. After a few seconds, Brice turned Dimitri's hand up again and took the bowl from Maeve. Maeve produced a cloth and tied it around Dimitri's hand.

The look the woman sent to Dimitri had Jaycee starting forward again, ready to rip out Maeve's throat if necessary. The woman had her own mate.

The male Shifters in front of Jaycee blocked her way again. Around them Jaycee saw Dimitri give Maeve a grateful nod and the smile that could knock Jaycee sideways. Dimitri smiled at everyone like that, but Jaycee was about to boil in her own blood.

Brice took the bowl to the brazier and trickled Dimitri's

blood from it to the flames. The liquid hissed and spat, the acrid scent cutting through the heavy smell of incense. The leopard inside Jaycee growled.

"The Goddess is pleased," Brice announced, setting the bowl on a table and lifting his hands. "The blessings of the Goddess be upon us all."

The Shifters cheered. This seemed to be a signal that prayer time was over, because the music started up again, thumping louder than before. The Shifters drifted apart, the atmosphere becoming more relaxed, conversations resuming.

The Shifters who'd blocked Jaycee ceased being statues. One shot her a grin before he walked away. "You ever want to ditch Red there, just let me know."

Sure, because a mangy-looking Feline would be worth the trade for the well-made, sexy, warmhearted Dimitri. If Jaycee hadn't been in a hurry she might have burned him with sarcasm. As it was, she only rolled her eyes and strode to Dimitri's side.

"You okay?"

Dimitri blinked down at her and showed her his bandaged hand. "Not much of a cut—I get w-worse at the fight c-club." His hot smile returned. "Want to k-kiss it better?"

"You're fine," Jaycee said, folding her arms.

"He is," Maeve said. She lingered at Dimitri's side, touching his bandage as though making sure it didn't slip. "Brice never cuts deep. How about we find you a beer, Dimitri?" She slid her fingers around his elbow.

Jaycee burned as hot as the brazier's flames. Did the Shifters accepting Jaycee as her own person mean they considered her mate fair game? Seriously, what the hell?

If she went leopard on Maeve and slammed her to the floor, what would the Shifters here do? Laugh? Try to kill her? Throw her and Dimitri out? That would end their mission before it started. She and Dimitri were supposed to be looking for evidence of sedition, not fighting mate battles.

Jaycee tightened her arms across her chest and hardened her voice. "Sure, Dimitri. Why don't you go get a beer? I'll make some new friends."

Dimitri's brow furrowed but he said nothing as Jaycee turned on her heel and stalked away from him and Maeve. Her leopard did *not* want to go, but Jaycee made her feet move.

Casey materialized next to Jaycee, regarding her in his nice-guy way. He handed her a cold bottle of beer. "Don't be too hard on Dimitri," he said in a friendly tone. "Maeve is only checking him out, seeing if he's trustworthy. I told her he was, but Maeve doesn't always take my word for things. Smart of her."

Casey was her *mate*. She should believe in him.

Then again, Jaycee would do the same thing, she admitted to herself. She'd double-check. She glanced back at Dimitri, who was watching her.

But I wouldn't be clinging to someone else's mate quite so hard, Jaycee thought with a growl.

She could always take her revenge on Maeve by crawling all over *her* mate, but she had no wish to. Casey was personable but nothing to get excited about, and Jaycee was not a female who could fake interest in a male.

She decided to prod Casey for information instead. "No cubs are here, I notice," she said.

Casey grew serious. "Brice's rules. These parties can get a little wild."

"Wild how?" A scan of the room showed her Shifters talking and joking together, but in a low-key way. At the last party she'd been to in the Austin Shiftertown, Connor Morrissey and the bear Scott—who had just come out of his Transition—had led a bunch of Shifters streaking. Shifters weren't much bothered by nudity, but to have a stark-naked Connor, Scott, and some of the wilder Felines and Lupines run screaming through the partying Shifters had quickly turned the backyard gathering to chaos.

And had been funny as hell. The boy called Olaf, a polar bear cub, had chased the older Shifters, not a stitch on him, yelling at them to wait for him. His foster dad, Ronan, in his gigantic Kodiak bear form, had run after *him*. Pretty soon, all the Shifters were throwing off their clothes and joining in, some Shifting, some simply running, screaming with their arms in the air. Dimitri had laughed so hard he'd fallen flat on the grass, laughing up at the sky. Jaycee had decided to lie down with him, curling around him as Shifters leapt over them in a flash of bare human limbs and furry animal legs.

In this house tonight Shifters lounged on sofas and chairs or walked about, conversing. This could be a boring human cocktail party in a chichi suburb.

Casey caught her skeptical look. "Just wait," he said.

"Whose house is this?" Jaycee asked. She sipped the beer Casey had given her, deciding not to mention that she liked wine better. Shifters were supposed to like the grain, not the grape, so she usually kept this preference to herself. Addie knew and made sure Jaycee could enjoy a glass every once in a while, but most Shifters who found out ridiculed her, forcing Jaycee to be a closet wine enthusiast.

"That, I can't tell you," Casey answered. "Not because Brice wouldn't want me to, but because I don't know. I assume a human. Or if a Shifter, that fact is hidden."

Jaycee figured as much. But what human would let their house be overrun with Shifters who were settling in to stay here past their curfew? That human would be arrested, fined, maybe even jailed for harboring dangerous Shifters.

Out of the corner of her eye, Jaycee saw Maeve lead Dimitri out of the living room, heading for the staircase hall. Jaycee definitely didn't like *that*. She started to follow, but Casey put a heavy hand on her arm. "Don't interfere."

Jaycee jerked back to him. "With a woman running off with my mate?" She opened her eyes wide. "Why not? She's *your* mate. Why aren't you going after her?"

Casey gave her a patient look. "Jaycee, there are certain things you don't rush to control. Let things go. Your life will be easier when you do."

Things like letting another woman drag off her *mate*? What the hell was this, a love-in?

Or maybe Casey was simply telling Jaycee not to jump to conclusions. A Feline wrapping herself around Dimitri

and pulling him toward the stairs didn't mean she was looking for a bedroom and sex.

Sure, and a leopard falling into a river she'd been certain
she could jump across hadn't meant to become a sopping
ball of fur rescued by a laughing red wolf.

Dimitri and Maeve had disappeared. Jaycee could let
them go, as Casey suggested, trusting that Dimitri wouldn't
give in to his natural Shifter horniness and his impatience
with Jaycee. Trust that Maeve didn't have more on her mind
than showing Dimitri the historic architecture of the old
house.

Or Jaycee could go after them and make sure.

She shook off Casey's hand, set down her beer, and headed
for the stairs.

"Jaycee, wait," Casey called behind her, but Jaycee didn't
stop.

The staircase hall was deserted. The staircase itself was
a graceful thing, lifting from the ground floor to a spindle-
lined landing above.

Casey hadn't followed her. He remained in the living
room, his unhappy expression telling Jaycee he fully expected her to find his mate and Dimitri up to no good.

Jaycee smothered a growl and headed up the stairs, her
fingers skimming the polished railing. The second floor had
a light-colored wooden floor, painted white walls, and paneled doors leading off the landing, all of this lit by old-
fashioned sconces.

Jaycee crept down the hall, moving as quietly as only a
leopard could, and opened the first door. Behind it was a
bedroom with furniture of dark old wood, but it was empty
of Shifters. The second bedroom was the same. After that
came a large bathroom with a claw-footed bathtub. The next
room along was another bedroom, this one holding a canopy
bed, a fireplace, a wide sofa, and Maeve and Dimitri.

Maeve was busily trying to push Dimitri onto the sofa
and unbutton his jeans at the same time. Dimitri, to his
credit, was clutching his waistband with one hand and fran-
tically pushing Maeve away with the other.

Jaycee was across the room in an instant, locking her hand around Maeve's throat and jerking the woman from Dimitri. Jaycee let her face turn to that of her half beast, her teeth becoming fangs. *"Back off."*

Maeve whipped from Jaycee with the speed of a wildcat, her fingers becoming claws. The two faced each other, snarls rippling from Feline throats.

Dimitri hastily buttoned his jeans and stepped between them. "Stop! D-don't fight over me. I feel like a p-piece of meat."

"Shifters don't cheat," Jaycee snarled around him at Maeve. "You have your own mate."

Maeve straightened up, her claws receding. "You don't understand, honey."

Jaycee didn't like women calling her *honey*. She'd used the term herself in the same way until she'd understood how nasty and condescending it could sound.

"I'll make you understand—*sugar*," Jaycee snapped.

"Cool it, Jase," Dimitri said in a hard voice. "I wasn't going to let her touch me."

Maeve regarded Jaycee coolly. "This isn't how we do things around here—fighting all the time. The Goddess didn't make us for that."

What the hell was she talking about? "The *Fae* made us," Jaycee said. "To fight for *them*."

"It's a common misperception," Maeve answered calmly. "The Fae created us because they were following the will of the Goddess."

"What?" Jaycee stared at her. "It was the Goddess's will we were enslaved by the Fae and forced to do battle for them? Then had to fight a long and bloody war to get away from them? The Goddess wanted all that, did she?"

Maeve nodded. "We learned how to fight and how to survive. See how we've grown?"

Jaycee's mouth hung open. "Right—all the Shifters slaughtered in all those Fae wars were thrilled to be cut to pieces so *you* could learn to survive. Bet you never had to fight twenty thousand armed Fae by yourself."

"Jase." Dimitri's sharp word cut through her speech. "Peace."

Jaycee drew a breath to keep arguing, then clamped her mouth shut. Dimitri was right—best to shut up, no matter how enraged she was that Maeve had tried to go for her mate.

Damn it, this job had been so much easier when she wasn't distracted by mate crap. It was going to drive her insane.

Before Jaycee could assure Dimitri she was finished arguing, the doorway darkened as Brice filled the opening. He filled it entirely—bears were big. He rested his broad fingers on the doorframe, his dark brown eyes taking in the scene.

"Maeve," he said firmly, though not sternly. "Don't scare them off before we've even said hello. Go keep an eye on Casey, sweetheart. You know he gets restless without you. Let me talk to these two for a while."

Maeve didn't look upset or apologetic—she smiled at Brice as though pleased he'd chosen to speak to her. Giving him a nod that was almost a bow, Maeve moved past Dimitri and Jaycee without a word and headed for the door.

Brice moved to let her by, and Maeve brushed her fingers over his arm as she slid around him. Brice caught her hand, squeezed it, gave her a warm look, and let her go. Maeve headed down the hall, calling over the banister to Casey in a sultry, promising voice.

"Come, my new friends," Brice said to Dimitri and Jaycee. "We'll find someplace less intimidating to talk." He waved his arm, indicating they should follow him, and turned away.

Jaycee exchanged a wordless look with Dimitri. He didn't nod, didn't even twitch his finger, but Jaycee knew he wanted to find out what Brice had to say.

Brice led them downstairs and through the big living room. Casey and Maeve were nowhere in sight.

The Shifters were finally loosening up and dancing to the music, some of them getting cozy with one another in corners. There were more males here than females, but the Shifters solved that problem by having several males cluster around each female, the females not looking unhappy about it.

Jaycee and Dimitri followed Brice to a door that opened to a stairway leading downward. As Jaycee prepared to descend behind Brice and Dimitri, she caught sight of someone across the living room, and she paused infinitesimally between one step and the next.

The man met her gaze with very black eyes, shook his head the tiniest bit, and went on flirting with a Lupine female who'd draped her arm around his shoulders.

Jaycee knew the man, had fought beside him. He'd gotten himself stabbed while trying to help Kendrick when Kendrick had faced dissension in his ranks, had been healed by a polar bear Shifter, and had gone on to help Jaycee and Dimitri defeat Kendrick's enemy.

The man called himself Ben, though who or *what* he was Jaycee couldn't say.

She turned wordlessly, hoping her expression hadn't betrayed her, and followed Dimitri down the basement stairs.

CHAPTER ELEVEN

The basement was well lit and held a pool table and a bar
with glasses hanging over it, a clear mirror behind the
bar reflecting facets of light through the glasses. It was a
setup Dimitri might like if he ever got his own place—that
was, one bigger than the two-room tiny house he'd built
himself on Kendrick's ranch.

No one was here at the moment, the large room empty
of Shifters. Brice stepped behind the bar, rummaged in a
refrigerator, and came up with bottles of beer.

"I have wine if you want it, Jaycee," he offered.

Dimitri watched Jaycee's eyes narrow. She liked wine—
why, Dimitri wasn't sure—but she was obviously wondering
how Brice knew that.

Jaycee gave Brice a stiff nod. "Pinot Grigio if you have
it. Chardonnay would be fine too."

"Pinot it is," Brice said. He shot Dimitri a glance as if to
say, *Ladies can be so adorable, can't they?*

Dimitri gave him a tight smile in return. They weren't
friends enough to share jokes about Jaycee—no Shifter took
to another that quickly.

Brice set the drinks on the counter and lifted his bottle of beer. Jaycee took up her glass, sniffed it first in suspicion, second in the way a wine lover tested its scent. Dimitri watched her rest the glass against her chest for a second, inhaling. She lifted the goblet to her chin, inhaled again, then finally stuck her nose in it.

"Nice," she said, then poured a large dollop into her mouth and swallowed. No dainty slurps or spitting it out for Jaycee—though she'd once told him that the way wine tastings were portrayed in movies and TV shows was bullshit.

"I don't know jack crap about wine," Brice said. "A human buys the stuff for me—I guess he has good taste."

"He can stock my wine cabinet anytime," Jaycee said in a light voice. "So, Brice, how did you stick your hand into the fire without burning it?"

Dimitri nearly choked on his beer. He coughed, set the bottle down, and banged his hand to the top of the bar. "Jaycee," he spluttered.

Brice only laughed. "It's a good question. What do you want me to say, Jaycee? That the Goddess protects me with her magic? Or that I used a flame retardant? A stunt performer showed me how to do the trick. It's impressive, right?"

Dimitri cleared his throat one last time and picked up his beer bottle. "Why t-try to f-fool everyone?"

Brice gave him a wise look. "Shifters, you know? They attend Goddess rituals and do the circle dances, but they don't always *believe*. My faith in the Goddess is true, and I want to bring other Shifters into that faith with me. But some can't be convinced without tangible proof of the Goddess's love. So I show it to them. I don't think she minds."

"But Goddess magic *is* real," Jaycee said. "You see it in the Guardians, in the healers, in the empaths. You don't have to trick Shifters into believing."

Brice heaved a patient sigh. "You wouldn't think so, would you? The Shifters who have come to me are looking for something more in their lives—answers, relief from the tedium of life in captivity. They want to know their sacrifice—taking the Collars, living in Shiftertowns—is worth something. That the Goddess hasn't forgotten them. She hasn't, but sometimes they need reminding."

"How do they not smell the flame retardant?" Jaycee asked. "How did *I* not smell it?"

Good question, Dimitri decided. Jaycee could scent a dropped acorn at a thousand paces. She could distinguish between five different wines Dimitri would swear were all the same, explaining in detail the multitude of odors within each.

Brice answered readily. "I mix it with scents I buy at a woo-woo shop in the French Quarter. The woman who owns it knows a lot about scent and masking it. *And* she likes Shifters." He grinned. "Win-win."

"You're—" Jaycee broke off and took another sip of wine. "Not what I expected."

Brice laughed with the deep vibration bear Shifters had. "Casey can be a bit of a fanatic. He recruits for me. I bet you expected an exaggerated version of him, maybe me foaming at the mouth while I prostrated myself in front of Goddess statues. That's not my style. The Goddess will lead us to great things, and I do her will, but I don't mind having a little fun on the way." He lifted his beer, toasting them with it. "Shifter style."

"Why do you w-want re-re-re . . ." Dimitri closed his mouth in frustration, the word not coming out.

"Recruits," Jaycee said. "What do you want recruits for?"

Brice fixed her with his dark gaze. "It's sweet that you want to finish his sentences for him, Jaycee," he said, leaning his elbows on the bar. "But you might also be damaging him. Making him even more inhibited."

Dimitri opened his mouth to say, *No, she isn't*, but Brice held up a hand, stopping him. Jaycee had flushed, her eyes sparkling with anger.

"You care for him," Brice said to Jaycee. "That's obvious.

But your caring might be hindering him rather than helping him." He turned to Dimitri. "Do you stutter all the time?"

"Not when I'm seriously p-pissed off," Dimitri answered. "Or shifting. Or making s-sweet love." He winked at Jaycee, who flushed redder still.

Brice gave him a thoughtful look. "Stammering can be caused by abuse early in life. Did that happen to you as a cub?"

"I have n-no idea." Dimitri didn't mind talking about his past, because there wasn't much to talk about. "I don't remember a lot about my cubhood. My dad was a Russian timber wolf. My m-mom a red wolf. I remember them fine, but not what h-happened to them. I was found abandoned in the woods in North C-Carolina, and the humans who found me couldn't understand me."

"Because of the stutter?" Brice asked in a kind voice.

"Because I only spoke R-Russian. Maybe I stammer because I l-learned English late."

Brice contemplated him with an interested gaze. "It can also happen because of a trauma. Something terrible that would leave a deep scar."

"If there was, I d-don't r-remember . . ." Dimitri trailed off. He felt a sudden flash of heat, as though something burned him, heard a scream. The basement lights went dim, and he could no longer see Jaycee.

No. He sucked in a breath and thrust out his hand, with Jaycee instantly clasping it.

As soon as Dimitri touched her, felt her hand solidly in his, the darkness cleared and the screaming ceased. Jaycee squeezed his fingers and sent him a *You okay?* look.

Dimitri knew he would be as long as he focused on her. Maybe Brice was right and a terrible memory lurked inside him, one that had wiped his brain of everything that had happened before the backwoods human couple had taken him home. They'd been surprised to find that the little boy they'd decided to take care of could turn into a wolf.

Dimitri let out a laugh but didn't move his hand from Jaycee's. "The first time my foster p-parents saw a red wolf sitting in the middle of their living room, they tried to sh-shoot me. Both of them. I turned back to human, and they freaked out. That could have c-caused an im-im-ped . . . im-ped . . . Screw it."

"Why didn't they kill you?" Brice asked in curiosity. "Humans didn't exactly believe Shifters existed before twenty years ago, and after that they thought we were evil."

"I don't know," Dimitri answered, shrugging. "We never t-talked about it. They were g-grateful to have a k-kid, I guess. They were m-mountain people. Off the grid. Drank a lot. But g-good people."

"What happened to them?" Brice's question was gentle. Jaycee who knew Dimitri's story, only listened, her beautiful golden eyes on him.

"H-homemade liquor, tobacco, and too much b-barbecue," Dimitri answered. "No doctors in the backwoods. They hit the human age of fifty-five and k-keeled over."

He said it lightly, as he always did, but Dimitri still grieved. David and Anna had taken him in, loved him, cared for him, and hadn't minded that he was a Shifter. They'd believed God had given them a demon-child for some reason, but being demonkind wasn't Dimitri's fault, they said, and they'd care for him as God apparently willed. They'd been a little crazy, but kind.

Brice only said, "Hmm."

"It doesn't b-bother me," Dimitri said. "That I c-can't talk, I mean."

"Other Shifters don't give you hell about it?"

"They do," Dimitri conceded. "Then I k-kick their asses."

"You've taught them to respect your fists," Brice said in understanding.

Dimitri nodded. "And my c-claws, teeth, elbows, feet . . ."

"Or he yells at them in Russian," Jaycee put in.

"N-no one understands that, though," Dimitri said. "Not as effective as a t-takedown."

He remembered Kendrick giving him a meaningful look when he'd assigned Dimitri and Jaycee this task. *They ridicule you, and it upsets you very much.*

Dimitri rearranged his face into a sorrowful expression. "It's h-hell."

Brice gave him a nod. "I promise you, Dimitri, I will find a way to make your life less hellish. The Goddess can work miracles."

Jaycee took another sip of wine. "Are you a healer?"

"Not exactly," Brice answered. "I can't put my hand on Dimitri's head and make him dramatically lose his speech impediment. But I know things about healing the mind, and the Goddess will lend us her strength and magic. Will you let me try, Dimitri?"

Dimitri gave him a skeptical look. Leaping at the chance would look more suspicious, not that Dimitri believed he could do anything anyway. "What do you want in return?"

Brice shook his head at the question and looked sad. "This is what happens when we live too long in Shifter-towns. We lose our trust, our sense of helping each other for the sake of it. We've picked up human ways—we believe no one gets something for nothing."

Dimitri shrugged. "I suppose that's true. S-sorry."

"You were raised by humans," Brice went on. "That also contributes to your lack of trust." He took on a patient look. "I don't want anything at all from you, Dimitri. I want you to live your life in happiness and freedom. Those Collars, for example." He gestured to Dimitri's throat. "Take them off."

Jaycee froze. Dimitri didn't move. "W-what?"

"I know they're fake," Brice said. "I don't invite Shifters to my hidden places without checking them out first. Kendrick's Shifters all wear fake Collars to keep the humans fooled." He gave them a grin. "Don't worry—your secret is safe with me. No webcams feeding to Shifter Bureau. You're welcome to look, of course." He waved his hand at the shadowy walls and ceiling.

"N-no," Dimitri said squaring his shoulders. If Brice wanted a gesture of trust, he could give him one. "Jase—will you do the honors?"

Jaycee wasn't as happy about this as Dimitri, but she rose

and moved behind him. Her fingers were warm on his neck as she pressed the catch to open the Collar.

Dimitri exhaled as he pulled the Collar from his throat. His neck was faintly sore—the fakes were designed to impress the skin like the real ones did. Shifters who'd managed to have their real Collars removed—a slow, arduous process if the Shifter didn't want to go insane with the pain—had raw and abraded skin around their necks for weeks.

"That is freedom, my friends," Brice said. He wore a Collar that looked plenty real, though Dimitri couldn't tell. The Morrisseys in Austin gave fakes to Shifters who'd had their Collars removed, and like Dimitri's, they looked authentic. "Jaycee?"

Dimitri undid the clasp of Jaycee's Collar before she could reach for it herself. He felt her flesh rise in goose bumps as he brushed his thumb and fingers over her neck, then her Collar loosened and released.

He took it from her and bunched it in his hand, the chain warm from her skin.

"Much better." Brice gazed at Jaycee in approval, the heat in his eyes making Dimitri bristle. Brice noticed. "She isn't your property, my friend. Females can make choices these days. A mate-claim isn't binding."

"What about a mating?" Jaycee asked before Dimitri could snarl at him. "Under sun and moon?"

"The Goddess didn't actually come up with those ceremonies," Brice said in a reasonable tone. "Shifters did. There was so much fighting over mates when we were left on our own that we created the ceremonies so Shifters would publicly recognize that certain females were off-limits. The human marriage ceremony is much the same—showing other humans that the two have made a pair."

"So, you don't believe in the official matings?" Jaycee persisted.

"I didn't say that." Brice didn't sound offended. "I said it wasn't a Goddess ceremony, though we've tied it to our beliefs. We use the sun and moon ceremonies to let other Shifters recognize the choices we've made. But you're thinking about Maeve trying to hit on Dimitri." Brice's lips twitched. "I'm sorry about that. She and Casey are sun and moon mated, but they have an understanding. There aren't as many Shifter females as males, as you know, and our gene pool is not large. So the females in my group choose the males, more than one if they want. But we're not having a free-for-all, I promise you. No orgies in my house." Another twitch of the corners of his mouth.

"Glad to hear it," Jaycee said. "If males I don't choose touch me, they're toast. I'll tear into them before Dimitri even has a chance."

"Which is why I allowed you here, Jaycee," Brice said. "You know what you want and aren't afraid to defend yourself. I like strong females. I don't want Dimitri to have to take time to fight for you—you can do it yourself. Some things will grow easier over time."

Dimitri wondered what he meant by the last statement, but he said nothing. Jaycee was good at asking blunt questions without making people angry at her. He'd learned to stand back and let her, absorbing the answers.

Brice lifted his beer, took a long drink, and set the bottle down on the bar. "You'll want to go back to wherever you're staying and think about it, I know that. Return when you're ready. But not here. Meet me at the bar. I don't want to give the human cops too many opportunities to find me."

He leaned his hands on the bar, in no hurry to leave. Dimitri took a last swig of his beer and set it back down, the bottle half full. Jaycee had finished her glass of wine.

"G-good night, then." Dimitri let Jaycee's Collar dangle from his hand. "Yours, my s-sweet."

Jaycee took the chain but Brice said, "Leave them off. Let the Shifters here know you're free. Plus, if you wear them outside, you'll have to dodge humans, and you're now out after curfew."

Jaycee glanced at Dimitri, shrugged, and slid the Collar into her pocket. "Aren't you afraid we'll betray your secret location?" she asked Brice.

"No." Brice gave them a tight smile. "You're curious, and I haven't done anything more sinister you can run and tell Dylan about than praying to the Goddess and doing my trick with the brazier. You're welcome to seek me anytime. I know you'll soon understand."

Brice came out from behind the bar, his bear size dominating even the basement's large space. He stood half a head taller than Dimitri and a good two feet above Jaycee.

When Brice's hand came down on Dimitri's shoulder, Dimitri flinched, but not because Brice hurt him—the bear's touch was almost gentle.

But something sparked deep inside Dimitri's brain, similar to what had flashed when he'd watched Brice with the brazier.

I know him from somewhere, his thoughts whispered. *It's going to drive me batshit crazy until I remember from where.*

D imitri decided to head straight back to Jazz's house, not stopping for a late dinner or a midnight snack even though without Collars they would have been able to go to a human restaurant. The indented line on Jaycee's neck had faded by the time they'd said good night to Casey and departed—Dimitri assumed his had as well.

As he pulled his motorcycle into the curved drive, he saw that several rooms of the house were lit and the front porch light shone out, though Dimitri knew neither he nor Jaycee had turned on any lights before they'd left. The front door opened for them again too.

Jaycee patted the doorframe as they went inside. "Jazz said it would be nice to us."

"*W-who* would be nice to us?" Dimitri asked, looking around in worry.

"The house." Jaycee gave the wood a final pat and strolled toward the staircase. "I'm beat. Mind if we talk about weird Brice and his tricks in the morning? Jazz told me to use her room. *You* can sleep across the hall."

She ran lightly up the stairs, no exhaustion showing. Dimitri watched her hips move in her tight pants, the light from the chandelier catching on her tawny hair. Every move she made was breathtaking.

Dimitri went to close and lock the front door, but the house took over that job too. It was unnerving to see the bolts slide into place on their own.

Dimitri decided to make for the kitchen, which was on the second floor, as the first-floor rooms had been left in their eighteenth- and nineteenth-century states for the tourists. He was starving—maybe he could find a box of stale crackers or something Jazz had left behind.

The pantry and the refrigerator in the cavernous kitchen proved to be well-stocked. Dimitri opened and ate half a box of crackers that were crisp and salty. A frozen apple turnover, warmed up in the microwave, served as his fruit. He washed everything down with a pint of milk—fresh, not spoiled—drunk from the carton, and turned off the light, ready for bed.

He didn't want to know where all the food had come from. Just didn't.

Jaycee hadn't locked her door. When Dimitri quietly opened it to check on her, he found her curled up under blankets on a four-poster bed, the tank top she slept in hugging her chest. Her eyes were closed, her breathing even. Jaycee could always drop off in a heartbeat and awake refreshed and ready to go.

Dimitri left her and entered the bedroom across the hall, which was filled with heavy furniture from the mid-nineteenth century. The ponderous bed had garishly carved head- and footboards, the carving repeated on the two night tables and vast dresser. A chandelier heavy with gilt and faceted crystals hung over the bed.

Dimitri eyed the chandelier as he shucked his clothes and turned off the lights, hoping the house wouldn't decide to drop the huge light smack onto his bed.

He lay awake for a time, watching shadows on the white

ceiling and plaster medallion that held the chandelier, thinking over what he'd learned.

He couldn't decide whether Casey and Brice were crazy
or only trying to make their life in captivity easier. Were
they working to betray all Shifters or simply finding refuge
in rituals to the Goddess?

Brice was right—he'd caught Dimitri's and Jaycee's curiosity. They'd go back.

Dimitri pondered until his eyes grew heavy and he slept.

He jumped awake, knowing by the shadows he hadn't
slept long. A groaning noise made him look up.

The chandelier above him swung alarmingly. Another
sound made him snap his head around, and he saw the
dresser sliding back and forth across the wall, and then his
bed started shaking. The curtains billowed at the windows,
and the paintings on the walls rattled.

Standard cliché horror-movie stuff. Dimitri admired
whoever had programmed the effects.

Then the giant bedstead abruptly came off the floor. It
hovered a couple of inches in the air and then slammed back
down, the impact sending Dimitri to its edge. He caught
himself with Shifter agility, landing on his feet on the car-
peted floor.

He was about to yell *Enough!* when he heard Jaycee
scream. In the next second, Dimitri was out the door and
sprinting for her bedroom.

CHAPTER TWELVE

Jaycee's eyes popped open as Dimitri burst into her bedroom, its door banging into the wall.

"Jase!" he shouted. "You all right?"

Jaycee struggled up. Dimitri stood next to her bed, moonlight shining fully on him, though she could have sworn she closed the blinds. The white glow outlined his body and red hair and shadowed the minute pair of briefs that hugged his hips.

Jaycee raked her hair back from her face, holding it in place with her hand, and looked pointedly at the briefs. "If those were any smaller, could they still be called underwear?"

"What?" Dimitri blinked down at himself. His abdominal muscles rippled as he did so, then he straightened, stretching his equally impressive shoulders. "Screw that. I heard you screaming. I th-thought—"

He looked around at the quiet room, his big hands balling to fists.

"You thought what?" Jaycee raised her brows. "I didn't scream. You must have been dreaming."

"No . . ." Dimitri continued scanning the room as though

he expected something to jump out of the closet. "Sure you're okay?"

"Yes." Jaycee looked him up and down. "Are you?"

"Yeah." Dimitri's balled fists came up and he jammed his arms over his chest. "N-no. This house is fucking weird. Furniture moving all over the p-place. S-screaming . . ."

"I didn't hear anything. Are you positive you weren't dreaming?"

"I damn well wasn't." Dimitri growled at her. "S-someone's messing with us."

"The house is haunted. Jazz told me all about it." Jaycee gave him a look under her falling hair. "You scared?"

"Of what?" Dimitri said in defiance. "I th-thought *you* were s-scared. Or h-hurt."

"Well, I'm not."

Dimitri remained planted in the middle of the room. The house was silent, refreshingly so, private and secure, not like Brice's place with Shifters crawling all over it. Jazz had confessed to Jaycee that she loved her house, where she'd lived happy years with her grandmother. She'd felt protected there.

Jaycee understood. The house was a little strange, but after her initial uneasiness it had ceased to frighten her. Dimitri, on the other hand, looked haggard, as though he viewed going back across the hall to his room with the same enthusiasm he would jumping into an active volcano. Dimitri was fearless in the fighting ring, but a few doors opened and shut on their own and his face was gray, and not because of the moonlight.

Jaycee flipped back the covers, letting in cool air. "You want to sleep with me? Just *sleeping*, I mean."

For once, Dimitri made no jokes. He was around the bed and slipping under the covers before Jaycee finished saying the words.

She had to admit that Dimitri snuggling down beside her, she spooning back into him, was nice. Dimitri warmed the bed—and took up most of it, but Jaycee didn't mind.

He settled the covers, then draped a heavy arm over her. "Your hair s-smells nice," he murmured.

"Aw," Jaycee said. "Good shampoo."

"Shut up and take a compliment," Dimitri said without a stammer.

"Sorry." Jaycee told herself she shouldn't tease him all the time, but it was difficult not to.

Dimitri burrowed his nose into her neck. "I'm j-just going to enjoy this."

"No sex," Jaycee warned.

"D-did I say anything about s-sex?" Dimitri asked indignantly. "I'm not even t-touching any intimate parts."

"But you're thinking about it. Like I said, that underwear is *really* small."

Dimitri chuckled, a warm rumble in the night. "Sweetie, I'll l-leave you alone tonight, but I c-can't promise not to *think* about it. I'm only so strong."

Jaycee was thinking about it too, that was the trouble. She went over the passionate encounters they'd had—the first one right after their Transitions when they'd been burning with hormones. It had been messy, awkward, and embarrassing.

The last time had been in Kendrick's house, when Kendrick and Addie had mated. A leader mating was powerful magic, which had permeated the entire Shifter group. Dimitri had come to check on Jaycee, as he had tonight, and they'd made hard, swift love to each other.

"You're plenty strong," Jaycee whispered.

"Not about you I'm n-not," Dimitri said, his voice low. "Now b-be quiet and let me hold you."

Jaycee closed her mouth. Dimitri's body was heavy behind her, his arm solidly around her waist. The house made Jaycee feel secure, and with Dimitri around her she'd never felt so safe in her life.

To moonlight, and Dimitri's snore, Jaycee drifted to sleep.

S he woke to music. A radio played loudly somewhere in the house, and sunshine poured through her bedroom window. It would be hot today, New Orleans sticky in August.

Dimitri was gone. Jaycee tamped down the cool wave of disappointment, rolled out of bed, and pulled a pair of running shorts from her duffel bag. She knew the bathroom down the hall was stocked with thick towels, waiting for her, and she dragged on the shorts and headed out of her room.

The door across the hall was open. Music blasted from it, along with Dimitri's voice. Apparently, he'd forgiven the house or his dreams for waking him up—he was in the middle of the room in nothing but a low-slung pair of jeans, his back to the door, singing at the top of his lungs.

Dancing too. His hips moved in time with the music, his voice rising to a falsetto to hit high notes. Jaycee didn't know what the song was, but the word *baby* featured in it a lot.

Jaycee leaned on the doorframe and watched. Dimitri was what she'd call aesthetically pleasing. His supple and strong back tapered to his very tight backside, which was cupped by the jeans, emphasizing his long legs and powerful build. She wondered if he'd put on a fresh pair of tiny underwear that morning, or maybe had left them off entirely.

Heat stirred inside her, building what had already been smoldering. She didn't need to stick her hand into a brazier to feel fire—she only had to look at Dimitri.

He must have showered while she slept, because his hair was damp, dark with water. A few beads of moisture lingered on his shoulders and his upper back. He leaned his head back at one point, shaking it, sending droplets flying. Jaycee laughed.

Dimitri spun around. He saw Jaycee, but instead of being abashed, he held out his hands and danced his way toward her, singing the whole way. He didn't stutter when he sang— he never had.

His voice wasn't true but Jaycee didn't care. He was singing for joy and being alive, for the sunshine and warmth. For Jaycee.

Dimitri caught her hands and spun her into the dance. Unlike when he'd danced with her at the roadhouse, he didn't pull her close or use it as an excuse to kiss her. He moved swiftly in a swinglike dance, shoving Jaycee away and pulling her back toward him, never letting her be off-balance.

He danced with the grace of his wolf, not missing a step. He guided the two of them around the room, pulling Jaycee out of the way of the massive furniture. The chandelier above them swayed in time with the music, as though the house danced with them.

As the song wound to its climax, Dimitri gathered Jaycee and spun with her in the middle of the room, pelvis to pelvis. His strong arms wound around her back, and at the song's last chord, he lowered her into a dramatic dip.

The DJ yelled, "Good morning, New Orleans!" and went on blathering about something or other.

Dimitri held Jaycee in his arms, still in the dip, his gray eyes on her. His face softened as he looked down at her, the corners of his mouth flattening. Jaycee hung there, knowing he'd never drop her, wanting the moment to hover forever.

Dimitri breathed hard with his dancing, his bare chest expanding. He had such strength, but it didn't make him arrogant. He barely acknowledged how strong he was, as though he didn't notice.

Jaycee needed his strength. She always had. And it had been there for her to reach out and touch.

She touched him now. Jaycee traced the curve of his pectorals, fingertips catching in the curls of damp red hair.

Dimitri abruptly raised her and set her on her feet, and Jaycee's hand fell away. Dimitri stood looking down at her for a long moment, and then he put his hand behind her neck and drew her up for a kiss.

A deep, breath-stealing kiss. Jaycee tasted the mouthwash he'd used and the spice of himself. Then Dimitri was gone, moving away in time to the next song, snatching up a shirt as he went.

"There's plenty of f-food in the kitchen," he said. "W-want breakfast?"

Jaycee could only stand in place, her lips tingling, her heart banging in her throat. "You cooking?"

"S-sure. Have a sh-shower and c-come on in."

Dimitri swayed past her, still dancing. He caught her again, pressed another heart-pounding kiss to her mouth, and danced out. She heard his laughter as he ran the hall, which sounded very close to a wolf howl.

"Why are you so happy this morning?" Jaycee asked half an hour later. She entered the kitchen after showering and dressing to find Dimitri juggling eggs, the ovals going up and up and up.

He faked almost dropping one, then laughed at Jaycee when she cried out, and broke the eggs into a bowl. He swished the yolks and whites together and poured them into a pan.

"Am I happy?" Dimitri asked as he rotated the pan, spreading eggs to all sides. Good, he was making omelets. "I'm b-being me."

Jaycee sat down at the table to watch him cook. The kitchen, on the second floor, was large, with stainless steel appliances and light wood, very modern. Obviously the kitchen was for the inhabitants of the house, not the tourists. Except for the ceiling beams and the wide window looking out to the sweeping front drive, there was nothing in here original to the house.

Downstairs, the house was exactly as it had been in seventeen hundred something-or-other. Humans loved to preserve the past, Jaycee noticed, and romanticize what had gone. Chances were the past had been no better or worse than the present—the human brain glossed over horror and hardship and revived what it wanted to glorify. Shifters who remembered the times humans glamorized thought they were nuts. A hundred years ago technology might have been simpler, but wars were brutal, a flu virus could wipe out a good percentage of the population, and only a privileged few lived in any comfort.

Shifter past had been even worse—they'd had to hide in remote parts of the world and keep humans from killing them. Many Shifters had begun to starve and fewer cubs had been born. Shiftertowns had saved Shifters from being killed outright and had also helped Shifters live in peace, have cubs, and get on with life. Kendrick had created his own "Shiftertown" for the same reasons, only without the Collars and human oversight.

"So, what do we do now?" she asked. "Go back to Brice? Report in to Kendrick?"

"I already reported," Dimitri said. "While you were in the shower. K-Kendrick says to look around a little longer, return to the club where we met Casey, check out Brice. We didn't find any s-sign of Shifters ready to do violence against other Shifters at Brice's h-house, but that doesn't mean there aren't any."

"Or maybe Kendrick sent us out here for a different reason." As Jaycee showered, she'd thought over the events from her disruption at the fight club to meeting Brice at his odd party. "To get us out of the way while he and Dylan go after another target?"

Dimitri turned around, spatula in hand. "Why the hell would they? We're Kendrick's top t-trackers, except for Seamus. If there was something d-dangerous going on around Austin, Kendrick would n-need us."

"But we're troublemakers, remember?" Jaycee idly picked up a knife and used its handle to trace a pattern on the placemat in front of her. "At least I am."

Dimitri swung back to the stove, lifted the omelet pan, and flipped the eggs with a flick of his wrist. The omelet folded in on itself perfectly, and Dimitri slid it to a plate. Jaycee rose and went to the stove for it.

"You're dreaming," Dimitri said, holding the plate out to Jaycee. He didn't release it when she tried to take it. "Kendrick has known you a l-long time. You break rules you don't l-like but they're usually ones Kendrick thinks are s-stupid anyway. Plus, he's not going to throw away his best trackers on a wild-g-goose chase."

Jaycee tugged at the plate, but for some reason Dimitri wouldn't let go. "Or maybe he's keeping Dylan off his back."

"C-could be." Dimitri finally released the plate, and Jaycee had to take a step back to catch her balance. "S-send us

out to make it look like he's t-taking the threat seriously."
He frowned. "Nah, Kendrick would t-tell Dylan to stick it
if he didn't agree with him."

Dimitri was most likely right, but the Shifters at Brice's
had been happy, not worried or constrained. They hadn't been
plotting, only hanging out, going through a Goddess ritual,
or pairing up. Nothing that didn't happen at any Shifter party.
And yet . . .

"Something weird is going on with Brice, I will agree,"
Jaycee said. "I didn't have a chance to tell you, but remember the guy, Ben, who helped us take down Kendrick's old
partner? I swear I saw him at Brice's last night."

"You did see me," came a deep voice from the kitchen
door.

Jaycee shrieked and leapt into the air. The plate with her
omelet spun like a Frisbee, and the perfectly made eggs
swirled off and splattered all over the floor.

CHAPTER THIRTEEN

Dimitri held the omelet pan like a weapon, a drop of hot oil falling to singe his foot, but he barely noticed. He was already halfway across the room to the man who lounged in the doorway, but Jaycee beat him to Ben, the leopard in her making her fast.

"How the hell did you get in here?" she demanded.

Ben stood about five foot seven, had a body full of muscles, black hair, and black eyes like windows to nothing. He had tatts up and down his arms and across his fingers, one flowing up his neck and onto his cheek. He regarded Jaycee without worry.

"The back door was unlocked. I heard you talking up here, so I came to say hi."

"What I mean is," Jaycee said tensely, "how did we not hear you or smell you? You have a distinctive odor." She sniffed at him.

True, Ben did carry the faint brimstone scent associated with the Fae. Not the guy's fault. He was from Faerie, but as he'd told them repeatedly, with heat, he was *not* Fae. In any case, Ben was old, powerful, and had a vast storehouse of knowledge behind those dark eyes.

"Hey, I took a shower," Ben returned, unoffended. "And I've learned to elude people, including Shifters who try to kill me for smelling like a Fae. Also didn't want to alert anyone who might be watching you that I came to see you. Cool house, by the way."

"Belongs to a friend," Jaycee said.

"Yeah, Jasmine. We've met. She and Mason are steaming up the sheets, from what I hear—she'll bring another cub soon, I'd guess."

Jaycee relaxed. "You might have called first," she growled at Ben. "You ruined my breakfast."

"There's p-plenty more," Dimitri said. "Someone s-stocked the fridge. Sit down, B-ben. I'll m-m . . ." He turned back to the stove, his powers of speech failing him. He could talk to Jaycee for a long time without worry—Kendrick and Seamus almost as much—but speaking to people he didn't know well could exhaust him.

"I'm not cleaning that up," Jaycee said, waving her hand at the eggs all over the carpet and sending Ben a glare.

"It's all right; I'll do it." Ben grabbed a roll of paper towels from the counter and started scooping the ruined omelet from the floor. "Even though *you* dropped it."

"Because *you* scared me." Jaycee watched him, hands on her hips, then sighed, grabbed more paper towels, and helped.

Dimitri kept cooking, determined not to laugh. "S-so," he said as Jaycee and Ben cleaned, "wh-what did you think of B-Brice?" If he kept his sentences short he'd be all right.

Ben continued to wipe up the floor, tearing off dry towels to finish the job. "I'm not sure what to make of him. His little band of followers likes him. Respects him—they don't fear him. I mean, they bend to his dominance, but they're not ter-rified. They joke with him, disagree with him, banter with him. The vibe I get isn't bad, but I'm not sure exactly what it is."

Jaycee nodded in agreement. "We need more dirt on him. Why did he let you join?"

Ben shrugged. "I explained who I am. What I am. You know, ancient being, screwed over by the Fae. I'm always looking for a place I can belong."

The last sentence had a ring of truth. Dimitri had felt the same way for a long time.

Jaycee laid a hand on Ben's shoulder. "You're always welcome at Kendrick's."

Ben's dark eyes softened. "Aw, you're so sweet. I'd hug you but I'm hungry, and Dimitri might throw that pan at me."

Dimitri, watching them, absently overstirred the eggs, which started to scramble instead of cook evenly. Screw it. He threw in some salt, pepper, and cheese and crumbled everything together.

Jaycee unfolded herself to her feet, keeping her hand on Ben's shoulder. He made a show of helping her up, then threw the paper towels away in the garbage can in the corner.

"You didn't explain how you got in here," Jaycee said. "We didn't see you coming, or hear you, or scent you." Her eyes narrowed. "Can you teleport?"

Ben barked a laugh. "I wish. Shit, what I wouldn't be able to do if I could pop from place to place? No, I used stealth. When you hide out from the Fae for a thousand years, you get good at it."

"If they exiled you to this world, they should leave you alone," Jaycee said indignantly. She approached the stove and looked at the mess in the frying pan. "Are you making that for yourself?"

Dimitri gave her an irritated look, dumped the scrambled eggs onto a plate, where they steamed, and wiped out the pan.

"I'll take those." Ben's broad hand snaked in and snatched the plate. He grabbed a fork from the counter and dug in. "Like I said, I'm hungry. Mmm. Not bad."

Dimitri set the pan down, cracked more eggs into a bowl, and quickly stirred them into a froth. He was mean with a whisk. Maybe he could introduce it as a weapon at the fight club. He spread out the eggs, which lapped to the edges of the pan. Perfect.

"The Fae exiled me," Ben said as he ate. "But that's never

good enough for them. The vendetta against me and my people was passed down from generation to generation. I'm the last of my kind now, but they won't be happy until we're all gone. Bastards."

Dimitri's sympathy for Ben went up a notch. They'd all had to put up with shit from the Fae, but Ben had a long history of struggling to survive.

He flipped the omelet once it was set, slid it to a plate, and presented it to Jaycee with a flourish. Jaycee smiled up at him, and suddenly nothing else in the world mattered.

He thought of sleeping against her last night, her lush body cradled into his, and dancing with her this morning. She'd laughed at him singing and dancing like a fool, and he hadn't been able to stop himself pulling her close and kissing her.

Dimitri almost did it now. Jaycee's smile was genuine and full of impish good humor. Her eyes sparkled, her red lips curving.

Ben looked over at the omelet. "What, no parsley?"

Dimitri handed Jaycee the plate. "B-bite me."

Ben grinned at him, and Dimitri returned to the stove.

By the time Dimitri had made himself an omelet, filling it with cheese and ham, both Jaycee and Ben had seated themselves at the table and were finishing the last of their eggs. As Dimitri ate, the other two talked about what they'd observed at Brice's party—Ben hadn't found out much more than they had, and he hadn't been taken down to the private bar in the basement.

Ben looked around the kitchen once they'd exhausted the conversation. "This house is interesting. Mind if I look around?"

"I'll come with you," Jaycee said, rising. "I haven't explored it much myself."

Dimitri bolted the rest of his omelet, wiped his mouth on a paper towel, and joined them.

Jaycee and Ben were already down the main staircase by the time Dimitri caught up to them. The chandelier that hung far overhead tinkled.

"Nice." Ben looked admiringly along the hall at the polished paneled wood and the doors that led to the large, lavishly furnished rooms. "I ran an old hotel back in North Carolina for a while. Left to me by the family who lived there. It's still nice. Haunted, of course."

"So is this house," Jaycee said. "I haven't seen any ghosts though, only doors opening and closing."

Dimitri clamped his mouth shut. He hadn't told Jaycee about the flying furniture in his room, because she apparently had heard and seen nothing. He put his hand on the staircase railing and felt a faint shudder move through it. No, not a shudder. More like laughter.

That feeling was confirmed as he stepped off the last stair. Jaycee and Ben were already out of sight. A whisper of laughter drifted past him, and far above him, the chandelier swayed.

Smart-ass, Dimitri growled silently and then hurried to catch up to Ben and Jaycee.

He reached them when Jaycee was unlocking the door that led to a small stair leading downward. Why Ben wanted to explore the dark recesses of the house, Dimitri didn't know, but the man seemed intrigued.

Dimitri peered into the square of blackness that the door revealed. He didn't scent anything dangerous, smelling only dust and mildew, which would be expected in an old root cellar.

Ben led the way down. Dimitri insisted on going ahead of Jaycee, and she let him after giving him an exasperated look.

The cellar was not so much a basement as a space under the house that had been enclosed. They were too near the river to dig down, too close to the water table.

The ceiling was about six feet high, forcing Dimitri to stoop. A breeze wafted through the space, keeping the air from being too dank.

"What d-do you think you'll f-find down here?" Dimitri asked Ben. "Dead b-bodies?"

"You never know," Ben said philosophically.

The cellar spread out in all directions, no walls dividing it off. Dimitri sniffed the air. "N-no death here."

"No," Jaycee agreed. "Only vegetables. And rodents. Snakes."

"Mmm-hmm," Ben said absently.

Jaycee and Dimitri exchanged a look.

It was weird that, while Brice acted like a fairly normal Shifter—all bears were full of themselves—Dimitri was highly suspicious of him. Ben, on the other hand, was as far from normal as a being could be, and yet Dimitri knew he could trust Ben with his life. *Had* trusted him. Something to think about.

Ben turned abruptly back to them. "I was wondering if the house was on a ley line," he said. "That might account for the weirdness."

Dimitri shook his head. "No one p-popping in and out of F-Faerie here that I can tell."

Jaycee had moved close to Dimitri, her body warmth touching him. "I don't think this house would let Fae in."

"It let B-Ben in," Dimitri pointed out.

"Who isn't Fae," Jaycee said.

"But most supernatural beings get a whiff of me and think I am," Ben said, sounding unworried. "However, my friends, a ley line isn't simply an entrance to Faerie. It's a way to *get* to Faerie if you have the right means, like a Fae artifact. But ley lines are more than gateways. They contain magic, a flow of power connecting to other power around the world. They're concentrations of raw energy that both carry magic and enhance magic used around it."

Dimitri hadn't known that. But then, he didn't have much chance to be around magic, other than the Sword of the Guardian Kendrick carried. Dimitri made sure he rarely had anything to do with magic at all.

"I'm a f-fighter," he said. "Not a sp-spell-c-c-c . . ."

"Neither am I," Jaycee said. "A spell-caster. I wouldn't know a ley line if it hit me in the face."

Ben circled the area, peering into dim corners. "Well, I

would. They hit me in the face a lot." He shook his head. "But if one is here, it's subtle."

He glanced around one more time, a puzzled look on his face, before he shrugged and led the way out.

Dimitri made for the veranda, Jaycee a step behind him. The stuffiness of the basement had bothered him—he wanted open air, a breeze.

The humidity of the August day smacked him as he walked out the door, the heat stifling. Dimitri peeled off his T-shirt and plumped down on a bench in the gazebo. He was outside, in the shade—this was fine. The rose vines that covered the house, yellow roses everywhere, cut the bright sunshine and some of the heat.

Jaycee sat down next to him. "Feels like it might rain."

Clouds were building in the south, the top of the thunderheads brilliant white in the sunshine, their undersides black.

"Good. Might c-cool things off."

"What do you want to do?" Jaycee was close to him on the bench, her thigh touching his. "Try to find out more about Brice before we see him again? Wait for him to call? I have the feeling those other Shifters wait by the phone for him to get in touch."

Dimitri's curiosity stirred beneath the heat and the heaviness of the air. "I wonder how they all c-communicate. Internet forum? Social m-media group?"

"We should have asked to join," Jaycee mused.

"W-we probably have to be invited." Dimitri leaned back, lacing his fingers behind his head. "W-we could t-try to search. But I'm n-not good with c-computers."

"Neither am I," Jaycee answered. "But I know someone who is. Broderick's mate Joanne. She used to be a hacker."

"T-true." The quiet-spoken young woman was a frigging genius, according to Broderick. Plus she had the fortitude to put up with Broderick, which made her a saint, in Dimitri's opinion.

"I'll call her," Jaycee said. She leapt to her feet, eager and energetic. "Better than just sitting here."

"I don't know." Dimitri ran his gaze down her body, lingering on her full breasts in her V-necked shirt, then moving to her beautiful face and shining eyes. "It's nice to s-sit once in a while. We do t-too much running around."

Jaycee put one hand on her hip. "We're trackers. It's our job to run around."

"But s-sometimes"—Dimitri traced Jaycee's fingers where they rested on the tight leggings she wore—"it's g-good to s-stop."

Jaycee's face softened. "I know." She scissored her fingers together, catching his larger ones. "We're not alone though. We *were* alone, but now there's company."

Ben hadn't followed them to the veranda. From inside came the banging of a door, and Ben's voice. "Well, *cool*."

Jaycee rolled her eyes. Dimitri shot her a smile. "Should we see what he's up t-to?"

"Probably." Jaycee didn't move. "I like it here—in this house, I mean. I feel like we're out of the way—*distanced* might be a better word. Distanced from all the worries about being caught outside a Shiftertown, without Collars; worry what other Shifters are up to. Here, I feel like all that's far away. Unimportant."

"A good place to stop." Dimitri firmed his hand on hers. "And sit." He tugged her to him. She started to sink down next to him again, but he caught her around the waist and pulled her onto his lap.

Jaycee relaxed against him, her restlessness fleeing. The humid air made her face bead with perspiration, a drop of it on her lips. Dimitri kissed it away.

Be my mate, Jase, he wanted to say. *We'll have every day like this, to hell with the world while we hold each other.*

Jaycee was looking at him, Dimitri very aware of her focus on him. Her breasts rested against his chest, every intake of her breath sinking her closer to him.

Jaycee's eyes drifted closed as she softly kissed him. Her lips were warm, damp from the heat, the flick of her tongue through his mouth enough to ignite him.

Ben had very bad timing. If he hadn't arrived, Dimitri

would carry Jaycee back upstairs to her bed for the day. They couldn't do much investigating until dark anyway, when the clubs opened and they could look for Brice and his followers. Once they got closer to Brice's group, if they could, or invited in to stay with them, he and Jaycee wouldn't have much opportunity to be alone together. They'd have to be alert for danger at all times, with no time to sit in quiet intimacy, letting the world go by.

This house, for all its strangeness, felt safe. They could remain within its walls and make love all day, and it would take care of them.

Dimitri shut out his thoughts and concentrated on kissing Jaycee. He felt her strong hands on his back, her mouth on his, her soft backside on his thighs, making his already hard cock harder still. Her hair in its ponytail was sleek against his fingers, her breath hot on his cheek.

This woman was the only one for him. Had always been. They'd been friends for years, always looked out for each other. Dimitri wanted that camaraderie to last forever, and he wanted this woman in his bed. He wouldn't mind cubs too, little leopards gamboling all over the place.

Jaycee drew back from the kiss and cupped Dimitri's cheek. Her eyes were half closed, the brown of them touched with gold. Leopards purred, and Jaycee was doing it now.

The last time Dimitri had made love to her, it had been quick and fierce, both of them grappling each other. Dimitri wanted the next time to be like this, the two of them lying in slow, sultry heat, making love as the day went by.

The only reason to get up would be to bring food back to the bed, maybe a run in animal form if they got too restless. A run would wind them up again, and they'd be making love with even more fervor.

Do it. Ignore Ben.

The words whispering through his brain seemed to come from outside him. Jaycee smiled at him, no more hesitation.

A crash came from inside the house. "Oops." Ben's voice drifted to them.

At the same time, a stiff breeze swept down the veranda,

dancing through the row of wind chimes. A rumble of thunder followed.

Then Ben said abruptly, "Okay, that's just wrong."

Jaycee jumped, her alertness returning. She and Dimitri exchanged a glance, then they both scrambled up at the same time and made for the house. Wind and thunder poured after them, as well as the first spattering of rain. The door, left open, slammed itself behind them, and the bolts clicked closed.

CHAPTER FOURTEEN

Dimitri pushed his way in front of Jaycee as they ran down the hall. He always would, she realized. Protect her. Of course, this did give her a chance to watch his ass move in his formfitting jeans, his bare back supple above it. He'd left his shirt on the veranda.

Ben was at the front of the house, in a small sitting room. There wasn't much to the room, only a few chairs and a small table in the eighteenth-century French style—a room more for sitting still and admiring the wallpaper and gilded furniture than for any kind of gathering.

Ben was rattling the knob of a door set into one wall, its doorframe curving seamlessly into the blue silk wallpaper that was painted with flowers and colorfully plumed birds.

"You have the key to this?" Ben asked as Dimitri and Jaycee dashed into the room.

Jaycee fought irritation that something so innocuous had brought them running. "Jazz said all the keys are in the hall table," she said as she caught her breath.

"Found those," Ben said, peering to examine the lock. "But this looks like no keyhole I've ever seen."

Jaycee darted around Dimitri before he could stop her. She was quick and curious, like the cat inside her.

She crouched down to see what Ben pointed out. The keyhole was odd, larger at the bottom than the top, and shaped, she thought, like a rosebud. An upside-down one.

"None of the keys fit," Ben said. "And do you notice something about this door?"

"It's on an outside wall," Jaycee said. "So? It might lead to the porch."

"Does it?" Ben's dark eyes were a mystery. "Take a look."

A long window opened in the wall about five feet from the door. Jaycee pushed back the lace curtains, undid the window's catch, and opened the casement, letting in a rush of wind and the smell of rain.

The window was tall enough that a person could use it for a door. Jaycee stepped over the sill and onto the front veranda. Dimitri came directly behind her, his body heat warm on her back, his breath on her neck.

The wall was blank where the door should be, the bricks running unbroken to the next window, which opened from the room beyond.

"All right," Jaycee said. "I agree, that is wrong."

Wind whipped down the porch, clouds blotting out the sunlight. Thunder rumbled, closer now, the ground vibrating with it. Jaycee shivered. She didn't like storms.

Dimitri ushered Jaycee back inside and shut the window. Rain began to come down, pattering loudly on the porch roof.

Ben was on his knees, scraping at the lock with a thin piece of metal. "Things like this bug me. I have to know." The metal slipped, and he muttered a word Jaycee had never heard before. "Wish my hands were a little more skilled."

"Let me." Jaycee slid in with leopard grace, dropped to her knees, and grasped the lockpick.

Ben gave it to her without argument. "You know how to pick locks?"

"You'd be amazed at what trackers learn."

She was as curious as Ben as to where this door went. She scented danger, but that did not erase her curiosity.

"Maybe it's a door to N-Narnia," Dimitri suggested.

Ben grunted. "Don't even say that in a house like this. You never know what kind of magic it can produce."

"They have t-talking animals there," Dimitri said. "We'd f-fit right in."

"I remember those stories," Jaycee said. "One had a were-wolf in it, but he was evil and got killed. So watch yourself."

"I liked the m-mouse," Dimitri said. "He had attitude."

"Will you two stop?" Ben growled. "Words are magic, all right? You never know what saying them will cause."

Jaycee snapped her mouth shut. She wasn't sure what Ben meant, but then, he'd lived a thousand years, part of them in Faerie, and was probably right about the dangers of anything smacking of magic.

Thunder cracked overhead. More rain poured down, and the windows rattled.

The lockpick slipped, came down on Jaycee's wrist, and nicked it, drawing a thin streak of blood. She snarled in irritation and patiently inserted the pick into the lock again.

A sharp gust of wind blew open the window Dimitri had closed. Rain pelted into the room before Dimitri could spring up and shut it again.

He halted at the window's opening. "Shit!"

"What?" Jaycee looked up, but she could barely see Dimitri in the swiftly fading light.

"I d-didn't think they had tornadoes here."

Jaycee scrambled to her feet and hurried to him, Ben behind her. The clouds to the south were low and black, roiling with wind. The same wind shrieked through the eaves, pulsing against the house and pushing Jaycee back a step.

A finger of cloud reached down from the thunderheads, scattering debris before it.

"You can have tornadoes anywhere," Ben said. "If conditions are right."

Conditions seemed to be right at the moment. The finger receded into the sky but another snaked down, then a second. Both disappeared, but another, larger one moved toward the earth.

Behind the noise of the wind came the sound of warning sirens. Ben's phone started dinging at the same time.

He snatched it from his pocket and looked at it. "Tornado warning," he said, reading his screen. "No, really?"

"Basement," Dimitri said firmly.

"Won't help in this case," Ben argued. "Nothing's underground."

"Bathroom," Dimitri said. Jaycee, experienced from living in Texas, understood what he meant. A first-floor bathroom with no windows and a sturdy walled shower might withstand the winds or at least provide some shelter.

"All on the second floor," Jaycee answered. "The ground floor is historically accurate."

"Great," Dimitri said, staring at the funnels appearing and disappearing into the cloud. "Where d-did historically accurate people hide from st-storms?"

"Hell if I know," Jaycee said. "How about under the dining room table? That thing's massive."

"Right." Ben turned to lead the way. "Dining room."

As she started to follow, something made Jaycee freeze, her Feline senses tensing. Her leopard wanted to arch her back and hiss.

She didn't know why she was having this reaction—her cat instincts had been alerted by something more than the storm. Then she saw the rose vines. Dimitri halted in the act of turning to follow Ben, and Ben came hurrying back.

Jaycee had thought the roses covering the house beautiful, blooming yellow, climbing over everything. Now, as Jaycee watched, the vines around the porch pillars began to flow toward one another, touching and then locking together. They created a mesh that covered the space between veranda posts, then flowed down like a river of green to crawl across the porch and up the windows to cover them.

Dimitri, closest to the sitting room window, backed away, herding Jaycee behind him. The vines crossed the window, blocking the rest of the light and most of the wind. Breezes slid between the cracks in the branches, but the gale that had blown through the room suddenly died.

Jaycee gazed at a lattice of rose canes crossing and criss-crossing, leaves squashed, blossoms drooping. Ben darted from the room, heading to the one next to it. Jaycee wanted to follow, but she found herself unable to move, fascinated by the intertwining vines.

"It's the same all over," Ben said, returning to them. "All the windows and the front door. Probably the back one too." He stared at the mass of branches over the windows and shook his head. "*So* not natural."

"It's the house," Jaycee said in a subdued voice. "It's protecting us."

The building shuddered—not with the strange vibrations it made on its own, but as though something had struck it.

Wind, Jaycee realized in the next moment. It hit the house with the momentum of a freight train, the sound a loud, echoing *boom*.

If the windows hadn't been covered with the vines, they would have broken. The walls continued to shake, the house rattling, bits of plaster falling from the ceiling.

Dimitri reached for her to gather her against him, and Jaycee didn't fight him. She leaned into his chest, hearing his heart beating rapidly, feeling the sharp rise and fall of his breath. He closed his arms around her as though he alone could shield her from the storm.

She let him hold her, his warm strength easing her. Jaycee didn't enjoy storms, and in Texas they'd had to ride out bad ones. When they'd lived in the underground bunker—where they'd sheltered when Kendrick had first led them to Texas—they'd been able to hide well from the weather, but since moving to the ranch, they'd had to face it.

Jaycee didn't know why distant rumbles of thunder made her tense, why a sudden change in humidity made her growl. Her leopard didn't like it, was all she knew.

Dimitri always laughed at her whenever she bolted indoors at the first flicker of lighting, but at the moment, he was as tense as she was. Of course, tornado winds striking the house were something to be afraid of. Those winds were deadly, and being Shifter wasn't going to save them. To the storm, they were just one more thing in its path.

Dimitri had his eyes closed, his arms tight around Jaycee. His face had gone gray in the darkness, his heartbeat off the scale. His skin was clammy with sweat, the dampness of it cool though his body was roasting hot.

"You okay?" Jaycee whispered.

Dimitri didn't respond. He was rigid, fingers biting down.

"This house is holding pretty good," Ben told them. "It's stood in this spot for this long. We'll be fine."

As if in answer, there was a horrendous crash from the hall. Ben leapt out the door. Dimitri jerked alert, unwound himself from Jaycee, and went after Ben only to find him right outside the sitting room, his arms out to hold them back.

"Wall came down in the front corner. We need to get *out* of here before the storm pulls down the rest."

"How?" Jaycee demanded. The window behind them was blocked with vines. The darkness in the hall told her all the others were too.

Ben had a flashlight beaming along the corridor. "Tear through the vines on the back door?"

"Then what?" Jaycee asked with a shiver. "We hope we don't get sucked up by a tornado?"

"We can't get out," Dimitri said in a hoarse whisper. "It's t-trapped us."

"Dining room table," Jaycee said decidedly.

She started that way, but she'd taken only three steps down the hall when Dimitri abruptly grabbed hold of her and hauled her back into the sitting room. Before Jaycee could argue, he'd pushed her to the floor and landed on top of her. Ben cried out, and then there was a crashing, splintering roar, the smell of dust, and then pain.

Dimitri kept Jaycee under him no matter how much she squirmed to get up. Debris rained down on them—boards, plaster, vines. His brain swam and spun, wind and dust smelling like the charred remains of burning wood, the ice-cold blast searing like fire.

Memories rose and then faded, past and present swirling together until Dimitri didn't know what was real.

The only thing anchoring him to the world was the soft body of Jaycee beneath him. She was his mate, and she was everything.

That fact cut through his strange terror and disorientation, giving him a focus. Jaycee. His love. His *mate*.

Rubble continued to fall down on them, beating on Dimitri's back; then, abruptly, it ceased.

Dimitri raised his head. Dust choked the air, rendering visibility almost nothing. He couldn't tell if the room was still there or not, if the house had fallen around them or was nothing but a ruin.

He heard a groan near him, and then Ben dragged in a rasping breath. "Everyone all right?"

"Yeah," Dimitri croaked. "Jase?" He put his hand on her cheek, found it cold. Stark fear plunged through him. *"Jase."*

Jaycee coughed. "Goddess, I swallowed half the storm," she said, voice grating.

Dimitri's relief made the terrifying memories kicking at him vanish. He lowered his head and kissed Jaycee's lips. And again. Her mouth, face, dusty hair. She was alive, and all right.

"When you're done." Ben's voice came from above them.

There was a crackling noise, and light poured into the room. The rose vines were coming apart, revealing gray light outside with gently falling rain. A beam of sunshine broke through the clouds, rendering the world a sparkling jewel.

"What the hell?" Dimitri looked around, and Jaycee took the opportunity to slither out from under him.

The room's walls were still standing, but the ceiling above them had been half peeled away. The upstairs must be gone, because a sunbeam poured through the crack.

"Oh, no," Jaycee said in sorrow. "Jazz's house. She'll be devastated."

Ben looked around, almost in awe. "I hope our bikes are

all right. Or else we'll be out looking for a ride as well as a place to stay."

"Doesn't matter," Dimitri managed as he climbed to his feet. He'd seriously mourn the loss of his motorcycle, but he knew he could buy another one when he was finished grieving. The house was irreplaceable.

"We should find out the extent of the damage," Jaycee said, her voice heavy. "I'll have to—"

Whatever she'd have to do was cut off by another noise. Not the boom and roar of the storm, but a crackling and rushing similar to what the rose vines had made.

Dimitri moved to the window, which was unbroken, the draperies around it barely moistened from the rain. The vines were receding from this wall but climbing upward, moving to the broken part of the ceiling and on into the wreckage above them.

"Holy shit," Jaycee whispered beside Dimitri. The three of them watched as the vines wrapped around the bricks and shattered wood of the house and started to pull them together.

Like a bizarre special effect, the house seemed to grow into itself, brick by brick, held in place by twining rose vines. Maybe that was why the entire mansion was covered with them, Dimitri mused—they were what kept the house from falling down.

Little by little, the ceiling above the sitting room solidified. Dust rained down as the walls rose and the roof was pulled back on.

Ben watched in wonder. "Some bitchin' magic was put into this place," he said, full of respect.

Dimitri turned back as the room darkened again, the ceiling now in place. He took Ben's flashlight from him and pointed it at the odd door they'd not been able to open.

But now that the house was distracted . . .

Dimitri moved swiftly to it, turned the handle, and wrenched it open.

CHAPTER FIFTEEN

Jaycee heard Dimitri shout. Her heart racing, she swung around to see him hanging on to the knob of the now-open door in the wall.

The doorframe outlined blackness. Jaycee hurried to Dimitri, who was leaning back from the dark rectangle as though trying to keep from being pulled in.

"What's in there?" Jaycee asked, peering around him.

Dimitri let go of the doorknob to grab the back of Jaycee's shirt and yank her away from the unnerving darkness. "N-nothing," he answered.

Ben was a few steps behind Jaycee. "What do you mean, *nothing*?"

He took his flashlight back from Dimitri and shone it through the door. The beam cut through the blackness but only rested on more darkness. Jaycee couldn't make out anything; not a wall, a corner, a floor . . .

"N-nothing," Dimitri repeated. "Like I said."

"Everything has to be something," Ben said. "Even deep space between galaxies has a few molecules floating in it."

He thrust the flashlight into the opening, but there was no

change—the blackness swallowed the beam a few feet in. Next Ben put a tentative foot through the door. "Whoops," he said as he tilted forward.

Jaycee and Dimitri, as one, seized him and pulled him to safety. Once Ben had cleared the threshold, the door slammed shut, the lock clicking loudly. Rose vines shot through the open window to crisscross themselves over the door. They crackled with the effort, then suddenly went still, all quiet.

Dimitri let out his breath. "Guess the h-house doesn't w-want us in there."

"Guess not," Jaycee agreed.

"How can a house want anything?" Ben asked.

He reached out and lightly touched one of the vines. It didn't move, didn't do anything, though one of the leaves on it twitched from the movement of his finger. It was just a vine.

"I'm not going to argue with it," Jaycee said. "The house kept us safe from the storm, didn't it? It's like a mother, almost. Or father. Both rolled into one. I'll have to call Jasmine. The house repaired itself, but didn't clean up inside. *We* have to do that, it looks like."

"Figures," Ben said, shrugging.

Dimitri gave the door a final look, then walked out into the hall. Jaycee followed and caught up to him in the staircase hall, where he cranked his head back to look up the stairs.

The chandelier, amazingly, was still in place, hanging high above the main hall. This part of the house, in the middle, had the least mess. Dust had mixed with water to coat the furniture with a fine film of mud, but otherwise all was unbroken.

Dimitri stared up at the chandelier as though transfixed by it. "We're lucky the house likes us," he said without a stammer.

"I'm understanding that," Jaycee said. "It likes Ben too or he'd have never been able to get in."

"Good point," Ben, who'd followed her, said. He righted

a table that had fallen and brushed it off with his hand. "Thank you." He gave the paneling a quick stroke. "I'm very grateful."

The house was silent, water dripping from its eaves, wind rippling the chimes outside. No rumblings, creaking, climbing plants, whispered laughter. It seemed like an ordinary house, one that had survived a strong storm.

Jaycee watched both men eyeing the building in admiration and heaved a sigh. "I'll get some brooms and dust rags. We'd better get started."

When Jaycee called Jasmine to tell her about the storm and the house's peculiar behavior, Jasmine didn't seem surprised.

"My grandmother told me about it doing something like that during a hurricane," Jasmine said, her light New Orleans accent coming through. "Though the house wasn't hit directly that time. Let me know if any furniture needs to be repaired or replaced, and I'll put my carpenters on it. They know how to make everything true to the period." She paused and added wistfully, "Tell it I said hello and will be back soon."

"Sure," Jaycee said. What was odder—the house or the woman who had a relationship with it? "Hopefully there won't be too many repairs."

"It's all right," Jazz answered. "When you live in a historic home, you get used to it." When Jaycee mentioned insurance, Jazz laughed. "We never could afford insurance. Cheaper to fix everything ourselves. Don't worry, Jaycee. Just enjoy yourself."

Jazz also seemed surprised when Jaycee mentioned the swimming pool. "I don't have a pool," Jazz said, then concluded, "The house looks after its guests, I guess."

Jaycee hung up, startled and envying Jazz and her easy outlook. But then, Jazz had a loving mate in Mason McNaughton, a growling wolf of a young man not long past his Transition. Her serenity came from happiness.

Jaycee, Dimitri, and Ben spent the rest of the day cleaning up from the storm. The downstairs didn't fare so badly, but upstairs they had to pile plaster and pieces of wood and brick into the corners to haul away later. Jazz would have to replace some of the furniture in the bedrooms, including curtains and bedding. The bedrooms Jaycee and Dimitri had slept in, however, were untouched.

The two men worked without fuss. Shifters had never considered cleaning a house to be "women's work"—possibly because, traditionally, male Shifters hadn't gone outside the home to find jobs. They'd hunted, gathered, and sometimes farmed on small plots. Both genders did the hunting and harvesting, and both genders took care of the house and raised the cubs.

Jaycee remembered when she'd first encountered human women who'd been expected to wash all the clothes, do the cooking and the cleaning, take care of the cubs, *and* go out and find a job to bring in extra money. She'd been amazed they put up with it, seemed to think it was normal. Jaycee would have to have a serious talk with any male who expected her to do all that.

Watching Dimitri bend double to sweep out the corners wasn't a bad thing either. Did he deliberately wear jeans that enticingly snug? Knowing Dimitri as well as she did, Jaycee was sure of the answer.

She realized she'd been polishing the same corner of a hall table for about five minutes, her gaze glued to Dimitri's ass, when she caught sight of Ben grinning at her, his dark eyes crinkling in the corners.

Jaycee flushed and whirled away to clean somewhere else.

Ben departed a couple of hours before Dimitri wanted to return to the club where they'd met Brice. Jaycee didn't see Ben go—one minute he was devouring a bag of chips in the kitchen, the next, he was gone.

When she and Dimitri went out to the shed to retrieve Dimitri's motorcycle, they saw no sign of Ben, no sign of the motorcycle he claimed to have ridden here. No tire tracks, nothing. Stealth indeed.

Jaycee rode behind Dimitri to town without question, not insisting that she drive. She held on to Dimitri as they pulled away from the house, enjoying the feeling of him moving against her.

As they headed into the city, Jaycee noticed something odd—in a long day of strange things. There were no puddles from the rain, no tree limbs down, no damage to the houses and buildings they passed. Jazz's property had been covered with mud and deep puddles, but once they turned onto the road that led to the 61, she noticed nothing amiss. It was as though the storm had been localized to the narrow strip of land where Jazz's house lay.

She didn't like that, and neither did her leopard. Ben had said the house might be on a ley line, which was a power flow of deep magic. Did it mean the storm was magical too? An attack against the house and the two Shifters and Ben inside it?

Or had it simply been crazy Louisiana weather? Tornadoes could be arbitrary. Jaycee had seen them do heavy damage to one house, while leaving a house across the street untouched. She'd have to think about that for a while.

They were in the city quickly. It was still light, as summer days were long, but by nine, twilight had fallen and New Orleans came awake.

Jaycee liked the city, which was different from any she'd visited. Tourists flocked here, of course, but as she and Dimitri walked down the street toward the Shifter bar, local women and men said hello, and while they waited to cross a street among a crowd, people asked how they were doing.

Groupies streamed toward the Shifter club by the dozen. No one on the street seemed to think it odd that both women and men had their faces painted to look like cats or wolves—a few bearded men going for the bear look—or wore ears, whiskers, and tails. One woman had forgone most of her clothing to wear a bikini, a tail, and cat ears. She drew looks of envy from those walking in the sticky heat. The heat was one reason no one hurried—strolling was much more pleasant than rushing.

The club was already going strong, though Jaycee knew from experience that Shifter clubs didn't become fully crowded until midnight. Shifters were supposed to be back in their Shiftertowns by then, and the partiers lived on the edge of excitement, anticipating a raid. Usually, the human police left the clubs alone, city police and Shifters having learned a long time ago how to give and take to keep the peace.

Not always, though. Dimitri slowed as they neared the club. "Not good."

The men outside the door checking IDs weren't Shifter bouncers or even human cops. They wore military camouflage and one carried a tranq rifle.

Sometimes this happened. Shifter Bureau would get a hair up its collective butt and decide to make sure Shifters were following the rules. No Shifters leaving their home states, no Shifters out after midnight, all Shifters in Collars.

Jaycee and Dimitri had resumed their Collars for the club—the humans there would know they were Shifter and many would have seen them the night before wearing Collars. No way to strip them off and fade into the crowd—the momentum of the people behind them, eager to reach the club, kept them moving forward.

"Shit," Dimitri said softly.

"Let's cross the street," Jaycee said. "Quietly, like we changed our minds and want to look in shops instead."

She glanced to where lit shops enticed the crowd with promises of real voodoo magic, the best New Orleans gumbo, and other temptations. A brass jazz band sat in the middle of it all, filling the air with wild trombone and trumpet runs.

"I can help," a young man said softly in Jaycee's ear. He was tall, blond, and wore wolf's ears, with whiskers painted on his cheeks. "I know the back way in. You won't have to show ID."

Dimitri said nothing. He turned so his back was to the crowd at the door and sharply gestured for the young man to lead the way.

Their guide was in his early twenties, Jaycee guessed, which for humans meant fully grown, able to marry and leave his family. Shifter males usually didn't leave their families at all, even once their Transition happened—brothers, wives, and cubs often lived in the same houses. The Shifter family who'd raised Jaycee had lived as such, though in their case, it hadn't been a good thing. They'd fought constantly, the entire pack at each other's throats most days.

The young man led them between two buildings, the passageway so narrow Jaycee hadn't realized anything was back here. Her nose wrinkled at the stench of garbage, urine, and animal droppings as they picked their way between walls of crumbling brick.

The passage opened to an alley, which smelled even more strongly of garbage. Bins lined the space, and back doors opened to kitchens, from which smells of foods and spices tumbled out. Men lounged by these doors, tips of cigarettes glowing.

They paid no attention to Jaycee, Dimitri, and their guide after one glance. Likely it wasn't unusual to see Shifters skulking in alleys around here.

The guide took them to a blank, black door, and knocked on it. A few moments later, a Shifter opened it, a Lupine by the look of him. He had black hair cut short against his head, an equally trimmed shadow of a beard, and clear gray eyes. His short-sleeved black shirt showed tattoos on his arms. He gave Dimitri a hostile stare.

"Who are you?" he growled.

Dimitri said nothing. He chose to do that sometimes, using his stare to intimidate in case his mouth wouldn't cooperate. Jaycee folded her arms and spoke to the Lupine for him.

"We're looking for Brice."

The Shifter didn't do a happy dance. In fact, his scowl deepened. "Brice? Figures. Fine, I'll let you in, but you keep the hell out of sight." He switched his glare to the groupie, who quickly bowed his head, curling in on himself.

The Lupine moved aside and let them past—Dimitri first, then Jaycee, and the young man scuttling in after them.

"Thanks," Jaycee said kindly to the groupie, and he was all smiles again.

The Lupine led them through the cubbyhole that was a kitchen—unused, as no food was served here—and to a hall that led to the main club. He paused before he opened the door at the end, behind which came the pulse of music.

"Anyone asks, I didn't do this," the Lupine rumbled. He looked Dimitri up and down. "What are you supposed to be, anyway?"

Dimitri kept up the silent stare, his gray eyes unwavering. Jaycee pinned the Lupine with her gaze, though she wasn't as good at it as Dimitri. "He's a red wolf," she said. "They're rare."

"I'm sure he's proud of himself." The Lupine kept his gaze on Dimitri, not Jaycee, certain Dimitri was the bigger threat. "You don't look like Brice's usual dickheads."

Dimitri dropped his silent alpha mode and asked, "What d-do they usually l-look like?"

The Lupine's eyes narrowed. "Glazed. Like they've sucked in too much incense dancing around naked to the Goddess." He looked Dimitri up and down again. "But you're new. Give it time." He reached for the door. "I'm Angus. One of the bouncers. If you want to ditch the Goddess fanatics, I can get you out again. My advice—go now and don't come back."

Dimitri studied Angus for a time, then gave him a slow nod. "Angus. G-got it. You going to l-let us in now?"

The Lupine eyed them in more irritation, then switched off the light in the hall, opened the door to the club, and led them through.

Turning the light off kept their silhouettes from showing in the open doorway, a consideration Jaycee appreciated. They followed Angus into a shadowy area near the bar, which was crowded with Shifters and humans. The groupie who'd shown them the way in faded into the morass, lifting his hand in greeting to other groupies, male and female.

"Brice is up there," Angus pointed upward to the top balcony of the club, where the winding iron-railed staircase led. "Holding court."

Dimitri nodded his thanks.

As they passed Angus on their way to the stairs, Angus casully put out a hand and tugged Jaycee back. She spun around, ready with a scowl, but Angus withdrew the touch immediately, leaned down, and spoke into her ear.

"Ditch this loser," he said clearly. "Really. Brice and his cult are weird about mates. You're worth more than that."

Interesting. Maybe she and Dimitri should talk more to this guy. For now, Jaycee kept to her role.

"I go with Dimitri," she said, making herself sound submissive and indignant at the same time.

Angus gave her a look of disgust, turned his back, and stalked away, as though washing his hands of her. Jaycee hurried to catch up to Dimitri, who was already climbing the stairs.

Brice had taken over the third floor. Jaycee saw Casey, Maeve, and other Shifters she recognized from last night. No Ben though.

The tables up here were small. Shifters had pulled chairs from them to cluster around Brice, the tabletops littered with bottles and mugs of beer. Brice rose immediately when he spied Dimitri and Jaycee, and Shifters moved aside as he made his way toward them.

Brice tonight drew Dimitri into a large Shifter embrace. Dimitri didn't like it, Jaycee could tell, but he went along with it. Brice engulfed him, rubbing his shoulder with one fist.

Brice released Dimitri and turned to Jaycee. There was nothing in his eyes but welcome as he came to her and hugged her. He was a leader, happy to see members of his clan.

Brice smelled of beer and bear, Shifter smells. Warmth and sweat. Jaycee caught her breath as he tightened his embrace, then exhaled sharply when he finally let her go. Brice noticed, and laughed.

"Bear hugs are tough," he said, patting her shoulder. "I'm glad you two came back." He signaled a waitress who was moving among the tables. "A round of their favorites for my friends."

The waitress seemed used to Brice and his commands. She asked Jaycee what she wanted—Jaycee asked for Dimitri's brand of beer and a glass of wine for herself. The waitress looked surprised at the wine order, but nodded and headed down the stairs with leggy speed.

"Saw Shifter B-Bureau set up outside," Dimitri said. "What's th-that about?"

Brice shrugged. "Every once in a while they check on us. This is New Orleans, a mecca for so many. Wouldn't want Shifters messing with the tourists."

"Huh." Dimitri sat down. Jaycee saw two of the female Shifters who were sitting together checking him out, which irritated the hell out of her. They noticed her gaze, put their heads together, and started talking, shooting her and Dimitri amused glances.

Brice settled down to talk, and so did the rest of the Shifters, continuing conversations any Shifters might have. They talked about football—the kind they played in Ireland and England—events going on in their Shiftertown, the difficulty in replacing plumbing.

Innocent, everyday things. No whispering about turning on other Shifters, no one mentioning the Fae, no fanatics foaming at the mouth.

Brice and his followers were strange, there was no doubt about it. Anyone who would stick his hand into fire to impress his friends had to be a little out there, and those who let him do it had to be equally strange.

But none of that made them evil. It might be that there was nothing to report, which was fine with Jaycee. She and Dimitri could pack up and go home, discuss their findings with Dylan and Kendrick, and move on to the next job.

Not that it wasn't nice spending time with Dimitri. Back home, he had his cottage, and she had her room in the main house so she could watch over Kendrick and his mate and cubs. She and Dimitri didn't usually have this much intensive time together.

Sleeping with him last night had been comforting—Jaycee hadn't slept so well in a long time. Conferring with him, eating with him, talking, laughing, surviving crazy storms together . . .

"Jaycee," Brice rumbled from directly next to her, and Jaycee started. Lost in thought, she hadn't seen him move. "Can I talk to you a second?"

He stood beside her chair, hand out to indicate he wanted her to follow him. Jaycee looked at Dimitri, who'd heard him, but Dimitri only gave her a nod. He knew she'd report to him whatever Brice said.

Brice seemed amused that she'd looked to Dimitri before she'd left him. Brice's dark eyes twinkled as Jaycee picked up her wineglass and followed him to an empty table in the far corner, well away from the others. Brice settled her in a chair, then sat down to face her.

Dimitri didn't look over at them, focusing his attention on Casey and other Shifters who were talking with him. Including, Jaycee observed to her annoyance, the two females who'd been watching him.

"Jaycee." Brice waved his hand in front of her face. "Let it go."

Jaycee traced the lip of the wineglass. "Sorry. Shifter females don't like others looking at their mates. You know that."

Brice leaned over the table toward her, keeping his voice down. "That's what I want to talk to you about," he said. "If you join us, I want you to give up your mate-claim with Dimitri." He gave Jaycee a nod when her mouth popped open. "Refuse the claim, and come to us as fair game."

CHAPTER SIXTEEN

Refuse the mate-claim. Jaycee stared at him in shock, but Brice wasn't joking. He studied her with brown eyes that were completely serious. Concerned, even.

Jaycee held back the hot words that tripped to her mouth. *Who the hell are you to tell a Shifter not to mate? What do you know about me and Dimitri?*

She curled her fingers on the tabletop, resisting the urge to lunge at him, claws extended. She was fast, but he was a bear—strong, deadly.

"Why?" she managed to ask.

Brice's gaze held sympathy. "We need you, and Shifter women like you. In the wild, we didn't produce many cubs, as you know. I don't want to see that happen again. As a free female in my group you would be able to choose your mates— two or three—to have as many cubs as you could from different fathers. To strengthen the gene pool. We should have been doing this as soon as we went into Shiftertowns, given the unevenness in gender populations."

"What about the mate bond?" The question slipped out

before Jaycee could stop it. "The binding between two true mates? The Goddess gave us that."

"I know." Brice nodded patiently. "Mate bonds still happen. But that doesn't mean you can't have more cubs with other males. If you choose a mate from among my Shifters, they'll understand."

"Dimitri won't," Jaycee said with conviction.

Dimitri had always been possessive of Jaycee. Even when they'd been close friends but friends only, and they had seen other people, Dimitri had considered Jaycee his special companion. The friend he went to before all others. The lover who'd shared the first taste of sex with him after their Transitions. The woman he always sought.

"Dimitri will come to understand," Brice said. "He's a good man. A good Lupine, I should say." He gave her the ghost of a smile. "I imagine he'll be happy with the woman who chooses him. That doesn't mean you two can't still have a relationship."

"What if I choose *Dimitri* as my mate?" Jaycee asked. "What if I don't want to change anything?"

"I hope you *don't* choose him," Brice said. "I would like to see you mate with Felines, to strengthen those lines. Strong Felines are a huge asset."

Jaycee sat back, letting herself smile. "Now I know you're shitting me. A bear saying Felines are wonderful?"

"I'm a leader," Brice answered without humor. "I do what's good for my clan. Whether I think bears are best or not isn't the issue."

Jaycee tried to remind herself of the mission. She was a tracker—this was her job. She should tell Brice that sure, she'd refuse the mate-claim, the very thing she'd been telling herself to do since Dimitri had made it. She simply hadn't had the right chance, a way to let Dimitri down easy.

Not that Dimitri would stay down. He'd already told her that.

But Brice's demand stirred something visceral inside Jaycee, a need to keep hold of Dimitri by any means necessary. Life without Dimitri in it would be . . . empty, colorless, wearisome. Watching him go to another woman, even for their cover, would kill her.

Brice had to guess what she was thinking. He leaned closer still. "It would have to be sincere, Jaycee. In front of witnesses. No lying to me."

Shit. Jaycee might have talked herself into a pretense at a refusal, she and Dimitri telling Brice she'd done it. But in front of witnesses . . . Rituals with witnesses were binding. Jaycee might lie when she said she refused, but her answer would be taken as truth by all other Shifters. It would make no difference that she crossed her fingers behind her back. In the eyes of Shifters, the mate-claim would be broken.

"If you don't want to do this, I can't force you," Brice was saying. "I also can't let you into my group. The others follow my ideas—you must as well. If not"—he spread his hands and leaned back in his chair—"then go back to Dylan and tell him all about us. And tell him that if he wants to know what I'm up to so much, he should come and ask me." He took a sip of beer.

"I don't work for Dylan," Jaycee snapped. Not a lie—she worked for Kendrick. If Dylan had asked her and Dimitri to investigate without Kendrick's endorsement, she'd have told Dylan to stick it.

Brice blinked at her vehemence. He knew she spoke the truth—he'd scent it as well as hear it.

"I have to admit, I'm surprised," he said. "Tell you what— you talk it over with Dimitri. If he understands, if you both agree, then we can work something out. You're a unique woman, Jaycee. Dimitri's a unique man. Who else has a red wolf in his group?" He grinned.

Kendrick, Jaycee thought but didn't say.

Brice stood up. "I'd love to have you both. If you and Dimitri can come to an understanding, we'll get you initiated as soon as possible. Oh, don't worry." His amusement deepened. "The initiation is nothing more intense than the usual Shifter ceremonies. No exchange of blood or bodily fluids of any kind. No tests. Just the Goddess letting us know you belong to her, and a party afterward."

So, I don't belong to the Goddess already? Jaycee thought. *Glad to know I wasted all those prayers and burned offerings my entire life.*

Brice noticed her disgruntled look, which seemed to please him for some reason. He held out a hand to help her to her feet.

A commotion began at the top of the stairs. Shifters had gathered there and now surrounded someone Jaycee couldn't see. Not Dimitri—his red head towered above the crowd, his gaze on whatever had caught their attention.

"Ah," Brice said, squeezing Jaycee's hand. "Let me show you how we deal with true spies in our midst."

Jaycee's heart went cold for a second, but Brice's focus was for the crowd of Shifters. He wasn't talking about her or Dimitri.

He kept hold of Jaycee's hand and pulled her with him to the stairs. On the top step, looking alarmed at the hostile Shifters facing him, was Ben.

"Hey," Ben said, sending Brice a worried glance as he approached. "What's up?"

The Shifters blocking Ben's way reached out and yanked him into their midst. Brice let Jaycee go as he wove his way through his Shifters, took handfuls of Ben's shirt, and lifted him high.

"Who are you?" Brice demanded.

Ben stared down at him in astonishment. "I told you. My name's Ben. I sometimes go by Gil. I'm the last of my kind. Creature of the Goddess."

"Not quite." Brice's voice was calm, cold. The Shifters around him fell silent. Below, the music pounded on, the crowd downstairs unaware of the drama high above them.

"You were expelled from Faerie," Brice said sternly. "You are the last of creatures who were evil, a far cry from the Goddess's chosen. You plotted with demons against Shifters."

Something dangerous flashed in Ben's eyes. He didn't seem to worry that he was held up in Brice's big hands, perilously near the edge of the balcony.

"Base slander," Ben said. "That rumor's been going around for a thousand or so years, long before you were born. You have evidence?"

Jaycee slipped through the crowd to Dimitri. He turned his head to see her at his side, his eyes holding a warning glance.

Brice's look was flat as he gazed up at Ben, no forgiveness in his eyes. "You and your people sided with the *dokk alfar,* the dark Fae," he said. "Abominations. They fought the high Fae, if you remember. You targeted the Battle Beasts, the Shifters, who fought at the high Fae's command. Shifters were killed, or caught and tortured."

"Beg to differ," Ben said, brows lowering.

Jaycee didn't know much about what Ben was. She expected him to change into something or lash out with magic, at least break Brice's hold. Ben was strong—she'd seen Shifters back down from him when he did little more than stare at them.

"I can smell lies," Brice said. "I can smell the stink of demons on you. Why have you come here? To torture more Shifters?"

Ben didn't struggle. "I can see someone's filled your head with fairy stories. Excuse the pun."

What was Ben doing? Jaycee reached for Dimitri's hand, and he closed his fingers hard around hers. Why didn't Ben defend himself instead of making feeble jokes? Brice's Shifters were angry, ready to tear him apart.

Jaycee took a step forward, but Dimitri tightened his grip and held her back. Jaycee understood his concern—if they interfered, they might be attacked as well—but Jaycee couldn't stand here and let Shifters kill Ben.

"It's been a long time coming, hasn't it?" Brice said, his tone fierce. His hands became the razor-sharp claws of a grizzly. "*This* is what happens to friends of the *dokk alfar,* who torment the Battle Beasts."

He lifted Ben still higher; then, with a savage snarl, Brice hurled Ben over the balcony. Ben pedaled his arms and legs in midair, then sailed down two stories to land on the hard floor, in the middle of the dancing crowd.

* * *

Dimitri heard Jaycee's shriek, but it was lost in the Shifters' collective howls, and the screams of the people below. Jaycee started forward, but Dimitri dragged her back.

"Let go of me," she told him, anguish in her eyes.

Dimitri shook his head. If Ben was dead, there was nothing they could do. With the mood of the Shifters up here, they might end up following him the same way if they expressed concern.

Brice had to be insane. Dealing with a perceived enemy was one thing, but to do it in a club whose outer door was monitored by Shifter Bureau was suicide. Did he want every Shifter in here to be tranqued and caged?

Jaycee went still under Dimitri's touch, but he felt her distress. They considered Ben a friend, a brother in arms, even if they didn't know much about him. They'd fought together. Kendrick trusted him, and so did Dylan.

Dimitri kept hold of Jaycee but managed to get them to the wrought-iron railing around the balcony. Jaycee clutched it as they both peered over.

Confusion reigned below. Groupies were screaming, Shifters swearing and shouting. The human employees were trying to calm people down, to prevent the soldiers on attachment to Shifter Bureau from storming inside. Dimitri saw the Lupine bouncer, Angus, move to stand by the main door as though ready to keep Shifter Bureau out himself.

In the middle of the floor, where Ben had fallen, was . . . nothing. Dimitri scanned the tiled dance floor and the area around it, looking for Ben's body, or blood, or people he'd fallen on, but he saw no sign of any trauma. Shifters and humans milled about in confusion, their collective daze heightened by the liquor being consumed. Ben had completely disappeared.

Dimitri exchanged a glance with Jaycee. Her brown-gold eyes were worried, but she said nothing.

Brice didn't seem to notice that Ben had vanished. He

laughed, his face relaxing into its good-natured lines. "That was fun. Let's have another round. On me!"

The Shifters cheered. Below, the screaming ceased and nervous laughter began. The wave of relief of the Shifters on the lower floors reached Dimitri. Brice had played a trick, they must think, but nothing terrible had actually happened.

Jaycee tugged Dimitri down to speak into his ear. "Why isn't he worried about Shifter Bureau?"

Dimitri shrugged. "Maybe he's got the local b-branch in his pocket. Or he knows that Angus guy will k-keep them out."

"Angus didn't like Brice, I thought."

"Might be p-pretending," Dimitri answered.

"I want to go," Jaycee said. She looked upset, and not only about Ben. "I need to talk to you."

"Yeah—what was B-Brice getting cozy with you about in the c-corner?"

Jaycee only frowned, motioning to the stairs.

Brice approached them before Dimitri could argue with her. "I agree—you should go," he said—Shifters had good hearing. "Come back here tomorrow, and let me know what you decided. Dimitri." He put an arm around Dimitri's shoulder. "Jaycee." He wrapped his other arm around her. "I think we'll make a good team." He hugged them tightly, then released them. "Go on now."

He gave Jaycee a meaningful look before turning back to his followers and raising his hands high. They cheered.

Casey, Dimitri noticed, looked unhappy, but his mate, Maeve, shouted for Brice. She made her way toward Brice, her body swaying in invitation.

Dimitri towed Jaycee to the stairs. He picked his way down, steadying Jaycee, though he knew she'd never fall. Jaycee steadied Dimitri in return.

When they reached the ground floor, Dimitri scanned the club once more but found no sign of Ben. He'd completely disappeared.

Angus moved to intercept them as they made their way

toward the shadowy door through which they'd entered. "I take it you'll need to go out the back way."

"If Shifter B-bureau is at the front d-door still, then yeah."

Angus gave Dimitri a sharp eye. "Brice has done this before," he said.

Jaycee looked startled. "Done what? Dumped someone off the balcony? Why is he allowed in here?"

"He has the human manager coerced. Why do you think?"

"What happened to the p-person he tossed off?" Dimitri asked.

"A Shifter," Angus said. "I recovered. Eventually."

"You tried to join Brice's group?" Jaycee asked in surprise.

Angus snorted, his eyes flicking to Shifter white. "Fuck that. I was doing my job as bouncer, trying to kick him out. I told him dickheads like him weren't welcome. He and his best friends tossed me down. I thought the bar's owner would have him arrested, but no. Brice and the owner have an understanding." He growled in Lupine disgust.

"Why do you still work here?" Jaycee asked. "If the owner doesn't mind if his bouncers are dropped from three stories up?"

"To keep an eye on Brice," Angus answered without pause. "And I need the money, sweet thing. Have a cub to take care of." He glowered at Dimitri. "If you two join him, don't talk to me anymore. I don't want to drown in shit."

With that, he stalked toward the back, leading them to the safe passage out.

The ride back to the house was silent and uneasy. Jaycee had kept an eye out for Ben as they'd walked back through the hot crowd to Dimitri's motorcycle, but neither she nor Dimitri had spotted him, dead or alive.

Jaycee hoped like hell they'd find him at Jasmine's house, but when they walked in—the door obligingly opening for them—the house was dark and empty.

"He's some k-kind of magical c-creature," Dimitri said, trying to sound reassuring. "He probably magic-ed his way out."

"Why was Brice so angry with him anyway?" Jay-cee asked as she dumped her helmet on the hall table, along with the fake Collar she'd pulled off. "Brice knows Dylan asked us to spy on him, but he threw *Ben* over the balcony, not us."

Dimitri shook his head. He looked up the dark staircase as though trying to decide whether to ascend it.

The floors were still dirty from the storm, grit beneath Jaycee's boots. Jasmine would have to get a cleaning service in here before the tourists were let in again.

"Dimitri," Jaycee began. Her throat hurt, and she couldn't make the words come out.

"What?" Dimitri asked absently, studying the dark chan-delier above them.

Jaycee took a breath and continued in a rush. "Brice doesn't want us back until I refuse your mate-claim."

Dimitri dragged his attention from the shadowy upper floors and fixed it on Jaycee. His gray eyes were stark in the dim light, the wolf in him looking out.

"What?" The word was hard.

Jaycee outlined what Brice had told her—the need for females to take several mates to strengthen the bloodstock, like cattle. Brice hadn't actually said that, but Jaycee knew that was what he meant.

When she finished, Dimitri stood absolutely still. "Ass-hole," he bit out. "Did he tell you one of the mates had to be him?"

"No." Jaycee shook her head. "He said mates would be my choice, and didn't mention himself."

"Good," he said quietly. "'Cause I would have killed him."

Every word was pronounced clearly. No stammering, no caveats—Dimitri hadn't said, *I might have had to kill him* or *I would have thought about killing him.* He meant, liter-ally, that Brice would be one dead bear if he had instructed Jaycee to mate with him.

"I'm not doing it," Jaycee said swiftly. "Not for him. Not for a job. I'm telling Kendrick it's off."

She started for the stairs, ready to run up to her room and

make the call, but Dimitri blocked her way. He gazed down at her, his gray stare holding her in place.

"You can refuse, Jase."

Jaycee blinked up at him, unsure she'd heard him right. "What?"

"Brice is right that it's your ch-choice. You've n-never said yes or no. I don't give a shit what you tell B-Brice. I only give a shit what you tell *me*. So which is it?"

CHAPTER SEVENTEEN

Jaycee dragged in a sharp breath that burned her lungs. Dimitri remained motionless, waiting for her answer.

"This isn't a good time to discuss this," Jaycee said, her voice cracking. "We're working. We have to keep our mission separate from our personal life."

"You just said you wanted to call off the m-mission," Dimitri said. "To t-tell Kendrick you're done. What's the matter, Jase? You don't like being t-told to make the decision?"

"No," Jaycee answered loudly. "It's none of anyone's business but ours."

"So tell B-Brice what he wants to hear, we'll figure out what he's up to, and g-go home."

"He wants me to refuse in front of witnesses."

Dimitri went very still, his eyes taking on a sharp light. "He said that?"

"Yep." Jaycee's chest was tight, her heart beating too fast. "If I do this, you know it will count whether I truly want to refuse or not."

Dimitri kept looking at her. "I'll just mate-claim you again, Jase. That's my right. No matter how many times you say no."

Jaycee shook her head. "He doesn't want me to choose *you* as mate. He wants me to mate with Felines, to breed more strong Felines." Jaycee wrinkled her nose. "I've never liked Felines. I've always been partial to wolves."

"You *are* a Feline," Dimitri pointed out. "So's Kendrick."

"I know. So I know how annoying they can be." Jaycee let out a breath. "I don't want to refuse. Not for Brice, and not in front of witnesses. It should be my real choice—*our* choice."

"It's only for the effing mission," Dimitri growled, the intense light growing in his eyes. "We g-go home, I'll claim you again, and we can f-fight about it then."

Jaycee folded her arms. "That easy, huh?"

"Sh-should be."

"I see," Jaycee said angrily. "If you take the claim so casually that watching me refuse it for Brice and his Shifters doesn't bother you, then maybe I should go ahead and refuse. For real." Her heart ached even as she said the words. "Then I wouldn't have this dilemma—the one where I'm worried as hell it will upset you. Bite me, Dimitri Kashnikov."

Jaycee swung away to storm off, make her way outside, maybe jump in the pool with her clothes on—she had no idea. She only knew she had to run, deal with this confusion and very real hurt Brice's request had caused.

Dimitri's heavy hand on her shoulder stopped her. Jaycee whipped around, ready to continue the argument, but Dimitri took hold of her and lifted her against the nearest wall.

The wind chimes on the veranda rang with a breeze that rushed into the house from the opening back door. No one came inside, only the wind and the scent of roses. Jaycee felt polished wood dig into her back, Dimitri's hot body hard against her front.

His eyes had gone very light gray, his red brows drawn, his mouth turned down. Lighthearted Dimitri was gone. In his place was a fierce man, a Shifter who'd survived many things and helped others survive them with him.

"You think I take it casually?" he asked in a quiet voice. Rage sparkled in his eyes, his strength unnerving, but he held himself in check. "Do you think I made the mate-claim because of some stupid hope that it would make you obey me, that I needed to dominate you?"

Jaycee didn't answer, her mouth too dry. Dimitri had snapped out the mate-claim when he'd wanted to prevent Jaycee climbing into a dangerous hole to save Kendrick. Jaycee had gone in anyway.

"I know it was more than that to you," Jaycee struggled to say. "That's why I thought Brice asking me to refuse would upset you."

"I'm not a little cub you have to placate," Dimitri answered, voice harsh. "I'm not the Lupine just past his Transition who wanted sex with you before his craving for you killed him. I mate-claimed *you*, Jaycee, my best friend. Not because I thought it would make you obedient—hell, I'm not that deluded. I did it because I fucking wanted to."

Dimitri never stuttered when he was furiously angry. Words came out without him having to think about them or stumble over them.

He glowered down at Jaycee, focused on *her*, not speech, caring only about what was enraging him.

"I claimed you because of your sassy mouth," Dimitri went on. He touched her lips with one finger. "Because your hair shines like gold in the sunshine, because as a leopard, you can hang upside down from a tree, for the Goddess' sake. Because your eyes look like topaz, because you can kick the ass of any Shifter who gets in your way. Because you jumped into the fight club ring to keep me from being trounced by a Lupine who tried to tranq me. Because you're hot, you drive me fucking crazy, and I don't want any other asshole Shifter to have you."

Jaycee stared up at him, the lump in her throat nearly choking her. Dimitri's eyes were like white fire, his hands strong but his touch on her lips gentle.

Another breeze blew down the hall. The chimes outdoors sang through the house, the wind light and cool.

Jaycee swallowed with effort. "In that case," she whispered. "Dimitri Kashnikov, I accept your mate-claim."

* * *

White heat seared through Dimitri's blood, the words sealing Jaycee to him with the ancient magic that beat through all Shifters. The acceptance was supposed to be in front of witnesses to be official, but who cared? In the old days, the claim and its acceptance were enough—the Shifters were considered mated.

Besides, the house could be a witness. Even as the thought went through his head, Dimitri heard the faint whisper of breeze that sounded like laughter. He ignored it to enjoy Jaycee's voice, her words rasping but strong.

"Don't," he heard himself say. *What?* his wolf howled. *She's my* mate. *She just said so!*

"Don't what?" Jaycee's eyes widened.

"Accept to shut me up. Accept and then change your mind. Accept because Brice p-pissed you off. I know how much you hate people telling you what to do. Don't accept because of that."

Her abrupt breath pushed her full breasts into Dimitri's chest. She and Dimitri were so different—she with her soft, lush body; he with his angular, hard one. They fit perfectly together.

"I don't play games with a *mate-claim*," Jaycee said, glaring at him. "I take it as seriously as you do. More, probably."

Dimitri gave her an incredulous look. "How can you take my mate-claim more seriously than I do? I claimed you in my head a hell of a long time before the words came out. I claimed you when I met you, Jaycee."

That stopped her. Jaycee stared at him in astonishment, her mouth hanging open. Dimitri had been tall and awkward when he'd first met Jaycee, on the verge of his Transition and messed up from it. Jaycee had been wickedly beautiful, sleek and lithe with golden eyes and hair shining in the sunlight. Kendrick had introduced her as a new member of their group and told Dimitri to show her around. Jaycee had smiled and changed his life.

Transitions were volatile things—Shifters moving from

cub to adult with all the hormonal fury of a charging bull elephant—and he and Jaycee had fought. And fought. With hot words as human, with teeth and claws as leopard and wolf.

The day they'd grabbed each other and found their rage metamorphosing into blatant need had been amazing.

They'd taken each other with a ripping of clothes, the lovemaking unashamed and unpracticed. When they'd come to their senses, Jaycee had been mortified. Dimitri had pretended to be, but he'd rejoiced. And never forgotten.

Jaycee must have been thinking about their first time as well, because she flushed a sudden dark red. At the same time, she drew him against her and covered his mouth with a full, deep kiss.

Dimitri's grip on her slackened, but he didn't let go. He pressed her into the wall, holding her up so he didn't have to bend far to kiss her back.

Her lips parted under his, the taste of her soul satisfying. Jaycee laced her arms around him, one foot hooking around his thigh.

Dimitri slid his hand under the hem of her shirt and tank top, working up to close his fingers around her breast. She wore no bra tonight, the tank top thick. Her nipple pushed into his palm in a firm, tight point.

He wanted to taste more of her. Lay her back on the stairs, lift up the top, and close his mouth around her breast. He'd suckle until she moaned, then he'd slide her jeans down and lock his mouth to the hottest part of her.

The wind outside built but lacked the ferocity of the earlier storm. It was a friendly breeze, caressing Dimitri, urging him on.

Jaycee dug her fingers into his back, pulling him closer. The movement pressed her breast into his palm, and she tightened her leg around him to bring the rigid line of his cock into the space between her thighs.

On the stairs, right now . . . He'd take her in mindless pleasure, stroking his hard cock into her sweet body, she hot and tight, squeezing him . . .

"Oh," someone said. "Hey. I guess I should have knocked."

Ben's voice floated from the dark hall, and Jaycee yanked her mouth from Dimitri's.

"Ben," she cried.

She tried to wriggle from Dimitri's grasp. He still had hold of her breast, and if she jerked again, she might hurt herself. Carefully, Dimitri released the breast in question and eased his hand out from under her shirt.

Jaycee unwound her leg and leapt impatiently to the floor. She landed with agility, but of course she did. Cats always landed on their feet.

Jaycee slapped on a light as she ran toward Ben, who stood near the back door, holding himself up on the wall.

"Are you all right?" she sang out. "What the hell happened to you?"

Dimitri remained where he was, resting one fist on the polished wood where Jaycee had been, his head bent as he fought to contain himself. Mating frenzy couldn't be switched on and off so easily, and as much as he was concerned about Ben, Dimitri's cock was fully tight. He'd have to wait a while before he turned around. Why did Jaycee have to turn on all the lights?

"I was thrown from a third-floor balcony," Ben was saying. "How do you think I am? But do *not* let me interrupt you."

"Don't be stupid." Jaycee's last word was muffled, and Dimitri looked over his shoulder to find that she'd embraced Ben.

Dimitri was supposed to be jealous—his mate had torn herself from his arms to rush to another—but he couldn't be. Ben looked haggard and bruised, but far better than someone who'd fallen several floors ought to.

His worry for Ben cut through his desires, allowing Dimitri to turn from the wall. "H-how did you get out of the club? I didn't see you l-land. No sign of you."

"Oh, I landed." Ben released Jaycee and put a hand to the back of his neck. "I created a little glam so I could slip away—everyone was looking everywhere but right at me. It's old magic, and I'm good at it. I'm also more resilient than most. Falling twenty-five or thirty feet makes me want to have a good stretch and go to bed, but won't break any-thing. The advantage of not being Shifter. Or human."

Dimitri didn't know what to make of his explanation, but it didn't matter. Whatever Ben had done to survive had worked. "I'm glad you m-made it back here. You'll s-stay with us."

"I don't have to. I just wanted to let you know I was still alive. Didn't want to use your phones in case Brice has found a way to tap them. Don't worry—his spies didn't see me come here. Like I said, I'm good at the glam."

Jaycee slid her arm around him. "Can you make it up-stairs? You can have something to eat and then go to bed."

"I said I'm all *right*." Ben didn't look all right, but he ducked out from under Jaycee's touch. "I'll go have a swim. I don't have a suit, so you know . . . give me my privacy. And I'll give you yours." He sent Dimitri a wink.

Jaycee flushed. "We were just working off steam."

Ben looked from her to Dimitri and back again. "Sure you were, sweetheart. You two kids have a good time. We'll talk later."

He turned away, gave them a gallant wave, and staggered to the back door, holding on to the wall as he went.

Dimitri joined Jaycee. "We sh-should go after him," he said.

"Don't you dare," Ben growled over his shoulder. "I need some alone time, not being bombarded with questions from two Shifters who are dying to jump each other."

Dimitri stopped, understanding. He knew how to tell when someone was being courageous and when they truly wanted to be left alone. As if to emphasize the point, the door to the back veranda closed itself with a decided slam as soon as Ben had exited.

"I g-guess that settles it," Dimitri said.

Jaycee ran a hand through her hair, which was mussed from their kiss. "I'm going to bed."

She didn't admonish him not to follow her, but she didn't invite him either. The moment had broken.

Dimitri suppressed a dart of frustration. Not Ben's fault—this kind of shit happened when you were a tracker. Personal feelings and needs had to take a backseat to the scouting and fighting.

Jaycee's fine ass made a nice picture as she went up the stairs ahead of him. The chandelier swung a little, its wrought-iron body creaking.

Dimitri followed her. He shut off the flooding lights with the switch at the top of the stairs and walked with Jaycee into the darkness. Moonlight poured through a window at the end of the upstairs hall, sharpening the edges of the shadows.

Jaycee entered her bedroom. She turned in the doorway, one hand on the handle, and studied Dimitri, saying nothing. He stopped in the hallway, equally silent, his heart pounding.

She wet her lips. "Stay with me tonight?" she asked, her voice the barest whisper.

Dimitri swallowed. He came forward, backed her into the room, caught the door, and closed it. He slid his arms around her, the fevered heat of ten minutes ago calmed into something deeper and more profound, and he kissed her.

J aycee opened herself to him. Dimitri could kiss like fire, and at the moment, she needed a little heat.

He held her close, his hand coming up to touch her face, the brush of his fingers incredibly tender. When he'd cupped her breast in the hall, Jaycee's mating need had burned, making her thrust herself against him, hungry for him.

She was still hungry, but the frenzy had cooled into something more beautiful.

The two times Jaycee had been with Dimitri, they'd both been desperate, in the throes of other forces. This time it was only the two of them, together because they wanted to be.

Jaycee had accepted the mate-claim and *still* Dimitri had argued with her, damn him. The mate-claim had wanted them to go straight to mating frenzy, ensuring they'd again be under forces beyond their control, but luckily Ben had happened by.

Maybe not luck. Ben had the uncanny knack of showing up the moment he was needed.

Dimitri's kiss held passion but not the savagery of their earlier kisses. He licked across Jaycee's mouth, his eyes closing, shutting out the starry gray.

Jaycee slid her hands down to his hips, then to his backside, enjoying the texture of his jeans over his tight ass. Very tight ass. Jaycee cupped firm flesh and moved her index finger along the indentation in the middle, the seam of his jeans giving her a nice path.

Dimitri lifted his head, opening his eyes. A gleam of wickedness lived there.

"You're a shit, Jase."

"Just checking out the goods," Jaycee said in all innocence. "Seeing what I'm getting."

"Yeah?" Dimitri's gaze was hot, and she heard the clink of his belt buckle opening. "Why don't you go for it instead of teasing?"

Jaycee's heart thumped. She'd started to enjoy him in the parking lot of the club outside Austin, but there again, she hadn't had the chance to finish. The mission always came first.

Dimitri's jeans sagged as she pushed at them, and her hands went to the fabric of his underwear, warm from his body. The small briefs he liked to wear clung to every crease—soft, thin cloth over Dimitri's nakedness.

It wasn't enough. Jaycee wanted all of him. She shoved the underwear down, smiling as she found the smooth skin of his backside.

"You're a fine man, Dimitri," Jaycee whispered, then winked up at him. "For a Lupine."

"And you're more beautiful than any woman I've ever seen," Dimitri said, his dark voice catching at her. "Lupine, Feline, human—doesn't matter. You win, Jase. No one can come close to you."

CHAPTER EIGHTEEN

Jaycee's smile died, and her heart squeezed into one painful ball. Dimitri's expression was serious, his eyes full of fire as he touched her face.

Her breath hitched in her throat, robbing her of words. Wind moved through the room, the curtains at the window fluttering. Jaycee was sure she'd closed that window before they'd gone, she thought distractedly.

Her arms and hands were full of Dimitri. He kicked his way out of his fallen underwear and lowered his head to nip her neck.

Jaycee's palms moved over his hips as she slid one hand to the front of him. Sensations came to her—wiry hair, hot flesh, the fascinating blunt weight of his cock. She wrapped her fingers around its wide breadth and held on.

Dimitri emitted a growl, his eyes closing again. Instead of standing still and letting her explore him, he grasped her shirt and tank top and pulled both off over her head.

Jaycee let out a breath as her breasts tumbled free of confinement, the cool breeze touching her skin. Dimitri gazed down at her in triumph, right before he hauled her against him and kissed her.

There was something strange going on in this room, and not just Dimitri kissing Jaycee the way he'd wanted to for a long time. The wind fluttering the curtains was cool and fresh, bearing none of the sticky humidity of the night they'd ridden through. And the furniture was moving.

Not much, but everything rocked a little, Dimitri saw out of the corner of his eye, like excited beings on restless feet.

This house was definitely creepy.

So said the back of his mind. Jaycee in his arms was capturing the best part of his thoughts.

Without doubt, the best part. She wrapped her sinful hand around his cock as they kissed, and squeezed him hard.

Lightning flickered on the edges of Dimitri's vision, real or imagined, he couldn't tell. His awareness moved to the point of Jaycee's gripping him and the hot taste of her mouth.

Jaycee. My mate.

Her words of acceptance rang in his head, heightening the spinning sensations. *Dimitri Kashnikov, I accept your mate-claim.* Didn't matter that she didn't say it in front of witnesses, and these days, it didn't count.

It counted to Dimitri, and he knew it counted to Jaycee. They were mates, had always been, even when they'd been trying hard to convince themselves they weren't.

Jaycee was shoving up his T-shirt with her free hand. Dimitri stripped it off, bunching it in his fists before he dropped it. All the while, she kept hold of him, her tight hand driving fire through his blood. His body wanted to thrust into her fist, let her release him that way.

No, he wanted to be inside her for that. Stroking was good, but the two of them joining was better.

Hard to think true thoughts while her fingers moved up and down, thumb caressing his tip, then the heel of her hand bumping his balls. Dimitri bit back a growl of need and fumbled open the button of her jeans.

Zipper next. Jaycee wasn't going to help. Her little smile told him that. Dimitri unzipped and pushed the jeans from her hips, then her sensible gray cotton underwear. No frilly strips of silk and lace for Jaycee. He'd have to buy her some and tell her to wear it for him alone. She was his mate now— she'd want to do it to please him.

That was a dream for another day. Right now, Dimitri sought the heat of her, his fingers slipping into her slick warmth.

Jaycee hummed in her throat. She swayed against him, the woman in her coming alive. Jaycee could fight, she could go toe-to-toe against alphas like Dylan and Brice, but under Dimitri's touch, she became sexy and sultry, her strength sinuous, beautiful.

He could make her release right now, he knew, stroking her until she writhed and went wild on his hand. She could make him release as well, her fingers learning him and working his desire to a fevered height.

The house seemed to approve. Furniture rattled on the floor, the curtains flapped, the unlit crystal sconces on the wall tinkled.

Earlier today, a natural tornado had whipped through the land. Tonight, wind swirled around Jaycee and Dimitri as they held each other, building each other to frenzy.

Dimitri needed her *now*. He wanted to be on top of her, sliding inside, her soft body beneath his, her hands urging him on.

He snaked one arm tightly around her, preparing to lift her. That would mean she had to let go of him, but he'd sacrifice for the hot joy of what was to come.

The bed spun away from the wall, slid across the room, and bumped gently into Dimitri's thigh. He let the momentum topple him backward, and he caught up Jaycee and pulled her along with him.

They rolled across the mattress, both of them bare except for their socks. Dimitri landed on Jaycee, his hands pinning her wrists, and he smiled down at her.

"I've never seen anything like you," he said. His words flowed easily, the disconnect between brain and mouth absent and unimportant. "My mate. You're hot, Jaycee." He released her to kneel back and draw his hand between the heat of her breasts. "Walking beauty."

"You're pretty good yourself." Jaycee gave him a flattering once-over. "Red-haired all the way down."

No denying that. Jaycee's was golden, the grace of her leopard coming through in her human body.

Dimitri admired her for a moment, then leaned down and licked the path his hands had taken on her breasts. He did what he'd pictured doing in the hall—drew his tongue around her nipple and pulled it into his mouth.

Jaycee let out a faint moan. She rose to him as he suckled her, her hands lacing through his short hair and drawing him close.

She tasted of salt and herself, the spice of Jaycee. All his. Dimitri had never been sure if she'd taken lovers other than himself, and he'd never wanted to ask, but it didn't matter anymore. They were together now, one for the other. No one else.

Jaycee stroked his hair, and then her hands landed on his back, fingers restless. Dimitri drew her nipple between his lips, enjoying the tip, then let it go and raised his head.

They looked at each other in the darkness, Jaycee's eyes tawny, her golden hair spread across the pillow. Her body was curved and firm, a Shifter woman in the height of her beauty.

Mate of my heart. She'd been always, would always be.

Jaycee ran her hands up Dimitri's arms. Her fingertips were soothing on his hot skin, leaving furrows of coolness.

Dimitri leaned down and licked her throat, where her fake Collar had left a faint line. He closed his lips over the skin there, suckled.

"Don't leave a mark," she whispered. "We'll have to put the Collars back on."

Dimitri growled and lifted his head. She had a smile on her face, as though she pictured herself with a Collar and a love bite peeping from behind it.

The image sent Dimitri over the top. He growled again, unable to hold back any longer.

The wind chimes on the veranda went wild as Dimitri came down on Jaycee, parted her legs with a strong hand, and slid inside her.

Jaycee cried out softly and rose to him, her back arching. Hot, tight, gripping—*Jaycee*.

Each time Dimitri loved her was better than the last. Mating frenzy rose, urging him to stay locked inside her until they emerged exhausted and starving. They'd eat, rest, and do it again.

Mating frenzy served a purpose, but right now Dimitri didn't care. He only knew Jaycee's strong body was closing around his, her scent enfolding him.

He thrust, then paused, then made another thrust. Goddess help him. Dimitri balled his fists, pushed them into the mattress as he thrust again. Jaycee lifted to him, her lips parting as she met his stroke.

She was made of beauty. There wasn't a time he hadn't loved this woman, this strong and sassy Shifter.

You're breaking me, Jase. I'm ready to do anything for you.

If she wanted to return to Kendrick and tell him she wouldn't investigate Brice anymore, Dimitri knew he'd go with her, face his leader for her. He'd a hundred times rather do that than listen to Jaycee tell Brice she refused Dimitri's mate-claim, even if she didn't mean it. Dimitri wanted to punch Brice in the mouth for even suggesting it.

My mate. My best friend. All other Shifters can eat shit.

He drove into her a little harder, a little faster. The bed rattled, shaking on its own. Wind whipped around them, clattering pictures against the walls. The chimes below pealed.

The sounds and jostling spurred Dimitri on. Jaycee wrapped her legs around his hips, pulling him down to her, her hands gripping his arms. She rocked her head back, her cries of pleasure echoing around him.

Jaycee was lost in sensations, begging him to take her, though Dimitri was doing that as hard as he could. She wasn't quiet, she shouted and yelled, to hell with whoever heard.

There was no one but the house. Dimitri knew damn well Ben had taken himself out of the way so he wouldn't *have* to hear them.

He rocked into her, Jaycee holding him tight, her feet pressing his buttocks. Dimitri felt his balls tighten, his release ready to overtake him. He resisted, wanting to stay inside her forever.

Slowing didn't help—it only heightened the sensation of her squeezing him, her hot body the only place he wanted to be.

"Damn it all to hell," Dimitri snarled as his climax refused to wait. White fire pulsed through him, he lost all coherence, and he drove into Jaycee over and over again.

Jaycee was plenty resilient. She held firmly on to him, lifting from the bed as her own climax came, her cries matching his. Her hair tangled on the pillow, her face flushed and wet.

Dimitri thrust into her one final time, holding himself inside until his shaking arms wouldn't brace him any longer.

He collapsed even as Jaycee, under him, finished riding out her release. She caught him in her arms, pulling him close, her kisses muffling his words of anger that it was all over.

The furniture ceased moving, the bed coming to rest with a thump. The wind died and the chimes below diminished to a whisper.

Jaycee gently ended the kiss, drew back, and looked up at him. She smiled, warmth in her golden eyes, and Dimitri's world was perfect.

When Jaycee stumbled to the kitchen at the end of the hall in the morning, Ben was at the stove cooking breakfast for about five hundred. Eggs overflowed the frying pan, and a plate piled high with bacon rested on the counter next to a stack of toast that had come from an entire loaf of bread.

Ben looked clean, rested, chipper. His close-cropped black hair was damp from a shower, his bruises and abrasions gone, his tatts stark on his dark skin.

"I thought you kids might be hungry," he said, flashing Jaycee a grin.

Jaycee put her hand to her hair. It was a mess, her face creased from the sheets. Dimitri had been in the shower when she'd climbed out of bed. He'd kissed her when he'd gone, walking out the bedroom door stark naked, giving her the best view in the house.

She'd thought about joining Dimitri in the bathroom, but she'd heard Ben moving around and grown hot with embarrassment. She'd pulled on the first shirt she found and some loose-legged pants, and hurried down the hall to the kitchen.

"Can I come to the sun and moon ceremonies?" Ben asked. "I love those."

"Nothing's been decided," Jaycee said quickly. Her stomach rumbled, confirming that she was ravenous. She grabbed a clean plate from the table Ben had set and filled it with bacon and toast.

Ben held out a spatula of eggs, and Jaycee shoved her plate beneath it. "A little more?" she asked as he dumped the eggs to it.

Ben laughed and complied. Jaycee seated herself, drew her feet up to sit cross-legged, and attacked the food. Ben gave her a knowing look, and Jaycee blushed again when she realized the shirt she'd picked up off the floor had been Dimitri's—his favorite black one with the red orange Harley logo.

"Are you really all right?" Jaycee asked Ben, delicately lifting a strip of bacon.

"I am. This house is great. I slept like a baby—heard nothing, thank the Goddess. The magic here speeded up my healing something wonderful."

"Good," Jaycee said sincerely.

"I wonder if Jazz would let me stay on here," he continued, turning back to the stove. "I could look after the place for her. It has a great vibe."

"Ask her," Jaycee said. "As long as you're not worried that it's haunted."

"That's the beauty. If someone comes in here who shouldn't, he'll have the shit scared out of him. Great security."

Ben returned to cooking, humming to himself.

Jaycee ate until her plate was clean, first hunger abated, then she rose and poured herself a large cup of coffee, dropping in a few spoonfuls of sugar. "Something I'm confused about." She sipped the hot, sweet mocha and closed her eyes in satisfaction. Nothing was better than coffee. Nothing. Well, maybe chocolate. And wine. And sex with Dimitri. Sex with Dimitri was definitely the best.

"What's that?" Ben filled a plate of food for himself and carried it to the table.

Jaycee leaned against the counter, cradling her cup against her abdomen. "A couple of things. You said you could cast a glam and not be seen, so you could get away. But when you were scouting for Kendrick a while back, you got stabbed. Remember? Zander had to heal you. Why didn't you use the glam then?"

"Wasn't paying attention," Ben said in irritation. "I was so sure I was being covert. I was careless, and I paid for it. Thanks for bringing it up. Next question."

Jaycee took a sip of coffee, thinking things through. "When Brice was reaming you out last night, he said something like—you and your people sided with the *dokk alfar*, dark Fae. Said you caught and tortured Shifters in whatever battles." She frowned. "But I thought the dark Fae were the good guys. The only one I know, Reid from the Las Vegas Shiftertown, is a *dokk alfar*. We like him because he hates the high Fae."

Ben slowed his chewing and rested his fork on his plate. He swallowed and cleared his throat.

"There are a lot of points of view," he said.

Dimitri entered in time to hear him. He wore jeans and a loose-fitting tank top, which showed the red curls on his chest at the neckline. He, like Jaycee, was barefoot.

He walked right past Ben and all the food to corner Jaycee against the counter.

"Morning, beautiful," he said. He moved her coffee cup aside and kissed her.

The kiss was hot, full of passion and afterglow, his lips warm, Dimitri taking his time. When he at last pulled away, he cupped Jaycee's face in his hands and looked down into her eyes. His were dark gray, holding a mixture of longing and satisfaction.

Jaycee wanted to say something like *Morning yourself, gorgeous*, but nothing came from her mouth. Dimitri brushed back her hair with a firm hand, then turned away and caught up a plate. Jaycee sagged against the counter, her heart beating rapidly, her body full of fire.

"What do you mean?" Dimitri asked Ben as though the conversation hadn't been interrupted. "A lot of points of view?"

"Well." Ben shot Jaycee a grin behind Dimitri's back. "If you love the high Fae, then the *dokk alfar* are demons to you. The *dokk alfar* are old beings, older than the high Fae, though the high Fae think they're so special. I'm not sure of the whole history, but the high Fae pushed the *dokk alfar* out of their traditional territories, wanting to take over, as they always do, the arrogant bastards. The *dokk alfar* decided they'd had enough one day, and fought back. Fought hard. They were ruthless, and taught the high Fae to be afraid of them. The two groups have been fighting ever since. Not an out-and-out war, but many struggles over the centuries. The *dokk alfar* got very good at hiding, very good at being stealthy. They taught me a lot."

Dimitri sauntered to the table with a loaded plate, low-riding jeans cradling his hips. "So you did s-side with them."

"Against the high Fae? You betcha. And my people—the goblins—paid the price. But I wouldn't take it back. If we'd fought on the side of the high Fae, we'd have become their slaves, like the Shifters were. Worse. The Fae wanted us for our magic. They'd have put us in hamster wheels, making us do magic for them until we died. Throw out the spent goblin, bring the next one in."

Anything lighthearted in Ben had vanished. His eyes showed an old rage, a determination that could flatten a city. Jaycee had seen the same flash in his eyes last night when he'd faced down Brice.

"What about the part about torturing Shifters?" Jaycee asked.

Ben scowled. "Fae like to say that. Poor Shifters, captured by the *dokk alfar* and the goblins. Torn apart or used for target practice. It's all bullshit. The high Fae tortured Shifters anytime they wanted—they're projecting their own evil deeds onto others. Whenever a Shifter was captured by a goblin, the Shifter was set free. I rescued a number of Shifters in my time, before they finally got themselves completely free of the Fae."

"Hmm," Dimitri said. He shoved his fork through eggs. "Then why w-would B-Brice be upset at you? He's a Shifter. He shouldn't believe high F-Fae c-crap."

"Where would he even hear high Fae crap?" Jaycee asked.

"Ah, that is the question," Ben said. "How did he figure out what I was? I didn't exactly volunteer the information. I had to explain the Fae smell, but all I said was that I was an ancient creature thrown out of Faerie, which is true. Who told him I'd worked with the *dokk alfar*?" His dark gaze landed on Jaycee.

"Don't look at me," Jaycee said. "I didn't even know. I hope you don't think one of *our* Shifters did."

"Not where my thoughts were going," Ben said. He rested his elbows on the table. "Why would a Shifter be upset that I'd fought the Fae? Sure, if he believed I hurt Shifters, I could understand, but doesn't he know about Reid? Everyone knows about Reid by now. Eric from Las Vegas and Dylan are good at sharing information with Shiftertown leaders. Shifters should know that the *dokk alfar* are allies with Shifters against the high Fae. So why did Brice call them evil demons?"

"Don't keep me in suspense," Jaycee said, though her tone said she knew what was coming. "Why did he?"

Dimitri answered for him, his voice subdued. "B-because Brice heard the high F-Fae's side of the story. Right? From a high Fae." He stabbed his eggs as though driving a knife through an enemy. "Which means D-Dylan is right about him. Brice is working with the Fae."

CHAPTER NINETEEN

Understanding and then fear flooded through Jaycee, making the coffee she'd just swallowed taste like bile. "Shit," she whispered.

"Yep," Ben said. "The question is—is Brice a fool who is being used by whoever his Fae contacts are, or is he selling Shifters out?"

"Why the hell would he?" Jaycee asked, her anger rising. "The Fae enslaved Shifters for what, a thousand years? Are they telling him it was all a misunderstanding? What about the Fae who are making swords to control Shifters through the Collars? The Collars are a Fae plot, remember? Which is why I thank the Goddess every day Kendrick kept us free of them."

"W-we should ask him," Dimitri said quietly. He didn't bluster or wave his coffee until it spilled, like Jaycee, but she sensed deep fury in him.

"Brice can't actually believe the Fae are going to save the Shifters, can he?" Jaycee demanded. She went to the table, plunked her cup to it and her butt to a chair. She refused to let Dimitri's bare arm, hard with muscle and brushed with red gold hair, distract her. "Every encounter we've had with the Fae has only proved they want us under their power again."

"Not all Fae do," Ben said. "There's one who visits the Morrisseys in Austin who's not evil. But that's one Fae out of, what, millions?"

"What about what happened up in Washington state? On the Olympic Peninsula?" Jaycee asked. "I heard all about that. Feral Shifters enslaved by Fae—Shifters captured and *made* to go feral. Does Brice have anything to do with that?"

"Which is why w-we're going to ask him," Dimitri said grimly. "Brice isn't f-feral. Neither are his followers."

"Fae don't all work together," Ben said. "There are many of the shitheads, in different territories, and most hate each other's guts. So the Fae with the swords that control Collars, the ones with the feral Shifters, and Brice's Fae might all be different."

"Or not," Jaycee said. "We need to find out." She gave Dimitri a look, her heart constricting. "Do we keep pretending? Do I tell Brice I'll refuse your mate-claim like an obedient little Shifter for the good of the group? Or do we grab him and interrogate him?" She hoped Dimitri would go for the latter. A little interrogation would be so very satisfying.

Dimitri resumed eating, a thoughtful look on his face. After he cleaned off his plate, he said, "I k-keep thinking I know B-Brice from somewhere. Can't think where." His red brows drew together, his face as handsome when he was pondering as when smiling, or over her in the dark making hard and fast love to her.

Jaycee lifted her cooled coffee. "I've known you since I joined Kendrick's Shifters twenty years ago. I've been beside you practically every moment since then, and I've never met Brice—I'm sure of it. So if you encountered him in the past, it must have been before that. We haven't been much out of each other's sights since."

Dimitri shook his head. "I didn't meet him when I was with K-Kendrick. Never saw m-many Shifters outside our group until this past year. Before that, I was with Anna and D-David, and I d-didn't know other Shifters then. Just me."

"Before that, then," Ben suggested.

Dimitri shook his head. "I don't remember m-much. You mean I m-might have met him when I was a cub, but it's b-blocked out like everything else."

"Could be," Jaycee said cautiously. Dimitri never liked to talk about when he was a cub, and not only because he couldn't remember. It distressed him that his memories were gone, especially the ones of his parents. He remembered them vaguely, but not in much detail.

Dimitri sent Jaycee a sharp look. "Are you thinking Brice had something to do with my parents' death? That's why I don't remember him?"

Jaycee didn't answer. It was a possibility, one to be carefully considered.

"That's a big conclusion to jump to," Ben said, lacing his fingers. "Could be you met him once long ago, that's all. Shifters have good memories. It might have stuck in your head even if you can't recall the actual encounter."

"I don't scent any guilt in him when he looks at you," Jaycee said. "No sign that he did anything to your parents. Even if he was remorseless about that, he'd be afraid you'd find out. I don't get that from him either."

"Neither do I," Dimitri agreed. "But it's b-bugging the hell out of me."

"I could hypnotize you," Ben said, then his face fell. "No, wait, maybe not. I've never done it to a Shifter. I might put you in a trance for a century."

"No hypnotizing," Jaycee said impatiently. "It's another thing we'll grill Brice about. If he's never seen you before, then we'll know you're remembering someone else."

Dimitri sipped coffee, still troubled. "Okay, whatever."

"What about Angus?" Jaycee asked. "The bouncer. He's less than thrilled with Brice. We could get some dirt on Brice from him, I'll bet."

"Unless he's a p-plant," Dimitri said. "You know—he

b-bad-mouths Brice and gets us to trust him. Then he t-tells Brice everything we say. Then Brice throws *me* off the balcony. Or w-worse—he throws *you*." He gave Jaycee a hard look. "Then I kill him." The stammer vanished on the last words.

"Angus seems like a decent guy," Ben said. "For a growly, constantly pissed off Lupine, that is. But then, most Lupines are like that."

"True." Jaycee rolled her eyes and drained her coffee.

"You t-two are h-hil, hil-lari . . . very funny," Dimitri said.

"We go back to the club, then?" Jaycee asked, rising to pour herself more coffee. "Corner Brice and find out exactly what he's up to? Or call Kendrick and have him send Dylan out here to scoop him up? Dylan's good at interrogation." Not as satisfying as doing it herself, but Jaycee had to admit Dylan was effective. The man only had to stare at his prisoner in silence, and that prisoner opened up and told him all he wanted to know.

"I'll c-call Kendrick," Dimitri said. "This is still his m-mission, his orders."

Jaycee agreed, though she could argue that trackers were supposed to take initiative when they thought it necessary. On the other hand, Jaycee had run into problems when she'd taken too much initiative and had been forced to endure Kendrick's wrath. But hadn't she caught humans planning to capture Shifters for bounty that time when she'd fallen through the broken skylights of the abandoned cabin the bounty hunters had taken over? She'd had them terrified and running by the time Dimitri, Kendrick, and Seamus had shown up. Kendrick had yelled at her anyway for making the big, bad male Shifters worry about her.

Dimitri gave Jaycee a stern look, as though remembering the incident, and pushed from the table. He didn't rise, only tilted his chair back, bare feet wrapping around its front legs.

"Club doesn't open until d-dark," he reminded her. "What did you want to do today?"

Jaycee knew exactly what she wanted to do. Hunger that hadn't abated surged through her blood.

"If you spend it in mate frenzy, will you keep it down?" Ben asked as he stacked dishes in the sink. "I can only stay so long in the pool."

"S-still a lot of the house to clean up," Dimitri said, lacing his hands behind his head. "We should m-make a start."

He felt as much yearning as she did, Jaycee could tell. She'd long been able to read Dimitri's moods, and this one was the lazy Lupine who wanted to make love and sleep in the sun all day, wake up and make love again.

"Third wheel, that's me," Ben said cheerfully. "You two do what you want. *I'll* clean up. No, I won't take the hint and vacate the premises. It's safer for me to stay here, and you kids need looking after. There's still something strange going on in this house, and you're distracted." He returned to the table and started picking up their used plates. "Take my advice, have the sun and moon ceremonies as soon as you can. Then maybe the rest of us can relax."

J aycee in the sunshine was a beautiful sight. Dimitri lounged in a wicker chair on the veranda in nothing but a pair of shorts, while Jaycee romped as a leopard around the grounds. He'd decided to give Ben a break and not chase her down and take her whenever he could, but it wasn't easy.

Dimitri had already broken the silent promise once. When Jaycee had gone to shower, Dimitri hadn't been able to walk past the bathroom, knowing she was there, naked under the water, gleaming with soap.

He'd have had to be dead to ignore that. He'd walked inside to see Jaycee peering out from around the shower curtain, soapy hand dripping suds on the floor. She hadn't said a word, only opened the curtain a little wider.

Dimitri had stripped in silence, then joined her in the small shower, the two of them sliding and laughing as he lifted her against the wall and desperately entered her.

It had been slippery, hot, fast, and crazy. Jaycee had stifled her cries by kissing him, Dimitri had growled and said not a word.

Afterward, he'd leisurely washed her body, then stood still while she washed him. Slick hands moving on his skin led to another wild round of lovemaking, this time the two of them falling out of the tub onto the floor.

Dimitri had driven inside her, bracing himself on the tile, while Jaycee laughed and groaned.

He'd been sore and exhausted by the time he'd climbed from her, helped her to her feet, and dried her off. After that, he thought it best he go find Ben and continue cleaning up the storm damage. Maybe he'd be so tired from that he'd be able to not stop and make love to Jaycee every time he touched her. *Maybe.*

By midafternoon, it was too hot to do much work, even for Shifters. Dimitri retired to the porch, Ben took a nap, but Jaycee, restless and impatient with the lazy males she'd been stuck with, changed to leopard and prowled the property.

Dimitri watched her from the veranda, sipping iced tea she'd made, while the wind chimes moved slowly above him, their music a muted whisper. Only scattered puffy white clouds today, no thunderheads. And sunshine, powerful and hot, rendering a strong and energetic Lupine a lazy man in a chair.

He propped his feet on the railing and answered his phone, which had begun to ring insistently.

"This is Dimitri. Smile if you're s-sexy."

"Glad you're in a good mood," Kendrick's deep tones came to him. "I've been talking to Dylan about what you told me this morning." Dimitri had called him after breakfast, before his shower with Jaycee. "For the record, Dylan doesn't think I'm sexy."

"But Addie does." Dimitri let out a laugh. "I s-see the way she looks at you, lucky t-tiger. Anyway, what did Dylan s-say?"

Kendrick's voice held a note of resignation. "He wants to pull you. Says it's getting too dangerous. He wants to talk to Brice himself."

Dimitri sat up, his feet coming to the floor. "P-pull us out? Why? We're g-getting close. Brice t-trusts us."

"Brice figured out that Ben was one of our agents. See what he did to him? Can you and Jaycee survive if Brice and his entire band turn on you?"

"N-no, h-he didn't f-f-figure . . ." Dimitri stopped in frustration. Usually his stutter went away when he was angry, but sometimes it came on full force. He held the phone away from his ear. "Jase!" he called. "C-come and t-t-t . . . *Fuck it.*"

He rolled to his feet and moved down the veranda steps, barefoot, into the cool mud and grass of the yard.

Jaycee came loping to him, her hindquarters moving right and left as though to keep her back legs from overtaking her front. She halted in front of Dimitri, her tawny leopard head covered with curved rows of black spots, her golden eyes pinning him without fear.

Dimitri held out the phone. Jaycee growled, her breath rattling as it went in and out. She plucked the cell phone out of his hand with her teeth, dropped the phone on the ground, and put one large paw on it. She didn't crush it; she simply pressed it into the mud.

Dimitri laughed, which calmed his voice. "You know that's K-Kendrick, right?"

Jaycee reared up and put her muddy paws on Dimitri's shoulders. She whuffed leopard breath in his face, then licked his cheek.

"Yeah, nothing says love like cat spit." Dimitri kept grinning, and Jaycee began to shift.

She hung her paws on his shoulders and morphed from gorgeous leopard to beautiful woman in about thirty seconds. Her paws were the last to change, becoming hands that held Dimitri and pulled him close.

Beautiful, *naked* woman. Her bare foot now shoved the phone aside, and then Jaycee rose on tiptoes and kissed Dimitri on the mouth.

Her breasts were cushioned against his chest, her tongue sweeping fire past his lips. His shorts were the only things between him and another satisfying round of mating frenzy.

"Jaycee." Kendrick's voice came through the phone, full of impatience but also amusement. "Talk to me."

Jaycee's tongue was busy in Dimitri's mouth, and Dimitri was in no hurry to shove her away.

Any other Shifter would have hung up and called them back when he calculated they'd calmed down. Kendrick held on, which meant that what he needed to say was important.

Dimitri heaved a sigh and eased Jaycee from the kiss. "He wants us to pull out and go home."

Jaycee gave Dimitri an incredulous look, then let go of him and dove for the phone. She had to scrape the mud from it. "Seriously?" She yelled at Kendrick. "You send us away on a crazy mission and now you won't even let us finish it?"

"I didn't say that." Kendrick's voice came clearly to Dimitri. "Dylan's putting together a team to head out there. Keep an eye on Brice but back off. Dylan will find out what he's up to. If Brice figured out Ben, he'll figure out you."

"It's more complicated than that," Jaycee said. Sunshine touched her honey-colored hair and her lovely body, shadows from the leaves above her dappling her skin like her leopard's spots. "Brice knows we're working for Dylan. He thinks he's turning us. And he didn't rumble Ben as a spy. Brice accused him of working with the dark Fae, hurting Shifters as part of their wars with the high Fae. He's more worried about Ben's past in Faerie than what he's doing hanging out with Shifters now."

"He believes Ben's a spy for the *dokk alfar*?" Kendrick said. "That's interesting."

"Yeah, we said *interesting* when we discussed it too," Jaycee returned. "If Brice is working with the high Fae, Dylan doesn't need to come out here and have a chat with him. We need to take him down and get him away from the Shifters he's already corrupted. They'll defend him if Dylan confronts him, and Dylan and his 'team' will have to fight them too. Brice's followers are just Shifters compelled by an alpha. They don't deserve to have Dylan and his posse on their asses."

She was thinking of Casey, Dimitri mused. Casey, as far

has he could tell, really was a good guy who was sure the Goddess would save them if they all prayed hard enough. Dimitri was willing to bet many of Brice's followers were much the same.

Then again, most of them had joined together to drop Ben in a fall that could have killed him if he'd been human— hospitalized him at the very least. Removing Brice's influence from those Shifters was a good idea.

"I want to know what Brice is up to," Kendrick said. "Is he a deluded Shifter thinking the Fae are his saviors, or is he going for a power play thinking the Fae will back him? And what are his Fae friends planning? If they're going to strike, I want to know when and where to expect them."

"So might the leader of the New Orleans Shiftertown," Jaycee pointed out. "Should we contact him?"

"Already have," Kendrick answered. "We're talking. He's not thrilled with Brice but won't move openly against him, knowing he'd have a mutiny, which will attract the attention of Shifter Bureau." Kendrick went silent a moment. "Dimitri," he said, knowing Dimitri was able to hear every word. "I want you to cut Brice from the herd and pen him up to wait for Dylan. Brice seems like the kind of Shifter who'd know exactly when Dylan was near, so we want him isolated before Dylan arrives. And then stick around. Don't let Dylan kill him until we know exactly everything Brice knows. Dylan tends to get . . . intense."

"We know," Jaycee said. "That's why we love you, Kendrick, and are glad you're our leader."

"Blech," Dimitri said, leaning over her shoulder. "Don't get m-mushy."

"New orders," Kendrick said. "Dimitri, catch Brice. Trick him, lie to him, duct tape him, jump up and down on him— I don't care. But get him away from his Shifters—quietly— and sequester him. Dylan will be there tonight."

"What about me?" Jaycee asked. "You haven't said my name. Dimitri can't do this by himself."

"I know that. But Ben's there. You, Jaycee, will stand down. It's too dangerous, and I can't afford to lose you."

"N-neither can I," Dimitri said.

Jaycee glared at Dimitri. "Hey, I'm your *partner*."

Kendrick's stern tones came from the phone. "You're also a female Shifter and valuable, not simply for your gender but for yourself. If something happens to you, Dimitri will kill me. So will Addison. I'd like to live. So stay put, Jaycee."

CHAPTER TWENTY

"You know I can't obey an order like that," Jaycee said heatedly half an hour later.

She crossed her arms over her chest—which was now covered with a T-shirt, her legs with shorts—and gave Dimitri her best angry stare.

Dimitri, who'd returned to lounging on the porch chair, his feet up, his strong legs enticing her to touch them, only returned her look calmly. As did Ben, who'd joined them for a confab after Dimitri had told him what Kendrick had instructed on the phone.

"A s-simple end to a boring mission," Dimitri said. "Ben and I nab B-Brice, bring him here, and l-let the house lock him in. D-Dylan shows up and qu-qu-qu . . ." He closed his eyes briefly. "Asks him about the F-Fae, and then offs him. We go home."

"You left out the part about you and Ben going up against Brice by yourselves," Jaycee snapped. "On *his* territory, guarded by who knows how many Shifters—or Fae, for the Goddess' sake. Are you just going to tap him on the shoulder and say *Hello, we want you to come with us?*"

Dimitri shrugged. "Maybe."

Ben leaned comfortably on a post. "We'll trap him without too much violence. Brice trusts Dimitri."

"He trusts me more," Jaycee pointed out. "Dimitri, you said you think you recognize him from somewhere in your past. Well, he might recognize you too, and be playing you. You don't remember, but maybe *he* does. You don't need to walk into his trap."

Ben gave her a stern look. "I agree with Kendrick that you're too valuable to lose in this mess."

Dimitri held up his hand. "Wait. What did you h-have in mind, Jase?"

Oh, finally, the mighty males were going to listen to her. Jaycee drew a breath to calm herself and hopped to sit on the veranda rail. "I tell Brice I've reconsidered about Dimitri's mate-claim and that I'm ready to refuse it. But I wanted to talk to Brice about it. I can even tell him I'd consider *his* mate-claim if he wanted to make one."

"Ah." Ben looked delighted. "A honey trap. I like it."

Dimitri growled. "And what if you trigger his mating frenzy making an offer like that? You ready to fight off a *bear*?"

"That's why you and Ben will be nearby, just out of scent range," Jaycee said, keeping her tone reasonable. "Males who are far gone in lust don't think straight. Dylan himself would probably be able to walk up behind Brice and knock him on the head while he's trying to look down my shirt."

Dimitri's growls grew deeper, and his eyes changed to light gray. "*I'll* knock him on the head. But you're p-probably right."

Jaycee made a show of gaping. "Really? Can I write this down? Ben, you're a witness. Dimitri said I was right."

"I s-say that all the time. We'll suss it out. If it l-looks like your plan will work, then we'll do that."

Ben's brows lifted. "Kendrick specifically told her to stand down, right? Am I hearing two Shifters questioning their leader's orders?"

Jaycee answered, "We always do, and Kendrick knows it. If we can get the job done, he's fine with it. And I bet

Addison was standing right next to him, telling *him* to tell *me* to be careful."

Dimitri nodded. Addie was protective of all of them, but especially Jaycee, whom she now considered her closest friend.

"I agree with Addison," Ben said. "But Dimitri makes sense too. How about I give my advice that if it gets dangerous, you butt out, Jaycee?"

Dimitri rolled his eyes. "Sh-she won't. That's why I mate-claimed her. Thought sh-she'd obey her m-mate. But, no."

Jaycee stuck out her tongue at him and walked past him to the house.

Dimitri's blood heated. *Bring that over here, sweetheart.*

Jaycee called back over her shoulder, "I'll go change into something enticing."

Dimitri growled after her. "You're f-fine. You're sexy no matter what you wear."

Truth. Jaycee was edible in the T-shirt that hung to her butt, shorts baring her strong legs, her hair scraped into a sloppy ponytail. Any Shifter would fall on her and lap her up.

Jaycee laughed as she disappeared into the house. "You're hopeless, Dimitri." She kept laughing, her silver tones floating out behind her.

Ben watched her go, then gave Dimitri a look of sympathy. "You're in deep, my friend. Congratulations to you. She'll never give you a dull moment."

"I know," Dimitri agreed. His heart burned with joy, but he kept his voice glum. "She drives me past crazy and out the other s-side."

"I can hear you!" Jaycee's voice came from the depths of the house, then an upstairs door slammed with vehemence.

Ben laughed at Dimitri, who realized he was staring into the house, picturing Jaycee stripping down to nothing.

"Definitely coming to the sun and moon ceremonies," Ben said, shaking his head. "I'll be there even if you forget to invite me. I'm going to make sure it happens. It so needs to."

* * *

Jaycee knew Dimitri wasn't happy with her choice of out-fits, but he'd have to live with it. She'd put on black leg-gings that had pink glittery stones down the seams and a leather tunic with a V-neck that showed plenty of bosom. She wore a close-fitting tank top under the tunic to keep male eyes from seeing too much.

The leggings were form-hugging but allowed her greater freedom of movement than jeans would—she could fight in them or quickly slide them off to shift. The tunic and top would also be easy to throw off if she needed to shift, and she liked how the entire outfit drew Dimitri's eyes to her.

Jaycee commanded plenty of attention as she, Dimitri, and Ben walked down the hot New Orleans street toward the club. Ben was casting a glam, he said, to keep people from noticing him. True, most guys watched Jaycee, most of the women looked with interest at Dimitri, but eyes glazed a bit if they rested on Ben, then moved right past him.

No Shifter Bureau tonight. They liked to be arbitrary, leaving Shifters alone for a time, then springing out of no-where to see who they could catch. Tonight Jaycee and Dimitri walked to the main entrance without hindrance, Ben quietly behind them.

Angus was on the door. He stood solidly in front of it, focusing on those who wanted to enter, checking ID of hu-mans who looked even remotely too young, growling at those he admitted even as he opened the door and ushered them in. The groupies seemed to find the process exciting, shivering and laughing in delight the more snarling An-gus was.

The Lupine's gray eyes narrowed as Dimitri and Jaycee made it to the front of the line. Angus glanced briefly at Jaycee, deliberately avoided looking at her for long, and returned his gaze to Dimitri. "He's not here," he said before either could speak.

Dimitri's brows rose. "B-Brice? He told us to m-meet him."

"I guess he changed his mind."

Angus gave Dimitri a challenging look, his eyes the white-gray of a wolf ready to shift. Something was wrong here. Was Brice in there and Angus didn't want to let them in? Had Brice told Angus to keep them out?

Jaycee slipped in front of Dimitri before he could stop her. "Do you know where he is?" she asked. She met Angus's gaze, which she immediately saw unnerved him. He was also trying to avert his gaze from the shadow between her breasts. "It's important."

Angus solved the problem of keeping his eyes off Jaycee by pinning Dimitri with a hard look. "Why? You two seem like a decent couple, except for this weird interest in Brice. Why do you want to be one of his Shifters? Go back home, wherever that is, and enjoy life. Keep dickheads like Brice out of it."

Jaycee glanced past him and up at the balcony where Brice had held court last night to find it empty and dark, the lights not even on. A chill seeped through her. He'd told them to meet him here—why had his plans changed? Without word to them? Did he know Dylan was coming? Did he have Dimitri's phone bugged? Or webcams at the house?

Jaycee doubted the house would put up with webcams, or even let one of Brice's underlings in to install them. Jaycee and Dimitri would likely smell any listening devices slipped into their pockets or attached to their phones, so that scenario was unlikely as well.

Brice not being here might have nothing to do with them at all. But Jaycee knew they needed very much to find him, and by the way Dimitri stiffened, he agreed.

"Seriously important." Jaycee drew a breath. "Where is he? His house?"

Angus kept his gaze on Dimitri. "Why do you want to know so much?"

Jaycee made a quick decision. She had to do that in the field sometimes—decide to trust someone to get the job done. "Let us in, and we'll tell you."

Her words were lost when Dimitri leaned toward Angus and said in a rumbling voice. "We want to c-capture him. You gonna h-help us?"

Angus's eyes widened. Then the belligerence vanished from his hard face, and he opened the door wide, hustling them both inside. Ben scuttled in before the door could bang shut on him.

Angus strode toward the office in the back, where they'd first met Brice, nodding at another bouncer to take his place.

The office was empty, fluorescent lights shining on desks strewn with invoices, a desktop computer nearly drowned in paper of all colors—like a still life depicting the futile dream of the paperless office. A chair had been pushed back from the desk by the last inhabitant and left there.

Angus shut the door, or tried to. It caught on Ben, who shoved his way in. Angus obviously could see him now, because he stepped back, his mouth open, before Ben quickly slammed the door.

"Where the hell did you come from?" Angus demanded.

"I'm with them." Ben motioned to Dimitri and Jaycee.

"I watched you sail off the balcony," Angus said, his voice not softening. "You look fine." He sounded annoyed by this.

"I heal fast. They're not kidding that we need to find Brice. You know where he is?"

Angus turned his angry gaze to Dimitri. "What is he?" he asked, jerking his thumb at Ben.

Dimitri collapsed into the office chair, leaned back, and planted his boots on the corner of the desk, displacing the invoices there. "We d-don't know. Now, here's your choice. Help us g-grab the d-dickhead, as you call him, or at least t-tell us where he is, and we'll leave you alone."

Angus didn't look any happier. "Are you fucked-up crazy? Brice's fanatics will fight to the death for him, he has them so brainwashed. You'd take your female into a sitch like that? Watch her be torn apart, or worse—given to the dickhead?"

Jaycee broke in. "His *female* can take care of herself. But we don't have time to argue. Brice might be making a break for it even as we stand here. Where is he, Angus?"

Angus took in the three of them—Ben's black eyes like

the night sky, Dimitri's intense gray stare, Jaycee's golden-eyed scowl—and shook his head.

"You're serious. Shit." Angus rubbed his whiskered face, then let out a long sigh. "All right. He was here for a few minutes, then he got a call, and they hightailed it out of here to his house—I overheard a couple of them saying that's where they were going. You know where it is?"

Dimitri nodded. "More or l-less. We'll find it."

"I'll go with you. I can lead you to it." Angus gave Dimitri a sharp look. "But only to keep your mate safe. Maybe she'll figure out to dump you and find a Lupine who can look after her."

"Not gonna happen," Jaycee said, her mouth turning down.

Dimitri, damn him, put on his laid-back, red wolf smile. "G-go ahead, try to k-keep her in line. I d-dare you. I'll laugh my ass off watching." He banged his feet to the floor and came up in a sweep of long legs. "Let's g-go."

Jaycee clung to Dimitri's back as they rode south through New Orleans in the direction of Brice's house. Though the night was sultry, she couldn't shake her coldness. This weather was meant for lazing on a porch, watching the stars, or being with friends at an outdoor café, drinking wine and laughing. Not for plotting an extraction that might turn into a nasty battle.

Angus led them on his motorcycle with Ben right behind him, Jaycee and Dimitri following. Jaycee felt Dimitri's tension in his body, though she knew the tension came from excitement, not worry.

Dimitri loved a good fight. He was hard to beat in the fight club ring, and the only reason he ever lost was because he had to follow rules.

Dimitri free of rules was unstoppable. She'd seen him bring down ferals or Shifter hunters without breaking a sweat. One moment his attackers would be pounding at him; the next, on their backs in a state of unconsciousness. Dimitri could be ruthless when he needed to be.

Brice's house was as dark and quiet when they pulled up as it had been when they'd first come here. The blackout curtains were in place, no vehicles in front. The porch lights were on to make the house look lived in, but there was no sign of who actually lived there.

Jaycee had to wonder what the neighbors thought, or if they knew who Brice was and chose to keep secret that Shifters hung out there. Because they were decent people and didn't want to see Shifters be hurt by Shifter Bureau? Or did Brice have them coerced with threats of some kind?

Angus and Ben waited for Dimitri and Jaycee to pull up around the back, where the entrance was equally dark.

"Sure you want to do this?" Angus asked Dimitri in a low voice. "He'll know you're coming."

"Yep." Dimitri hung his helmet on the handlebar. "I'm t-tired of this guy. I want him shut away and waiting for . . ." He stopped before he said the name *Dylan*. Angus only needed to know so much.

"Let's do this," Jaycee said softly.

Dimitri, of course, took the lead, too impatient to do it any other way. Angus insisted on walking behind him and wanted Jaycee behind *him*, Ben to bring up the rear. Ben readily agreed, and Jaycee conceded. It made sense. If Brice got around Dimitri and Angus, Jaycee could bring him down with leopard swiftness, and Ben would be on hand to back her up.

Dimitri waited in the shadows of the garage behind the house. The porch light to the back door wasn't on, but there were a few lights shining in upper windows.

Jaycee heard Dimitri's wolf snarl come. He stripped off his clothes, leaving them behind a shrub, then began to shift, arms and legs sprouting fur and claws, teeth and muzzle growing. When he was halfway between beast and man, he turned to Jaycee, giving her a look from his gray-white eyes.

She knew what he meant, what he always said when they went into danger on a mission. *Stay safe, sweetheart. See you on the other side.*

They didn't have to say it anymore. Jaycee knew. She

gave Dimitri a nod, acknowledging him. *You got it. Mate of my heart.*

Mate of my heart was new, but Jaycee had always known it was true. It had simply taken her a long time to acknowledge it.

Dimitri growled again, charged across the open space between garage and house, and kicked the back door in.

It fell open after one blow. Dimitri was already inside, ducking away from the doorframe in case someone was there waiting to attack. He slipped into the shadows, and Angus followed him as quickly.

Jaycee moved even faster than the wolves, skimming down the back hall and coming to land in a crouch near the opening that led to the main hall. The room beyond was dark, no lights on, no one partying or cleaning up.

Ben sauntered inside last and stopped near Jaycee. "You guys know no one's in here, right?" he asked in a normal voice.

Jaycee rose and began to make her way to the living room. Dimitri got there first, as did Angus. Jaycee sensed Ben following her closely, his warmth on her back.

The entire first floor was dark, silent. The Shifters moved soundlessly, and Ben didn't make any noise at all. Jaycee wondered if his glam could affect hearing as well as sight.

The only light they could see came from the upper hall. Dimitri swarmed up the stairs without hesitation or discussion. He knew, as Jaycee did, that they had to do this with shock and surprise, catch Brice and his people off-guard so they didn't have time to fight back or flee.

Except Brice's people didn't seem to be around. Jaycee caught Angus by the shirt as he prepared to ascend after Dimitri.

"You said they were here," she said in a fierce voice. "What are you leading us into?"

"I thought they were." Angus's scowl increased. "They said they were coming. They should be here."

Jaycee let him go. Angus's surprised bafflement seemed genuine, and she scented no deceit on him.

As Angus moved up the stairs after Dimitri. Jaycee paused to pull her leather tunic off over her head, leaving her in the form-fitting tank top, easier to move in than the tunic.

She hurried up after Angus, wanting to catch Dimitri before he kicked in any more doors. If Brice was behind one waiting to strike, she wanted to be next to Dimitri to defend him.

A noise came to them. Very faint, but it had all three Shifters and Ben freezing in place. The light at the top of the stairs illuminated them, including Ben, who must have dropped his glam.

Jaycee heard it again. A vague thumping, followed by a muffled groan.

Dimitri's between-beast's hearing pinpointed it. He strode down the hall on strong legs and knocked in a door to a bedroom with a double-kick.

"Honey, I'm *home*!" he sang out.

Angus was right behind him, and Jaycee ran to catch up. She made it to the bedroom to see Dimitri stop abruptly in surprise, shrinking back down to his human form.

On the floor, alone in the empty bedroom, was Casey, feet and hands tied, duct tape over his mouth. He'd been beaten to a bloody pulp, his face dark with bruises and abrasions. The sounds were groans in his throat and the pathetic tapping of one of his wolf paws he'd managed to move on the board floor.

CHAPTER TWENTY-ONE

Dimitri dropped to his knees beside Casey, but before he could reach for the man, Jaycee was there. Her competent fingers closed around the duct tape, easing it gently from his mouth.

"Casey," she said, her hand on his shoulder. "We're here. Tell us what happened."

Dimitri waited as Casey tried to look at them. One of his eyelids had been ripped, the eye so smashed Dimitri wondered if he'd ever see from it again. Dimitri rested his hand on a relatively blood-free patch of Casey's shirt, knowing touch comforted and could start the healing process.

Casey would need more than touch—he'd need a doctor or a Shifter healer. For now the man edged toward Jaycee, seeking her comfort.

"Brice," Casey croaked.

"Brice did this to you?" Jaycee asked in a dangerous voice. She bent closer so Casey wouldn't have to strain to speak. "Or had his Shifters do it?"

Casey managed a nod. "I didn't want to go."

Angus bent down on his other side, suddenly alert. "Go where? Case, it's me, Angus."

"Yeah, I thought I saw your ugly mug." Casey attempted a smile, but it died quickly. "He took them. I didn't really believe he would."

"Took them where?" Dimitri asked without a stumble.

Casey turned his working eye, bloodshot and full of tears, toward Dimitri. "He liked you. He wanted to wait for you."

So maybe Brice *didn't* know Dimitri and Jaycee had been planning to betray him tonight. But maybe Brice had figured out that Dylan was coming for him and had taken his Shifters to some remote place Dylan would never find him.

Jaycee asked gently, "Wait for us to do what, Casey?"

"They wouldn't let him," Casey said, giving her an imploring look. "They took them all. I didn't want to go. So they beat me down."

"Who did?" Dimitri asked urgently. "Come on, Casey. Where did Brice go?"

"Basement," Casey whispered. "Down there."

Dimitri remembered the cellar turned rec room and bar. "What's so special about the basement?" And why would Brice have Casey beaten if he didn't want to go down to it? Dimitri didn't ask the last question, not wanting to task Casey with too much at once.

"Maeve went," Casey said sadly. "She let them hurt me. Didn't protect."

"What?" Jaycee said, rage in her voice. "She's your *mate*. She had no business not protecting you, even if she disagreed with you."

Good to know Jaycee felt that way, Dimitri thought, his heart warming. "Peace, Jase. Why the basement, Casey? What's down there? What's going to jump out at us when we go to rip the bastard apart?"

Casey looked a bit surprised. "I've been praying. Praying to the Goddess to help me. I didn't really think *you'd* be her angel of mercy, Dimitri." He tried to laugh and coughed up blood.

Ben knelt next to him. "Do *not* move. I'm going to take

care of you, all right? But you have to tell Dimitri what to
expect. Are Brice and his crew waiting in the basement?"

"No," Casey said, his voice a croak. "*They* came. And
the Shifters went. Maeve is gone." He started to cry, shaking
with sobs.

Dimitri knew they wouldn't get anything more coherent
out of him. He rose. "Angus, Jase, with me. Ben . . ."

"I'll help him the best I can." Ben gave Dimitri a black-
eyed stare. "If you need me, you scream. I'm short, but I'm
great in a fight."

"No," Casey whispered. "All of you go. Find out what
happened. They can't hurt me anymore."

Ben didn't like that, and neither did Jaycee. Dimitri became aware that they all turned to him, the alpha in the
room, to make the decision about who did what.

It was true that Dimitri could use Ben and his strange
senses that were Shifter-like but different. He also didn't
want Jaycee out of his sight, and he didn't trust Angus
enough yet to leave him behind.

He drew a breath. "M-make him as comfortable as p-possible, Ben, and join us. Angus, Jase, you're with m-me."

Jaycee had risen next to him, and now she slid her hand
into Dimitri's, her fingers cool and strong.

"Let's go see what we see," she said.

She tugged at Dimitri, but Dimitri made sure he led the
way out.

The house remained silent as they descended. Jaycee liked
that Dimitri didn't shake off her hand or again insist that
she bring up the rear. Her position put her next to Dimitri,
where she could protect him.

They moved quickly and noiselessly to the door to the
basement stairs, which led into more darkness. Jaycee's
nerves prickled, and she wanted to shift. Her skin itched
with it, her leopard growling.

Don't go into the basement. Wasn't that the first rule of
horror movies? Jaycee had always considered that the hu-

mans who rushed down the steps at the first noise were fools. Why didn't they wait, listen, scent for danger? But humans weren't good at that, and humans in movies always seemed too stupid to live.

Dimitri led the way, the tension that came through his hand telling her he felt the same uneasiness. There was danger there, though Jaycee couldn't smell much. Shifters, yes, but she didn't scent a group, not the several dozen Shifters that had filled this house the first time they'd come.

She did smell smoke—not of fire, but of something sweet and stuffy, like incense. Sage, she recognized as they descended. Jasmine used it when she did psychic readings.

The incense had been burned in a brazier. Jaycee knew that not from the scent but because she saw the brazier on the stand as Dimitri carefully opened the door at the bottom of the stairs—no reckless kicking this time.

The brazier glowed faintly, its flames already spent. Its dim light glinted on the glasses hanging over the bar and on the mirror in its frame. The mirror looked misty, as though the smoke dusted it.

No one was here. No Shifters, no humans, nothing. Angus fumbled along the wall and flipped a switch, flooding the room with light.

A chalk circle had been drawn on the floor in front of the bar, the outline smudged here and there with a brown-red substance. Blood. Jaycee's leopard growled, and her nose wrinkled in distaste.

"I don't like this," Angus said. "The whole place stinks of magic."

"Brice is a Goddess fanatic," Jaycee said. "Maybe this was another of his rituals. Whatever it was, it's over now, and everyone's gone."

Dimitri moved behind the bar, keeping his eye on the mirror. Beer bottles, open and unopened, rested on the counter. Dimitri put his hand around an unopened one.

"Still c-cool."

Ben had come in while they checked over the room. "They haven't been gone long, then," he remarked.

Jaycee turned to him. "You were already here, in the group, before we arrived that first night. Did you have time to explore the house? Are there secret exits? Tunnels? Kendrick always made sure we had a back way out for whenever we had to escape and scatter. Did Brice have a similar thing?"

Ben shrugged. "Not sure. He was good at having his Shifters come and go without being seen by humans in the neighborhood as long as they didn't leave all at the same time. No mass exodus. But think about it—if all his Shifters had escaped through a secret door or tunnel, we would have noticed Shifters milling around as we rode into the neighborhood. We didn't see much of anyone."

Angus growled softly. His hair had become a little shaggier, his eyes so gray they were almost white. "I'm thinking they didn't leave here alive," he said.

"I don't smell death," Jaycee countered, and Dimitri gave a slight shake of his head. He didn't either.

"Not death. Taken." Angus's voice grew more guttural as he shifted to his half beast, a huge black wolf, his shirt tearing. "Death comes later."

"I don't think he's wrong," Ben said. "What ritual did they do here? What did it summon? Or do to them?"

Jaycee slid out her phone. "I'll call Kendrick. He's a Guardian—he'll know about Goddess rituals. Or if this even was a Goddess ritual. Plus, he can tell us if Dylan is close."

"Dylan?" Angus swung around. "Dylan Morrissey?"

Jaycee started and looked up. She hadn't meant the name to come out of her mouth, but then, she supposed it didn't matter now. The Shifter Dylan expected them to have ready for him was gone.

"What do you have to do with Dylan Morrissey?" Angus demanded, his voice edged with fury.

"As little as p-possible," Dimitri answered. "But he wants Brice."

"You're from the Austin Shiftertown?" Angus's glare didn't soften.

"Not exactly," Jaycee said. "But we occasionally work with them."

Angus swung on Dimitri. "You know that Dylan's been pulling Shifters out of Shiftertowns and carting them off Goddess knows where, right? Some have gone from our town, and our leader is not stopping it from happening."

Jaycee moved to face Angus. "What are you talking about? Dylan's an arrogant pain in the ass, but I don't think he'd do *that*."

"You're naive, then." Angus switched his glare to her. "It's been going on for a few years now. What is he doing with these Shifters? Killing them? Imprisoning them? Selling them?"

Jaycee listened with disquiet. She trusted the Morrissey family now, though she hadn't when they'd first moved to Texas, before she'd seen how Liam and Sean took care of their families and their Shifters. Dylan was a little more frightening—he was an old-school Shifter, having lived a long time before Shiftertowns were ever conceived. He'd lived longer than most Shifters, period.

She knew Dylan always had something going on, whether he was tracking Shifters like Brice, or keeping his eye on Shifter Bureau, or working with Shifter leaders in other towns, especially those in Las Vegas, North Carolina, and Montana.

If what Angus said was true, and if he wasn't wrong, then Dylan must have a reason for making Shifters disappear. She wondered if Kendrick knew, and what he thought about it. Or, Jaycee went on, her heart sinking, if Kendrick was helping him.

Jaycee glanced at Ben. He was examining the circle on the floor, keeping his face averted. Jaycee noticed, with heightened Shifter concern, that Ben was perspiring and breathing faster than usual.

"Ben, you knew about this?" she asked sharply. "About what Dylan is doing?"

Ben lifted his head, his eyes carefully neutral. "Why should I?"

Jaycee folded her arms. "Because you run a lot of errands for Dylan. I'm guessing that you're here because of him too, but that he sent you on a *different* errand from the one he sent us on. The fact that we're in the same place is a coincidence."

Ben's usual good-natured expression died as he straightened, the friendly light in his eyes vanishing. As he looked sharply at her, Jaycee became fully aware that she faced an ancient being, one who'd existed for a thousand years and who did things for his own reasons. If Ben was ever helpful and companionable, that was by his choice.

"It's nothing I'm going to discuss with you, Jase," he said quietly. "There are reasons for everything. That's all I will say."

Angus grunted. "Maybe Brice was right to throw you off the balcony."

Ben held up his hands. "I wouldn't go that far. Pain does *not* get easier to bear with age, trust me. But about all this . . ." He gestured around the room. "I'm in the dark. I don't think Dylan had anything to do with it. The circle and the brazier are used in Goddess rituals, but I'm not thinking the Goddess reached down and snatched them all to the Summerland."

Jaycee shrugged. "Who knows? Casey believes it."

"Casey is gullible and wants to believe something wonderful will happen to faithful Shifters," Ben said. "That's how he strikes me."

Angus snorted a laugh. "You have him spot-on. He's one of my clan. I told him not to trust Brice, but Casey is too nice for his own good. He's why Brice lit into me, and why I stuck around to keep an eye on him and the fanatic Shifters."

Good for Angus. Jaycee felt more affinity for him. She'd have done the same thing if Shifters from Kendrick's group had been enticed to join Brice.

No, she'd have been more direct, like knocking the deluded Shifters upside the head and dragging them home. Or taking down Brice, which is what she wanted to do now.

Dimitri was rummaging behind the bar. He came up with a butane lighter in this hand. "How about if we s-see what they were up t-to?"

Jaycee did *not* want him to touch the lighter's flame to

the brazier, but Dimitri had already done it before she could protest.

Sage smoke began to rise almost immediately, sweet smelling and making Jaycee cough. Ben didn't seem to mind it, the man standing in a cloud of smoke without wincing. Angus sneezed.

Dimitri had come alert while Jaycee coughed, her eyes tearing up until her vision blurred. He abruptly hauled himself across the bar, caught Jaycee around the waist, and yanked her backward so hard she came off her feet.

He'd do that only for a good reason, Jaycee knew, even as she fought to regain her balance. Angus was moving hastily back from the brazier as well, though Ben stayed still, curiosity in his bright eyes.

Smoke had fallen to curl around the outline of the circle. The thin haze rose like a curtain, a barrier between the basement and the inside of the ring. Growls filled Jaycee's throat.

Light flashed behind the smoke. With it came noise. Not a roar or strange sounds, but the noises of people shouting, arguing, and, incongruously, laughing. Jaycee also heard snarls and growls—Shifter sounds. Over all this was a stench like acrid smoke and sulfur.

The noise abruptly cut off, but the light remained, growing brighter and brighter until Jaycee had to screw up her eyes and turn away.

She met the bulk of Dimitri, who wouldn't move. Fine. She didn't mind hanging on to him, burying her face in his warm chest.

When the light died and Dimitri stiffened, Jaycee looked around. Angus shifted all the way to wolf, the rest of his clothes falling in shreds around him. Ben remained stoic, folding his arms. Dimitri growled, the sound rumbling in his chest.

Two people stood inside the circle. One was Brice, who glared at them in fury. The other was a tall, thin man with hair the color of old bronze and eyes as black as Ben's. He wore clothing made of leather and fur with rings of metal clinking in them, and he held a sword.

The thin man stared around him with a look of amazement, right before Angus leapt at him.

The man's astonishment dropped away. He spun out of the circle, sword ready, meeting the attack with professional skill. Angus, just as skilled, redirected his leap to land on Brice, his teeth and claws tearing into the big man, his impact shoving him through the smoke and into the bar.

The rest of them had already moved. Jaycee charged to assist Angus, and Dimitri shifted to half beast and went for the guy with the sword, even as the man turned to continue his sword strike on Angus.

Dimitri and the swordsman went down in a tangle, Ben throwing himself in to help. Brice began his shift to bear—once he became grizzly, he'd be very tough to fight. Shifting obviously took him a few minutes, however, plus Brice was hampered by Angus's attacking him. Both Angus's and Brice's Collars were sparking, but neither paid attention.

Jaycee was much faster at shifting. She had her party-fighting clothes off in a second, and in the next second, she was leopard.

Bears were big, strong, deadly, but leopards were quick and precise. Jaycee sprang, her claws finding Brice's throat as it grew thick with fur. She connected, blood coating her paws, but the fur and wattles on the bear's neck saved him.

Brice threw her off, rising on his hind legs to full bear height. He had a huge grizzly muzzle and the razor-sharp claws of his breed, the claws twice as long as those on a wild bear.

Jaycee dodged as Brice slashed at her. She leapt onto the top of the bar, all four paws landing easily on its polished wood; then she pushed off in the next heartbeat, straight for Brice. He lifted his claws to catch her, but Jaycee could change direction in midair. Angus took advantage of Brice's distraction to tackle him, making contact with his stomach, allowing Jaycee to land on top of Brice's head.

Brice roared, trying to twist around to grab Jaycee with his mouth, finishing her with one bite. Jaycee clawed streaks of red into his ears and leapt away again. She landed on the other side of the room, spinning to gauge her next attack. This was fun.

So she thought until she saw Dimitri. He was fighting the sword guy, his red fur bristling, his teeth and claws moving. He should have been able to take down a non-Shifter in a short moment, never mind his sword, but the guy was an amazing fighter.

The man writhed and spun in Dimitri's grip, stabbing fiercely, coming to his feet with his sword bloody and a knife flashing into his other hand. Dimitri was hurt, but not badly, not that he ever let wounds slow him down. He plunged back into the fight without stopping.

Ben had a knife as well, a long dark blade with a wicked point that looked old but deadly. His expression furious, he plunged the blade at the swordsman.

The swordsman saw it coming, his eyes widening with the first fear Jaycee had seen in him. He spun away at the last minute, avoiding the blade, which sent him directly into Dimitri.

The swordsman engaged with Dimitri, and the two of them went down in a ball of fur and blades. Ben circled them, trying to find an opening, but the fighters moved too fast.

Jaycee saw all this in a flash before she was leaping back at Brice. Brice had turned his attention to Angus, bringing his great paws around in an attempt to catch Angus around the rib cage. Angus dropped, trying to slither out of reach, but Brice's claws dug a gouge into his back. Angus howled, the howl cutting off as he sank his teeth into Brice's paw behind his claws.

Jaycee landed on Brice's back. Brice shook himself to dislodge her, which also hurtled Angus back and forth. But wolves, once they had a death grip, didn't let go. Angus held on, biting to the bone, Brice snarling in pain.

Jaycee raked her paws across Brice's face and neck, contacting with his Collar, which was sparking. Brice roared in pain and rage.

Jaycee tasted triumph. They'd have this bear down and

nearly meat, ready to hand him on a platter to Dylan and Kendrick.

What she and Dimitri would do with the swordsman, which her leopard knew was one of the hated Fae, she didn't know. They'd have to get his weapons away from him and truss him up in iron chains, maybe knock him out with a tranq. Dylan might simply kill him. Dylan was careful about humans, knowing hurting any would blow back on all Shifters, but he didn't give a shit about the Fae.

Jaycee saw a flurry of movement from the corner of her eye; then Angus began to scream. His mouth opened involuntarily, releasing Brice, and he fell to the floor, wolf howls turning to human cries of deepest anguish as he shifted. Jaycee stared in surprise, her start allowing Brice to throw her off.

She tumbled backward from his grizzly strength but got her feet under her and landed easily.

The swordsman had managed to twist away from Dimitri, who was scrambling up, having shifted all the way to his wolf. The Fae had his sword firmly in his hand, the point stretched out and touching Angus's Collar. The Collar flared with blue light, and Angus howled in pure agony.

Jaycee's leopard scream filled the room as she went for the swordsman. Dimitri reached him first, tackling him to the floor.

The swordsman spun to his feet with astonishing agility and slammed his sword to Dimitri's Collar.

Nothing happened. The swordsman looked puzzled but he held the sword to the fake Collar, his bare arms stiffening with muscle.

Dimitri shifted back to human. Stark naked, he remained flat on his back on the floor and tucked his hands behind his head as he looked up at the swordsman. "Psych!" he yelled.

CHAPTER TWENTY-TWO

Cold fear flooded Jaycee. Dimitri continued to laugh, lounging in front of the Fae as though they were on a beach and he teased a clueless human. The point of the sword was right at Dimitri's throat, an inch away from ending his life.

She saw the Fae realize that too. His brows came down and he eased the sword back the smallest bit to drive the point home.

Dimitri slapped the blade between his hands, his laughter gone. He jerked, and the sword came out of the Fae's grip.

Brice, bleeding and hurt but furious, hurtled himself at Dimitri. Jaycee ran at Brice to stop him. Angus, released, could only lie on the floor, rocking in agony.

The Fae recovered almost instantly from being disarmed and had his knife ready, slashing it at Dimitri, who lay between his booted feet.

Ben had circled behind the Fae, ready to thrust his black knife into the man's back. Jaycee reached Brice.

The moment Jaycee made her leap, Brice pummeled into

the half-sitting Dimitri and the Fae swordsman. His momentum took all three of them into the circle, where wisps of brazier smoke still drifted.

Angus rolled out of the way, his face gray, his breathing hard. He came to all fours, shifting creakingly back to wolf.

Jaycee's paws connected with Brice. At the same time, light flashed within the circle, and something bright and hot, like an explosion, ripped her from Brice and sent her tumbling back.

She landed and whirled, ready to charge again. Angus, closer, went for the circle, but Ben leapt in his way. "No!"

The light flared brighter and brighter, but Jaycee remained in place, determined not to turn away. Her mouth went dry, her heart hammering. Dimitri was in there. *Dimitri* . . .

The light cleared and died. The smoke curled upward and dispersed to show an empty circle drawn with chalk on the floor.

The swordsman, Brice, and Dimitri were gone.

"*No!*" The cry burst from Jaycee's human throat, her leopard flowing away as every fear engulfed her. She sprinted across the room, landing facedown in the circle, beating the floor with her bare hands. "No! Bring it back! Bring it back! *Dimitri!*"

The smooth cement floor yielded nothing. Jaycee's hands stung, her skin scraped away as she pounded the floor.

A strong grip pulled her from the circle, but Jaycee fought back. "Light the brazier. Bring him back!"

It was Ben who lifted her to her feet with incredible strength and turned her to face him. "Jaycee—stop."

Tears streaked from Jaycee's eyes, no rational part of herself able to make them cease. She beat on Ben's chest with her fists. "Find him! Why aren't you doing anything? Open it!"

Angus, bleeding and winded, staggered toward them. "Fire's gone."

Jaycee jerked from Ben's grasp to swing toward the brazier. The coals inside were gray, spent, and collapsed to ash before her eyes.

"A fire doesn't die that quickly," she said, rushing to the brazier and shaking it. "It was burning high."

The ash lay cold at the bottom of the bowl, no glow to say it had been lit anytime today. The sage likewise was nothing but cinders.

Jaycee screamed. She flung the brazier and its contents to the middle of the circle. A cloud of ash rose, stinging Jaycee's eyes and making Angus and Ben cough.

Nothing happened. The circle was nothing but chalk, the floor dirty with dead coals and burned sage.

Jaycee jerked herself around to face Ben and Angus. "We have to go after him. We have to find him."

"And we will." Ben looked grim. "I'll get you there, Jaycee. Promise. Dylan's coming. He can—"

"Screw Dylan," Jaycee said viciously. "*He's* why Dimitri has been snatched by the Fae. We were doing Dylan a fucking favor."

"I agree," Angus said, his voice rasping, though sounding stronger. "What can Dylan possibly do anyway? Brice is a Fae lover. Damn it, I should have just killed him when I had a chance."

"If you two will let me finish . . ." Ben's hard voice cut through their words. "Dylan knows a Fae, one who takes the Shifters' side. He might be able to find Dimitri."

Angus huffed. "Dylan is friends with a Fae? I should have known."

"This Fae's not that bad." Ben drew a breath as if to argue his point, then shook his head. "Not important right now. Let me talk to him."

Jaycee broke in. "I know the Fae you mean—Fionn, right? The father of Sean Morrissey's mate? That only works if Dylan and Fionn think it's worth it to find Dimitri. Dimitri's a nobody in the eyes of someone like Dylan. Dimitri's not a leader, not a Guardian, not a healer. He's a tracker. Expendable."

"Kendrick wouldn't think so," Ben said.

That observation calmed Jaycee's panic slightly—of course Kendrick would make every effort to help Dimitri—but it didn't curb her impatience. "I can't stand here and wait for Dylan—he might be hours away." She marched to Ben. "You, Fae creature, are going to help me figure out how to open a way and find Dimitri."

Angus had one hand on his own shoulder, working his arm as though trying to put his muscles back into place. "How?" he asked her. "Gates to Faerie need some kind of magic, like the circle here or standing stones. No standing stones in New Orleans that I know of. Not real ones, anyway."

"No, but I know where there is probably a ley line and a house with a ton of magic in it," Jaycee said before Ben could speak. "That weird door leads to somewhere. You can work with that."

"*I* can?" Ben placed his hands on his chest. "Sweetheart, no one is going to let me into Faerie. Banished, remember? Do you know what *banished* means?"

"You don't have to go inside. You only have to open a way. If Dylan arrives before you figure it out, fine. Otherwise, it's on you, goblin."

"*I'll* go with you, Jaycee." Angus picked up the remains of his T-shirt, studied it, and dropped it with a look of resignation.

"Thanks, Angus, but I'll travel faster without you."

Angus gave her a gray-eyed wolf stare. "I'm not letting an unprotected female into a place full of Fae and dumb-ass Shifters. You'll need someone to help you fight. I've got your back."

Jaycee's next words died on a breath of anguish. She and Dimitri always said that to each other, which often led to a bantering argument. *Don't worry, Dimitri, I've got your back.*

No, I've got your back, Dimitri would growl in return.

We can't both be watching each other's backs, Jaycee would say. *Someone has to be in front.*

Yeah, Dimitri would counter. *Me.*

Jaycee, triumphant. *Like I said, I've got your back.*

She almost broke down and cried. But if she did that, she wouldn't be able to see, and she now had to ride Dimitri's motorcycle all the way to the house.

D imitri woke with a groan. Something heavy and smelly lay on top of him, and it was raining—a cold, sharp rain scented with resin.

Dimitri pushed. His hands contacted with a body, large and hard with muscle. The smell was scared Shifter. *Not* what he wanted to wake up with.

He preferred Jaycee, with her soft curves and sweetly scented hair, her kisses of heat. Shit, who *wouldn't* want to wake up with her?

Dimitri shoved again with both fists. The Shifter on top of him, as naked as he was, toppled slowly off.

It was Brice. The man had been knocked out, his face bruised and bloody, most likely from Dimitri's wolf.

Dimitri's awareness flooded back, and with it, worry. He remembered the fight in the basement, the Fae with the sword, the flash of light, and then nothing.

He sat up straight. He lay in woods full of dead leaves, the air cold, the rain like fine needles. No more August in southern Louisiana. He might have been high in the mountains in the western United States or Canada, though he felt no effects of altitude.

Wherever it was, Dimitri was cold and wet, and a fucking Fae was running around loose somewhere.

Dimitri climbed to his feet. He was naked, his clothing still folded neatly outside Brice's back door in New Orleans. His phone was back there too, though he had a feeling he'd never find a cell signal in this woods.

He flowed down into the red wolf, thick fur being much better for this climate than uncovered human skin. Brice smelled worse when Dimitri was in this form, and his nose wrinkled.

There was no sign of the Fae with the sword. Had he run off when they'd landed here, or was the guy still in Brice's basement? Dimitri didn't like that idea, but at the moment, he could do nothing about it.

Brice would die if left out here exposed in the cold. On the other hand, if Dimitri woke him up, Brice might try to kill him again.

Dimitri gave an inward sigh, cursed himself for being such a nice guy, and smacked Brice's face with his paw. Brice groaned, feebly batted at the paw, and finally opened his eyes.

Dimitri growled, sticking his nose into Brice's face. *Stay down and tell me where the hell we are.*

Brice drew a breath, looked around, and relaxed. "It's all right, my friend. We've come home."

That settled it. Brice was bat-crap crazy. He was awake now and could shift to bear and survive, so Dimitri gave another growl, turned his back, and trotted away into the woods.

So . . . all he needed to do now was figure out where he was and how to get out of here.

Putting his nose to the ground and sniffing didn't help much. He picked up his own back trail, but it led about twenty feet to another spot in the woods and died there. Presumably, Dimitri had staggered from there to the place he'd woken, and collapsed.

He did pick up the acrid smell of the Fae with the sword; that trail led from the place Dimitri was now, deeper into the woods. So he *had* run off. Why he hadn't stopped to stab Dimitri to death while Dimitri was passed out, he had no idea.

Dimitri sniffed hard all around the place his trail ended, knowing he must have entered Faerie in that spot. The white light, the circle, the sage, the fire—all the magic shit he hated—had transported him here, and he knew it. Gates to Faerie could be anywhere, as long as there was a ley line nearby and something Fae to take a person through. Dimitri had been fighting an actual Fae, right on top of a magic circle, so no big surprise that he was now in the mystical land of Faerie.

Dimitri's ancestors had been born here. Many centuries before, diabolical Fae had jumbled together DNA laced with magic, probably by means more disturbing than test tubes, and had come up with Shifters. Bears, big cats, and wolves, bred to be their fighting beasts. Shape-shifters with the emotions and cunning of humans and the strength and agility of whatever animal they turned into.

Home, Brice had called it. Deep inside the wolf, Dimitri's human brain was troubled. This asshole truly believed Shifters should return to Faerie, to once again work for the Fae—be slaves to them, more like. Dylan had been right.

The other fear that streaked through both wolf and human side was for Jaycee. She'd been running toward the circle when the light had flashed. Had she been pulled inside as well? Was she even now in chains with that Fae bastard with the sword, and what was the guy doing to her?

The thought made Dimitri charge back to Brice, who was still trying to stand up.

Dimitri shifted to his half beast, which allowed his mouth to form words. "Where are they?" he demanded. "Where would they have taken her?"

Brice blinked, then shook himself and got stiffly to his feet. He was a big man with no clothing, which was not something Dimitri wanted to see, but he was too agitated to worry about it at the moment.

Brice rose all the way, smoothed back his dark hair, and looked down at Dimitri with a hint of a smile through his bruises. "Dimitri, my friend, you didn't stammer once when you said that."

"You're not my friend, and I don't give a rat's ass. Where would they have taken Jaycee?"

Brice shook his head, more like he was trying to clear it than to express a negative. "Jaycee's not here. She didn't make it."

"Didn't make it?" More ice seared his veins. "What do you mean, she didn't make it?"

Brice lifted his hands. "Relax. I mean she didn't come

through the gate with us. She didn't make it in time. Calm down—really. You're safe now."

Dimitri glanced around the woods, which looked endless in all directions. "We're in Faerie, you idiot. No wonder it stinks. By no stretch of the imagination are we safe. How do we get back?"

"*We* don't. Only the Fae know how."

Dimitri snarled. He lunged at Brice, putting his claws around the man's big, stupid throat, where the cool ring of a Collar rested. "We're going back. *Now.*"

Brice only looked at him. Dimitri saw him regain his strength, his confidence, right before he raised his arms, now giant bear paws, and broke Dimitri's hold. Dimitri took one step back but no more. Brice regarded him narrowly, planting his bear paws on his human hips—which looked ridiculous. The man had lost all sense of shame.

"Simeon's fort isn't far. You'll understand once you talk to him."

"Talk? How can I talk to a Fae? I don't understand their language. And who the fuck is Simeon? That Fae who tried to control me with his sword?" Satisfaction seeped through Dimitri's worry. "Surprised the hell out of him when it didn't work."

Brice didn't share his amusement. "No, he was just a soldier. Simeon is the leader of this area, which are the lands of his clan. I told him about you and Jaycee. He'll want to see you."

Dimitri allowed himself some measure of relief. If Brice wasn't lying, then Jaycee hadn't been pulled into Faerie, at least not that Brice knew of. She'd be in New Orleans, with Dylan on his way. Dylan would take her to Kendrick, and Kendrick would keep Jaycee safe. She'd be all right.

Sure. Dimitri knew Jaycee. She'd fight like hell to come after Dimitri, to search for him. She'd be up in Dylan's and Kendrick's faces until they mounted a rescue, the crazy woman. One reason why he loved her.

Yes, he loved her, Dimitri thought, his heart filling with

exultation. No shame in it. Shifters—and humans—who tried to fight falling in love, who tried to convince themselves they didn't need love in their lives—were just stupid.

Fall, you idiots. The landing is fantastic.

"You don't need to be afraid of him, Dimitri," Brice was saying. His kind, patient voice was back. "It's not what you think."

"I think your mind has been warped by fast-talking Fae," Dimitri said. "Why'd you run from the club tonight? Or was it last night?" He looked around at the gray sky above the trees. It seemed to be daytime again, so they must have been out a while, though he'd heard time probably ran differently in Faerie. "Whenever. Did you hear Dylan was coming for you?"

"I did, yes." Brice gave him a nod. "I have eyes and ears everywhere, my friend. I wanted to take my Shifters to safety before he found us."

"So they're all here?" Dimitri asked. "Your followers, including Maeve, who deserted her own mate?"

"She knows we need her." Brice spread his hands. "I'm sorry I lost Casey, but it couldn't be helped. Is he all right?"

"Hurt, but he'll live," Dimitri said in clipped tones. "Why did you come back through the circle? For us?"

"No, you pulled us back when you lit the brazier. The spell must not have dispersed yet. I'm glad you opened the way again, though. I didn't want to lose you."

"I'm touched." Dimitri stepped back. "Make another spell—send me back."

Brice gave him a pitying smile. "I can't. I'm not a mage or a Fae."

"Can this Simeon person do it?"

More of the smile. "I imagine so. He's the most powerful Fae around."

"Good." Dimitri folded his arms. "Let's go see him, then. Better than running around naked in the woods."

"I am pleased I will not have to force you. You will understand, Dimitri, and be glad. The Goddess sent you to me for a reason."

"Blah, blah, blah." Dimitri gestured toward the trees. "Lead on. And stay ahead of me. I want to keep my eye on you."

"Certainly." Brice, happily for Dimitri, closed his mouth and started to walk into the woods—which looked exactly like the woods in all other directions.

Dimitri morphed down into wolf to follow, but Brice stayed human. Just what I need, Dimitri growled to himself. *Instead of cuddling up to Jaycee, I'm following a big bear ass through freezing rain.*

Jaycee would laugh at the pun. Dimitri resolved to do everything he possibly could, including destroying all of Faerie if necessary, to get back to her and hear her laugh again.

The house's front door swung open as soon as Jaycee rumbled up the drive on Dimitri's big Harley. The lights were on as well, the hall's chandelier putting out enough glow to spill past the porch and out into the night.

Jaycee shut off the bike, leapt from it, and raced up the steps as Ben and Angus pulled up behind her. Angus did his best to reach Jaycee so he could enter the house first, Shifter-like, but Jaycee ignored him and pounded inside. She ran into the front sitting room, Angus on her heels.

"Jaycee, will you *stop*?" Angus demanded.

Ben followed them into the small room and leaned on the doorframe to catch his breath. "Never try to keep up with a leopard," he said to Angus. "You'll just hurt yourself. But it's all right. This house is a safe haven."

Angus's dark brows lowered as he took in the room. He'd found replacements for his ripped clothes at Brice's, so he could at least ride through the city and down the highway and not be arrested. The shirt and jeans were too big for him, but Angus didn't seem to notice. He sniffed. "It doesn't smell safe."

"You'll have to trust me on that." Ben pushed himself from the doorway and moved to Jaycee.

She'd stopped in front of the narrow door that led nowhere while Ben and Angus had argued. Rose branches still covered it.

"Can you open this?" she asked Ben. "Where are your lockpicks?"

Ben shook his head. "I don't think it's up to us. We never found the key, remember? I think if the house wanted us to open it, it would have led us to the key."

"What's in there?" Angus asked.

"I don't know." Jaycee's heart beat thick and fast. She had no idea what to do, only her leopard's instinct, which had told her to race to this house and try to wrench open the door.

"There's nothing to say that leads to Faerie," Ben said gently.

Jaycee put her hand on the rose vines. The leaves trembled but only from her jostling the branch. "Maybe it leads wherever you need it to go. This house is full of magic, you said, on a ley line, you think. Who knows what the people who lived here needed?"

"You could be right," Ben conceded. "That doesn't mean I can wave my hand and make the door take us to Dimitri."

Jaycee shook the vines. "Come on. Let me in!"

"Whoa." Angus gripped Jaycee's shoulder, not to yank her away, but to calm her, one Shifter trying to soothe another. "Let's think about this a little bit. Faerie is no place you want to go."

"If Dimitri is there, then it's where I have to be," Jaycee said, her voice breaking.

Angus's hand was warm and comforting. "Dylan's on his way, right? He probably knows a lot more about this than we do."

Jaycee turned to him. Angus watched her with gray eyes that held intelligence and compassion. "I thought you didn't like Dylan," she said.

"I don't, but he has resources. That's why he knows what's going on in every Shiftertown in the country. Probably in the world."

Jaycee knew damn well that if Dylan reached her before

she had this door open, he'd stop her from trying to find Dimitri. He'd chain her up, tranq her, something, and she'd be back at Kendrick's ranch, locked in the basement, by the time she woke up. What the hell would happen to Dimitri then?

"He's my mate," she said to Angus. "I have to go."

Angus, she saw in his eyes, understood. He'd mentioned a cub when they'd asked why he worked at the club, which meant he'd had a mate. Gone now, Jaycee suspected, seeing his pain deep down. It happened too often.

Angus released her. "If you go in, I'm going with you. My mate . . ." He stopped, swallowed. "I'm going with you."

Jaycee turned back to the vines, held on to them with both hands, and put her forehead against the leaves. "Please," she whispered. "Help me find him."

The vines shivered. Jaycee raised her head and then realized that the movement didn't come simply from the vines but from the wall itself. The house was shuddering, not hard, but enough to make the chandelier in the hall clink and the paintings in this room rattle.

Jaycee lifted her hands as the vines slithered out from under her fingers, the door coming into view once more. The rose branches curved themselves around the doorframe, forming a leafy arch.

The bolts on the door drew back on their own, the handle turned, and the door creaked open, showing Jaycee blackness.

She drew a breath, glanced once at Angus and Ben, and took a resolute step forward.

CHAPTER TWENTY-THREE

Angus this time managed to get through the door before Jaycee did. He sprang to her at the last moment, shouldered her aside, and plunged into darkness, Jaycee a step behind him.

Jaycee thought that *nothing* would feel different. Her feet landed on a firm surface like hard-packed earth, and cold air touched her face. She could see only darkness at first, though she swore a gray light like first dawn smudged the edges of her vision.

She turned back. Ben was outlined in the doorway, the bright artificial lights of the room behind him. He couldn't come in, he'd said. Ben leaned forward but was stopped by an invisible barrier, like a reptile trapped behind glass. "Wait," he called. "Take this."

Angus spun back to him before Jaycee could, stepping into the house and closing his hand around the dark-bladed knife Ben had used in the fight in Brice's basement. Angus gave Ben a grim nod and returned to Jaycee.

"Tell Kendrick," Jaycee said to Ben. "Tell him—"

Her words cut off as the door behind her suddenly winked

out, taking Ben with it. At the same time, the world around her lightened with actual dawn.

She and Angus stood just inside a wood. Beside them was an overgrown stump or some kind of pillar, completely covered with moss and ivy. A marker of some sort, perhaps.

Beyond the wood was a swath of grass, not wild but carefully trimmed, and beyond that were hedges and beds full of blossoms that wound in neat patterns around gravel walkways. A stone wall rose at the end of this, with a gate surrounded by rose vines similar to the ones around Jasmine's house.

The rising sun didn't give much light from behind a bank of thick clouds, but enough to glitter on the high, narrow windows of a huge house beyond the wall.

"Not what I expected," Angus growled. He handed Jaycee the knife Ben had given him and adjusted the too-large black T-shirt he'd grabbed from Brice's closet.

"No," Jaycee agreed. This landscape looked tame, civilized. Jasmine's haunted house, overgrown with vines and giant trees, the land fighting the encroachment of the industrialized river, looked far more crumbling and old than this place. As the sky grew lighter, birds began to chirp, like normal birds anywhere.

"Are we in Faerie?" Angus asked. "It's not Louisiana— the woods are wrong. Plus, mountains."

He pointed to the wall of mountains that were becoming visible behind the house as morning light brushed them. High mountains, with snow on their peaks, though the air where Angus and Jaycee stood was cool but not icy.

Jaycee shrugged. "Best way to find out where we are is to look."

She started forward. Angus, doing is best to be alpha, moved to put himself in front of her. The look he gave her as he passed her told her she'd damned well better stay in the rear.

If Jaycee weren't so worried about Dimitri, she'd find his behavior amusing. Dimitri always tried to put Jaycee behind him, but he also trusted her when she wanted to run ahead, knowing she was more cautious about true danger than most other Shifters. If Dimitri were here, they'd be strategizing about how to approach the place, dividing the scouting between them.

She could almost hear his voice, see the eager light in his eyes as they made their plans. Jaycee's throat tightened and sobs threatened to emerge. She gritted her teeth and took a long breath, trying to keep herself under control. She'd find him. She had to.

The gate in the wall opened. Angus and Jaycee halted, fading without speaking into the shadows of trees on the walkway, doing their best to blend with leaves and flickering light.

The person who strolled out was not what Jaycee expected either. It was a woman, tall, with brilliant red hair pulled up under a wide-brimmed hat. She wore flowing garments of dark blue, but they were slim against her body, caught with a belt around her waist, her loose pants tucked into thick boots. She had a basket over one arm and a pair of pruning scissors in the other.

As they watched, the woman walked along the path, stopping every so often to stoop and tug a weed loose with her gloved hand. At one point she tamped down a protruding tuft of earth in a flower bed with her boot, muttering under her breath.

She might have been an ordinary woman coming out to have a look at her garden on a summer morning, except for the fact that her hair in its complicated braids was a brighter red than Jaycee had ever seen before, even from a salon, and the ears that showed when she turned her head were pointed.

The woman lifted her shears to snip a flower from a bush and lay it in her basket, then another. She snipped a third, then she looked up and focused her gaze directly on Jaycee. She had green eyes, so bright Jaycee could see them from twenty feet away.

"You there," the woman said in a perfectly good, clear English. "Shifter woman. Yes, *you*. What the devil do you think you are doing in my garden?"

* * *

When Brice had said "fortress," Dimitri pictured ones he'd seen replicas of in North Carolina—wooden forts against the wilderness in colonial America.

He'd never been to Russia, but he assumed the straight tower he saw on the hill before him could be right out of the European Middle Ages. The stone didn't gleam or have flags snapping in the wind—it wasn't a fairy-tale castle. The fortress was utilitarian, with no windows from ground to roof, except for narrow arrow slits near the top, under the crenellations.

Brice led him to it up a trail that couldn't be called a road by any stretch of the imagination. Dimitri had hiked canyons in Arizona when he'd ducked out for a vacation—pretending he was human, of course. In those canyons and mountains, rocky trails switchbacked up sheer cliffs under wide skies, with not much vegetation to stop a fall if one happened. In the southern part of the state, what would stop you was a cactus or equally prickly brush; not a good way to go.

This trail made those look like paved highways. He and Brice began in woods, on a slope made precarious with loose dirt and dead pine needles. They came out of the woods to cliffs above the tree line—here the path was a foot wide with a solid wall on one side, a sheer drop to vicious-looking rocks on the other.

The tower loomed above them as the trail twisted toward it. As they drew closer, Dimitri saw that the thing had an honest-to-the-Goddess portcullis and drawbridge.

"It's never been taken," Brice said proudly, as though he'd built the castle himself.

"No shit." An attacking army would have a hell of a time making it up this trail, especially if soldiers were in place on top of the castle's walls to shoot downward. "You'd n-need aircraft." Dimitri had reverted to human to climb, wanting to use his hands. With the change, his stammer returned.

"Exactly. Which Fae don't have."

"Why d-didn't they make eagle Shifters?" Dimitri asked. "Eagles c-could at least shit on them."

Brice considered the question thoughtfully. "I don't know. Maybe they tried but the process didn't work. Birds are of lower classification than mammals. Brains are different."

"Birds can fly, and they d-don't put C-Collars on each other," Dimitri said. "Seems like a good trade-off to me."

He closed his mouth then, saving his breath for climbing.

When they reached the drawbridge, which was down, Brice approached the soldier guarding it. The bridge didn't cross a moat; it led over a sheer chasm with who-knew-what at the bottom. Water? Rocks? Dimitri peered over the edge but saw only mist. From this height, it wouldn't matter what was down there—whatever he fell on would make him just as dead.

The soldier wore chain mail woven from silver and so thin it moved with him like a second skin. How it protected him, Dimitri didn't understand, but it was probably overlaid with spells of some kind. Fae loved spells. The soldier had covered this with a few animal skins, one of a wolf knotted around his waist. The skins were of wild animals, not Shifters, but even so, Dimitri's wolf hackles rose and stayed up.

The soldier wore a fierce scowl under light brown hair, his face so thin it looked like skin stretched over an elongated skull. Dimitri had met a Fae—a man called Fionn Cillian, who was the true father of Sean Morrissey's mate. Fionn wasn't a bad guy once you got to know him, but while he resembled this Fae superficially, he looked different in all other respects. Fionn had a heavier build, his face squarer, his hair almost white. But maybe Fae looked different depending on from what part of their world their ancestors originated, as did humans in the human world, or as species of Shifters differed from one another.

Brice spoke to the Fae in the Celtic language Dimitri didn't understand. The fact that Brice spoke it fluently made Dimitri's temper splinter. Brice must have been hanging out with Fae for a while, or at least had made a study of the language, which meant he'd been planning whatever he was up to for some time.

The Fae grunted words back at Brice and jabbed his finger at Dimitri, the finger lowering to point at Dimitri's exposed balls.

Brice sent Dimitri an apologetic look. "The Fae don't like nudity, at least not in public. They think it's barbaric."

"So do h-humans," Dimitri said. "Tell him to move that f-finger or I'll make him eat it."

"I don't think I'll tell him that. He says there are clothes in the guardhouse we should put on."

"F-Fae clothes?" Dimitri's brows shot up. "Forget it."

"Simeon will insist," Brice said, and added, "You don't want him to insist."

The Fae soldier snarled something at Dimitri, his lip curling. Dimitri couldn't answer him in words, so he made his favorite sign with his middle finger. Was it truly universal? From the flash of rage in the Fae's eyes, it was.

"Fuck him," Dimitri said to Brice. "If he doesn't like my h-human shape, I'll use m-my wolf's."

Without waiting for the Fae or Brice to argue with him, Dimitri let his fur ripple out to cover himself as he lowered to all fours. Dimitri hid a wolf grin. Sometimes his shift was awkward, with his hair popping out all at once or each limb changing at a different speed. Jaycee would laugh at him, which made her eyes light.

This time Dimitri's change was as elegant and honed as if he found shifting the easiest thing in the world. He knew he shouldn't get cocky, because next time, it would probably be as tough as usual, but he felt grim satisfaction at the even deeper scowl on the Fae soldier's face.

Dimitri also noted that the soldier was a little warier of him in this form. Good to note.

Brice gave the soldier a shrug as though to say, *Poor, uncivilized Shifter; what does he know?* He then ducked into the guardhouse and came out in an ungainly pair of leggings and a tunic that barely fit his large build.

Dimitri wanted to tell him he looked asinine, but he didn't want to shift again to speak. He satisfied himself with a wolf yip and let Brice lead the way.

The soldier shouted a word through the gate tunnel, and the portcullis began to creak upward. It rose only about five feet before stopping—whether that was as high as it could go or whoever worked the controls saw no reason to raise it all the way, Dimitri had no idea. Brice, in human form, had to bend nearly double to duck beneath it, but Dimitri trotted under it without a problem.

The arched tunnel beyond the portcullis was about twenty feet long, ending in another metal gate. Not iron, but bronze. No iron for the high Fae.

The tunnel's ceiling contained several square holes covered with wooden trap doors. "Murder holes," Brice said. "They can pour boiling oil through them, or throw down boulders, whatever it takes if an enemy gets this far."

Dimitri had heard of murder holes, having at least watched documentaries about European castles on television. He made no sound, only plodded stoically onward.

The guard at the second portcullis unlatched it and pushed it upward. This guard looked almost identical to the first, down to the scowl—Dimitri wondered briefly if they were twins.

Brice gave him a cordial nod and led Dimitri across an open courtyard toward a massive wooden door.

The courtyard, which was paved with surprisingly smooth stones, showed Dimitri the first hint that some of the Fae in this place might actually be regular people. In one corner, men were building something out of wood, sawing and hammering, sleeves rolled up, yelling to each other over noise as they concentrated on the project.

In another part of courtyard men were repairing a wall with mortar. Fae tended to wear their hair long, and these men had theirs looped up in braids, pinned out of their way. More men and a few women scurried across the courtyard between small doors, carrying bags, boxes, or baskets of whatever was needed for the day-to-day working of the fortress.

Soldiers were here as well, keeping to one side of the activity. These soldiers were training, so didn't wear the mail the guards did—rather they had short tunics and close-fitting leggings that allowed them to move. Some were doing such prosaic exercises as sit-ups under the tongue-lashing of a sergeant, a few practiced with swords, others sparred hand to hand.

The Fae in the courtyard ceased what they were doing when Dimitri strolled through, following Brice. Those who didn't see them right away were nudged by their neighbors until they turned around and stared.

No one paid much attention to Brice—his novelty must have worn off, another indication he'd been coming and going to Faerie for some time. They apparently hadn't seen anything like Dimitri, however. No red wolves in Brice's makeshift clan.

Dimitri glanced around him, occasionally meeting the eyes of a Fae, who either became fixed in place or looked quickly anywhere but at Dimitri.

That's right, soak it in. I'll be doing some serious damage later.

In truth, Dimitri knew there were far too many here for him to fight. If he tried to run, one of the guards only had to push him off the drawbridge or wait until he was on the precipitous path below and shoot him with arrows—end of problem.

Dimitri continued to look around, taking in the lay of the land. The people working at the castle had to be able to bring supplies up here with relative ease—no wagons or even horses would be able to make it up the switchback trail to the front gate.

He wondered if they hauled their goods up the side of the castle with pulleys and winches or carried them up through tunnels in the hill to a back door. Dimitri liked the idea of tunnels. Kendrick's underground bunker had been chock-full of tunnels—he and Jaycee had become experts at navigating them.

Brice walked through the courtyard without challenge, again confirming he'd been here many times before. Had the run of the place.

Dimitri followed him, his senses alert. He'd chosen wolf form not because it would make the Fae more comfortable with his nakedness, but because he could hear, scent, even see things his human self wouldn't. He could let his instincts take over.

His instincts did not like the smells he found inside the castle. The large door opened to a wide space encircled by a staircase that led up through the square of the keep. The stairs that twisted upward were stone, flanked by a rickety-looking wooden railing.

The space between the stairs was filled with people occupied by ordinary things—making more repairs to the walls, scrubbing the stone floors, lugging baskets of food into a low-ceilinged hall that must lead to a kitchen. From the smell of things, they kept livestock up here too.

Brice led Dimitri up a flight of stairs, then another. Dimitri peered down through the railings at the working Fae who, like the ones outside, stared at him in amazement with a touch of fear.

So not all Fae were comfortable with the Battle Beasts around. Another good thing to note.

On the second landing, Brice moved down a short hall that ended in a double door. This entrance was guarded by two Fae in the thin silver chain mail. One opened a door and called inside. A sharp voice answered, and then both doors were opened, the Fae stepping back to admit Brice.

Dimitri knew immediately that they'd been admitted into a war room. About a dozen men filled the room—no women in sight—and were studying maps and books with the intensity of generals preparing for battle. The room was high-ceilinged, rising right to the top of the keep, where small openings let in light. There wasn't much sunshine today, so braziers had been lit for warmth and illumination.

A huge tapestry, which must have taken decades to weave, covered one wall. It depicted a battle with plenty of blood and slain horses, Fae, and to Dimitri's distaste, Shifters.

One area of the tapestry caught and held his interest. It showed three white tigers—one on the ground, covered in blood, the other two battling another Shifter, a Lupine, over the body of the fallen tiger. The white tigers seemed to be with a man wearing a gold diadem, the wolf with several soldiers in black armor, their heads covered in helmets with full face guards.

The black metal looked like steel or iron, but that couldn't be. It must be bronze armor painted black, or else those fighters weren't Fae. Hard to tell with their heads completely covered. Plus, it was a tapestry, not a photograph, and there was no telling whether the weavers were depicting real events or ones in their imaginations.

More disquieting than the tapestry was the glass case that rested near it. Dimitri's nose wrinkled as he went to it, rose to put his paws on it, and peered inside.

In the case lay a collection of skulls and bones. They were large and not human—Dimitri saw wolf, bear, and big cat. A stretch of hide bore the black and white stripes that had become familiar to Dimitri since Kendrick had accepted him into his clan. White tiger.

Dimitri turned from the cabinet with a snarl for Brice. *You're in with people who kill your own kind and keep their bones as trophies? The Shifters in this case never had the chance to be sent to dust, to the Summerland, you asshole.*

Dimitri's heart squeezed in horror as his wolf growled the last observation. A Shifter's greatest fear was to die without a Guardian near—the Guardian's sword freed the soul from the body, letting the Shifter enter the afterlife and rest in peace. A soul floating free could be captured, used, tortured.

What had happened to the souls of these dead Shifters? Were they still floating in Faerie, trapped? Dimitri said a silent prayer to the Goddess for them, and for himself. If he died here, he'd suffer the same fate.

"Dimitri." A deep male voice cut across the room. The words were clear as ice and just as cold. "Welcome. I have heard much about you."

CHAPTER TWENTY-FOUR

Jaycee stepped out from under the tree and faced the Fae woman. That lady halted on the path, the shears in her right hand held like a weapon.

"Well?" the woman asked. "How did you get here? Did you come in by the sundial?"

Jaycee resisted glancing behind her to look for a sundial. "No."

"It's in the woods," the woman said impatiently, gesturing with her shears. "Overgrown now. We wouldn't use it as a sundial anymore, would we?"

Jaycee thought of the ivy-covered pillar she'd passed. "We might have seen it."

The woman lowered her shears and gave Jaycee a pitying look. "Of course you did, dear. The only way in from that direction is the sundial. You don't look simple. Are you?"

Jaycee lost her patience. She came forward, keeping a wary eye on the shears, and stopped about ten feet from the red-haired woman. "Who are you?" she demanded. "Why do you speak English so well?"

"You are on *my* property," the woman answered. She was

taller than Jaycee, her cheekbones high and brushed with pink. "Who are *you*, Shifter? Did you wander in here by mistake? Or out of curiosity? Or do you belong to that awful Lord Simeon? He's a—what do you English people call it?—a prat."

"I've never heard of anyone named Simeon," Jaycee answered. "I'm Jaycee Bordeaux."

"Française?" The woman looked interested, then began speaking in French.

"I don't understand a word of French," Jaycee interrupted her. "I'm not English either. I'm Shifter, living in the States. For now."

"And your friend?"

Jaycee was conscious of Angus growling under the tree not far away. He didn't step out to confront the danger—not because of fear, she knew, but because his position boxed the Fae woman between them. He could be at Jaycee's side swiftly if necessary, or he could cut off the woman's retreat or block the path of whomever she summoned from the house.

"That's Angus," Jaycee said. "I don't know his last name."

The Fae woman straightened the flowers in her basket. "You're very free with names. You do know that names have power?"

"I do," Jaycee said. "That's why we have secret names no one knows. I'm sure you're the same way."

The woman smiled, but the smile was in no way warm and friendly. "Excellently parried, dear. I am called Lady Aisling Mac Aodha, and these are my lands. I speak English as well as you say, and French also, because I am fond of going past the sundial into the ancient world of my ancestors, now overrun by ordinary mortals."

Jaycee was intrigued enough to move a little closer. "Your ancestors?"

Lady Aisling regarded her without worry. "The Fae came from *there*, dear, not here." She gestured toward the woods with her shears. "Millennia ago. Thousands of years BC, as you would say. We came here when iron began to prevail,

our presence in your world lessening by the century until
we could no longer live there. This is our refuge. I'm something of a historian and archaeologist, so I like to visit our
old home now and again and see how things are going."

"I thought there was too much iron for you," Jaycee countered, her voice steady.

Lady Aisling shrugged her elegant shoulders. "There
are talismans one can carry that help for a time until they
are overwhelmed. I enjoy going to the shops. The clerks are
quite respectful and helpful to an elderly woman."

Jaycee blinked. Lady Aisling might speak like a woman
who'd experienced life for a long while, but the clerks in her
shops wouldn't think so. They'd see a beautiful woman with
sleek red hair and green eyes that could pierce armor. She
doubted Aisling shopped at discount stores—this woman
would go into boutiques where she sat on antique furniture
and was served tea or wine while the employees brought her
what she wanted. Male proprietors probably fell all over
themselves to wait on her.

"So, you walk past the sundial, and you're . . . where?"
Jaycee asked. "In Jasmine's house?" Jasmine had never mentioned a Fae woman popping in and out of her sitting room.

Aisling didn't change expression. "I have no idea what
you're talking about, dear. The other side of the sundial
moves, depending on the shadows. It's a *sundial*." She emphasized the word as though Jaycee would have known this
if she'd paid attention in school. "I have learned to read it
so I can go where I like. I quite enjoy what you call France—
Paris, Strasbourg, the south coast. I speak French far better
than I speak English—you'll have to put up with me."

She was apologetic, a well-bred woman politely explaining her lack.

"That means we can get back through there," Jaycee said.

"To your exact point of entry, when the shadow is in the
correct place." Aisling nodded, pleased her pupil had been
listening. "You did make a note of it, didn't you?"

Not exactly, but Jaycee would figure that out when the
time came. It didn't really matter if they fled through the

Fae gate and found themselves in Paris. Kendrick was good for a plane ticket.

"You don't seem to be worried about Shifters," Jaycee said, her gaze going to the shears, which now hung negligibly in Aisling's hand.

"Because there is nothing to worry about." A breeze ruffled Aisling's tunic and the ends of her hair. "Fae are terrified of the creatures, but I have always found that if you don't provoke Shifters, they are fine. Like snakes. Not that I see many Shifters on my journeys, but I have noted them from afar. They seem to have adapted nicely to the human world in the centuries since they've eschewed Faerie. Shifters are bit rough around the edges, but then, you were bred to be part animal. A pity about the Collars and the Shiftertowns. Human beings seem to be unhappy unless they are living in fear of *something*."

No, not at all what Jaycee had expected from a Fae. Either this woman was very unusual, or Jaycee would have to revise her definition of Fae.

"We're looking for a friend." The words caught in Jaycee's throat. *My mate. I have to find my mate!*

"Another Shifter?"

"Yes." Jaycee swallowed.

Aisling resettled her basket on her arm. "And how did he or she get to Faerie, dear? By the sundial?"

"He went through a circle, in a basement," Jaycee said, the tightness inside her barely letting her get out the words.

"I see. So, you believe you can ask me where your friend is—who did *not* come through the gate outside my house—and I will be able to find him for you?"

"Not exactly." Jaycee moved restlessly. She longed to spring forward and say, *Look, bitch, can you help us or not?* but she kept herself under control. The woman couldn't answer questions if she was shredded.

Aisling looked Jaycee up and down and seemed to reach a decision. She dropped her shears into her basket and said briskly, "Come with me. I want to show you something. You too, Angus."

Without waiting for them to agree or argue, she turned and strode toward the gate, her tunic fluttering.

Jaycee started after her, only to be stopped by Angus's hard grip on her elbow. "You're going to rush into a Fae house?" he growled.

Jaycee shook him off. "If she can help me find Dimitri, I'll follow her to hell itself."

Angus shuddered. "Don't even say that around here. But I get it. He's your mate. Don't worry—I'm with you."

Jaycee hurried after Aisling, who waited for them inside the gate in the wall. Behind it was another garden, this one a kitchen garden, with neat rows of vegetables planted in parallel lines. A knot garden of pungent-smelling herbs wove through the center.

A gardener—a Fae in what looked like burlap clothing—forked up clumps of earth at the edge of a bed. He glanced up in alarm as Aisling led the two Shifters through.

The gardener jerked his long fork from the soil and rushed to Aisling's side. He began gabbling rapidly, jabbing the fork in the direction of Jaycee and Angus. Aisling listened coolly, then responded in her crisp tones. Jaycee didn't understand the words, but she imagined what she was saying. *Don't worry. Go back to what you were doing, my good man, and don't be silly.*

The gardener stepped away, but he gave Jaycee and Angus a sharp eye. He wasn't as tall as Fae Jaycee had seen before, but shorter and broader of shoulder. He was still Fae though.

"Come along," Aisling said to Jaycee, quickening her pace. "And best you keep that iron hidden. I can feel it, but I'd appreciate it if you didn't bring it out into the open."

Jaycee realized she still held the knife Ben had passed her, an antique-looking thing with a leather-wrapped hilt. The metal was cool under her hand, the blade thick but sharp.

Jaycee slid the knife into a pocket along the pink glittery stripe of her pants. The pocket, which she'd altered for her need, was lined with leather so that she could carry a small blade close to her hip if she wanted it. She mostly didn't bother with knives as leopard claws were more efficient, but having a touch of iron in the middle of Faerie wasn't a bad thing.

Aisling led them out of the kitchen garden and along a hedge-enclosed walkway, then through a glass-paneled door into a long hall paved with slate. The hall opened to a large vaulted space with a staircase running up one side, the wide stones of the ground floor covered with carpet. Divans and chairs set about conveyed a sense of comfort as well as luxury.

Other Fae were moving about upstairs and down, cleaning, carrying things, and when Jaycee and Angus walked in, openly staring. Jaycee noticed that the staircase had no railing, but this did not seem to bother the agile men and women skimming up and down it.

A Fae woman who did show some age through her white hair and lined face emerged from another room, gaped in astonishment, then raced to Aisling and began scolding her. Her mother? Jaycee wondered. No, from the imperious way Aisling gazed at her, then said something dismissive, she must be an old family retainer. A nanny or governess or housekeeper, or something. Whoever she was, the woman turned a narrow-eyed glare on Jaycee and Angus and directed the scolding at them.

"They don't understand you," Aisling said with tired patience, in English. "Come along, you two. The sooner I explain, the sooner we can find your friend."

She handed the basket and shears to the retainer, then breezed up the stairs. Jaycee followed with Angus close behind her. The stone staircase bent around itself, moving upward into the shadows. A fall from the stairs to the floor below would be painful—as they wound higher, Jaycee revised the word to *fatal*.

Though possibly not for a leopard. Jaycee spotted a number of niches and stone carvings that would make good hand and foot gripping points on the way down. A wolf, however, would be dead. Jaycee made sure to put herself between Angus and the drop.

Aisling skimmed up the steps without worry, her stride quick and agile. At the top, she walked around a gallery, then down another hall, which ended in an open doorway that led to a beautiful room.

Jaycee considered it beautiful because it was so full of light. Windows made of many panes of glass covered most of one wall, with equally tall though narrower windows on the other walls. The ceiling lifted high, the room near the top of the house, with stone arches and corbels holding it up. Cathedrals in the human world had ceilings like this.

The wall opposite the windowed wall was covered with maps. Below these rested a long table filled with scrolls of paper and cloth, boxes, small glass cases, and canvas bags like those a person might take on a long hike. A chair had been pulled up to one end of the table, where notebooks were stacked, and a vase full of pens waited.

Aisling led them up to the table and pointed at the largest map stretched across the wall. "This, my dear, is Tuil Narath, what you call Faerie."

The outlines of the map resembled that of Europe stretching through Russia all the way to the Pacific Ocean. At least the top half did. The bottom half was also filled with land, cut in the very south—if the bottom represented south—by a huge sea.

Jaycee studied it in some dismay. If the place depicted was the equivalent scale, Faerie was as a large as Europe, Africa, Asia, and Australia combined. And that only if this was a complete map of it.

"You see my point?" Aisling asked. She picked up a slender stick and touched a dot nestled against a curve of mountains. "We are here. If your friend came in through a circle on a ley line, he could be anywhere *here*." She moved the stick to encompass the entire map. "Where would you like to begin looking, dear?"

D imitri sat on his wolf haunches as a Fae detached himself from a group and strode to where Brice and Dimitri waited. Dimitri refused to shift back to human—this Fae could just deal with talking to a wolf.

The man—Dimitri figured he was Simeon—wore the same kind of getup the guard at the gate had. His silver mail was no different, nor were the skins he wore or the supple boots. The kind of general proud to wear the uniform of the men beneath him, Dimitri supposed. *I'm just one of the guys.*

"A red wolf Shifter," Simeon said, sounding impressed. "I've never seen one before."

"They're rare," Brice told him. He looked smug, as though he'd personally been responsible for finding Dimitri. *Dickbrain.*

"A Collarless Shifter as well," Simeon went on. "My lieutenant was caught off-guard by that. He's still pissed off. He'd have killed you when you came through, but he's under orders not to destroy Shifters." He laughed, amused that Dimitri had torn a piece out of one of his own men.

Double dickbrain.

Simeon had dark brown hair and gray eyes, again putting to flight the stereotype that all Fae were pale-haired, black-eyed creatures. The Fae seemed to be as different from one another as were Shifters.

This Fae also spoke perfect, and idiomatic, American English. It chilled Dimitri to wonder where he'd learned it.

"Is he housebroken?" Simeon asked Brice, a grin on his high-cheekboned face. "Should I put down papers?"

Dimitri didn't dignify this with a growl. He merely sat, staring up at Simeon with his wolf eyes in a calm wolf face.

The Fae on the other side of the room watched Dimitri nervously, obvious about it. Simeon tried to be nonchalant, but he was tense as well. Dimitri could smell it.

"Lupines don't have senses of humor," Brice said, as though confiding a secret. "So be careful. They're not like bears."

Yeah, bears are a load of laughs.

"He is a beautiful creature," Simeon went on. He cast a look of true admiration at Dimitri. "I will be pleased to have him fight at my side."

I might rip out your side instead. Is this guy for real?

Brice had to know that Dimitri was not thrilled with his

pet Fae. But Brice seemed oblivious to Dimitri's body language, not catching what was in his head. Jaycee would have. Jaycee would be laughing her ass off by now.

Actually, she'd be busy shredding bits of Fae and bear between her agile paws. Watching her land on Brice's head and begin clawing his ears had been so funny . . .

Damn it, Jaycee. I'm getting out of here and back to you. Then we're going to say to hell with all the Shifters and tracking jobs, hole up and make love in the sunshine. We'll stay in Jasmine's house and tell it not to let anyone in for weeks.

Brice's ears still bore lines of red, though the wounds had mostly closed up. "He'll be a terrific fighter," Brice said. "My scout spotted him at their sparring arena and reported back to me."

Yeah, after he tried to drug me, and my mate kicked his ass.

"Good," Simeon said. "I rely on you to bring me the best. Do you think he'd mind a little, ah—how do you say—test drive?"

Dimitri stiffened. Brice, on the other hand, relaxed. "I don't think he would. What did you have in mind?"

Simeon smiled the chill smile of a true sociopath. *Brice, you poor deluded asshole, what the hell did you get yourself into?*

Simeon turned abruptly to his cluster of soldiers and said two words sharply in Fae.

Three men fell all over themselves to head out the door to obey the command, probably happy for the excuse to get out of the room and away from Dimitri.

Simeon didn't speak while they waited, and Brice didn't offer conversation. No, *So, how's it going? Did you catch that last episode of* Shifters Who Stupidly Trust Fae? They stood in companionable silence like old friends.

Three Fae soldiers returned, but they were different men, Dimitri saw. Probably the others had said, *Not going back in there. It's your turn to put up with Simeon's shit.*

The soldiers who returned seemed less intimidated by

the two Shifters in the middle of their war room. They pulled a half-conscious man between them—no, not a man, Dimitri understood when he caught his scent. A Fae, but not one like Simeon and his ilk.

And I've already been in Faerie too long when I'm using words like ilk.

The man was a *dokk alfar*—a dark Fae—like Stuart Reid who now lived in the Las Vegas Shiftertown, a man Dimitri had come to respect. Reid looked after a Shifter bear female and about a dozen orphaned cubs. Dimitri was willing to bet that Simeon and his high Fae wouldn't be tough enough for *that* job.

The soldiers pulled the *dokk alfar* forward. They held on to him as though worried he'd break free, but it was clear the guy was in no shape to stand up on his own. He'd been beaten and looked starved, the thin limbs that poked from his ragged clothes battered and cut, new gashes open over closed ones.

He had black hair and ropy muscles, and when he lifted his head, Dimitri saw dark eyes like Ben's, these filled with fury and hatred. The Fae might have beaten this man until he could barely stay upright, but they hadn't broken what was inside him.

"You, wolf," Simeon said to Dimitri. "This is a traitor to me and my army, my clan, my people. He was arrested and confessed, and is being held for execution. I can't think of any more fitting way for him to die than to be mauled by the Shifters he betrayed. But we'll give him to you alone, Dimitri. Show me what you can do."

CHAPTER TWENTY-FIVE

Dimitri growled. The *dokk alfar* had the sense to look afraid, though resignation overrode his fear. He was tired of the Fae, tired of pain, ready to end this—screw them.

I hear you, friend.

Dimitri needed to speak. Heaving a wolf sigh, he morphed out of his comfortable furry state and rose to become his man shape.

The air was cold to his human body, but he wasn't about to beg for clothing. For one thing, it bothered the Fae that Dimitri stood in nothing but his skin. For another, he wasn't about to stay around long enough to wait for them to bring him clothes. For a third, he had no intention of putting on something a Fae had worn.

The *dokk alfar* watched Dimitri warily but squared his shoulders as though deciding to face death without flinching. He took on a slow, feral smile, as though welcoming it.

The high Fae encircling them regarded Dimitri expectantly. All eyes in the room were on him, something Dimitri never liked.

He gave them a slow look in return and said in an exaggerated voice, "Eh . . . What's up, D-Doc?"

There were puzzled frowns from all, including Brice, which was truly sad. A life without Saturday-morning cartoons had to be pathetic.

The *dokk alfar* hadn't understood a word, but he seemed to realize Dimitri was making fun of the Fae. A glint entered his eyes.

Dimitri didn't know much of the Fae's Celtic language, but he'd learned a few words in *dokk alfar* from Reid. He barked out a phrase that sounded to him like a cat hacking a hairball, but apparently it meant *You okay?*

The *dokk alfar's* eyes flickered. He answered in words Dimitri didn't know, but he caught *czul*, which meant *bastards.*

Dimitri grinned, then turned to Simeon. "You want me to k-kill *him*? Why? What's he d-done?"

"Besides being a demon?" Brice answered before Simeon could. "He killed Shifters, Dimitri. Isn't that enough?"

The *dokk alfar* had no idea what Brice was saying, that was clear. They probably hadn't even told him what crime he'd been accused of. The high Fae hated the *dokk alfar* though, so his simply being alive had likely been enough.

If Brice didn't lie, then the guy did deserve punishment, but Dimitri didn't trust Brice. "Tell me what h-happened," Dimitri said to Simeon. "Exactly."

Brice was shaking his head, as though trying to silence Dimitri, but Simeon began without balking. "There was a battle. Shifters went in to take out the *dokk alfar*. Three Shifters went down. The *dokk alfar* dragged them away with them. This one was caught."

Simeon waved his hand at the man, who watched without worry.

That was all Dimitri would get, he knew. He turned to the *dokk alfar*, wishing Ben were here. He could use a translator about now.

Dimitri conjured up another word Reid had taught him. He spit it out. *Shifters?*

The *dokk alfar*'s eyes widened slightly. He gave Dimitri a nod and said back in his language, *Are okay*.

Hmm. Who was telling the truth? The Fae who'd made friends with Brice and had him bringing Shifters to Faerie to be Battle Beasts once more? Or the *dokk alfar* thinking he was about to be gouged to death by a wolf?

"Doesn't matter," Dimitri said out loud. "F-forget it, Simeon. I'm not doing your dirty w-work for you."

Simeon's brows rose. "He killed your people, Shifter."

"The name's *Dimitri*. You're trying to enrage me so I'll g-go Shifter on his ass and rip his heart out. Let me put it in t-terms you'll understand." He folded his arms and pinned Simeon with his best alpha wolf stare. "Fuck you."

Simeon gave Brice a patient look. "Brice."

Brice shrugged. "He's not used to the idea. Give him time."

Simeon's eyes hardened. "I don't have time. The trouble with this red wolf is you can't control him."

Yeah, life's a bitch.

The *dokk alfar* was giving Dimitri a worried look now. He spread his hands and looked straight at him. *Kill me,* he said in his language.

Dimitri replied, *No*, then turned back to Brice. "Hey, before we g-get into whatever Simeon wants to d-do to me, I have to ask. Where do I know you from? It's b-bugging me."

Dimitri was rewarded with a warm, sad, nostalgic smile. "Dimitri, my old friend," Brice said. "You don't remember? I rescued you."

Something flickered on the edges of Dimitri's memory. "Rescued me from what? When?"

"You were just a cub. There was a fire. I know you really *don't* remember—I don't see the knowledge in your eyes. Your parents were killed. I heard you crying out—you were in a trailer deep in the woods. I tore my way in and carried you out. I couldn't rescue them. I'm sorry."

Dimitri stood still. Flames, bright with heat, rose up before him, and he heard his own howls. Tiny, terrified, calling for his mom and dad.

Dimitri's breath left him. He felt the fire in his lungs, the burning, choking smoke. He was alone, surrounded by flame, trapped, trapped . . . *Jaycee.*

Into the picture swam an image of Brice. Younger, just past his Transition, but with much the same bulk he had now, the same intense dark eyes.

But the picture wouldn't complete. Dimitri reached for memories, for the feeling of being carried out by the scruff into clean air. Nope, wouldn't come. He could see only fire, Brice, the walls collapsing, and feel the despair and grief in his heart.

Jaycee. Dimitri closed his eyes.

He pictured her vividly, Jaycee with her tawny hair falling in a thick wave down her back, her sexy smile, her beautiful eyes watching him, unafraid. He brought back the sensations of making love to her in the crazy house, her body under his, her softness wrapped around him.

Thoughts of Jaycee made the flames clear, and Dimitri could once again draw a breath.

He opened his eyes. "What happened after that?" he asked Brice. "If you rescued me, why d-didn't I stay with you? Why was I sitting in the woods for D-David and Anna to find me?"

"You ran away," Brice said regretfully. "I looked for you everywhere, but you'd gone."

Must have been a reason, Dimitri thought but didn't say. Cubs had the instinct to go to those who would keep them safe, even if they didn't like that person. What about Brice had made cub Dimitri run off?

"Now I've found you again," Brice said. "I've been watching you, glad you were able to grow up safe and sound."

Dimitri folded his arms and regarded him stonily. "You were so glad that you dragged me to Faerie to be used by the Fae. Interesting."

"It's not what you think." Brice's good-natured patience became tinged with anger, a flash of rage that didn't look healthy. "I brought you home."

"No," Dimitri said, letting his own anger surface. "Home

is on Kendrick's ranch, in the shack I built with my own hands and am fixing up for my mate. Home is with my friends and the people who have come to be my family. Not here. Not with you."

Brice, if anything, looked hurt, though the dangerous fury lurked behind it.

Simeon, all business, broke in. "He had a chance. No, Brice, you tried, and your way is done." He snapped his fingers at one of the soldiers who'd dragged in the *dokk alfar*, and shot him a command.

The soldier, without changing expression, stepped forward. He pulled something out of his pocket as he did so and dropped it into Simeon's hand.

Dimitri's chest constricted and the flames returned to dance in his brain.

Simeon held up a chain of silver laced with gold, which ended in a Celtic knot pendant. "Bring him forward," Simeon told Brice, then bent a hard gaze on Dimitri. "It's time for *you* to take the Collar."

B en watched the three large Shifters he'd admitted to the house stand in front of the open door in the sitting room and gaze into the darkness.

One was Dylan. His dark hair was just going gray, his deep blue eyes that had seen so many things peering warily through the opening. Next to him was the hulking bear Shifter called Zander Moncrieff, a healer, a complete nutcase, and the most caring person Ben had ever met.

Filling out the threesome was Tiger.

Tiger had no other name. He stood still, his large fists curled to his sides, the overhead light glinting on his red and black hair as he looked through the doorway. He growled softly—that is, softly for Tiger. The rumble of it filled the room.

"Why'd you let her go?" Dylan asked Ben sternly. His words were accented, the three hundred years in Ireland tingeing them. "You could have stopped her."

Ben shook his head. "Dimitri's her mate—in her heart if not officially. She would have gone straight through me."

Dylan's stare became pointed. "You could have stopped her," he repeated.

Ben knew that. He had powers even Dylan didn't know about. Yes, if he'd tried, Ben could have prevented Jaycee from running through that door. She'd have hated him for the rest of her life, but she'd have been alive to do it.

"I decided not to," Ben said calmly. "Jaycee's no fool. Plus she has a Lupine with her who is more than capable in a fight. I've witnessed it."

Zander turned around. His eyes were as dark as any Fae's, the hair on his head as white blond. His beard was black and closely trimmed, like Angus's.

"He'd better be more capable than that poor guy at Brice's house," Zander said. "He's recovering. His wounds were easily closed, but it still hurt like a bitch." Zander always paid for his healing gift by taking on the pain of the person he healed.

"Angus can look after Jaycee," Ben said. "And Jaycee can take care of him."

Zander pointed into the void. "Where does this go? Doesn't look fun."

"Faerie, probably," Ben said. "But I don't know."

Dylan turned silently from Ben, his look managing to convey vast disapproval. Ben supposed the man had wanted to find Dimitri and Jaycee here safe and sound with Brice tied up between them.

"Tiger?" Zander asked. "You haven't said anything yet."

Tiger never spoke much. He had a mate now and a tiny cub called Seth, who was adorable. He carried himself in a more relaxed way these days, knowing his years of terrible ordeal were over.

"The land of the Fae is one possibility," Tiger said without moving. "Wherever this leads, Jaycee is there." No doubt in his voice.

Zander sighed. "Then we go. We need to fetch her back so Kendrick doesn't play jump rope with our guts."

That earned a sideways glance from Tiger, but the large man didn't answer. He'd learned to let things Zander said slide right by.

"Agreed," Dylan rumbled.

Kendrick himself was on his way to New Orleans with more backup, but he was hours behind them. Kendrick's language on the phone had burned Ben's ears, and let him know that he was furious at Ben for losing his two best trackers.

They were more than trackers to him, Ben understood from his tone, the number of swear words, and the fear in the back of Kendrick's voice. Dimitri and Jaycee were two of Kendrick's closest friends, and he cared for them deeply.

Zander glanced in surprise at Dylan, then turned to Ben in mock horror. "If *Dylan's* worried about what Kendrick will do to him, then we'd better get in there and find Jaycee." His look softened. "Tell Rae I love her."

"Better send the same message to Glory," Dylan said. "If she lets you speak when she finds out where I've gone."

Ben gave him a silent nod. Glory, Dylan's mate and a formidable wolf, was a terrible sight when enraged.

Ben and the other two Shifters waited expectantly for Tiger to say something, but he remained quiet, looking into the opening as though he could see what lay beyond. And maybe he could.

"Tiger?" Ben asked. "Any message for Carly and Seth?"

Tiger turned his head and pinned Ben with steady golden eyes. "Carly and Seth know I love them. And I will come back."

Without further hesitation, Tiger walked through the doorway.

"Shit," Zander said. "Say a few prayers to the Goddess for us, Ben. Dylan?" Dylan gave him a nod. Dylan started to walk forward, but Zander moved ahead of him, his bulk filling the doorframe. "A polar bear, a tiger, and a lion walk into Faerie," Zander said as first he, and then Dylan, vanished. "I wonder how this joke will end?"

And they were gone. Their voices cut off, and blackness filled the doorframe.

"Goddess go with you," Ben whispered, then touched the

wall of the house when it creaked. "Let's make sure they come back, all right?"

The house shivered, as though as worried as Ben. Ben patted the wall, then went to go make a few more phone calls.

Zander didn't like the smell or feel of the woods, the clouds, the sky, the thin rain. He didn't like the house that rose across the meadow on the edge of the woods, though he figured some might call the stone mansion with flowering garden and mountains beyond pretty.

Tiger halted just inside the line of trees. Next to him was an ivy-covered stone pillar, which Zander saw was an overgrown sundial. Weird place to put it where the sun would barely reach it. Maybe it had been placed here before the woods grew around it.

Tiger gazed unblinkingly at the house. "Jaycee is in there."

"Good," Dylan said, sounding relieved. He'd been the one to insist on Jaycee and Dimitri traveling to New Orleans to investigate Shifter activity, Zander knew. Kendrick would play jump rope with his guts too. "What about Dimitri?"

Tiger shook his head. "Not Dimitri. Jaycee, and one other Shifter. And Fae."

The other Shifter must be Angus, the bouncer from the club Ben told them about.

"All right, what's the plan?" Zander asked.

"We go in," Dylan said. "And we bring her out."

"Can't get more simple than that," Zander agreed. "Tiger, you want to—"

He cut off as Tiger started forward, his stride determined as he headed for the gate in the wall beyond the garden.

"—to lead the way," Zander finished. He strode after Tiger. "Here we come, a lion, a tiger, and a bear. Think any of the Fae inside will say, *Oh my*?"

"No idea," Dylan answered, falling into step with him as they followed Tiger across the garden.

"I hope they do," Zander said. "That would be seriously funny . . ."

His voice trailed into the morning as mists gathered to obscure the sunlight.

"Fuck that," Dimitri said, and attacked Simeon.

Brice snarled in fury and hurled himself at Dimitri but couldn't reach him in time.

The Collar Simeon held was real, Fae-made and full of spells—Dimitri could smell them. It was more potent than even the Collars most Shifters wore. Made sense. Here in Faerie, the Fae would be able to come up with more Fae gold, the key ingredient to making the Collars work.

Dimitri rammed into Simeon, shifting as he went, letting his claws land on Simeon's wrist. Simeon jerked, his fist opening, and the Collar clinked to the flagstones.

Brice swept it up. Dimitri completed his attack, sending Simeon to the floor, but Simeon, like the Fae soldier in Brice's basement, was battle hardened and experienced. He twisted even as he went down, a hard bronze knife coming out to slice at Dimitri's throat.

Bronze might not be as relatively hard as steel, but a sharp knife was a sharp knife. It cut through Dimitri's fur to draw blood as Dimitri pushed himself back to avoid a death blow.

He wished for Jaycee's agility. Dimitri recalled how he'd lazed on the porch watching Jaycee run and romp as her leopard at the house, Dimitri admiring her lissomness. Jase was beautiful, whatever form she took.

Images of Jaycee flitted through the back of his mind while he fought for his life—she dancing against him at the club, wrapping her foot around him in the hall at the house, her leopard running from him as they chased each other across the wide lands of Kendrick's ranch.

A kind of crazed joy washed through Dimitri—this was what his wolf had been made for. Fighting, springing, slamming paws into his opponents, spinning, lunging, teeth and claws working. Battling without the rules, without refs making sure no one got seriously hurt.

Dimitri was always happy to fight—he just refused to do it at the behest of a Fae.

Out of the corner of his eye, he saw the *dokk alfar* slam himself to the floor, which broke his captors' hold. He then rolled to his feet, a knife appearing in his hand. Where it had come from Dimitri didn't know, but the Fae the *dokk alfar* touched with it screamed and backed away in horror.

The knife had iron in it, Dimitri concluded. *Nice one.*

There were too many soldiers in the room, and Dimitri knew it. He had to find an area where he could fend them off while he figured out how to get away. The only place he had to run was outside into Faerie, where Shifters were enslaved, and he had no clue how to get home—but one thing at a time.

Dimitri became a whirlwind, his red fur rippling as he attacked, feinted, twisted aside, all the while making his way to the large door.

Dimitri always hated when people called him *coyote*, Lupines implying he was lesser than they were. But maybe there was something to that. He had a light-footedness that other wolves did not and the cunning to make people look one way while he did something unexpected.

Like dropping and rolling across the floor, avoiding two Fae trying to jab him with swords, and avoiding Brice as he threw off his makeshift clothes and shifted to bear.

The grizzly took up space in the chamber and many of the Fae scrambled away from him. *Terrified of Shifters. Wusses.*

Dimitri kept rolling, coming up on his paws with all the Fae on one side of the room and no one between himself and the door. Now to open it. The second or two it would take to shift and turn the handle might be the difference between his life and death, but what the hell?

The *dokk alfar* did a running vault over two Fae who penned him in, rushed past Dimitri, and opened the door. He politely let Dimitri barrel out first, then he ran after him, keeping up with Dimitri's long stride.

Dimitri made for the stone staircase, but the *dokk alfar*

grabbed a handful of Dimitri's scruff and made a motion
for him to turn down a side passage. Dimitri didn't know
whether he could trust the *dokk alfar*, but he turned. The
man needed to get away as much as Dimitri did—he certainly wouldn't be treated kindly by the Fae running around
this citadel.

The *dokk alfar* wrenched open another door, this one less
polished and carved, and plunged down a wooden staircase
beyond. *Aha. The back stairs.* With any luck, the steps went
all the way down and out through the hill.

They were steep, wherever they were taking them, dim,
and treacherous. The *dokk alfar* leapt down them without
fear, but Dimitri's wolf stumbled. He could move much
faster as wolf, but that wouldn't help if he tripped and ended
up with a broken neck at the bottom.

He shifted back to human, his bare feet unhappy with
the splintery wood beneath them. But his balance was better, and he could hang on to the walls on either side—no
railings for servants.

Screaming sounded lower down, maids and workmen
scrambling out of the way of the crazy *dokk alfar* and his
iron-bladed knife. Dimitri hit the bottom floor and ran into
a kitchen full of terrified people pressing themselves out of
the way. One of the younger maids took in Dimitri, all six
foot plus of him in his gleaming skin, and stared unabashed,
her mouth open.

Dimitri nodded to her. "Ma'am," he said, then charged
after the *dokk alfar*.

They made it to a trapdoor outside the kitchen, which the
dokk alfar yanked up a moment before twenty Fae soldiers
stalked forward and surrounded them, swords drawn. One
kicked the *dokk alfar* in the groin, sending him to his hands
and knees, then stepped on his hand that still clutched at the
ring to the trapdoor.

Brice came running up, panting, in human form once
more. The Collar Simeon had held was clenched in his giant
fist. "Take it like a Shifter, Dimitri."

Fight or surrender. Dimitri's choice. His ally, the *dokk*

alfar, was down. Brice wasn't going to help him. The only reason the Fae weren't killing Dimitri right away was because their leader, Simeon, had some weird fixation with Shifters.

Fight or become Simeon's pet, like Brice.

Dimitri flowed into his wolf and attacked the nearest soldier.

His limbs began to tingle, a lethargy quickly working its way through his body, and his legs buckled. The Fae he'd been fighting stepped back, and Dimitri fell all the way to the floor.

He looked up to see Simeon standing over him, a dart in his hand. The man didn't need a tranquilizer gun, did he? He only needed to corner Dimitri and stick a tranq dart into his shoulder when Dimitri was distracted.

Effective. Dimitri's body shifted back to human before he could stop it. He tried to make his arms and legs respond, make himself get up and run, but his limbs lay still, unresisting. Dimitri's brain became cloudy, his vision blurred.

He could see well enough to observe the Collar coming down to his throat, and the triumphant look in Brice's dark eyes as the silver and black chain locked around Dimitri's neck and Dimitri's first screams rang out.

CHAPTER TWENTY-SIX

J aycee gazed at the huge area Lady Aisling tapped with
her pointer, feeling hope drain out of her.

She reached over the table and touched the bottom of the
map, the parchment stiff under her fingers. "How am I going
to find you, Dimitri?" she asked softly.

Lady Aisling sniffed, hearing her. "Well, you could start
by postulating where he would be most likely to go. Why
did he disappear through a circle in someone's cellar? Did
a hole simply open up? Or was he playing with magic he
should not have?"

"Dimitri didn't set up the circle," Jaycee said. "We were
trying to find out where other Shifters had gone."

"A Shifter called Brice," Angus put in with a growl. "And
his crew. Brice was the one messing with Fae magic. He
probably sent a whole mess of Shifters into Faerie through
that hole."

"A group of Shifters?" Lady Aisling's brows rose. "You
see? That narrows things down." She lifted her pointer again
and moved it south and east of her house—a hundred miles?
A thousand? Ten? A map scale would be helpful.

"The lands of Simeon Mac An Bhaird. He has a keen interest in Shifters and even has managed to bring some to Faerie. And as I said, he is a prat."

"How do I get there?" Jaycee said, her heart thumping with impatience.

"Calmly, my girl. Then there is Orag du Galbrath and Walther le Madhug." The pointer moved to locations to the north of Simeon's patch and northwest of that. "Alarmed at Simeon's buildup of his army, reinforcing them with Shifters, they too have been bringing in Shifters. Whether by force or willingly, I have no idea. *The Battle Beasts should come back to Faerie*—that is their theory. Not all of us agree. The power hungry are mad for Shifters. It's the new fashion."

Jaycee shivered. Lady Aisling meant it was the new fashion regardless of what the Shifters thought.

Shifters had been captured and living penned up by the humans for the past twenty years or so. Now Fae were stealing them out of that captivity and dragging them into combat. Which, according to some evidence, had been the Fae's plan all along—half Fae passing as humans had influenced the creation of Shiftertowns and Collars. Brice had been brainwashing Shifters to follow him to Faerie and be slaves to the Fae again. And he had Dimitri.

"How far are these?" Jaycee swept her hand to indicate the map. "This one." She pointed to the closest, which belonged to the Fae called Orag. "And what kind of transportation do you have?"

"It is, as you measure distance, thirty kilometers. Or a little less than twenty miles for those in your world who have not converted their measurement preference. I have a carriage and four horses that can cover that distance in a few hours. However, I have not said that I will help you, dear."

Aisling gazed calmly at Jaycee, her green eyes unblinking.

Jaycee's breath came faster, her leopard restless inside. She could shift and take this woman before her retainers could help—plus she had a nice iron knife in her pocket.

Angus moved to Aisling's other side, looking every inch

a bouncer approaching an unruly bar patron. "We might not give you a choice," he said.

Lady Aisling gazed back at him without concern. "Hmm. Perhaps, you know, I would like a few Shifters of my own."

Jaycee closed in on her. "Would you? Are you worried about these Fae who are bringing in Shifters attacking you? You don't need to. Shifters won't obey the Fae. We're born hating them."

Aisling turned to her. "You're not, you know. Born hating Fae, I mean. Your anathema is taught. But I was teasing. I don't want Shifters in my house. You are far too uncivilized, if you won't take offense. And I have no fear of men like Simeon attacking me. He would not dare."

"Why not?" Jaycee observed the wide window, thought about the stone sides of the house that were full of carvings, the low garden walls. "This place isn't defensible. Far too many opportunities for an enemy to get in. You'd be taken very quickly."

Aisling gave Jaycee a small smile. "What you say is true, but my neighbors will never attack me."

"Huh," Jaycee said. "I wouldn't put it past the Fae to do whatever they want."

"Neither would I," Aisling answered. "But I know they won't touch me."

Her words distracted Jaycee from her unceasing worry. "Why not?"

Aisling raised her shoulders in a simple shrug. "My dear, *you* see a harmless elderly Fae woman who likes to putter in her garden and visit your world to shop as a treat. *They* do not."

"You keep saying *elderly*," Jaycee broke in. "But you don't look elderly to me. Shifters live a long time, but I'd think you weren't that far into your first century. In human terms you'd be in your late twenties at most."

"Kind of you." Aisling preened, a woman pleased to be complimented. A glance into her eyes, though, showed she was far from young. Those eyes bore the weight of years, of things seen, endured. "You might be surprised to find that I am at least a thousand years old, and that I am not an ordinary Fae."

"I don't consider Fae ordinary at all," Jaycee said. "But what do you mean?"

"I mean I am one of the Tuil Erdannan."

She paused significantly, as though waiting for Jaycee to gasp and clutch her chest in awe.

Jaycee shook her head. "Means nothing to me."

Lady Aisling sighed. "I ought to have known. What do they teach young people these days?" She stepped to the middle of the room and cleared her throat as though beginning a lecture to uninformed pupils.

"The Tuil Erdannan are the descendants of unions with gods and the Fae," she said. "That is the legend, anyway. But we are feared the length and breadth of Faerie. I have no idea why—I have no interest in the petty wars between Fae clans—but it's convenient when I want to be left alone." Aisling's smile grew, crinkling her green eyes at the corners. "How do you think I learned your languages so quickly? And resist iron as well as I do? Most Fae are hopeless at both. No, the clan leaders will not bother me here."

She raised her hand, her long fingers splaying, and instantly the room was engulfed in flame.

Not true flame, Jaycee realized after she'd dropped to the floor. The stone crackled with fire, the windows glowed, and glass ran like water, but nothing in the room truly burned, and Jaycee felt no heat. An illusion?

"I assure you, it is real," Aisling said as though reading her thoughts. "I can make it destroy or not, as I choose."

She closed her hand and the flames died instantly. A few papers from the table fluttered to the floor in the breeze created by the sudden vacuum, and the room returned to its innocuous appearance.

Aisling no longer seemed as harmless, though. Jaycee sucked in a breath as she rose to her feet, and knew she'd never look at the woman the same way again.

"Enough showing off for the day," Aisling said with a

faint smile, as though admonishing herself. "Your friends are here. Shall we go down and greet them?"

D imitri peeled open his eyes and wished he hadn't. He'd been in the middle of a wonderful dream about Jaycee— he was licking her bare skin all over—but for some reason someone was trying to strangle him at the same time.

Metal bit into his throat, stinging Dimitri's skin and choking off his breath. He coughed and woke. The image and taste of Jaycee dissolved, but the choking remained.

With awareness came pain, deep biting pain that clung and didn't let go. Every one of his nerves was on fire, his bones couldn't move, and white heat flared behind his eyes.

Close on the pain came memories of more pain—Brice locking the Collar around Dimitri's throat, Simeon touching his sword to the Celtic knot, and Dimitri's screams piercing the air until his throat was raw and the screams turned to hoarse rasps. Simeon had closed the circuit between his sword and the Collar until Dimitri's limbs were jerking on the floor, and blood and tears flowed from his eyes.

No wonder Shifters went feral. That flooding pain had forced Dimitri's body into that of his half beast, but the shift had only made the pain worse. The Collar, new, had to learn Dimitri's change in shape, and it had dug into his neck until he could no longer breathe.

Somewhere after he'd instinctively shifted to human again, Dimitri had passed out.

Now only a groan came from between his lips as the Collar sparked, reminding him of its presence.

As he became more awake, he realized he lay on a stone floor with a grate about five feet above him. In the movies, people thrown into dungeons at least had dirty straw to lie on, or a high window to look out of and be reminded of the sky.

This was a real dungeon, which meant uneven stones, a low ceiling, and a bad stench. A very faint light showed through the grating, probably from some window far, far

away down a twisting hall. No handy torches, which always
seemed to be burning in subterranean passages in movies.
Who tended the torches? he'd always wondered. Kept them
lit, stocked with fuel, took them down, cleaned them and
re-lit them when they died out?

Frivolous thoughts to distract him from pain, thirst, more
pain, and pure rage. When Dimitri got out of here, Brice
was one dead bear.

Where were Brice's followers? Dimitri wondered. The
poor, messed-up Shifters who'd decided Brice was a dy-
namic leader? Were they in similar dungeons? Elsewhere
in the fortress? Kept in some kind of barracks or kennels
until they were needed?

Some of them would have followed Brice willingly. Others had probably gone to him out of curiosity and had been
dragged here by their fellows. Dimitri knew, even as he tried
to catch his breath, that he couldn't leave them behind for
the Fae to use. Yes, they were here by their own stupidity;
yes, they'd let Brice throw Ben off a balcony; but that didn't
mean Dimitri would let Shifters suffer and die as Fae slaves.
He was a tracker—rescuing Shifters was part of his job.

Right now, it was all Dimitri could do to breathe.

He heard a stirring on the cobbles to his right. Dimitri
stiffened, which rippled pain down his spine again, causing
another groan.

A voice said in guttural English, "You okay?"

Dimitri blinked the haze from his eyes and slowly turned
his head. The *dokk alfar* sat not far away, his head nearly
touching the low ceiling. His long limbs were folded up, his
clothes rags, his smell unfortunate. Not that Dimitri smelled
any better.

"You understand me?" Dimitri asked.

The man only stared with eyes darker than night. Dimitri realized that the *dokk alfar* had probably picked up that
phrase and nothing more.

"No," Dimitri said. "Not okay. What's your name?"

More staring. He understood *No*, and that was about it.

"All right, let's do this the basic way." Dimitri pressed

his hand to his chest. *"Dimitri."* He pointed to the *dokk alfar* and gave him a questioning look.

The man didn't change expression—probably cursing his luck that in all the dungeons in all the lands of all the Fae, he'd been stuck in this one with a complete moron.

"Cian Tadhg Cailean an Mac Diarmud," he said.

"Oh." Dimitri drew a breath, flinched as every muscle pulled in different directions, and let it out again. "Assuming something in there is your name, how about I call you Cian?"

The *dokk alfar* again had that *Goddess-help-me-I'm-stuck-with-an-idiot* look, but he gave a nod. "Cian." He pressed his hands to his chest in imitation of what Dimitri had done, then pointed at Dimitri. "Dimitri."

"Yes." Dimitri let out his breath, which didn't hurt as much. As long as he didn't breathe *in*, he'd be fine. "At least we have that sorted out. Now what do we do?"

Cian only looked at him in silence a few moments. He unfolded his legs after a time and closed the distance between them, then carefully touched Dimitri's chest. The slim hand pressed down, as though feeling Dimitri's heartbeat, then moved along his ribs, touching with the impersonal prodding of a doctor.

It hurt, but Cian seemed to know exactly where to press on every one of Dimitri's internal organs. Not hard but competently, as though checking Dimitri for injuries. Had Dimitri lucked out and been locked up with a healer? Would it do either of them any good?

Cian found a rib that hurt like hell. Dimitri let out a shout of pain, and Cian withdrew his hand. It was back a second later, his palm warm on Dimitri's side as he found the injury. He probed gently with his fingers, then announced something, shaking his head.

What? Broken? Only cracked? Who knew?

Cian stripped off what was left of his shirt and tore it in half. He put a strong hand under Dimitri's side and lifted him enough to slip the cloth underneath, then he looped it around Dimitri's ribs and tied it tightly. Dimitri growled and swore in Russian but once Cian was done yanking him around, the rib stayed in place and felt better.

"Shifters heal fast," Dimitri said, his voice faint. "I'll be all right."

Cian rested his hand on Dimitri's shoulder again, then withdrew. The touch was comforting, something Shifters needed for healing. Did Cian know that? Or was he just doing what *dokk alfar* did when tending their wounded?

Dimitri tried to remember the words Reid had taught him. He knew *Shifters*—which was *Horkalan*—also *hoch alfar czul*—high Fae bastards—and several words for alcohol.

"I s-say we blow this joint, kick some *hoch alfar czul* asses, and then get drunk on *gularain*."

Cian gave him a dark-eyed stare and then burst into a gravelly laugh. He nodded and said something in agreement, ending with *Horkalan*.

Dimitri laughed with him, which hurt like holy hell, so he calmed himself. After that, he and Cian watched each other again, out of conversation.

Cian crawled back to the other side of the dungeon, lost in the shadows. When he returned after a time, he had something in his hand. He put it into Dimitri's, hiding the movement with his body, in case a Fae *czul* guard was watching them from overhead.

Dimitri felt the cold hilt of a knife, the blade honed but heavy. *Iron*, he realized. Cian was a cunning shithead. He'd either hidden it from their captors, or the Fae had been too afraid to take it away from him.

He grinned at Cian. "Nice one."

Cian pointed upward, then backed away a little until he reached the edge of the grating. He reached up to rest his hands on the brick, closed his eyes, and drew in a breath, as though gathering strength or resolve. He opened his eyes again and curled his fingers.

Damned if he didn't dig right into the brick. Pieces of brick and mortar started falling around Cian to the floor. Dimitri gaped at him until Cian scowled and made the motion upward again.

Ah, got it. *Watch for guards.*

Dimitri tried to lace his fingers behind his head in his usual lounging position but gave up when his ribs pulled. He settled for simply lying very still.

He saw nothing above them beyond the grating, which must be made of some non-iron metal. Fae had become experts at smithing and forging in silver, gold, bronze, copper, and tin, manipulating these in amazing ways, or so Dimitri had been told.

No one came, though a shadow would flit past the light occasionally—a guard, perhaps, or someone simply passing through that hall, but no one stopped, and no one looked in.

Cian continued to claw at the bricks, which came out easily. Dimitri wondered if this was some latent *dokk alfar* ability, or whether the stone had simply rotted enough to be pulled away.

The falling debris made noise when it hit the floor, so Dimitri began to whistle, then to sing. He chose a wavering country song, full of all the clichés anyone could think of. The songwriter had known it was cliché-ridden and had had fun with it.

Jaycee would laugh. Dimitri was filled with a sudden and gripping longing for her, a heat in his heart that began to cut through the agony.

He stopped singing for a moment as knowledge filled him like cool, soothing water.

The mate bond. The image of Jaycee rose before him, her smile that made her eyes glow, the sassy way she cocked her head while she told him exactly what she thought of him. Dimitri needed a woman who could stand up to him, go toe-to-toe with him, and he had it in Jaycee.

Plus, she was simply beautiful. Her human form with her breasts that fit well into his large hands, hips he loved to nibble, legs that were strong from running and fighting. Her leopard was gorgeous too, a golden body with mottled black and dark gold markings and dark spots in pleasing patterns on her face. Jaycee could leap like nothing he'd ever seen and fight like a wild thing.

The mate bond wrapped around Dimitri, settling in his chest, shimmering down into his cracked rib and making it whole. The Collar seemed suddenly to choke him less, and his pain began to ease.

"I love you, Jase," Dimitri whispered. "And I swear by the Goddess, I will come back to you."

CHAPTER TWENTY-SEVEN

Jaycee leapt down the stairs as the terrified gardener rushed in through the back door, leaving a trail of mud from his boots. Behind him strode three Shifters Jaycee knew—Dylan, Zander, and Tiger.

Immense relief flooded her along with renewed energy. If anyone could help her find Dimitri it was three of the most powerful Shifters around, most especially . . .

"Tiger!" Jaycee sailed off the last five steps, landed lightly on her feet, bounded to the large, quiet Shifter, and threw her arms around his waist. "Am I glad to see *you*!"

"Hey," Zander said behind her, mock hurt in his voice. "What about the rest of us? Liver? Chopped?"

"Glad to see you too, Zander," Jaycee said.

She kept her arms around Tiger, who gazed down at her with his strange and enigmatic eyes. While male Shifters were wary of Tiger and wouldn't dream of flying to him and grabbing him in an embrace, females and cubs had no problem with it. Tiger would never hurt them, and they knew it.

Tiger put one strong arm around Jaycee's waist and gave

her a firm hug in return. "We came to take you home. And
Dimitri. Where is he?"

Jaycee pulled back. "I was hoping you could tell me that.
I don't know."

"Hmm," Zander said. "That's not good." He swung around
to sit on the stairs, his black duster coat swinging. The Fae of
the house encircled them, some fearful, others angry, but
Zander only swept his gaze across them and turned back to
Jaycee. "Where did you lose him?"

Dylan had said nothing, only took in his surroundings
and the Fae without comment. Wherever his gaze landed,
the retainers suddenly found something else to look at.

Jaycee began to explain what had happened at Brice's
house in New Orleans, but Lady Aisling's imperious voice
interrupted.

"And who might you be?" She stood on the landing above
them, straight and unyielding. Her clothes were fairly plain
and dotted with soil from gardening, but Jaycee had a feeling Aisling would be intimidating whether she wore rags or
the finest couture.

The same went for Dylan. In a dusty T-shirt and oil-
stained jeans, he dominated the space. Angus and even
Zander conceded to him. Only Tiger was oblivious to who
was dominant, but Tiger was always like that. He'd been
raised in a cage, isolated in a basement, never seeing the
sunlight until he'd been released forty years later. He didn't
give a rat's ass about dominance.

Zander, leaning back to look up at Aisling, said, "We
might be Shifters. Might not. Who knows?"

Aisling let out an impatient sigh. "Do not be impertinent,
young man. And I'll thank you to get off the stairs. They
were just scrubbed."

Zander raised his hands in an apologetic gesture and
heaved himself up. With his white braids and duster, he
looked the oddest of the three, beating Tiger's mottled hair,
topaz eyes, and immense stillness.

Dylan, by contrast, looked almost harmless. He spoke to

Aisling in a respectful voice, his expression calm. "I am Dylan Morrissey of clan Morrissey, former leader of the Austin Shiftertown. Am I addressing one of the Tuil Erdannan?"

Aisling's frown smoothed. "You impress me, Shifter. Difficult to do. I was coming to realize that young Shifters know nothing about the Tuil Erdannan. But never mind about that." She lifted her chin. "I have decided to help you locate this missing Shifter, Dimitri Kashnikov. Yes," she said to Jaycee's surprised look. "I made the decision as I descended the stairs. Not because your friends came to find you, but because I like *you*, Jaycee. And because devilish clan lords like Simeon and Orag should not prevail. I ought to have moved against them long ago, but I tend to forget about petty things. When you live a thousand years, people who annoy you tend to die off."

She spoke matter-of-factly, but Jaycee saw something raw flicker in her eyes. The other side of her statement was that people she cared for also died. Jaycee had seen a similar look on Ben's face a few times.

"We still don't know where Dimitri is," Jaycee said, her voice less sharp than it had been. "Which is why I'm so happy to see Tiger. He's like a tracker extraordinaire. Can you tell where Dimitri is?" she asked Tiger.

"I cannot," Tiger said without worry. "Not yet."

"But you will." Jaycee spoke with conviction, more to reassure herself than anything else. "Come upstairs and look at the map."

"I don't need a map," Tiger said. "I need to look."

He closed his mouth, pivoted to the right, and walked out to the garden the way he had come. The gardener sidled out of his path, holding his fork in a defensive stance. Tiger strode by him without a glance.

Zander started after Tiger with a growl. "Damn it, he can't run around Faerie by himself."

"Who's going to stop him?" Jaycee asked.

Zander turned back at the open door. "Good point, but even Tiger can't fight the next Shifter-Fae war singlehand-

edly. But he might try. I'll see if I can rein him in." Zander
turned in a swirl of his coat and headed after Tiger.

That left Dylan, who turned his blue gaze on Jaycee. "I
asked Kendrick to put you on this mission because you broke
the rules," he said. He sounded resigned, even apologetic.
"I suppose I have only myself to blame. We tried to tell you
to stand down when it grew too dangerous."

Jaycee folded her arms and looked Dylan in the eye, not
an easy thing to do. "Kendrick can't give me an order that
will keep me from protecting my mate. Neither can you."

Dylan, to her surprise, gave her a conceding nod. "I
know. But when we discussed the mission a few days ago,
you weren't calling Dimitri mate."

"That changed," Jaycee said. "I accepted his claim."

She lifted her chin, ready to defend herself. She'd always
denied out loud that she and Dimitri were anything but
friends—not because she'd been ashamed of her feelings,
but because it wasn't anyone's business but theirs.

They'd always been more than friends though. She'd
known it in her heart. Not many Shifters accepted female
trackers, but Dimitri had always believed in her, had from
the day they'd met. That must have been when Jaycee had
started loving him, but she hadn't noticed the love blossoming until it had grown too big to ignore.

Now the love sang in her heart, binding Jaycee to Dimitri with a surety she could never dismiss. The mate bond
had formed between them so quietly, Jaycee had not realized
it, not until now, when his absence threatened to tear it
from her.

"Good," Dylan said firmly. "I'm thinking it's about time.
Now tell me how you became separated from him."

Aisling listened, eyes alight with curiosity while Jaycee,
with Angus filling in some details, related the tale of how
she, Dimitri, and Angus had rushed to Brice's to find the
Shifters gone, about the circle in the basement, the fight,
and ending with Dimitri being pulled with Brice into Faerie.

Presumably into Faerie. The circle might have gone anywhere.

Jaycee finished before her voice could break on a sob. The fact that Dimitri could be anywhere in the universe, well beyond Jaycee's reach, scared the hell out of her. She wasn't ready to let him go. Not now. Not ever.

"Hmph," Aisling said. "That's what comes of playing with magic beyond your ability. Fae soldiers have no business making circles and doing sage spells, and neither do Shifters."

Dylan looked past Jaycee to Aisling, his gaze assessing. "What Fae would have the knowledge to use such a spell?"

"Any of them" was Aisling's dampening answer. "It's common, if not sensible. But Fae these days think they can wield magic because they find a ley line and know a chant. In my day, they studied for at least a century before they were allowed to so much as light a candle." She sighed. "No wonder they lost their hold of the world to the humans."

The garden door burst open, and Zander returned with his usual gusto. "Tiger's pinpointed Dimitri."

Jaycee whipped her attention to him in shock. "He did? Where?"

"I don't know." Zander's irritated look softened as he took in Jaycee's agitation. "He stood in the field looking around, and then said, *That way*, and took off."

Aisling started down the stairs. "*Which* way?"

Zander let out a breath, went to the nearest window, and pointed. "That direction, more or less."

Aisling halted next to him. She was only a few inches shorter than Zander, her red hair a sharp contrast to his white. "That could mean Simeon or Orag. Can you catch your tiger friend?"

"No." Zander growled. "He's gone. He's not your average Shifter."

"He wouldn't be," Aisling said. "Tigers were bred by the princes and kings. They mostly liked white tigers, but they'd take an orange in a pinch. Tigers are a special breed."

"We noticed," Zander said dryly.

"We'll go to both," Dylan broke in. "Zander to Orag, and

me to this Simeon's lands. Zander can take Angus to back him up, and I'll take Jaycee."

"No," Aisling said firmly. "If either of you rush out beyond the boundaries of my estate, you'll end up a Shifter skin on a castle wall. I don't think much of my neighbors, but they are powerful warriors, and they have no use for Shifters they don't control."

"I wasn't planning on letting them catch us," Dylan said. "They won't know I'm coming."

Aisling shook her head. "You will die, Shifter. I don't care how much power you have with your own people. You will come with *me*, in my carriage, and we will visit Orag and Simeon in turn. Neither will deny me entrance, and you will be under my protection." She tapped her lips, looking Dylan up and down. "Best that you be in your animal forms, I think. They already believe me eccentric, and if I turn up with a wolf, a polar bear, and a lion, they'll worry quite a lot. And Jaycee next to me as my leopard . . . Jaycee?"

Her voice faded as Jaycee loped from the house, already in leopard form, her sensitive nose catching Tiger's scent.

The rest of them could debate all they wanted about how to best approach the Fae near Aisling's lands, but Jaycee knew her easiest way in. Herself, with Tiger.

She heard Zander and Angus shouting for her, fear for her edging their voices. She doubled her speed, focused on Tiger's scent and sprinted after him. Tiger could move swiftly, but Jaycee was a leopard, fast enough to catch a tiger.

Dimitri sang, talked, and otherwise made plenty of noise to cover the rattle of stones as Cian dug them out. At one point, Dimitri felt well enough to crawl over and try to help, but he got only a faceful of brick dust for his trouble. He coughed, cleared his throat, and went back to singing.

He segued from country to Chris Isaak, so he could croon. Cian screwed up his face and shook his head whenever Dimitri hit a high note. Everyone was a critic.

After a long time, when Dimitri's voice was hoarse and his lungs hurt, Cian motioned him over. Dimitri slunk on elbows and knees, keeping up the insane humming.

Cian had scraped mortar, brick, and stone away from the channel that held the grating in place. He indicated where he wanted Dimitri to grip the bars, then once Dimitri had a firm hold, they began to work the grating free.

That took awhile, since they had to be quiet. Dimitri was too hoarse to sing anymore, so he talked, loudly, about anything and everything. His stammer came out as annoyingly as ever, but Dimitri didn't fight it. If his captors wanted to think he was crazy—either from the Collar or because that was just him, so what?

He wound down as he and Cian slowly lowered a piece of the loosened grate to the floor, leaving a yard-sized square hole out of the cell. Dimitri kept talking even though he could barely rasp now. If the cell suddenly went silent, a guard might decide to investigate. If he simply thought Dimitri had talked and sung until he'd lost his voice, he might not.

No matter what, this was going to be tricky. Cian climbed through the hole first, his long limbs folding and unfolding like an acrobat's. He must have been faking his pathetic weakness when he'd been brought to Simeon, because he was now nimble and strong. He turned around and helped Dimitri climb out, Dimitri now the pathetic one.

They traversed the corridor noiselessly, Cian seeming to know where he was going. As Dimitri had suspected, the light he'd seen came from a window that opened at the top of a stone staircase. He glanced up the stairs as they passed, but Cian didn't stop, leading Dimitri deeper into the keep.

At one point, they had to duck into shadows as two Fae soldiers wandered past. They were talking easily to each other, not seeming to be on any kind of patrol. Off duty, probably.

Cian's hand shook as he touched Dimitri's after they'd gone. As strong and smart as this *dokk alfar* might be, he was scared. They were deep in enemy territory without a clear way out.

Dimitri lowered his head to Cian's ear and whispered the word for Shifter. He pointed to his nose, then sniffed, trying to convey that if he turned to wolf, he could smell the Fae coming so they could hide more quickly. Cian caught on and nodded. Dimitri took a breath and changed into his wolf.

When he'd shifted in front of Simeon, he'd congratulated himself on how effortlessly he'd done it. *Like I'm some kind of bad-ass.*

The fluidness he'd achieved then was long gone. Dimitri's limbs jerked, and his body shuddered, the shifting arduous. Fire shot from the Collar through every nerve, making the process even more painful.

As he fought his way into wolf form, Dimitri realized he'd grown cocky about being a Collarless Shifter—the Shifters who'd taken the Collar long ago had seemed like suckers to him. Maybe the Goddess was teaching Dimitri a lesson, making him understand what the Collared Shifters went through every day of their lives. Maybe the Goddess was mad at him for mocking her children, or maybe Dimitri was going as crazy as Casey or Brice.

Even so, the awareness shamed him. Dimitri vowed a new purpose in life, to help the Morrisseys get Shifters the hell out of their Collars—no more delays.

Dimitri landed on all fours as wolf, winded and panting. His throat was tight, the Collar slow to expand to fit him. Part of its mix of magic and technology was to adapt to the Shifter, no matter what form he took, but apparently a new Collar took time to figure it out.

They moved along the corridor noiselessly, Dimitri's sense of smell thankfully undamaged by the Collar. He scented Fae, both nearby and far away, their trails clear.

Dimitri moved ahead of Cian, searching also for scents that might show them a way outside. The trapdoor they'd reached where they'd been caught lay in the other direction, but this fortress probably had more than one back entrance. The kitchen had looked well stocked—the supplies had to be coming from somewhere.

The problem with Dimitri's being good with scent was

that other Shifters were too. Dimitri smelled them coming, caught the stink of Shifters who hadn't bathed in a while, one or two of whom were going feral. They were close, seeking.

He shoved Cian down a side passage into darkness, but too late. The stink grew stronger, and Dimitri turned around slowly to find about a dozen Shifters hemming them in. He'd seen most of the Shifters at Brice's party, but they didn't look cowed or enslaved at all. They watched Dimitri, some as humans, some in their animal forms, all with eyes bright with glee.

A Lupine pushed his way to the front. Dimitri recognized him as the wolf he'd battled at the fight club, who'd stuck a tranq dart into him, causing Jaycee to dash into the ring to help.

The Lupine grinned, all the evil Dimitri had sensed in him that night plain on his face. "Hey there, C-c-coyote," he sneered. "Show us what you can do."

He really shouldn't taunt an enraged red wolf in serious pain. Dimitri growled with the fury of a dozen ferals and launched himself straight into him.

CHAPTER TWENTY-EIGHT

Jaycee knew Tiger heard her coming. He had better senses than any Shifter alive. He slowed his steps and waited as Jaycee came bounding up to him.

He had changed to tiger, his large paws pressing huge indentations into the grass and mud. He growled softly, a frown on his tiger face, as Jaycee reached him.

I'm coming with you, Jaycee tried to convey. *He's my mate.*

Jaycee hadn't had a lot of interaction with Tiger, but he always seemed to understand her. He gave her an acknowledging look from his golden eyes and led the way onward.

Jaycee wanted to race ahead, Tiger's steady pace too slow for her, but she understood the wisdom of sticking with him.

The scents of Faerie came to her as they went—which strangely weren't that much different from those she'd smelled when she'd lived in the northern United States. Pine woods, fresh earth, grasses, wildflowers. Birds flitted, insects buzzed. It wasn't an exact mirror world of Earth—some of the birds had odd plumage, and a few flying insects were about a foot long—but for the most part the woods seemed familiar.

From what Jaycee had read, scientists now believed there were many different possible worlds existing all at the same time. She didn't understand their mathematical explanations, but they were basically talking about a place like Faerie and its threadlike connection to the human world. The professors might not *know* they were talking about Faerie, but then, no one had believed Shifters were real until recently either.

Tiger proceeded in a straight line, never mind stands of trees, hills, streams, in his way. He walked as the sun slanted to the west, then disappeared beneath the horizon.

Two moons appeared in the sky, one smaller than the other, both cool and white. Tiger walked on, Jaycee beside him. She wondered whether Aisling would reach wherever Tiger was going before them, but she doubted it. If her horses and carriage were like the kind in the human world, they'd have to traverse this terrain on a road, which Aisling had said would take hours. Tiger's route would be faster.

More difficult as well. Jaycee shook nettles from her fur and flung water from her feet when she climbed out of a stream Tiger led her across. She growled. Her cat hated getting wet.

After a long time, when Jaycee's paws were beginning to hurt, glittering lights showed ahead of them. The lights were high above the horizon, so at first Jaycee thought they were stars, but they resolved into warm lights, winking in and out.

Tiger halted. He shifted to his human shape and stood silhouetted against the sky, the double moonlight shining on his multicolored hair.

Jaycee morphed to human with him. "Is that where Dimitri is?"

"Yes." Tiger said the simple word, and it pierced Jaycee's heart.

"Thank the Goddess. He's—is he still alive?"

A lump lodged in her throat, cutting off her breath. She didn't want to ask the question, but she had to.

"I don't know," Tiger said, his deep voice rumbling. "But it is Dimitri. He is a good fighter."

He was. Jaycee drew a breath, the cool air making her

shiver. Dimitri could outfight most Shifters in the Austin Shiftertown, and most of Kendrick's as well. He lost fights only when his opponent cheated—such as sticking him with a tranq dart.

Jaycee's shivers turned to ice-cold fear. "If he's in there— he's alone. No help." Tears stung her eyes and trickled to her cheeks. "I can't let him be alone, Tiger. He needs me. So don't even think about telling me to stay behind."

Tiger looked down at her with eyes that were wise. "If you are hurt, Addison will be angry. So will Carly." He said nothing about Dimitri's or Kendrick's anger, she noticed.

Jaycee swiped at her tears with the back of her hand. "I'll tell them you couldn't stop me. They'll believe it. And if Dimitri is already gone . . ." She drew a shuddering breath. "Then it doesn't matter."

If Dimitri died, the mate bond that had been growing between them would be severed, and Jaycee would succumb to grief. Shifters did this, sometimes never coming out of it.

She'd long pretended the mate bond wasn't there, pre- tended Dimitri meant nothing to her beyond their close friendship. But the bond had wrapped her heart so well, had become so familiar, that it had become part of her existence. If the bond broke, she'd lose not only Dimitri but herself.

The only thing that gave Jaycee hope as she gazed at the gleaming citadel on the hill was that she still felt the mate bond. If it existed, then Dimitri was alive.

Waiting for her. Needing her.

"I've got your back," she whispered to him across the distance. "I'm coming, love."

Tiger heard her. In silence, he shifted to tiger and led her onward. Jaycee changed into her leopard form and followed, but it was a long time before her eyes ceased blurring with tears.

Dimitri charged the Lupine, ready to lock his jaws around his throat and go for the kill. The Lupine managed to duck out of the way, but not fast enough to escape entirely.

Dimitri gave him a heavy blow with his paw, spun, charged again, and locked his teeth into the stunned Lupine's shoulder.

The Lupine howled and began to change to his half beast, but his Collar went off, tingling sparks around his neck. A heartbeat later, Dimitri's Collar did as well.

Son of a *bitch*.

What ran through him was pure agony. The Collar shocked deep into Dimitri's neck, biting into his nerves, turning every movement into torture.

How the hell did Shifters fight like this? Dylan and his family had trained themselves to not let their Collars hurt them until well after the event, and others could battle straight through the pain—he'd seen Shifters like Spike and Broderick do it often enough at the fight club. He'd admired them for it, but not until now did Dimitri understand the phenomenal thing they'd accomplished.

I will never sneer at Dylan Morrissey again as long as I live. And wouldn't it be nice to have him here right now?

The other Shifters had hung back while the Lupine had taunted Dimitri, as though hoping for a good show. But now that the Lupine was snarling, trying and failing to shake off Dimitri, they waded in.

In spite of the Collar, Dimitri hung on, biting down on the Lupine, tasting blood.

This wasn't the fight club. This was real, a battle for Dimitri's life.

Dimitri's anger helped him focus. If he killed the Lupine and got away, the Collar would cease torturing him.

Cian was there next to him, battling like a whirlwind, his knife flashing, Shifters yowling when he cut them. They should put *Cian* in the ring at the fight club, Dimitri thought distractedly.

He'd observed that the high Fae soldiers were crazy fighters, but Cian put them to shame. He kicked, spun, punched, slashed, and knocked down, keeping the Shifters away from Dimitri. He could have run, could have made it to freedom, but he'd stayed to help Dimitri fight.

Stupid of him. The odds were bad. These Shifters were spoiling for violence, despite the happy, hand-holding chants to the Goddess they'd been making at Brice's. They probably thought the Goddess blessed their bloodthirstiness, endorsed it even. Shifters like that were doubly dangerous.

And just when Dimitri thought he and Cian might break free, along came Brice, the big grizzly running in to spoil the party.

Brice roared, his bear voice vibrating through the stones. He shoved the bleeding Lupine aside, breaking Dimitri's hold, and went for Dimitri himself.

Dimitri fought with all his strength, his wolf more agile than the lumbering bear, but the bear made up for it in size and power. Dimitri's Collar slowed him down, while Brice managed to ignore the sparks from his.

Damn it. So close. Dimitri's fur became coated with blood as he entered a battle to the death.

The pain from Dimitri's Collar was a river of fire, coupled with the bite of Brice's grizzly claws raking across his stomach. Dimitri decided to do what wolves did best, and went for Brice's throat. Brice's claws were deadly, but so was the wolf's bite. Dimitri clamped his jaws around Brice's throat and hung on.

Cian fought the other Shifters, their screams and shouts echoing, but Shifters weren't trying to rush to Brice's aid, maybe sensing Brice wanted to finish this himself.

Dimitri went down, blood pouring from his stomach. He wouldn't let go of Brice, the bear's blood raining over him. The stench was horrible, but Dimitri knew his only chance was to hang on.

Somewhere in the back of his brain, he thought he heard a leopard's furious cry, one from a very familiar leopard. He must be imagining things. Death throes were making him delirious.

She came hurtling down the hall, past the Shifters who were busy fighting the whirlwind of Cian, followed by a gigantic Bengal tiger.

The leopard sprang from the stone floor, her legs nearly

straight, flew over the heads of the Shifters, easily avoiding their swiping claws, and hit all four paws into Brice's head.

Dimitri quickly let Brice go, scrambling backward as Jaycee ripped into Brice's face, her cat claws moving too fast for Brice to stop them. Brice howled and batted with his huge paws, but Jaycee was instantly out of his reach, hitting a wall with her back feet and using it to propel her into Brice again.

Dimitri's Collar quit sparking, letting him draw a sharp breath. His sides hurt where Brice had torn them, but the sight of Jaycee made him feel suddenly stronger.

He gathered strength and charged back in, again locking his jaw around Brice's throat, while Brice desperately tried to bat Jaycee away.

Meanwhile, there was Tiger. Where the hell he'd come from, Dimitri didn't know, but at the moment, he didn't care. Tiger seemed to be busy letting loose all the pent-up rage that stemmed from being locked in a cage most of his life, and the Shifters were terrified of him. Watching usually gentle Tiger put his tiger ears back and do battle with his huge paws, never missing, was seriously scary. No wonder Tiger never fought at the fight club. No one would be courageous enough to ever go back.

One by one, the Shifters managed to flee, until Tiger was alone, roaring down the hall.

The Fae would be coming any second, and they might have tranq rifles and other more nasty weapons. Dimitri and Jaycee needed to finish Brice and get the hell out of there.

Brice at last managed to knock Jaycee out of his way. Instead of running after the other Shifters, he grabbed Dimitri, who still hung on to his throat, put his bear paws around Dimitri's neck, and began to crush him.

Dimitri was forced to unlock his jaw and release the bear's throat. He kicked out with his paws, breaking Brice's hold, and fell, gasping for breath. Then Jaycee was there, landing on Brice's back and digging in.

Brice ran. He headed for the bowels of the castle, back

toward the dungeon, Jaycee on his back gouging out clawfuls of his fur.

Dimitri shifted to human, landing hard on his butt on the stone floor, his breath clogging his throat. "Jaycee!" he croaked.

She sprang straight into the air, releasing Brice, whipped her body around, and came down running. She made a leap at Dimitri and landed on him, shifting to human as they both fell to the stones.

Dimitri was a mass of hurt, he was covered with blood, and he could barely breathe, but who cared? His mate was on top of him, kissing his face, crying his name, crying, period. Jaycee's tears dripped to his face, salt and sweet, her breasts soft against his chest.

"Mate of my heart," she sobbed. "Dimitri. I love you, love you, love you, so much."

"Hey now." Dimitri smoothed back her tangled hair. "I love you too, Jase." He stroked her hair again, enjoying the silk of it and the heat of her body against his. His pain began to recede, the touch of a mate healing.

Then he blinked. "Shit, what the hell are you doing here? Tiger? Why the *fuck* did you let her come?"

Tiger, remaining a tiger, had ceased roaring. Now he turned and stared stoically at Dimitri, offering no explanation.

"I wouldn't let anyone stop me," Jaycee said, touching Dimitri's battered face. "I had to find you. Nothing was going to keep me away."

Every word was hard, harsh, the tears in her eyes heartbreaking. Dimitri closed his arms around her, breathing her, losing himself in her.

Cian returned from the passage down which Brice had escaped and barked a few urgent words at Dimitri. Tiger shifted to human with a quickness Dimitri envied.

"He says we must go," Tiger rumbled.

"I figured." Dimitri started to climb to his feet, his arms full of Jaycee. She helped him stand, and he helped her.

They leaned on each other, as they ever had. "You s-speak *dokk alfar*?" he asked Tiger.

"I know all languages of the Fae." Tiger said something to Cian, who listened as though amazed Tiger understood his language, then he answered. "He knows the way down," Tiger translated.

"Good. Let's g-go."

Dimitri could barely walk. He didn't mind so much though, with Jaycee to lean on.

Cian led them through narrow passages that were deserted and very dark, night having fallen outside. A small glow came through isolated arrow slits, but not enough to illuminate the halls. Tiger, who could see perfectly fine in the dark, led the way with Cian.

Jaycee touched Dimitri's Collar, concern in her eyes. "What the hell?"

"D-don't ask," Dimitri said. "When we get home, I'll have Dylan take it off me. If we c-can get home."

"We can," Jaycee said. "I know the way."

Of course she did. She was his mate, and she was the most amazing woman alive.

"Tiger," Dimitri said. "I t-take it you were part of the t-team Dylan was sending out to grab Brice?"

"Yes," Tiger said.

"Dylan's a smart g-guy."

"Yes," Tiger answered.

Dimitri tightened his hold on Jaycee. She said nothing more, but that was fine. Words were superfluous between them, not really needed. With Jaycee, it was never a problem that Dimitri couldn't always speak smoothly. They understood each other without the need for mindless babbling.

"One thing." Dimitri had wondered about this since Simeon had dragged Cian in for Dimitri to kill. "The Fae b-bastard who runs this place said that Cian had betrayed and m-murdered Shifters. Tiger, ask him what that's about."

And if Cian had killed Shifters, Dimitri would make him pay for it, no matter that the guy had helped him break out of prison.

Tiger began speaking in the harsh-sounding language of the *dokk alfar*. He kept the questioning short, as was Tiger's way, and Cian answered as succinctly.

Tiger's expression turned angry as he listened, which did not bode well for whoever was on the receiving end of the anger. "Shifters led by the high Fae attacked the *dokk alfar*," he said, his words tight. "Several Shifters were injured. The *dokk alfar* took them back to their caves with their wounded and tended them. They are alive."

Dimitri deflated with some relief. He gave Cian a nod of thanks, which the man returned deferentially.

"We'll rescue them," Jaycee said. "But *after* we take Dimitri to safety."

Dimitri looked sideways at Jaycee. "We'll argue about who g-goes on the rescue mission l-later."

Jaycee just gave him her best *we'll see* look. It was an old argument between them, and Dimitri rejoiced that he was with her to have it again.

Cian led them through a door, not to the stairs or tunnels Dimitri expected, but to a lower courtyard, an open space on the side of the citadel. A low wall with more arrow slits encircled it.

Above them rose the sheer sides of the main citadel. Below the wall of this courtyard, jutting rocks led down to a steep slope covered with trees. Dimitri understood the logistics of this parapet—if an enemy managed to climb up the backside of the hill, soldiers would stop them. Even if they didn't, the attackers would never be able to scale the wall up to the main keep. It was too high and too sheer. The door Cian had led them through could easily be blocked and hidden, and anyway the maze of halls inside would be perfect for ambush by the castle's inhabitants. And the dungeons were not far, waiting . . .

Jaycee looked over at the rocky slope. "I can climb this. So can Tiger, I bet. Dimitri?"

Her golden brows were drawn together with worry. She was so sweet. Dimitri kissed her lips.

"Of course I c-can, darlin'. Try to stop me."

Cian went first. No one agreed to this—he simply vaulted over the lip of the wall and began to descend. Dimitri watched him pick out hand- and footholds with ease and precision.

"Go," Tiger said. "Go *now*."

Dimitri heard them coming as well. Brice's enraged growls, Simeon's voice yelling commands in Fae, the soldiers' pounding footsteps.

"Change to wolf," Jaycee said to Dimitri. "And pick up your feet."

Do what? Dimitri was already shifting and couldn't ask with his mouth. The shift, difficult now, took too long. He was still trying to pull himself into his wolf shape when the Fae charged out the door, pouring onto the open cobbles.

Fortunately, the door was so narrow they could only emerge one at a time. Tiger herded Dimitri and Jaycee toward the wall, turning to defend their escape.

He couldn't hold off a horde of Fae by himself. Dimitri began to turn back, as unsteady as he was, but Jaycee was in front of him, already leopard. *Don't you dare.*

Tiger, becoming his huge, terrifying tiger-beast barked a growl at both of them. *Go!*

Hope you know what you're doing, big guy, Dimitri thought, and then he was all the way wolf, running with Jaycee to the wall.

I said, pick up your feet! Jaycee growled. She loomed above him, grabbed the scruff of Dimitri's neck, and plunged over the wall with him.

CHAPTER TWENTY-NINE

Dimitri felt his neck fur stretch, the Collar going with it, which made for some serious pain. But Jaycee held him firmly in her jaws, her teeth nowhere near cutting him, as she dragged him down the hill, her agile paws finding the projections to take them safely along.

Dimitri's mate was rescuing him by carrying him off like she would a cub. The alpha male inside Dimitri should have been offended—if it weren't so fucking funny.

He heard Tiger roar above. Damn it, they couldn't leave him. Dimitri started to struggle only to find that he couldn't. Jaycee's mouth was firm, and Dimitri hung limply in her grip, unable to move. Jaycee growled deep in her throat— *Quit squirming, damn it.*

She descended slowly but steadily. Dimitri had no idea how she found the handholds—pawholds—but Jaycee did it without hesitation or clumsiness. She was Feline grace in all its perfection.

A strange, twanging sound made Jaycee flinch. She froze on the rocks, suspending the two of them above the tops of the trees, still a couple hundred feet from the ground.

A tiny rock next to them pinged, then split apart. Next, a wooden shaft with a barbed arrowhead bounced off the side of the cliff and tumbled downward. Archers, shooting at them.

The Fae were famous for their archery. Back when Shifters had been Battle Beasts for the Fae, the archers would clear the way for the Shifters to run in and fight on the field. The best archers could put an arrow through another Fae's eye at fifty yards. Even the least competent in the squad would be marksmen—they weren't chosen if they weren't.

The few arrows increased to more and more. Jaycee twisted this way and that, Dimitri flailing, while arrows flew by. It would be only a matter of time before one of them hit them.

Jaycee yowled. She clamped her jaw quickly closed before she could drop Dimitri, but she slipped. Dimitri saw the arrow sticking out of her back haunch, blood staining her fur. She tried to grab on to the rocks with her claws, but her leg was too weak, and her hold failed.

Dimitri felt his stomach drop as they fell, with Jaycee desperately trying to find footholds and hang on to Dimitri at the same time.

Dimitri drew on all the strength he had left, swung himself in her jaw, and sailed to plant his feet on the nearest boulder. It stuck out of the cliff face at a sharp angle, and was slippery as hell, but with his front paws, and then Jaycee's coming over his, they might stick here for a while.

They did until the next arrow struck, this time hitting Dimitri's dangling back leg. He yelped, scrambled, and then they both were falling, nothing to stop them.

I love you, Jaycee.

I love you, Dimitri. Mate of my heart.

The mate bond wrapped them as they fell, body to body.

It hurt very much when two giant hand-paws grabbed Dimitri and hauled him and Jaycee back up every torturous inch to the parapet.

Dimitri landed on his stomach on the flat surface of the courtyard, his leg numb, but the arrow hadn't gone through the deepest part of it, only the sinews. Jaycee, on the other hand, lay panting on the stones, bleeding from the wound in her back hip.

Tiger stepped back from where he'd dumped them and continued fighting the enraged Fae who surrounded him. The soldiers battered him with swords, knives, and kicks, and the archers threw down their bows and joined in. There was a movement behind Dimitri, and Cian reappeared, returning to help them fight.

Dimitri didn't see Simeon, but that didn't mean the man wasn't around, waiting to spring. He'd likely sent his underlings to wear them down, whereupon he'd wander in and finish them off.

Brice pushed through the fighters. He was bear, bloody, with deep cuts across his face and neck where Jaycee had clawed him. He limped but still moved quickly as he charged across the open space for Jaycee.

Dimitri struggled up as Brice grabbed Jaycee in his grizzly paws, raising her high. Jaycee fought, but she was hurt, slowed, her claws swiping empty air. Brice lifted her higher, then began to squeeze.

Dimitri was on his feet, charging—or trying to. His hind leg didn't work. But his three other legs did and he propelled himself onward. He leapt . . .

And was brought down abruptly by the Collar, tightening as it bombarded him with electric shocks. Dimitri shook his head, trying to clear his vision, but the shocks kept coming, the Collar designed to prevent him from making the killing blow he planned.

He went down on the cobbles as Jaycee screamed.

Pain stole his vision. All was dark while Dimitri lay groaning, the Collar cutting off his breath and rendering his body one mass of agony.

Dimly, he thought he caught a whiff of smoke, then saw the flicker of flame.

No.

Fire boiled around him, flames crawling on every surface, coming at him to devour him. Dimitri blinked, exerting himself to resolve the stones under him, Jaycee fighting Brice, but all he could see was fire.

It wasn't real. Dimitri lay on cold stone under a moonlit sky while Fae did their best to slay Tiger, and Brice was killing his mate.

Brice . . .

Dimitri saw him, but a much younger Shifter seemed to be superimposed over him. As Dimitri's vision cleared, he found himself no longer halfway up a stone castle in Faerie, but in a small trailer house in the middle of nowhere America. The house was aflame, heat searing his lungs, his throat closing up from the smoke. He was a cub, howling hard, calling for his mom and dad.

But they'd died in the first part of the explosion, the tank that heated the trailer going up in flames. The tank had been set alight by a young bear, angry that Dimitri's mother and father had driven him away.

The grizzly had arrived that night, drunk and angry— apparently he had become fascinated with Dimitri's mother, a red wolf, at the local roadhouse. When Dimitri's father had kicked his butt and they'd gone home, Brice had followed.

Brice had rocked their small trailer house until Dimitri had become terrified. Just as his father had morphed to wolf to run outside and deal with the bear, the large tank of fuel had exploded, fire engulfing his father, and his mother, who had been right beside him, joining her mate to help him do battle.

The grizzly had blinked heavily, astonished at what he'd done, then he'd fallen forward into the burning house.

Dimitri the cub scrambled over him and out into the empty air. His heart was breaking, grief consuming him and stealing his reason. He had to get away, run, run, run . . .

But the bear was screaming, being burned alive. Dimitri's memories began to dim as he turned back, his Shifter instinct spurring him to save the living. The cub in him needed an adult, an alpha, to take care of him, to help him.

He ran as fast as his small legs could move to the trailer, grabbed the bear by the back foot, and dragged him out of the fire. The bear gulped air, rolled to put the flame out of his fur, then rose on shaky legs.

He'd stared at Dimitri with the same dark eyes that had welcomed him as an adult at the bar in New Orleans, and then had tried to kill him.

Memories long suppressed beat through Dimitri's brain—he saw the bear realize he couldn't let this little cub tell anyone how he'd stalked Dimitri's mother and then blown up the trailer, causing her death and that of her mate.

Dimitri had to run. He turned and fled into the woods, his red wolf legs moving in terrified rapidity. He heard Brice following, snarling with fury, but Brice had been too hurt by the fire, too winded by smoke, and had dropped behind.

Dimitri had run until he could run no more, passed out, and woke with no memory of what had happened to him. His cub brain had blotted out the trauma, his adult self reasoned now with clarity. He'd protected himself by cutting off the horror and grief that might have led him to his death. He'd sat where he'd fallen for a long time, until kind human strangers had found him and taken him into their home to tend him.

The memories fell away, and Dimitri was back on the stone courtyard in the land of the Fae, where Brice was busy murdering his mate.

Dimitri rose on stiff legs, the Collar desperately trying to shock him. Brice had taken away Dimitri's beloved father and mother, and now he was trying to take away Jaycee, his best friend and his mate.

The sound Dimitri made was a cross between a howl and a scream, a terrible cry of rage and bloodthirsty need for vengeance.

The damned Collar wouldn't cease, arcs of blue electricity streaming into Dimitri's throat. Dimitri became his half beast with little effort and dug his fingers into his own flesh, sinking them around the chain. Just as Cian had burrowed his fingertips into the stone, jerking it loose to free them from the dungeon, so Dimitri sank his fingers into his neck where the Collar had embedded itself.

Dimitri no longer cared about petty things like pain. He

wrapped his fingers around the Collar and ripped it from his throat.

Collars were designed to burrow in, to become one with the Shifter, and removing a collar was usually a long and harrowing process. Dimitri cut the process short by tearing the chain away, his nerves screaming where they let go, blood pouring from his neck. He threw the blood-smeared chain to the stones, and it skittered across the parapet with a clinking sound.

Dimitri roared—every sorrow of his past, all the anger, the grief that Brice had caused him, streaming forth. Brice had told Dimitri with a straight face that *he* had rescued Dimitri from the fire, twisting the tale so Brice became its hero.

Fucking asshole.

The words came from Dimitri's mouth as he closed both arms around Brice's body and yanked Brice from Jaycee.

Jaycee fell, panting, coming up again covered in blood. Dimitri crushed Brice's ribs, the bear howling, before Brice squirmed around and began to fight.

Dimitri knew he should be half dead from the battle, then from falling, being shot with an arrow, and last, gouging the Collar out of his throat, but the feral beast that existed inside every Shifter had taken over, infusing him with strength. Dimitri's past and present merged into a continuous line, the cub and the adult finding each other at long last.

Both of them seriously wanted Brice dead.

Dimitri saw real fear enter Brice's eyes. He could no longer hide from Dimitri, or from himself.

He'd fight to the end, though. Brice became his half beast, a giant of a bear-man, and met Dimitri in a crash of bodies. They fought, hand to hand, claw to claw, Dimitri feeling nothing but the bright need to kill. Survival didn't matter anymore, only destroying the man who'd taken his family.

Dimitri was going down under Brice's greater weight, but he didn't care. He kept on battling, the cub striking out at the beast who'd killed his parents, the adult beating on the man who'd tried to kill his mate.

Brice opened his mouth, his bear maw with its huge teeth coming at Dimitri's neck, ready to rip out his throat.

Jaycee let loose her best leopard scream. She landed on Brice, her clawed paws going to *his* throat, tearing it open. Blood streamed down on Dimitri, and Brice roared, swinging around to hurl Jaycee off. They were too close to the wall— if he threw Jaycee from him here, she'd go over the side.

She didn't, of course. Brice managed to jerk her loose and toss her away, satisfaction in his eyes as she flew toward the parapet's edge.

Jaycee twisted herself and landed atop the parapet's low wall, bounced on her three good feet, and came into a crouch once more at Dimitri's side.

Where she belonged. Dimitri heaved himself up, and together he and Jaycee seized Brice and sent him to the ground.

"Payback's a bitch," Dimitri growled, and then he grabbed the terrified Brice by his great head and broke his neck.

Jaycee clung to Dimitri as she lay panting, the stones beneath her cutting into her hurt leg. Shifting back to human was painful, but she wanted to hold Dimitri, just hold on to him.

Dimitri lay beneath her, his throat wet with blood, so much that at first Jaycee feared Brice had managed to get in a killing blow. But no—a Collar, bloody, rested on the stones. Someone had put a real Collar on Dimitri, and he'd torn it off when it had tried to prevent him from rushing to fight for Jaycee.

If Dimitri hadn't managed to reach her, Brice would have broken Jaycee's body and flung her from the precipice. She wouldn't have had the agility to save herself—she knew that with chilling clarity.

"Thank you," she whispered.

Beneath her, Dimitri shifted to his human body and wrapped one shaky arm around her. "Hey, baby. I've got your back, remember?"

Jaycee kissed him, though her lips hurt, and from his wince, his did too.

Tiger roared, the sound vibrating the stones. The Fae had surrounded him, swords flashing, but they couldn't get close to him. The Fae whom Jaycee had recognized as a *dokk alfar*, like Reid, fought the Fae savagely, stabbing at them with a dark knife like the one Ben had given Jaycee.

She and Dimitri should rise, fight, help Tiger and the *dokk alfar*. Too bad Jaycee had an arrow in her leg and no energy left.

"What is *that?*" a deep voice asked. "I want one."

Dimitri jerked his head up and let out a groan. A Fae soldier had emerged from the castle, this one standing calmly as he stared at Tiger in amazement.

"Damn," Dimitri said. "I wondered when he'd show up."

"Who is he?" Jaycee asked, looking the tall Fae up and down. He wore silver armor and animal skins and carried a sword, but he simply watched the fight instead of joining in.

"That's Simeon," Dimitri said. "He owns the place."

"Ah—Simeon Mac An Bhaird."

Dimitri looked at her in astonishment. "You know him?"

"Heard the name. Looks like a jerk."

Dimitri shook with laughter, then moaned in pain. "You got that right."

Simeon moved on light feet to stand over Dimitri and Jaycee, his right boot near Dimitri's face. He moved his sword to tap Jaycee. "You. You're comely. I'll take you for my own."

"*Comely?*" Jaycee turned a scornful gaze up to him. "Seriously? And get that sword out of my face."

"Jase," Dimitri said worriedly, but Jaycee didn't care who this guy thought he was. Aisling had called him a prat, and Jaycee decided she agreed.

Simeon's brows drew together. "You're even more insubordinate than *he* is. I shall enjoy myself taming you. Soon you'll beg to come to me."

"Oh, please." In a sudden swift movement, Jaycee rolled

over, grabbed Simeon's sword between her hands, and yanked
it out of his grasp, just as Dimitri had done with the Fae in
Brice's basement. She and Dimitri had practiced that move
for a long time.

Jaycee flung the sword away, triumphant, right before
Simeon grabbed her by the hair and pulled her up, a silver
knife at her throat.

Dimitri kicked him in the balls.

Simeon grunted, loosening his hold on Jaycee's hair
enough for her to squirm away. She rested on her good leg
and her hands, ready to leap. Dimitri kicked out again,
laughing when he caught Simeon high up inside his hip.

Simeon stumbled but was back in an instant, murder in
his eyes. He raised his knife and brought it down at Dimitri's
throat.

"That will be quite enough of *that.*"

Relief washed through Jaycee as Lady Aisling's clear,
imperious tones rang through the courtyard. "Oh, thank the
Goddess she's here," Jaycee whispered.

"Who's here?" Dimitri asked, cranking his head around.

Lady Aisling swept onto the roof, and she could truly
sweep in the silver and green robes she'd put on over a shimmering blue tunic and leggings. Fur lined the cloak and the
tops of her boots—she'd dressed for the occasion. Flanking
her were three Shifters in animal form—a black-maned lion,
a black wolf, and a very large polar bear.

Tiger let out a roar and scattered the Fae who'd been
trying to cut into him. The soldiers caught sight of Aisling
and her new friends and went ashen. Swords fell from hands,
clattering on the stones, and a few of the Fae dropped to
their knees.

The soldiers' reaction annoyed Simeon, but he turned,
gave Aisling a brief bow, and spoke to her with some defer-
ence. "What brings you here, my lady?"

"You do, Simeon," Aisling said, pinning him with her
green-eyed stare. "You and your ill-advised actions. I am
taking the Shifters with me. All of them."

Simeon's eyes flared with rage but Jaycee saw him tamp

down his anger. He swept his arm to indicate Jaycee, Dimitri, and Tiger. "Fine. Take them," he said bad-temperedly.

"I mean all of them," Aisling said, her voice firm. "Including the ones hidden in your stables."

Simeon scowled. "Those Shifters are here of their own free will."

"I am sure you told them that. The bear is dead." Aisling glanced at Brice's limp body lying in the bright moonlight. "The others will come with me."

Simeon shrugged. "Those that wish to, will."

The lion changed to human with a crackle of sinew. "Where are they?" Dylan asked in a harsh voice.

"As her ladyship indicated, in the stable." Simeon waved a dismissive hand. "Go. My men will not prevent you."

Without another word, Dylan headed back into the castle. Angus, the black wolf, after only a moment's hesitation, went with him.

Zander remained, his polar bear taking in the surroundings. Jaycee saw by the look in his eyes that he was enjoying scaring the Fae shitless very much.

Except that Jaycee suspected their fear had more to do with Aisling than any of the Shifters. Aisling had done nothing more than walk in and look regal, and she had the Fae quaking in their boots.

"Tiger, polar bear," Aisling said. "Help Jaycee and her mate down to my carriage."

Zander rose on his back legs, stretching his arms upward as he shifted to his human form. He finished standing at full height, extremely nude and large all over, as bears were.

He moved to Jaycee and Dimitri, his path taking him right by Simeon, who eyed him in great distaste. No one could be more naked and obvious about it than Zander Moncrieff.

Zander deliberately brushed against Simeon, then paused and tweaked his nose. "Hi there," he said in a loud voice; then he was past him, kneeling to Jaycee and Dimitri.

Zander's expression changed to worry as he laid one hand on Dimitri's shoulder and the other on Jaycee's. "I'll fix you up," he whispered. "Don't worry. But we have to get away first. Are you up to it?"

Tiger made the question irrelevant. He strode to Jaycee, lifted her in his arms, and carried her away.

Jaycee squirmed, looking back to see Zander helping Dimitri to his feet. "Put me down," she said to Tiger as he ducked into the castle. "I have to make sure Dimitri is all right."

"You have an arrow in your leg," Tiger said. "Zander will help him."

"Dimitri is my mate." Jaycee's fighting strength was waning, and she heard the tears in her voice.

"Zander is a healer. The best thing for your mate is for you to not hurt yourself more."

He had a point, but the emotion rocketing through Jaycee's body wouldn't listen to logic. Tiger gave her a look of sympathy, understanding, but he wasn't about to put Jaycee down.

"Zander will help him. He is a good healer." Tiger grunted. "Even if he is a very large pain in the ass."

Jaycee laughed, and ended up crying. She covered her face with her hand and gave up struggling as Tiger carried her down many flights of stairs and all the way down the hill to a luxurious carriage, painted sparkling gold, that waited at the bottom.

CHAPTER THIRTY

The Shifters didn't want to go home. Dimitri heard Dylan telling Tiger this in disgust when Dylan finally emerged from the castle.

Zander had carried Dimitri down the hill in surprisingly gentle arms to a coach where Jaycee already waited.

"I can heal you," Zander had said to Dimitri as they'd descended. "But not on this hill. I'd pass out from the pain, and then we'd fall, and then we'd both need a healer. Can you hold on until we get back to the Fae woman's house?"

"Yes," Dimitri had said, resigned. Not very dignified, being carried over a large, naked man's shoulder, but what choice did he have? "Who *is* the Fae woman?"

"Apparently a very powerful person," Zander answered. "Those Fae soldiers turned green when they saw her, and these are guys who weren't scared of *Tiger*."

"Ignorance," Dimitri said, his teeth clenching as Zander took a hard step. "All Fae should be afraid of Tiger."

"True," Zander said. "But it's good to note."

Jaycee was waiting in the carriage, dressed now in a silver silk garment that clung to her curves. She drew Dimitri close when Zander set him on the seat beside her. Never mind that he was bloody and getting it all over the pretty silver robe—Jaycee simply held him. That was when Dimitri knew everything would be all right.

When they reached the house, Zander healed Jaycee first— Dimitri insisted—then he closed Dimitri's wounds. After that, Zander headed out into Aisling's garden to lie on his back and breath heavily while he studied the stars. He'd be all right, he said to Jaycee's worried questions. He'd healed Shifters who'd been hurt much worse. But she should leave him alone for a time—and then bring him a beer.

Jaycee watched him with concern, but she concluded that Zander knew from experience what he needed to do to recover. She let him be.

Angus and Dylan returned with Brice's body. Brice was of his Shiftertown, Angus said, and needed to be taken to his Guardian. He was a shit and a murderer, but Brice couldn't be left inside, with his soul floating free for the Fae to enslave.

Aisling lent Angus a cart and sent him off toward the sundial, explaining what shadows he should look for to ensure he went back to the right place.

Dylan had convinced a few of the Shifters to return with him, ones who'd realized they'd gotten in way over their heads. They were subdued as they followed Dylan to the sundial and out of Faerie. Maeve wasn't one of them. According to Dylan, when Jaycee asked him, she'd said she wanted to stay—Simeon was going to take her as mate.

"Poor Casey," Jaycee said to Dimitri later as they lounged in a large room in Aisling's house, one with a glass roof. The two moons hovered straight overhead, bathing the room in white light.

"*Lucky* Casey," Dimitri said. "Losing a mate who'd rather be with a Fae is no loss. He's a nice guy, if gullible. He'll find someone who appreciates him."

Cian, the *dokk alfar* Dimitri said had gotten them out of the dungeon and had fought valiantly for them, had departed.

He'd come down the hill with Dylan and Angus, stopped to say something to Tiger, then turned to Dimitri and saluted him. He made a low bow to Aisling, who studied him in surprise, and then ran off into the woods, disappearing quickly from sight.

"He said *Goddess go with you*," Tiger told Dimitri. "And that he will send the Shifters his people have healed back home when they are ready. He also salutes you and your lady warrior. May you be happy and strong."

"A very *dokk alfar* thing to say," Aisling remarked. "And they don't like very many people."

"He's a good guy," Dimitri said.

"For a *dokk alfar*?" Aisling had asked, brows rising.

"For an anything," Dimitri had answered, before he'd turned to Jaycee and closed his eyes.

H ome. Or at least Jasmine Samuelson's weird-ass house. Jaycee felt the usual prickle of strangeness as she crossed the threshold of the door that led to the sitting room, but she also felt the house's welcoming, plus a little of its relief. The house had worried about them, she thought.

It was afternoon here—late, from what Jaycee could see. Clouds covered the sun, rendering the landscape light gray, but it was peaceful and serene, the tall trees around the house deepening the shadows.

Ben hurtled into the sitting room as Jaycee and Dimitri emerged. Jaycee had resumed the black pants and tank top she'd left in Aisling's garden but Dimitri had lost his clothes in Brice's New Orleans house. Jaycee didn't mind him walking beside her without them.

Ben slammed his arms around Jaycee and Dimitri at the same time, kissing Jaycee soundly on the cheek. "I am damned glad to see you. Goddess, I thought I'd lost you both." He hugged them tighter, the homey, slightly smoky tang of his scent an agreeable change from the acrid odor of the Fae.

"We're fine," Dimitri said. He pulled back and grinned at Ben. "Didn't realize you loved us so much."

"Hey, you stand here and watch your friends be swallowed into Faerie and see how you like it." Ben gave Dimitri a severe look. "On second thought, don't. It sucks."

Zander and Tiger came through as he finished speaking—Dylan and Angus had already gone, Angus to carry Brice's body back to the New Orleans Shiftertown and Dylan to escort the Shifters who'd wanted to return home. Dylan had also rescued the bones and skins of the long-dead Shifters from Simeon's war room, taking them back to be released by a Guardian. Likewise, Cian had promised to return the Shifters his people had healed.

"What sucks?" Zander asked. "Coming back out of Faerie doesn't. Whew! Thank the Goddess for *this* world. Those Shifters who want to stay in Faerie are fucking nuts." He sobered. "Goddess go with them. They're going to need her help."

As Tiger stepped through the door after Zander, it slammed, one vine twining itself around the doorknob.

Tiger looked at the door, then did a careful scan of the room, taking in every aspect of it, including the vines that arched over the doorframe. "The house is lonely," he said. His tone went wistful. "Like I was."

Dimitri put his hand on Tiger's shoulder. "Not anymore, big guy."

Tiger lost his pensive look. "That is true." His eyes glinted with the wisdom he hid from so many. "I will go home now to Carly and my cub."

He squeezed Dimitri's hand, then went to Jaycee and enfolded her in a tight embrace. "Take care of your mate," he said. "Congratulations." He moved his finger to Jaycee's abdomen then, before she could ask what he congratulated her for. Tiger strolled out of the sitting room, making for the front door.

"Gotta go," Zander said quickly. "He's my ride. You two take care of yourselves. Rae and I are staying in Austin a few days, so now's good time for your sun ceremony." He pointed both forefingers at Jaycee and Dimitri. "Later." He swung around, coat flying. "See you, Ben!" he shouted, then the front door banged, letting in a blast of warm, humid air.

A moment later, a motorcycle rumbled to life. Jaycee heard Zander shouting for Tiger to wait; the motorcycle paused, then revved and drove off, its roar disappearing into the distance.

Jaycee wanted to fall into Dimitri and hang on. She was exhausted and starving, and a little nervous about what Tiger might have been trying to tell her.

Dimitri's gray gaze rested on Jaycee, no doubt about what was on *his* mind. The love in his eyes was plain too, and Jaycee felt the mate bond tighten around her heart.

Ben eyed them both and cleared his throat. "I should get going. I'll stop by and make sure Casey's all right, take him home. I'll just . . ." He began drifting toward the door. "I'll let myself out."

Jaycee knew she should be polite, ask Ben to stay, offer him dinner maybe, but she couldn't find the words. She needed to be with Dimitri, to reassure herself he was all right, that they'd survived. Hell, they'd even completed their mission to find out what was up with Brice and his Shifters.

Out of the corner of her eye, she saw Ben grin, then drift away. After a moment or two, another motorcycle started up and the sound of its engine faded into the afternoon.

Dimitri put his arms around Jaycee and tugged her close, their mouths meeting in a hungry kiss . . .

The door to Faerie burst open. Ice-cold wind blew through the house, shriveling the vines around the door.

Dimitri spun from Jaycee, thrusting her behind him at the same time. Jaycee tried to shove her way to his side, but Dimitri's strong arm held her in place.

Simeon strode through the door, his sword drawn, his face twisted with terrible rage. Maybe the iron in this house wasn't enough to impede him from entering the human world, maybe he knew spells that mitigated the effects, or maybe he just didn't care.

He kept advancing, his sword poised to kill. "You murdered my best Shifter," he snapped at Dimitri. "I promised his people I'd avenge him."

Jaycee's growls filled the room as she became leopard. Her

party clothes shredded and fell from her, then she rushed Simeon with Feline speed.

Simeon whirled to face her, sword ready, but Dimitri grabbed his sword arm with his human hands, his strength renewed from Zander's healing. He twisted, but Simeon kept hold of the sword, snarling as he whipped it around to strike at Dimitri.

"Shit!" Dimitri danced out of the way and aimed a round-house kick at Simeon's middle. Simeon anticipated and spun away, only to find himself facing a leopard.

Jaycee read the flash of irritation in his eyes, annoyance at himself for miscalculating. Jaycee sprang before he could recover his surprise, landing on him full force.

He fought her, but Jaycee's impact pushed them both into the nearest wall. Which shook.

The house began moving, every beam rattling, the crystal sconces tinkling, the chandelier in the main hall creaking noisily. The windows shivered, the shutters clacked, and the floor heaved.

The house was furious. Why it had let Simeon in, Jaycee didn't know, unless it hadn't been paying attention. Or maybe it had wanted him there . . .

Jaycee leapt from Simeon as the wall behind him bowed backward. The paneling split open, showing red, crumbling brick, which itself began to part. Mortar shattered, brick dust fell, and a gap behind it opened to nothing.

Simeon's eyes widened as he was sucked into this gap, then the bricks rushed together around him. His sword clanked to the floor and he screamed, looking to Jaycee imploringly, his hands reaching for her.

Jaycee started for him, but Dimitri yanked her back. She shifted to human, landing against Dimitri, his arms enclosing her.

The vines around the door shot to the bricks. They slithered between them and whipped around Simeon's body where it was pinned, wrapping him tighter and tighter. Vines covered his face, and then there was a sickening crunch, and Simeon's screaming ceased.

The vines tightened once more, and then Simeon's body dissolved to dust, much like Shifters did when their hearts were pierced by the Guardian's sword. Pieces of brick and mortar rained down with the dust, then the vines withdrew, the paneling closed again, and all was silence.

"My, my."

Lady Aisling stood in the doorway to Faerie, once more in her gardening clothes. She wore her broad-brimmed hat and carried a basket and trowel.

"A sentient house," she said, stepping through the doorway and making her way to the pile of dust that used to be Simeon. "Quite a rarity. They are very protective of their people." She put a light hand on the painted paneling that looked none the worse for wear. "I will just take care of this, then leave them alone," she said to the house. Aisling knelt, scooped the dust with her trowel into her basket, and rose again.

"Actually, I came to give you this," Aisling said to Jaycee and Dimitri, who clung to each other as they watched her in stunned silence. She took a stone from her pocket, an amethyst wrapped with gold wire. "You two seem to have a nose for trouble. But I like you. If you ever have need of my assistance, hold this and say my name. I'll hear you." She seemed to understand that neither Jaycee nor Dimitri wanted her to approach while she held the basket, and she set the stone on a table. "My felicitations on your upcoming nuptials," she said, then gave them a brisk nod and turned away.

She stepped out the door, calling ahead to someone beyond. "Stop worrying, my good woman. I was only collecting what was left of Simeon Mac An Bhaird. Good riddance to bad rubbish, I say."

Her voice drifted away, then the door slammed shut, its lock clicked, and then the door itself winked out of existence. Bare blank paneling was left in its place, white-painted and innocuous. The vines that had encircled it withdrew all the way out the window, until there was no evidence that they'd ever entered the house in the first place.

Jaycee turned in Dimitri's arms, shaking all over. "I think I want to go home."

"Yeah," Dimitri said. "Me too. Let's grab our stuff and hit the road."

They went up the stairs hand in hand. The house was quiet, the wind chimes whispering on the veranda, late sunlight slanting through the windows.

Jaycee's room was bathed in warm light, the clouds on the horizon stained gold, red, and orange. A cool breeze blew through the open window, curtains moving softly.

Jaycee lifted her bag of clothes, then put it down. The house made no sound, but she sensed its tension, its worry that it would be left alone again. "On the other hand," she said to Dimitri. "It will be dark soon. We could make a start after breakfast tomorrow."

Dimitri leaned on the doorframe, his tall, honed body unclothed, his wanting showing plainly. "What did you have in mind to do until then?"

"Oh, I don't know." Jaycee folded her arms and leaned back on a bedpost.

Dimitri started for her at a leisurely pace, his gaze never leaving her. She'd noticed that since they'd left Simeon's fortress, he hadn't stuttered, as though some switch had been thrown inside him. She decided not to mention it.

She didn't have the chance. As soon as Dimitri reached her he pulled her against him, drawing her up for a slow, need-filled kiss.

The wind chimes jangled in the breeze, the air cooling as the sun slipped over the horizon. Jaycee was plenty warm as Dimitri lowered her to the bed, coming over her with his heated body. He skimmed the hair back from her forehead as he slid inside her, his kiss slow and full of fire.

When he eased from the kiss, he looked at her with eyes heavy with desire. "I love you, Jaycee. Mate of my heart."

Jaycee touched his face. "Always my mate," she whispered. "My friend, my love, my other self."

Dimitri grinned. "Shut up and kiss me."

Jaycee did, then she wrapped her legs around him and drew him in, surrendering to love, desire, and the hot-bodied man who was her best friend and the truest mate of her heart.

EPILOGUE

One week later, Kendrick conducted the first full sun and moon ceremonies he'd done at his ranch, the new home for his Shifters. With his mate, Addison, by his side, he blessed the union of Dimitri Kashnikov and Jaycee Bordeaux—in the afternoon under the blazing Texas sun; then that night under the gentle full moon.

Shifters from Kendrick's ranch and the Austin Shiftertown went crazy at the party after that, celebrating a new mating, a new hope.

Kendrick had snarled and shouted and growled at Dimitri and Jaycee when they'd come home to the ranch, more furious than Dimitri had ever seen him. Kendrick had kept up the severe, pissed-off leader stance for a while, then had grabbed Jaycee and hugged her hard, tears in his green eyes.

He'd continued yelling at Dimitri for not keeping Jaycee safe and then for nearly dying himself, and losing his best trackers. Then he'd pulled Dimitri into a firm embrace.

They'd been joined by Addie and the cubs, everyone crying, the cubs in turn yowling and hugging them. Once they'd settled down, Addie had seized Jaycee by the hand and taken her into the kitchen for girl chatter. Their laughter and squeals had pierced the air.

Everyone came to the sun and moon mating—Zander and his mate, Rae, she with a Sword of the Guardian on her back; Ben, who'd brought beer for Dimitri and a bottle of a very fine Côte du Rhône for Jaycee; Dylan and his family; Tiger and his—Tiger carrying the very tiny boy, Seth, with great pride but also much care. Casey had come, brought by Angus, who'd said that attending a mating ritual would do the man good. Casey was grieving from his mate leaving him, Dimitri could see, but he did seem cheered by the party and meeting new Shifters. Hopefully he'd get over Maeve and find someone worthy of him.

Angus brought a boy of about ten with him, explaining that he was his cub. A troublemaker, he'd said, pride in his voice. Raising him on his own was hell. The cub, a Lupine with a serious expression, agreed it was tough taking care of his dad by himself. Dimitri wondered if Angus had told the kid about his adventures or if he'd decided not to mention what danger he'd been in.

The party lasted well into the night; Charlie happy to keep supplying beer, burgers, pizza, even champagne. Cubs ran wild, Kendrick's cubs romping and playing without worry.

One day soon, according to Tiger's prediction, Dimitri and Jaycee would be watching their cub run with them.

Dimitri enjoyed hanging out with his friends, but after a while, he wished they'd all disappear so he could be alone with Jaycee. But Shifters loved a good shindig and weren't about to leave anytime soon.

They all wanted to talk to Dimitri and Jaycee. Ben cornered them on the back porch of the ranch house while Shifters in various forms did a conga line around the outer cabins.

"So," Ben said, slamming himself into a porch chair and shoving his feet onto the railing. "Dylan just told me you met one of the Tuil Erdannan. No way. He's making that up, right?"

"You mean Aisling?" Jaycee asked. She'd curled up next

to Dimitri on the porch swing, his arm around her, her warm head resting on his shoulder. "I think that's what she said she was. She was nice."

"Nice?" Ben came up, feet thumping on the porch floor. "Sweetie, the Tuil Erdannan are not *nice*. They're crazy, powerful, ultra-magical killing machines. You met one, and you're still alive? That's what you should be asking yourself."

Jaycee started but Dimitri soothed her, stroking her shoulder. "She helped us," he said. "She liked Jaycee."

Ben stared at them. "Seriously, you two . . . You're amazing. Totally amazing."

"Are they that dangerous?" Jaycee asked. "I'd never heard of the Tuil Erdannan."

"That's because you don't care what goes on in Faerie. The Tuil Erdannan don't pay a lot of attention to lesser mortals, thank the Goddess. Can't be bothered. They're very old, can wipe out their enemies with their pinkies if they want to, and some say they created the *dokk alfar*. Just for fun. To see if they could. I don't know if that's true, but they seem more disposed to leave the *dokk alfar* alone, while they are happy to beat the high Fae to a pulp. They didn't help my people though." Ben scowled. "I bet they didn't even notice."

"If you ever meet Aisling, you can ask her," Jaycee said.

Ben blew out a breath. "I doubt I ever will. Maybe that's best."

"You could," Jaycee said. "She gave me a talisman to summon her. But she said only in need. You asking her *what the fuck?* probably doesn't qualify as great need."

Ben's eyes widened. "She gave you a talisman? Shit." He ground the heel of his hand to his forehead. "The most powerful beings around, except for the Goddess, and she just hands you a summoning talisman?"

"Yes." Jaycee started to smile. "I think I *will* ask her to meet you. Might be fun to watch."

Ben rose, making an *I-give-up* gesture. "What you call fun and what I do are vastly different, sweetie. You two enjoy each other." He started down the steps, then turned back.

"Congratulations," he said, his voice softening. "Really. I knew you belonged together."

He sent them a grin, shook his head again, and headed back for the party.

"Everyone did," Jaycee said softly. "Addie too. She told me when she first came here that we should be mates."

"We knew," Dimitri said, kissing her hair. "We just took our time admitting it. At least, *you* did. I always said you were the one for me."

Jaycee turned to him, her eyes lit with her love. "You're a shit."

"Yeah, but you adore me."

Dimitri bent to kiss her, but no, they couldn't be left alone even long enough for one hot kiss. Dylan climbed to the porch, sent them an unapologetic look, and sat down.

"I wanted to talk to you alone."

Dimitri spread his hands. "Here we are. Alone. Mates on their moon ceremony night—how weird is that?"

Dylan shot him an exasperated look. "I won't keep you. My own mate is feeling the power of the sun and moon mating. But I haven't had a chance to speak to you."

Dimitri conceded. "Speak, then. Before Glory comes and drags you off. She will, you know."

"Yes. I do know." Another wry glance. "During the last year, I've been rounding up Shifters," Dylan said. "Ones I handpick—Kendrick has been helping me."

Dimitri remembered what Angus had said when they'd found the circle in Brice's basement, that Dylan had been pulling Shifters out of Shiftertowns for who-knew-what reason.

"I heard," Dimitri said. "Sort of. Angus mentioned it."

"I've talked to Angus too," Dylan said, unruffled. "I asked him to join."

"Join what?" Jaycee asked.

"My army. Fae are recruiting Shifters—coercing, promising, or out-and-out abducting. They want their Battle Beasts, as you saw. Simeon was only one of the Fae gearing up. They are mainly fighting each other at the moment, trying to decide who will lead them. They want back into this world, which they ruled in the deep past. They want to use Shifters to do it—are using them already. I want to fight back. So I'm picking the best Shifters I know to gather them and train. I need Shifters like you, who are not only good fighters but can make decisions without leaders there every second to guide you." He sat back. "It's entirely up to you. Are you in?"

"Yes," Jaycee answered immediately.

"No," Dimitri said.

Jaycee blinked at him in shock. "What?"

Dimitri braced his bare foot on the porch floor, stilling the swing. "They nearly killed us in there. Nearly killed my *mate*. Jaycee's going to have a cub. I want her safe—I want the cub safe. If you want me to answer now, I can't."

Jaycee's mouth was open. "Speak for yourself."

"I am," Dimitri told her. "And our cub."

Jaycee watched him a moment longer, then drew a breath. "He's right. I need to think about the cub. Maybe later?"

Dylan rose, seeming unworried by Dimitri's answer. "I don't know how long the Fae will wait. If you change your mind, let Kendrick know." He sent Jaycee a faint smile. "*Now* I will leave you alone. The blessings of the Goddess be upon you."

With that, he walked down the stairs, along the path to the cabins. A tall woman with very blond hair was striding toward the house, and when Dylan reached her, he slid an arm around her and led her into the shadows.

Jaycee didn't speak for a time. Dimitri held her, the swing rocking, the night breeze kind.

"I can't tell whether I'm having a cub or not," Jaycee said after a while. "I might not be."

"Tiger thinks so." Dimitri caressed her bare arm with his thumb. "I haven't known him long, but so far, he's never been wrong."

Jaycee smiled, her golden eyes glinting in the darkness. "We could always make sure."

"That we could." Dimitri grinned back at her. "Should

we try to reach my cabin without being intercepted, or use your room?"

"My room's closer."

They studied each other a moment and then as one sprang to their feet and made a mad dash into the house. Jaycee bounded ahead of Dimitri, laughing, flowing into her bedroom and spinning in place to wait for him.

Dimitri kicked the door shut. "Vixen."

"Leopard," Jaycee corrected him. She came to him, beautiful as ever, and Dimitri's heart soared. She was his—his love, his life. Jaycee slanted him a sly glance. "My sexy red wolf."

"Y-yep." Dimitri had observed that his stammer was mostly gone, though once in a while it returned. But not enough to hamper him. Something had resolved within him when he'd finally been able to remember what had happened to him. Knowledge had brought grief, but the terrible blank, the uncertainty, was gone.

"Or maybe it's *coyote*?" Jaycee said, toying with the front of his shirt.

"Oh, sweetheart, them's fighting words."

"Hope so."

Dimitri growled. Jaycee laughed, then shrieked when he lifted her and threw her onto the bed. He came down on top of her, the two of them wrestling, Dimitri alternately growling and kissing her.

Their clothes managed to come off as they sparred, until they were skin to skin, face to face. Dimitri stilled, kissing his beautiful mate.

"All right," she said in a low voice. "Red wolf."

"That's my girl." Dimitri kissed her, then slid inside her, finding heaven. "No, my *mate*."

"Always." Jaycee's eyes drifted closed as she rose to him, passion taking her. Her strong hands slid to his back, then his hips, pulling him into her, her whisper ending on a groan. "Always, my love, my mate. Don't worry—I've got your back."

Dimitri laughed, then got down to the business—and joy—of loving his mate.

Wind chimes from the New Orleans house, a mating gift from Jasmine, tinkled at the window, and the moonlight touched them, the Goddess pleased.

CHAPTER ONE

LONDON
MARCH 1881

I had not been long at my post in Mount Street, Mayfair, when my employer's sister came to some calamity.

I must say I was not shocked that such a thing happened, because when a woman takes on the dress and bad habits of a man, she cannot be surprised at the disapprobation of others when she is found out. Lady Cynthia's problems, however, turned out to be only the beginning of a vast tangle and a long, dangerous business.

But I am ahead of myself. I am a cook, one of the finest in London, if I do say it, and also one of the youngest to be made head cook in a lavish household. I worked some time in the winter at a house in Richmond, and it was a good position, but the family desired to sell up and move to the

Lake District, and I was loath to leave the environs of London for my own rather private reasons.

Back went my name on the books, and the agency at last wrote to my new lodgings at Tottenham Court Road to say they had found a place that might suit. Taking their letter with me, I went along to the house of one Lord Rankin in Mount Street, descending from the omnibus at South Audley Street and walking the rest of the way on foot.

I expected to speak to the housekeeper, but upon arrival the butler, a tall, handsome specimen who looked as though he rather preened himself, took me up the stairs to meet the lady of the house in her small study.

She was Lady Rankin, wife of the prodigiously wealthy baron who owned this abode. The baron's wealth came not from the fact that he was an aristocrat, as the butler, Mr. Davis, had already confided in me; the estate had been nearly bankrupt when Lord Rankin had inherited it. However, Lord Rankin was a deft dabbler in the City and had earned money by wise investment long before the cousin who'd held the title had died, conveniently childless.

When I first beheld Lady Rankin, I was surprised she'd asked for me, because she seemed too frail to hold up her head, let alone to conduct an interview with a new cook.

"Mrs. Holloway, ma'am," Davis said. He ushered me in, bowed, and withdrew.

The study in which I found myself was small and overtly feminine. The walls were covered in yellow moiré and the curtains at the windows were white lace. Framed mirrors and paintings of gardens and picturesque country lanes adorned the walls. A delicate, gilt-legged table from the last century reposed in the middle of the room, with an equally graceful chair behind it. A scroll-backed chaise, covered with shawls, sat near the desk.

Lady Rankin was in the act of rising from the chaise as we entered. She moved listlessly to the chair behind her desk, sat upon it, and pulled a paper in front of her with a languid hand.

"Mrs. Holloway?" she asked.

Davis had just announced me, so there was no doubt who I was, but I nodded. Lady Rankin looked me over. I remained standing in the exact center of the carpet in my second-best frock, a brown wool jacket buttoned to my throat, and my second-best hat—made of light brown straw—perched on my thick coil of dark hair.

Lady Rankin's garment was white, filmy, and high necked, its bodice lined with seed pearls. Her hair was pale gold, her cheeks thin and bloodless. She could hardly be thirty summers, but rather than being childlike, she was ethereal, as though a gust of wind could puff her away.

She glanced at whatever paper was in front of her—presumably a letter from my agency—and then over the desk at me. Her eyes were a very light blue, and in contrast to her angel-like appearance, were rather hard.

"You are very young," she observed. Her voice was light, as thin as her bones.

"I am nearly thirty," I answered stiffly.

When a person thought of a cook, they pictured an older woman who was either a shrew in the kitchen or kindhearted and a bit slow. The truth was that cooks came in all ages, shapes, and temperaments. I happened to be nine and twenty, plump and brown haired, and kind enough, I hoped, but I brooked no nonsense.

"I meant for a cook," Lady Rankin said. "Our last cook was nearly eighty. She is . . . gone. Living with her daughter." She added the last quickly, as though fearing I'd take *gone* to mean to heaven.

I had no idea how Lady Rankin wished me to answer this information, so I said, "I assure you, my lady, I have been quite well trained."

"Yes." Lady Rankin lifted the letter. The single page seemed too heavy for her, so she let it fall. "The agency sings your praises, as do your references. Well, you will find this an easy place. Charles—Lord Rankin—wishes his supper on the table when he arrives home from the City at eight. Davis will tell you his lordship's favorite dishes. There will be three at table this evening, Lord Rankin, myself, and my . . . sister."

Her thin lip curled the slightest bit as she pronounced this last. I thought nothing of it at the time and only gave her another nod.

Lady Rankin slumped back into her chair as though the speech had taken the last of her strength. She waved a limp hand at me. "Go on, then. Davis and Mrs. Bowen will explain things to you."

I curtsied politely and took my leave. I wondered if I shouldn't summon Lady Rankin's maid to assist her to bed but left the room before I did anything so presumptuous.

The kitchen below was to my liking. It was nowhere near as modern and large as the one I'd left in Richmond, but I found it familiar and comfortable.

This house was what I called a double town house—that is, instead of having a staircase hall on one side and all the rooms on the other, it had rooms on both sides of a middle hall. Possibly two houses had been purchased and knocked into one at some time and the second staircase walled off for use by the staff.

Below stairs, we had a large servants' hall across a passage from the kitchen. Past the kitchen on the same passage was a scullery—which also connected to the kitchen and had a door that led out and up the outside stairs. On the other side of the kitchen was a larder, and beyond that a laundry room, a room for folding clean linens, the housekeeper's parlor, and the butler's pantry, which included the wine cellar. Mr. Davis showed me each, as proud as though he owned the house himself.

The kitchen was a large square room with windows that gave on to the street above. Two dressers full of dishes lined the white-painted walls, and a hanging rack of gleaming copper pans dangled above the stove. A thick-legged table squatted in the middle of the floor, one long enough to prepare several dishes at once on, with space at the end for an assistant to sit and shell peas or do whatever I needed done.

The kitchen's range had been neatly fitted into what had

been a large fireplace, the stove high enough that I wouldn't have to stoop or kneel to cook. I'd had to kneel down on hard stones at one house—where I hadn't stayed long—and it had taken some time for my knees and back to recover.

Here I could stand and use the hot plates that were able to accommodate five pots at once, with the fire below behind a thick metal door. The fire could be stoked without disturbing the ovens on either side of it—one oven had racks that could be moved so several things could be baked at once, and the other spacious oven could have air pumped though it to aid roasting.

The sink was in the scullery, so that dirty water and entrails from fish and fowl could be kept well away from the rest of the food. The larder, a long room lined with shelves and with a flagstone floor, looked well stocked, though I'd determine that for myself in due time. From a cursory glance, I saw bags of flour, jars of barley and other grains, dried herbs hanging from the beams, spices in tinned copper jars with labels on them, and crates of vegetables and fruit pushed back against the walls.

The staff that ran this lofty house in Mayfair wasn't as large as I would have expected, but they seemed a diligent lot. I had an assistant, a rather pretty girl of about seventeen who seemed genial enough—she reminded me of myself at that age. Whether her assistance would be useful remained to be seen. Four footmen appeared and disappeared from the servants' hall, as did half a dozen maids.

Mrs. Bowen, the housekeeper, was thin and birdlike, and I did not know her. This surprised me, because when you are in service in London, you come to know those in the great houses, or at least *of* them. However, I'd never heard of Mrs. Bowen, which either meant she'd not been in London long or hadn't long been a housekeeper.

Mr. Davis, whom I soon put down as a friendly old gossip, gave me a book with notes from the last cook on what the master preferred for his dinners. I was pleased to find the dishes uncomplicated but not so dull that any chophouse could have provided them. I could do well here.

I carefully unpacked my knives, including a brand-new sharp carver, took my apron from my valise, and started right in.

The young assistant, a bit unhappy that I wanted her help immediately, was soon chatting freely with me while she measured out flour and butter for my brioche. She gave her name as Sinead.

She pronounced it *Shin-aide* and gave me a hopeful look. I thought it a beautiful name, conjuring mists over the green Irish land—a place I'd never been—but this was London, and a cook's kitchen was no place for an Irish nymph.

"It's quite lovely," I said as I cut butter into the flour. "But I'm sorry, my girl—we can't be having *Sinead*. People get wrong ideas. You must have a plain English name. What did the last cook call you?"

Sinead let out a sigh, her dreams of romance dashed. "Ellen," she said, resigned. I saw by her expression that she disliked the name immensely.

I studied her dark brown hair, blue eyes, and pale skin with some sympathy. Again, she reminded me of myself— poised on the edge of life and believing wonderful things would happen to her. Alas, I'd found out the bitter truth too soon. Sinead's prettiness would bring her only trouble, well I knew, and hopes dashed by life again and again.

"Ellen," I repeated, trying to sound cheerful. "A nice, solid name, but not too dull. Now, then, Ellen, I'll need eggs. Large and whole, nothing cracked."

Sinead gave me a long-suffering curtsy and scuttled for the larder.

"She puts on airs," Mrs. Bowen said as she passed by the kitchen door. "Last cook took a strap to her." She sounded vastly disapproving of the last cook, which made me begin to warm to Mrs. Bowen.

"Is that why the last cook was dismissed?" I already didn't think much of this elderly cook, free with a strap, whoever she was. Sinead's only crime that I could see so far was having dreams.

"No." Mrs. Bowen's answer was short, clipped. She ducked away before she could tell me anything more interesting.

I continued with my bread. Brioche was a favorite of mine—a bread dough made rich with eggs and butter, subtly sweet. It was a fine accompaniment to any meal but also could be served as pudding in a pinch. A little cinnamon and stiff cream or a berry sauce poured over it was as grand as anything served in a posh hotel.

It was as I began beating the flour and eggs into the milk and sugar that I met Lady Rankin's sister. I heard a loud banging and scrabbling noise from the scullery, as though someone had fallen down the stairs. Pans clattered to the floor and then a personage in a black suit burst through the scullery door into the kitchen, bootheels scraping on the flagstones, and collapsed onto a chair at the kitchen table, flinging out arms and legs.

I caught up my bowl of dough before it could be upset, looked at the intruder, and then looked again.

The person wore black trousers, a waistcoat of watered silk in a dark shade of green—a shining watch fob dangling from its pocket—a smooth frock coat and loose cravat, a long and rather dusty greatcoat, a pair of thick leather gloves, and boots that poked muddy toes from under the trousers. The low-crowned hat that went with the ensemble had been tossed onto the table.

Above this male attire was the head and face of a woman, a rather pretty woman at that. She'd done her fair hair in a low bun at the back of her neck, slicking it straight from a fine-boned face. The light color of her hair, her high cheekbones, and light blue, almost colorless eyes were so like Lady Rankin's, that for a moment, I stared, dumbfounded, believing I was seeing my mistress transformed. This lady was a bit older, though, with the beginnings of lines about her eyes, and a manner far more robust than Lady Rankin's.

"Oh, Lord," the woman announced, throwing her body back in the chair and letting her arms dangle to the floor. "I think I've killed someone."

CHAPTER TWO

As I stared in alarm at the woman, she looked up at me, fixed me with a gaze that was as surprised as mine, and demanded, "Who the devil are *you*?"

"I am Mrs. Holloway." I curtsied as best I could with my hands around my dough bowl. "The new cook."

"New? What happened to the last one? Nasty old Mrs. Cowles. Why did they give her the boot?"

Since I had no idea, I could not answer. "Has something happened?"

The lady shoved the chair from the table and banged to her feet, her color rising. "Good God, yes. Where the devil is everyone? What if I've killed him?"

"Killed who?" I asked, holding on to my patience. I'd already decided that the ladies of this family were prone to drama—one played the delicate creature, the other something from a music hall stage.

"Chap outside. I was driving a rig, a new one, and he jumped out in front of me. Come and see."

I looked at my dough, which could become lumpy if I left it at this stage, but the young lady was genuinely agitated, and the entirety of the staff seemed to have disappeared. I shook out my hands, wiped them with a thick towel, laid the towel over the dough bowl, and nodded at her to lead me to the scene of the problem.

Fog shrouded the street onto which we emerged from the scullery stairs, Lady Cynthia—for that was Lady Rankin's sister's name—insisting we exit the house through the servants' entrance, the way she'd come in.

The fog did nothing to slow the carriages, carts, delivery wagons, small conveyances, and people who scurried about on whatever business took them through Mount Street, which was situated between Grosvenor Square and Berkeley Square. Mud flew as carriage wheels and horses churned it up, droplets becoming dark rain to accompany the fog.

Lady Cynthia led me rapidly through the traffic, ducking and dodging, moving easily in her trousers while I held my skirts out of the dirt and dung on the cobbles and hastened after her. People stared at Lady Cynthia in her odd attire, but no one pointed or said a word—those in the neighborhood were probably used to her.

"There." Lady Cynthia halted at the corner of Park Street, a respectable enough place, one where a cook should not be lurking, and pointed.

A leather-topped four-wheeled phaeton had been halted against the railings of a house on the corner. A burly man held the two horses hitched to the phaeton, while a lad patted them, trying to keep them calm. Inside the vehicle, a man slumped against the seat—whether dead or alive, I could not tell.

"Him," Lady Cynthia said, jabbing her finger at the figure inside the phaeton. "He popped out of nowhere and ran in front of me. Didn't see the bloody man until he was right under the horses' hooves."

I was already moving toward the phaeton, Lady Cynthia behind me, pressing myself out of the way of carts and carriages rumbling through. "Did you summon a doctor?" I asked her, raising my voice to be heard over the clatter of hooves and wheels.

"Why?" Lady Cynthia gave me a blank stare with her pale eyes. "He's dead."

I reached the phaeton and opened the door to study the man slumped in the seat. I let out a breath of relief—he was quite alive. I'd unfortunately been witness to those brutally and suddenly killed, but the one thing I'd observed about the dead was that they did not raise their heads or open their eyes to stare at me in bewilderment.

The burly man holding the horses called to Lady Cynthia. "Not dead, my lady. Just a bit bashed about."

"You, lad," I said to the boy with him. "Run for a doctor. Perhaps, my lady, we should get him into the house."

Lady Cynthia might have worn the clothes of a man, but she hesitated in the fluttery way young ladies are taught to adopt these days. Cooks, I am pleased to say, are expected to be a bit more formidable. While the boy raced away at my command to summon a physician, I had no compunction about climbing into the phaeton and looking the fellow over myself.

He was an ordinary person, the sort one would find driving a cart and making deliveries to Mayfair households, though I saw no van nearby, nothing to say who his employer was. He wore a plain but thick coat and a linen shirt, working trousers, and stout boots. The lack of rents or stains in his clothing told me he was well looked after, maybe by a wife, or perhaps he could afford to hire out his mending. Or perhaps he even took up a needle himself. But the point was he had enough self-respect to present a clean and neat appearance. That meant he had work and was no ruffian of the street.

I touched his hand, finding it warm, and he groaned piteously.

Lady Cynthia, hearing him, looked much relieved and regained some of her vigor. "Yes, inside. Excellent idea, Mrs. . . . Mrs. . . . ."

"Holloway," I reminded her.

"Holloway. *You.*" She pointed a long, aristocratic finger at a sturdy youth who'd paused to take in the drama. "Help us carry him into the house. Where have *you* been?" She snapped at a gangly man in knee breeches and heavy boots who came running around the corner. "Take the rig to the mews. *Wait* until we heave this man out of it."

The thin man, who appeared to be a groom—indeed, he would prove to be the head groomsman for Lord Rankin's town stables—climbed onto the box and took the reins, sending Lady Cynthia a dark look. His back quivered as he waited for the youth and the burly man to help me pry the hurt man out of the phaeton.

I looked into the youth's face and nearly hit my head on the phaeton's leather top. "Good heavens," I said. "James!"

James, a lad of about fifteen or so years, with dark eyes, a round, rather handsome freckled face, and red-brown hair sticking out from under his cap, shot a grin at me. I hadn't seen him for weeks, and only a few times since I'd taken the post in Richmond. James didn't move much beyond the middle of London, as he made his living doing odd jobs here and there around the metropolis. I'd seen him only when I'd had cause to come into London and our path crossed.

James, with his father, Daniel, had helped me avoid much trouble at the place I'd been before Richmond, and I'd come to count the lad as a friend.

As for his father . . .

I could not decide these days how I regarded his father. Daniel McAdam, a jack-of-all-trades if ever there was one, had been my friend since the day he'd begun deliveries in a household I'd worked in a year or so before. He was charming, flirtatious, and ever ready with a joke or an encouraging word. He'd helped me in a time of great need last autumn, but then I'd learned more about Daniel than perhaps I'd wanted to. I was still hurt about it, and uncertain.

After James and the burly man worked the injured man from the carriage, I pulled myself upright on the phaeton's step and scanned the street. I have sharp eyes and I did not have to look far before I saw Daniel.

He was just ducking around a corner up Park Street, glancing behind him as though expecting me to be seeking him. He wore the brown homespun suit he donned when making deliveries to kitchens all over Mayfair and north of Oxford

Street and the shapeless gloves that hid his strong hands. I recognized his sharp face, the blue eyes over a well-formed nose, the dark hair he never could tame under his cloth cap.

He saw me. Did he look abashed? No, indeed. Mr. Mc-Adam only sent me a merry look, touched his cap in salute, and disappeared.

I did not know all Daniel McAdam's secrets, and I knew he had many. He'd helped me when no other would, it was true, but at the same time, he'd angered and confused me. I was grateful and could admire his resolve, but I refused to let myself fall under his spell. I had even allowed him to kiss me on the lips once or twice, but that had been as far as *that* went.

"Drat the man," I said.

"Ma'am?" the groom asked over his shoulder.

"Never mind." I hopped to the ground, the cobbles hard under my shoes. "When you're done in the stables, come round to the kitchen for a strong cup of tea. I have the inkling we will all need one."

A doctor came and looked over the man Lady Cynthia had run down. He'd been put into one of the rooms in the large attic and pronounced to have a broken arm and many bruises. The doctor, who was not at all happy to be called out to look at a mere laborer, sent for a surgeon to set the arm. The surgeon departed when he was finished, after dosing the man with laudanum and giving Mrs. Bowen instructions not to let him move for at least a day.

The man, now able to speak, or at least to mumble, said his name was Timmons and begged us to send word to his wife in their rooms near Euston Station.

At least this is what Mr. Davis related to me. I had scrubbed my hands and returned to my brioche when the hurt man had been carried upstairs, needing to carry on with my duties if I was to have a meal on the table when the master came home. Lady Rankin had said he returned on the dot of eight and expected to dine right away, and it was after six now. Ellen/Sinead, though curious, obediently re-sumed her kitchen duties.

As Sinead and I worked, Mr. Davis told us all about the doctor's arrival and his sour expression when he'd learned he'd come to see to a working-class man; the surgeon, who was much more cheerful; and the fact that this Timmons would have to spend the night. One of the footmen had gone in search of his wife.

By that time, I had shaped my rich bread and was letting it rise in its round fluted pan while I turned to sorting out the vegetables I'd chosen from the larder—plump mush-rooms that were fresh-smelling, asparagus that was a nice green color, a firm onion, and bright tomatoes.

"Lady Cynthia is beside herself," Mr. Davis said. He sat down at the kitchen table, propping his elbows on it, doing nothing useful. My chopping board was near him, and I thumped the blade menacingly as I cut through the onions Sinead had peeled for me. Mr. Davis took notice. "She's a flibbertigibbet but has a kind heart, does our Lady Cynthia," he went on. "She promised Timmons a sum of money for his trouble—which Lord Rankin will have to furnish, of course. *She* hasn't got any money. That's why she lives here. Sort of a poor relation, but never say so."

"I would not dream of it, Mr. Davis." I held a hothouse tomato to my nose, rewarded by a bright scent, the tomato an excellent color. I longed to bite into it and taste its juices, but I returned it to the board with its fellows and picked over the asparagus. Whoever had chosen the produce had a good eye.

Mr. Davis chuckled. I'd already seen, when he'd led me through the house, that he could be as haughty as anything above stairs, but down here in the kitchens, he loosened his coat and his tongue. Mr. Davis's hair was dark though gray at the temples, parted severely in the middle, and held in place with pomade. He had a pleasant sort of face, blue eyes, and a thin line of a mouth that was usually moving in speech.

"Lady Cynthia and Lady Emily are the Earl of Clifford's daughters," Mr. Davis said, sending me a significant look.

Interesting. I left the vegetables and uncovered the fowl

I was to roast. I'd cook potatoes and onions in its juices and throw in the mushrooms at the end, along with the tomatoes for tang. For fish, I had skate waiting to be poached in milk, which I'd finish with parsley and walnuts. Early March could be a difficult time—the winter fruits and vegetables were fading, and spring's bounty barely beginning. I enjoyed cooking in spring the most, when everything was fresh and new. Biting into early greens tasted of bright skies and the end of winter's grip.

I had heard of the Earl of Clifford, who was famous for being a bankrupt. The title was an old one, from what I understood, one of those that kings had been bestowed for centuries—reverting to the crown when the particular family line died out but given to another family when that family pleased royalty enough to be so rewarded.

I did not have my finger on every title in Britain, but I had heard that Clifford was the eighth of this earldom, given to a family called Shires. The present Lord Clifford had, in his youth, been renowned for bravery—deeds done in Crimea and that sort of thing. He'd come home to England to race horses, tangle himself in scandals, and have notorious affairs with famous beauties. He'd finally married one of these beauties, proceeded to sire two daughters and a son, and then gambled himself into ruinous debt.

His son and heir, as wild as the father, had died tragically at the young age of twenty, going slightly mad and shooting himself. Lady Clifford, devastated by the death of her favorite child, had gone into a decline. She was still alive, I believe, but living in poor health, having shut herself away on her husband's estate in Hertfordshire.

The daughters, ladies Cynthia and Emily, had debuted and caught the eyes of many gentlemen, but they'd not fared well, as their father's debts were common knowledge, as were their mother's nerves and their brother's suicide. Lady Emily, the younger, had married Lord Rankin before he was Lord Rankin, when he was but a wealthy gentleman who'd made much in the City. Lord and Lady Clifford must have breathed a sigh of relief when he'd put the ring on her finger.

I had known some of the Clifford story from gossip and newspapers. Now Mr. Davis kindly filled in the gaps as I plunged a tomato into hot water, showing Sinead how this loosened the skin so it could be easily peeled.

"Lady Cynthia was not so fortunate." Mr. Davis stretched out his long legs, making himself as comfortable as possible in the hard wooden chair. "She is the older sister, and so it is a scandal that the younger married and she did not. And, of course, Lady Cynthia has no fortune. She is agreeable enough, but when she found herself in danger of being on the shelf, she chose to become an eccentric."

While I left Sinead to finish peeling, seeding, and chopping the tomatoes, I warmed butter and basted the hen, which was a plump, well-juiced specimen. Lord Rankin, it seemed, spared no expense on his victuals. Happily for me, as a cook's job is made ten times easier with decent ingredients.

"Poor thing," I said, shoving the fowl into the roasting oven and licking melted butter from my thumb. I closed the door and fastened it, and snapped my fingers at the lad whose task it was to keep the stove stoked. He leapt from playing with pebbles in the corner and grabbed a few pieces of wood from the box under the window. He opened the grate and tossed in the wood quickly, but I was alarmed how close his little hands came to the flames. I'd have to make up the balm I liked of chamomile, lavender, and goose fat for burned fingers.

The boy returned to his game, and I wiped my hands and looked over Ellen's shoulder as she moved on to tearing lettuce for the salads. I liked to have my greens washed, dried, and kept chilled well before serving the meal.

"Lady Cynthia took at first to riding horses in breakneck races," Mr. Davis continued. "Amateur ones, of course, on the estates, racing young men fool enough to take her on. She has a light touch with a horse, does Lady Cynthia. She rode in breeches and won most of her gallops, along with the wagers. When our master married Lady Emily, he put a stop to Lady Cynthia's riding, but I suppose she enjoyed wearing the breeches so much she didn't want to give them up. Our lordship don't like it, but he's said that as long as

Lady Cynthia stays quiet and behaves herself, she can wear trousers if she likes."

Mrs. Bowen chose that moment to walk into the kitchen. She sniffed. "Speaking of your betters again, Mr. Davis?" She studied me getting on with the meal, then, with head held high, departed for the servants' hall, disapproval oozing from her.

Mr. Davis chuckled. "Mrs. Bowen puts on airs, but most of what I know about the family I learned from her. She worked for Lady Clifford before she came here."

I pretended to absorb myself in my cooking, but I was curious. I have a healthy interest in my fellow beings, unfortunately.

As Davis went momentarily silent, my thoughts strayed again to Daniel. He popped up here and there throughout London, always where something interesting was happening, and I wondered why he'd chosen the moment when Lady Cynthia had run down a cart driver.

"If Lady Cynthia hurt this man for life with her recklessness," I observed, "it could go badly for her."

Davis shook his head. "Not for the daughter of an earl decorated for bravery and the sister-in-law of one of the wealthiest men in London. Lord Rankin will pay to keep our Lady Cynthia out of the newspapers and out of the courts—you mark my words."

I believed him. Wealthy men could hide an embarrassment to the family, and Lady Cynthia viewed herself as an embarrassment—I had noted that in her eyes. I myself saw no shame in her running about in gentlemen's attire—didn't we enjoy the courageous heroines who dress as men in plays of the Bard? Cheer for them in the Christmas pantomimes?

I saw no more of Lady Cynthia that evening, or indeed of anyone, as I turned to the business of getting the supper done. Once I gave my attention solely to cooking, 'ware any who stepped in my way.

Sinead proved to be capable if not as well trained as I would have liked, but we got on, and she burst into tears only once. She ceased her sobbing after she cleaned up the salt she had spilled all over the lettuce and helped me pull the roasted fowl out of the oven, bubbling and sizzling, the aroma splendid. I cut off a tiny piece of meat and a speared a square of potato and shared them with her.

Sinead's face changed to rapture. "Oh, ma'am, it's the best I ever tasted."

She exaggerated, I knew, although I suppose her comment was a testament to the previous cook's abilities. I thought the fowl's taste could have been richer, but I would not be ashamed to serve this dish.

Mr. Davis and the footmen were already in the dining room above. I rounded up the maids to help me load a tureen of steaming asparagus soup into the lift, followed by the lightly poached skate, and then, when it was time, the covered plate of the carved fowl with roasted vegetables and the greens. I hadn't had time to fix more than the brioche for pudding, and so I sent up fruit with a bite of cheese alongside the rich bread.

It was my habit never to rest until I heard from the dining room that all was well. Tonight, I heard nothing, not a word of praise—but not a word of complaint either. The majority of the plates returned scraped clean, although one of the three in each course was always only lightly touched.

Such a shame to waste good food. I shook my head over it and told the kitchen maids to pack away the uneaten portions to distribute to beggars.

I'd learned long ago that not every person on earth appreciates good food—some don't even know how to taste it. Instead of growing incensed as I had done when I'd begun, I now felt sorry for that person and distributed the food to the cold and hungry, who better deserved it.

"Who is the faint appetite?" I asked Mr. Davis when he, Mrs. Bowen, and I at last took our supper in the housekeeper's parlor, with Sinead to wait on us.

"Tonight, Lady Cynthia," Mr. Davis said between shoveling in bites of the pieces of roasted hen and potatoes I'd held back for us. "She is still most upset about the accident. She even wore a frock to dinner."

Apparently, this was significant. Mrs. Bowen and Sinead gave Mr. Davis amazed looks.

One of the footmen—I thought his name was Paul—tapped hesitantly on the door of Mrs. Bowen's parlor and entered when invited.

"I beg your pardon, ma'am," he said nervously. "But his lordship is asking for his evening cup of coffee." He swallowed, his young face rather spotty, his Adam's apple prominent. He darted Mrs. Bowen a worried look. "He's asking for Sinead—I mean Ellen—to deliver it."

An awful hush descended over the room. I was struck by the paling faces of Mrs. Bowen and Mr. Davis and the unhappiness in the footman's eyes, but mostly by the look of dread that came over Sinead.

She set down the teapot she'd lifted to refill Mrs. Bowen's cup and turned to that lady pleadingly, distress in every line of her body.

Mrs. Bowen gave her a sorrowful nod. "You'd best be going on up, girl."

Sinead's eyes filled with tears, every bit of cheerfulness dying. She wiped her hands on her apron, curtsied, and said, "Yes, ma'am," before she made for the door.

She found me in the doorway, blocking her way out. "Why?" I asked the room, not excluding the footman. "What is the matter with Ellen taking the master his coffee? Mrs. Bowen, Mr. Davis, you tell me this minute."

Mr. Davis and Mrs. Bowen exchanged a long glance. Sinead would not look at me, her cheeks stark white and blotched with red.

It was Mrs. Bowen who answered. "I am afraid that his lordship occasionally believes in the idea of . . . I suppose we could call it *droit de seigneur*. Not often, fortunately."

"Fortunately?" The word snapped out of me, my anger, which had touched me when I'd seen Daniel in the street, finally finding a vent.

I was well aware that a hazard for young women in service, no matter how grand the household, was that the master, and sometimes his guests, saw no reason not to help themselves to a maid, or a cook's assistant, or, indeed, even a cook, when they fancied her. The young woman in question was powerless—all she could do was either give in or find herself another place. If she fled the house without reference, gaining new employment could be difficult. If she gave in to the master's lusts, she risked being cast out with a stain on her character. If her own family would not let her come home or if she had no family, she had no choice but to take to the streets.

I had learned as a very young cook's assistant to keep myself buried in the kitchen and rarely cross paths with the gentlemen of the household. As cooks seldom went above stairs, this had worked well for me. My ruin had been entirely my own fault and nothing to do with any house in which I'd worked.

"It does not happen often, does it?" I asked testily.

I was pleased that at least Mr. Davis and Mrs. Bowen looked ashamed, with Mrs. Bowen bordering on wretched. "Only when his lordship has been made unhappy," Mr. Davis said.

And he'd been made unhappy today by Lady Cynthia's running down a man in the street, a story everyone in Mayfair likely knew by now. "Good heavens—why on earth do you stay here?" I demanded of all present. "There are masters respectable enough in other houses, and wives who will not put up with that sort of thing."

Mr. Davis regarded me in some surprise. "We stay because it's a good place—you'll see. His lordship is generous to the staff. Always has been."

"I see. And sending a young woman as sacrifice every once in a while is a small price to pay?" My mounting anger made my blood fire in my veins. "Well, I will not have it. Not in my kitchen."

"Mrs. Holloway, I understand your unhappiness," Mrs. Bowen said. "I share it. But what can we do? I try to keep the maids occupied away from his lordship, but it is not *my* house. Her ladyship ought to keep him under her eye, but she cannot."

I full well knew Mrs. Bowen was right. Some gentlemen are highhanded enough to believe *everything* they do is justified. Those who have power and wealth behind them are only encouraged in their prideful thinking. The frail Lady Rankin likely knew what was going on but hadn't the strength to confront him about it.

My heart sank at the thought of having to look for another place when I'd only just found this one. The kitchen was well stocked, the house efficiently run, and the street near to an omnibus that would take me easily to the place in London where my heart was. Why, oh why, did the master and his base needs have to ruin a perfectly good situation?

My fury made me reckless. "I won't have it," I repeated. "Ellen, sit down and calm yourself. *I* will take Lord Rankin his coffee."